The Masked Avenger

A Fable

by

Peter Alexei

Published by the Author

Visit the author's website at www.peteralexei.com

First Printed Edition: May 2012

ISBN: 978-0-9852354-1-3

*For my father, who read every word first,
and my mother, who saved my life on more than one
occasion.*

Fable *n.* 1. a short tale to teach a moral lesson, often with animals as characters 2. a story not founded on fact 3. a story about supernatural or extraordinary persons or incidents; legend.

I

The sun cascaded through the gaps between the buildings, the early morning mist causing the light to seem thick, as if passing through incense. Silhouetted against the gleaming atmosphere of Ellis Street, a figure emerged, a shimmering image at first, gradually becoming more distinct as it grew closer.

But distinct did not mean more real.

The traffic seemed to freeze around him, the people crossing the street moving in slow motion. The steam coming up from the manhole covers caused him to slip in and out of focus, until he burst through the intersection, revealing himself in all his splendor.

He wore a cape, with a cowl that covered the top part of his face. This was all made out of a black garbage bag, which snapped in the breeze behind him. Across his chest and around his back crisscrossed silver chains, which he used to lock up the bicycle on which he rode. His enormous Black body was clad in a gray, stained sweat suit, with black basketball shorts. The Doc Martens, which had been duct-taped together, enclosed the feet that were peddling in a stately rhythm.

The effect was not yet complete.

A belt, from which were suspended a pair of handcuffs along with an assortment of household utensils, came close to capping the image, but it was the toilet plunger, worn through the belt at a rakish angle as if it were a saber, that pushed this vision from the common-place San Francisco weirdness into the realm of something more sublime. Add to this the stateliness and purpose with which he weaved in and out of the Tenderloin traffic, and he became beautiful.

As Maddy Stevenson sat in her car at the intersection, long after the light had shifted to green and the cab behind her began to honk, she thought:

I have never seen anything like it.

II

"I have never seen anything like it," Maddy said to her friend in the next cubicle.

Maddy was just one month into her internship at the San Francisco Clarion, Northern California's leading daily newspaper. After graduating with a degree in Communications from Stanford University, she felt lucky to have landed such a sought-after position. Her friend in the next cubicle, Carlos, was also an intern, having come from the Central Valley, by way of Columbia University. He was still sipping his hot Peet's coffee and trying find his way out of the fog produced by a previous night's revels in the Castro.

"Seen anything like what?" said Carlos, his eyes bleary and his voice hoarse.

"This amazing homeless Black man – at least I'm pretty sure he must be homeless - riding a bicycle through the Tenderloin. I think it was at the corner of Hyde and Ellis…"

"That's an icky spot. When was this? Not last night…"

"No, it was this morning, on my drive in." Maddy felt self-conscious about driving to work when she lived only two miles up the street in Russian Hill. But she was never sure what errands she would be sent to run, and she preferred the drive to the crowded and often smelly MUNI buses. She was also fortunate enough to have parents who could afford to offset her meager intern's stipend and provide her with an apartment that included the most precious of San Francisco amenities: parking.

"So, what was so amazing about this guy?"

3

"He looked... well, he sort of looked like he wanted to be Batman. I mean, he had the cape and the belt and everything, but it was all made out of found objects – garbage bags, bicycle chains..."

"I love this town. I was lucky enough to score some tickets to the opera the other evening, and the most exquisite gowns were being worn by the men. The society women simply couldn't compete. Face it. This city is a magnet for the sartorial Avant Garde... and the weird."

"No, it's not just that – the... weirdness," said Maddy thoughtfully. "There was something about him. A confidence, a sense of real purpose."

"A lot of homeless people are like that. They stride across intersections in the path of oncoming traffic as if where they were going was the most important thing in the world, and fuck everybody else. As soon as they cross, of course, they stop and realize that they've forgotten what they even crossed for." Carlos' eyes suddenly got wide. "Head's up!"

At that moment, a compact but very intense woman came striding towards them.

"I've got an assignment for you," said Carey Portman. Carey was a Pulitzer Prize-winning journalist who had won her recognition through a series of articles detailing corruption in the San Francisco police department. She had coined the term "Burritogate," after a sorry sequence of events involving drunk off-duty police officers, two gay men, and a burrito led to a mammoth cover-up within the department. Like most ambitious people, she refused to rest on her laurels.

"I need you to spend the next week interviewing homeless people."

"Homeless people? Just any homeless people?"

"I'd prefer it if you were to travel a little farther afield than the fifty or so who camp out on our doorstep," said Carey, with a sour look on her face. The Clarion was located South of Market, just a block from the infamous Sixth Street corridor. There were more homeless people per square inch in that part of San Francisco than almost anywhere outside of Calcutta, due to its proximity to Union Square and the cable car turn-around, two of the biggest tourist attractions in the City. The staff of the Clarion routinely had to pick their way through a gantlet of panhandlers, junkies, and prostitutes. "I think it would be ideal if you found out where the 'nodes' of homelessness in San Francisco are, and interview people at each node."

"Nodes," nodded Maddy, as if she knew what Carey was talking about. "Yes, ma'am. Is there an angle?"

"Not sure yet. But this town leads the country in homelessness per capita, with no answers in sight, and it's time for a periodic check-up of the demographic. We'll see where all of this leads."

"Should I take photo support?"

"No. Once we have a game plan, with a few names and locations, I can do the follow up with a photographer."

Such was the life of an intern. The grunt work would, of course, be done by Maddy. Even, if she was lucky, the bulk of the actual writing. With a few "refinements" and the odd "punch-up," however, Carey would elevate the material into the kind of reading that occupied the liberal elite on Sunday mornings as they sipped their coffee - and further cement her reputation as a journalist of national importance.

"Take Carlos with you for moral support. Don't be nervous. Most homeless people, at least here in San Francisco, are pretty mellow. There are the screamers, of course, but their bark is usually worse than their bite."

"Where I should start?" asked Maddy, trying very hard to suppress a nervous quiver in her voice.

"The only truly dangerous spot is 16th and Mission. I'd work up to that place, and only go there during daylight. Start at the 'Island' – I'm sure from there you can piece together the other places where the homeless call home. Check in with me at the end of each day, and we'll map out the next day's activities. Okay? Go get 'em."

And Carey strode off.

"The 'Island?'"

"It's at the intersection of Mission and South Van Ness. A half-dozen people live there. I pass it every day as I go to and from work," said Carlos. "It's a pretty depressing spot. Just a little chunk of concrete in the middle of the street, not much bigger than the bathroom in your apartment."

"And a half-dozen people live there?"

"Not that I've counted, but there's quite an encampment. A pile of shopping carts and cardboard boxes."

Maddy thought for a second.

"Any provisions we should take with us?"

"We should requisition some cigarettes, some bottled water and some Clif bars. They might open up to us if we bear gifts."

"I'll print out a map. See you downstairs in the lobby in five minutes."

"Oh," said Carlos, as he put his computer to sleep, "you might also want a healthy supply of Handi-Wipes. It's pretty gross out there."

III

As he parked his bicycle in the alley behind the Orpheum Theater, he sighed. This is getting harder every day, he thought. The feeling of omnipotence that used to wash over him when he rode through the City was fading. But he had to project the same confidence, nonetheless. Otherwise, the forces of darkness would sense his growing weakness, his weariness, and then, who would stand before them? The police were useless, less than useless, and there was no elegance or panache to their efforts. They were bullies, mostly, and a constant torment to him and those he was sworn to protect.

I can't afford to be this tired, he thought.

The squeak from the milk crate rallied him.

"Robin! Come to me, my friend." And from the milk crate a small, furry head appeared. The kitten was still very young, but it knew that breakfast had arrived. It climbed up out of the blanket that had been tenderly shoved into the crate that served as its nest. Robin hopped down to the popping sound of the air-sealed lid being removed from a can of cat food.

"The food of the Gods. Why they make any flavor other than tuna is beyond my comprehension."

The black and gray clad man pulled out a plastic fork from a plastic bag that contained little packets of soy sauce and Chinese mustard. He carefully divided the contents of the can, placing half of it onto a paper napkin before the kitten. To the remainder, he applied some mustard. He sat down on a packing blanket and leaned wearily against the wall. The kitten, purring furiously, gobbled the food with quick bites.

Oh, for a drink.

No.

A warrior must always keep a clear head. Too many decisions to be made within a split second. I must maintain my edge.

I must also get some sleep. Night, now that winter is approaching, comes much too soon. God, I'm tired.

Having finished his breakfast, the man in black and gray carefully arranged his packing blanket, adjusted a piece of cardboard to shut out the sun, and curled up in a ball. The kitten rubbed up against him, purring, and finally settled into a curl next to his face. Within a few minutes, the purring was drowned out by the laboured breathing of his troubled sleep.

IV

That did not go badly.

I mean, really. Not badly, at all.

Peter Kohler strolled through the magnificent, gleaming new lobby of the Museum of Asian Antiquities, pausing to catch his reflection in the window of the museum's gift shop. He adjusted his tie and ran his fingers through his leonine mane of silver hair. As he buttoned the jacket of his Wilkes Bashford suit, he smiled and reflected on how he stood at the precipice of greatness.

Or at least great wealth.

As Director of the Museum, he had overseen the construction and grand opening of the new museum building, designed by one of Europe's most prominent architects (a real bitch, he sighed, but that went with the territory). The museum was located on a prime spot opposite City Hall, constructed partly out of the old San Francisco Library. Its frontage was a prime location, anyway – the back of the museum, however, sat on Hyde Street, just across from the Orpheum, and the western edge of the Tenderloin. Even so, the museum was heralded as a bright spot within the City and had received excellent reviews for its architecture and its permanent collection. The exhibit within was, without question, unrivalled in the western hemisphere for its depth and scope. With the quality of the artifacts, and the star quality of his architect, Kohler and his museum had achieved international recognition. With this new-found cachet in his pocket, he was finally able to meet with the Chinese authorities capable of granting him access to the rarest of Tibetan sacred artifacts. His planned exhibit, Tibet Revealed, would be a blockbuster.

His meeting with the Chinese contingent was all he could have hoped for. With the help of his board chairwoman, Madeleine Chang, he convinced them that he, and his museum, were the best option for presenting Tibet to the rest of the world. The terms were easy to accept: for exclusive access to huge warehouses of sacred objects that had been plundered by the Chinese during their occupation of the mountain country, he would curate and construct an exhibit that would, if not whitewash, at least ignore China's brutal suppression of the Tibetan people.

But that's only the beginning, he thought. As with any large shipment of goods, certain items might just "fall off the truck." He had seen for himself how cavalier the Chinese were about documenting their stolen treasure. It had been enough for them simply to suppress the religious beliefs and the dreams of independence of the Tibetan people. It had only just occurred to them that there was capital, both political and financial, to be gained from opening their treasure trove to the world. So, there would be few, if any, questions asked, should certain objects, whose value Kohler could assess better than anyone, slip off the manifests.

Kohler laughed to himself at the wicked irony of it. There were more than a few collectors in the Bay Area, and in Hollywood, who would pay enormous sums for authentic Tibetan religious artifacts, no questions asked. They would then, when they died, more than likely bequeath these artifacts to his very museum. What was there to feel guilty about? So what if it took another decade or two for the pieces to finally see the light of day? What was that compared to centuries of obscurity?

In the meantime, Peter Kohler would make millions, and his retirement villa in the Greek islands would be that much closer to reality.

V

"We're going to lose the contract," said John Sanders.

He was nervous. It was Monday morning, and he already wished the week was over. The email he had received from the director of MagicLand Theatrical first thing that morning was quite clear. And his employer, Cheryl Niederman, was the sort of woman who was more than likely to kill the messenger should the message fail to please.

"You know we can't afford that."

Cheryl Niederman stared out of the window of the 22nd floor office of Niederman Productions. She sighed. There was a time when being a theatrical producer was fun. Working with her husband's substantial microchip fortune, she carried considerable clout within the producing community. She owned or operated all the major commercial theatre venues in San Francisco and was often instrumental in providing the funding and the infrastructure for large productions preparing for Broadway. As "out-of-town try-out" locations went, San Francisco beat the hell out of New Haven.

A small, whippet-thin woman, she radiated nervous energy. At an opening night party, she was a vivacious hostess. Behind the scenes, however, she was as fierce and relentless as any old-school male Broadway impresario. She turned away from the sight of a California Street cable car climbing up towards the top of Nob Hill, and fixed Sanders with an icy stare.

"So, what the fuck are *you* going to do about it?"

Sanders winced. The "you" cut like a knife.

"I'm not sure what remaining options we have. We

shot our wad with the Channel 5 expose, and the Mayor's response was..."

"Both flashy and flaccid. What an asshole. He's so concerned about keeping his mistresses provided for that he can't get it up for something that really matters."

The situation was this: MagicLand Theatrical was mounting the national tour of its enormously successful Broadway musical, *The Leopard Prince*, which was based on the equally successful animated film of the same name. They had been in negotiations for months with Niederman Productions over using the Orpheum Theatre for the first stop of the tour. By providing the Orpheum for the "production" phase of the tour, during which the technical kinks were worked out prior to a potential decade-long run through the provinces, Niederman Productions would receive a healthy percentage of the profits, which were guaranteed to be spectacular.

The sticking point in the negotiations was that the Orpheum, the only theatre in the Niederman chain of theatres large enough to house the spectacle that was *The Leopard Prince*, was right in the heart of the Tenderloin. It was unforgivable in the eyes of the MagicLand executives that the ultimate family entertainment should be performed at the cross-roads of homeless squalor.

In an effort to shame the City into doing something, *anything*, about the problem of public urination and crack dealing that routinely took place in the plaza behind the Orpheum, John Sanders had several video cameras installed on the roof-top of the theatre. The videos of defecation, panhandling, bathing in the public fountain, drug dealing, and random violence were then released to Channel 5 News.

The response from the Mayor's Office was rapid, and ineffectual. A lot of noise was made about a pre-dawn police blitz that removed all of the benches from the plaza. But that effort backfired, as the homeless simply slept on the ground. And the political fallout was only to be expected. The Mayor, who was perhaps the most liberal politician governing a major metropolis in America, was still considered a reactionary compared to his Board of Supervisors, who took the latest efforts to do something about the homeless as a call to arms. The Mayor spent the next few weeks back-pedalling, huffing and puffing, and the benches were restored.

"A lot of sound and fury signifying nothing. So, I repeat, what are *you* going to do about it? If this falls through, the homeless population in San Francisco will be augmented by at least *one* certain individual."

"Mark Eichler, the Chairman and CEO of MagicLand, will be making a tour of the theatre on Wednesday for a final buy-off prior to load-in. If we can present a better face than last time he was here, even if it is only for the duration of the visit, we might pull this off."

"Present a better face? What are we going to do? Bus that squalid refuse of humanity to some off-site holding area, like the Chinese did with their homeless for the Beijing Olympics? Get real. God save me, and this city, from those people. If they simply disappeared off the face of the earth, no one would miss them, and we might actually turn this city around. Seriously, they could all fucking die."

John Sanders was silent for a moment.

"Do you know Richard the Second?" he asked slowly.

"What does that have to do with anything? And yes, of course, I know Richard the Second. You mean Shakespeare's Richard the Second?"

"The part where Henry the Fourth says something like 'If only someone would rid me...'" Sanders pursed his lips and thought better of going any further with that thought. "Leave everything to me," he said, finally. "Say no more. The necessary steps will be taken."

"What*ever*."

And with that cold dismissal, John Sanders bowed his head slightly, and exited the office. Cheryl Niederman returned her gaze towards California Street. The cable car was slowly working its way down the hill.

VI

As Paul MacDougall snapped his cell phone shut, his temples began to throb.

I need some air, he thought.

He headed out of his office and walked out to the second level of the ballpark. The deck was redolent of garlic from the famous garlic fries that were being prepared for twenty-thousand orders that night, and maintenance crews were steam cleaning the brickwork of the beautiful new façade. He flopped into a seat in the shade under the upper deck balcony and watched the grounds crew prepare for the evening's game. TBD Park was the gem in baseball's crown, easily the most beautifully situated park in the major leagues, and home to the San Francisco Goliaths. And Paul MacDougall was the majority shareholder of a team that was steamrolling towards the playoffs. One last home stand remained, five games, and the Goliaths, behind the hitting of Benny Cashman, were a virtual lock to win the pennant. Even if they lost all their remaining games, the wild card was still theirs. And Benny Cashman was closing in on one of baseball's most hallowed records, Hank Aaron's 755 home runs. Sure, there was Barry Bonds' *statistical* record of 762 homers, but few people took that seriously anymore. At the pace Cashman was driving balls into the water in the cove beyond the right field fence, he would break the record during the World Series, should the Goliaths get that far, if not before.

Things should be great.

Except for that phone call.

What had been an open secret for several years was now on the verge of becoming one of the worst scandals in baseball. Benny Cashman had tested positive for steroids. The call had come from the lab where the testing was done. MacDougall had taken the precaution of "engaging" an inside technician to alert him should the worst happen. Now it appeared that the test results were bound for the office of the Commissioner later that day. There was almost nothing that could be done. After the scandal involving Bonds, and the congressional hearings into steroid abuse by other overperforming older ballplayers, Major League Baseball had to take what it considered a "hard" stance: mandatory fifty game suspensions for all who tested positive for their "first" offence. The timing could not be worse. With Cashman batting clean-up, the Goliaths were better than even money to make it to the World Series. Three rounds of play-off baseball. The Goliaths would have home field advantage should they close out the regular season strong. A potential of almost a dozen home games of additional attendance. Tens of millions in additional revenue, which would go a long way towards paying off the debt on the gleaming new, privately funded, ballpark.

Without Cashman in the line-up, all of that evaporated. Should the suspension begin by the end of the week, the playoffs would be without the most formidable slugger in baseball. In an era where statistics ruled, and the slightest adjustment in slugging percentage could mean the difference between the pennant and the cellar, Cashman was the difference. It had been documented: he was worth, between runs scored and runs batted in, a full run per game. There was not a pitcher or coach in all of baseball who didn't pull their hair out trying to negate his effect on the game.

But he had cheated. Even worse, been caught cheating.

How could he have been so stupid?

But what was cheating, anyway? thought MacDougall. Gone was the day when pitchers pitched complete games. Pitch counts were everything.

A position player would be out on the field six days a week, but a pitcher would only throw 100 pitches every five days. Batters faced a level of strength and a battery of arms that Babe Ruth never did. MacDougall wondered how many of Ruth's or Aaron's home runs came in the final couple of innings, when the starting pitcher's arm became rubber, and the balls they threw became as large as softballs. A hitter now would need to do whatever he could to keep an edge.

I wouldn't call it cheating. Just levelling the playing field.

But the fans would never see it that way, and Major League Baseball had to be responsive to the fans.

The thought of all those lost millions made MacDougall sick. He sat in despair as a team of five men slowly worked their way across the outfield with a hose, watering the grass methodically. There had to be something he could…

It's not cheating, just levelling the playing field, he reminded himself as he picked up his phone and hit the Send button, connecting him to the last number that had been an incoming call.

VII

They had decided to walk the long seven blocks to Homeless Island. Carlos had argued that a good reporter had to feel the ground under his feet, and pound some serious pavement. Maddy, as they passed the porn cinemas along Market Street, was not convinced.

She reflected on the irony of her assignment. Growing up in a guard-gated community in Orange County, she had never seen a homeless person, except on television. Nick Nolte, she thought, in *Down and Out in Beverly Hills*. And, of course, Dan Ackroyd's turn as a homeless stockbroker in *Trading Places*. They were funny. It was not until she went to Stanford and started coming up to the City for shopping sprees in Union Square, that she encountered the real thing. The homeless in Union Square were the most entertaining of the lot. Although initially startling to a sheltered white girl, they were relatively benign, and almost good natured. It was survival of the fittest in a very competitive market, so a non-threatening vibe was essential. There was the Dolphin Man, who wore a dolphin puppet on his right hand, and made it dance and sing. There was the Gospel Quartet, who would miraculously appear at half hour before shows at the Geary and Curran Theatres entertaining arriving theatregoers with clapping hands and soulful renditions of gospel classics. There was the remarkably clean-cut man who simply walked throughout Union Square mumbling to no one in particular, "Money for something to eat," over and over. And most gently moving of all was the older gentleman, in his thread-bare business suit, who stood quietly on the corner holding a Street Sheet for sale, without saying a word.

It had been at the end of one such shopping spree that Maddy had her first truly bone-chilling encounter with the down and out. She and her friend, Annika, had just left Macy's on O'Farrell when a horrifically skinny Black woman in a super mini skirt, her hair in straggles of ribbons and feathers, flopped to the sidewalk in front of them and began howling like a wild animal. The woman spasmed, then dragged herself along the ground screaming profanity, then spasmed again. After a few minutes of this agony, she collapsed completely. Maddy had feared she was dead. The police came shortly and woke the woman up. She then staggered to her feet and went on her way, screaming obscenities. Maddy was quite shaken by the scene, and it was many months before she returned to downtown, preferring, instead, the convenience and cleanliness of the Stanford Shopping Center, or, if she did make to the City, heading straight for the more rarefied shopping streets of Chestnut and Union.

Now she was going to be up to her eyebrows in life's rejects.

I'm sure this will be good for me, she thought. All part of life's rich pageant. A learning experience, to be sure.

They crossed Van Ness and approached the Island. It was now around eleven in the morning, and the fog from the night before was finally breaking up and the sun was coming out. It promised to be a hot day. The little-known secret of the Bay Area was that late September through early October provided the most gorgeous weather of the year. Living in Russian Hill, on Lombard Street, Maddy would encounter during the early part of the summer legions of freezing tourists who had arrived in California on vacation anticipating the glorious, Californian golden sun they had seen on television. Instead, they encountered the reason San

Francisco was affectionately known by its inhabitants as the Fog City. Maddy reflected that owning a sweatshirt stand down on Fisherman's Wharf would be a path to great riches.

But today, the heat was already beginning to make Maddy sweat a little, and she took off her pink cashmere sweater and wrapped it around her waist.

As she and Carlos approached the Island, Maddy thought that there was no one there, just a pile of boxes with a few shopping carts positioned forlornly at odd angles. As they crossed the street, however, she could hear a wailing coming from one stack of boxes. They approached cautiously. Suddenly, a little girl in a mini skirt came out of the stack, tears streaming down her face. After a moment, Maddy realized that she was not a little girl at all, but a midget, and her face was terribly worn.

"He's dead!" the woman wailed. "What will I do now?"

Maddy's initial repugnance was replaced by real concern. "Who's dead?" she asked, pulling out some Kleenex from her little black backpack and handing them to the little woman. The little woman took the Kleenex and blew her nose.

"Old Jack. He was my man. We took care of each other, you know? Looked after each other. Now he's dead, and I have no one to protect me."

"That's not true, and you know it, Mary," came a voice from behind Maddy and Carlos. They turned to see a heavy-set woman in a wheelchair rolling up the handicap ramp onto the Island. The woman was missing both of her legs.

"You know the rest of us are here for you. You'll be okay."

The woman in the wheelchair pulled up to Mary, and then wheeled around and faced Maddy and Carlos.

"Who are you two? What have you got to do with Mary?"

Maddy hesitated, so Carlos stepped forward.

"We're with the Clarion, ma'am. We hoped you might have a couple of minutes to answer a few questions for us."

"A few questions, eh?" She eyed both interns warily.

"We brought some Clif bars and some cigarettes," blurted Maddy. "Would you like some?"

The woman in the wheelchair suddenly laughed.

"I'd rather have five bucks, but if that's what you've got, then sure. What flavor Clif bars?"

"Apricot and Cherry Almond."

"No Peanut Butter Chocolate?"

"Um. I'm afraid not."

"Well, I'll take the cigarettes, then. Mary, you want the Clif bars?"

"I'm not hungry," said Mary. She had plopped herself down on the sidewalk. She began to wipe her face with the Kleenex, mopping up tear-smeared makeup. Her skirt was hiked up around her waist, revealing some very shabby black and white striped underwear. Maddy was not sure where to look.

Carlos gave the woman in the wheelchair a packet of cigarettes. The woman tore open the package, tapped out a cigarette, and put it into her mouth.

"Got a light?"

Carlos pulled out his lighter and held the flame to the woman's cigarette. She lit the cigarette and inhaled deeply. Her features relaxed visibly as she exhaled.

"So, what do you want to know? You're awfully young to be wandering around out here. Both of you. How old are you, anyway?"

"Twenty-three," said Maddy.

"Same for me," said Carlos. "We're both just out of school and interning at the Clarion."

"And they sent you babies out to interview us." The woman turned to little Mary. "They do this every few years. 'A check-up of the demographic,' or some such bullshit. At least you're not census takers. So, what do you want to know?" she repeated.

"May we start with your name?" asked Maddy, pulling out a note pad.

"Beth."

"Beth…"

"Just Beth. We sort of do without last names out here. Not much point in them. If I told you my last name, and it got in the paper, it might embarrass somebody somewhere. Most of us are out here because we don't want to be a part of our families or pasts anymore."

"If my father knew where I was, it would break his heart," said Mary. She was now applying eye shadow. A garish amount, thought Maddy.

"You were upset a moment ago about a friend of yours… Old Jack. What happened to him?"

Mary started to wail again. The tears that ran down her cheeks started to make her eye shadow run. Beth answered for her.

"The police found him dead in a doorway. He had that skin-eating disease…"

"Tissue Necrosis," said Carlos.

"Yeah. That stuff. It's horrible. Ate him alive."

"He got it from an infected needle. He… he was a user. He wouldn't get treatment for it," sniffed Mary. "Now he's gone…"

Beth rolled over to comfort Mary. Maddy pulled out some more Kleenex, which Beth took and used to dab Mary's face.

"He was sort of our unofficial leader. Our Tribal Elder. Kept us together. He was good with the police, whenever they came by." Beth started to get teary-eyed herself. "We'll miss him."

"When did he die?" asked Maddy.

"Just last night," replied Beth. "He could barely walk, but he still headed out to make his rounds. His feet were just bloody bone. The flesh had been almost completely eaten away."

Maddy felt sick to her stomach.

"His feet?" asked Carlos.

"He had run out of places to stick a needle," sniffed Mary.

There was an uncomfortable pause.

Finally, Maddy screwed up her courage. She turned to Beth.

"How did you... end up here?"

"Why do I live like shit, you mean."

"I, I wouldn't..."

"We live like shit. Some of us enjoy it, but I don't. This is a stupid, pathetic way to live. It's really just a slow death. But I hang in there because people like Mary need someone.

"I ended up here after a car accident. I was already near the bottom rung. I was so depressed after the birth of my little girl that I started drinking. My husband eventually gave up and divorced me, taking my baby with him. That made me more depressed, I drank even more, got fired from my job as a cashier at an auto shop, and got in an accident a few months later, which took my legs. I had no insurance, so every last penny went to pay medical bills no decent person could pay. Once I was released from the hospital, I had no place I could go. After overstaying my welcome on the couches of the few friends I still had, I found it less stressful to just be out here."

"How do you feed yourself?" asked Maddy.

"I work the end of Van Ness, before you get on the freeway. I do alright. With my sign, and when I can manage a smile, I can make about twelve bucks a day." She smiled a gap-toothed smile at Maddy. When she did so, her face transformed, and Maddy thought she looked years younger.

"Do you mind if I ask how old you are?" said Maddy.

"I'm thirty-two," said Beth.

"I'm nineteen," added Little Mary.

Maddy felt as if she had been slapped in the face. Beth looked as if she was in her fifties. Mary's face was worn in the way little old ladies in Russia were. It was a brutal indication of the wear that life on the streets could have. She wasn't sure what to say.

"What else do you want to know?" asked Beth.

Carlos jumped in.

"We've been asked to find out where the 'nodes' of homelessness are in San Francisco."

"Nodes?"

"You know, where do homeless people gather. Where do they call home, as it were?"

"'As it were,'" laughed Beth. "Well, that would be giving away trade secrets, don't you know."

As Maddy and Carlos looked disconcerted, Beth took pity on them.

"Well, you found this place. There's about six or seven of us who crash here. Does that make this a 'node'?"

"I think so," said Maddy.

"Well, then. Other places where more than a dozen or so people get together include the UN Plaza, of course, and along Taylor at Ellis. Big 'node' there. Then there's the Park…"

"Golden Gate Park?" asked Maddy.

"Yeah. Whole tribes of people live in the bushes out there. I couldn't do it, too fucking cold. Fog comes in fierce there almost every night. And then there's Dogpatch, down along Third Street near China Basin."

"If we were to go to those other places, are there any people we should ask for?"

"Most places, people get nervous if you're asking for specific names. Look, sure there are some pretty scary people in any big city, but for the most part, we're a pretty quiet bunch. We didn't end up homeless because we could stand up for ourselves, you know. And any of the screamers, well, they're just screamers. All bark, no bite."

Mary, at this point, had fallen asleep.
Suddenly, Maddy had an inspiration.

"Have you ever seen or heard of a Bla... I mean, African-American man who wears a black cape and rides a bicycle?"

"The Masked Avenger? Sure, I've seen him."

"The Masked Avenger... is he really called that?"

"I'm not sure what else you would call him. He's a good man. No one knows his real name, and he's not spotted all that often. A lot of lurking in shadows. He thinks he's a superhero. He's not, but he has helped a lot of people."

"Do you know where I might find him?"

"I don't know for sure, but the one time I saw him was in the Civic Center area – around McAllister and Hyde. He won't be out during the day, though. I'm sure he's a 'creature of the night,' don't you know." She laughed.

"'Creature of the night'... you mean like Batman?"

"Well, yeah, but also there are half of us who do the day shift, and half of us who do the night shift. For some of us, it's just safer to be awake at night. At night is when the real scumbags come out, and you don't want to be caught napping."

"But you're up now," said Carlos.

"Well, that's because I work the rush hour trade. I'll try to catch some sleep, and then head back by around three. Then I stay up until the sun comes up, catch an hour or two, then head back."

"That means you're only getting a few hours of sleep a day," said Maddy.

"Why do you think I look like I'm fifty?" Beth laughed again and wheeled herself towards Mary. "Come on, baby, if you're going to sleep, why don't you curl up with me. I'll take care of you."

Mary nodded slowly and allowed herself to be led to her cardboard box. She curled up inside. Beth hopped out of her wheelchair, crawled into the box, and started to tug one of the flaps closed.

"Good luck to you," she said to Maddy.

"Good luck to you, too," said Maddy. Beth just smiled.

Maddy just felt awful.

VIII

Jason Stillman had some fast work to do. And some urine samples to generate. He drained his bottle of Fiji water and headed off to the men's room. He thought of the one hundred thousand dollars he would make from this trip to the bathroom. Somehow, the revision of certain test results should be worth more than that. The man he was being paid to protect made that much per game, if he got a hit or not. As a former Little League player, Jason shook his head. He had had his dreams of playing Major League ball like any young boy, but reality reared its head in high school. Or rather, a predilection for getting stoned, and hanging out in the lab with his stoner chemistry teacher after school. Thank goodness he had an aptitude for chemistry. He parlayed that into a degree from UC Santa Cruz and this job for UriLabs. He was grateful that he hadn't toked in over a week, so his urine would be clean of all foreign substances.

It wouldn't do to screw this up with a positive result for some other contraband.

He sighed as he wiped himself, began to pee, stopped, and put the container into the stream. As he filled up the cup, he pondered the remaining steps he had to take. The sample would have to be analyzed and the old results would have to disappear. The new results would be attached to the numbered file that "protected the identity" of the test subject, and it all had to happen before the 5pm FedEx deadline. Thank God it was a slow afternoon, and his colleagues were taking a long lunch. Even if his supervisor returned early, if Jason looked as if he was simply going about his business, all would be fine.

Now, what to spend that money on?

IX

A full day behind her, Maddy pulled her bright yellow Beetle into the garage of her apartment building. As the door closed behind her, she jockeyed her car into the smallest parking space on earth. After the usual three maneuvers, she turned off the ignition and grabbed the small bag of groceries she picked up at Whole Foods on the way home.

Maddy shared her apartment with a young French woman, Angelique. Angelique was one of a large contingent of young foreign women who lived in San Francisco, working for international firms that needed bi-lingual staff. Angelique worked for an import/export company that dealt with French gourmet foods. Though difficult to live with, Angelique was worth her weight in delicacies, such as pate, mustards, cheeses, and wine. It was worth putting up with everything else, thought Maddy.

It wasn't that Angelique wasn't nice, or that she was messy. Well, she was messy in a certain way. She had a fairly pragmatic attitude towards her relationship with her boyfriend, who was still in Paris. If he wasn't here, that wasn't going to stop her from enjoying herself. With her short, chopped, black hair, long legs, and French accent, she created something of a sensation within the local straight male population. Maddy sighed as she caught her reflection in the lobby mirror before she hiked up the stairs to her second floor flat. Angelique kept her even keeled. In most any situation, Maddy could hold her own. She was blonde, pretty, and bright. Although little, at five foot two, she was built like the swimmer that she used to be in high school - firm and lean. She used to have more than her share of admirers gathered around Lifeguard Tower Number 5 down at Big Corona Beach. But when she went out with Angelique, she felt like chopped liver.

Angelique felt no awkwardness about the men who followed her home. Maddy had gotten used to sleepy morning introductions with complete strangers and finding the toilet seat left up in the middle of the night. All part of life's rich pageant, she kept telling herself.

Maddy, however, was going through an extended period of celibacy - not that it was desired, or even intentional. The truth of the matter was that she simply didn't have the energy for the San Francisco scene, and despaired of ever finding the right boy. Every man she met was either gay, married, or working through the post-college immaturity that drove her crazy. There was plenty of sex to be had if she wanted it. All she had to do was hang out in any one of a number of bars and pubs on Union Street or Fillmore. But she wasn't willing to put up with the bullshit that came with it. She didn't have the *sang froid* that Angelique had – the love 'em and leave 'em attitude.

I'm really just a good girl, she thought. I really just love snuggling, walks on the beach, movies, and good conversation. Bleh. Like every other girl in the Guardian want ads. She felt *very* special all of sudden.

The smells emanating from her apartment made her feel better. Another advantage to the French roommate was her way in the kitchen. Maddy could barely boil water, having grown up in a household where her mother wouldn't think of using a pot or pan or knife for fear of breaking a nail. But she was learning by osmosis, living with Angelique, and she was grateful for that.

As she entered the kitchen she stopped in her tracks. Angelique was locked in a passionate embrace with a handsome, dark-haired man. She was sitting on the kitchen counter with her legs wrapped around his back. Before Maddy could discreetly remove herself from the kitchen door, Angelique looked over the man's shoulder and called out.

"Maddy! How wonderful! Jean-Michel has just come from the airport. He is able to visit for the week. We are just so happy to see each other."

The young man turned and smiled sheepishly at Maddy. He took her hand and said, "A pleasure, mademoiselle." He was beautiful, thought Maddy. Blue-green eyes with black hair, and that mouth that only French people had. No wonder Angelique was faithful to him in her fashion. She might play with other men, but it was now obvious why there was never a significant attachment, or even anyone who lasted more than one night. Jean-Michel was the man who truly held her heart.

"I'm sure you want to be alone together..." Maddy stammered.

"Mais, non!" cried Angelique. "I have brought home all sorts of treats, and we would love nothing better than to have a small party here with you."

"Bien sur," said Jean-Michel, as he poured a third glass of wine for Maddy, the other two half drunk on the counter. "Please stay with us."

As Maddy sipped her glass of burgundy, and started to unload her groceries, she was hit by how lucky she was to live and eat so well. The day's adventure gave her a completely new appreciation for the simplest of luxuries: food, a clean home, a place to sleep out of the weather, running hot water.

She thought wistfully that she knew what to do with their leftovers.

X

The three teenagers were just regaining consciousness as Detective James Wang arrived at the crime scene. The old man was being wheeled on a gurney towards the ambulance, having been cleaned somewhat and bandaged by the paramedics prior to being taken to the hospital for observation. As the boys, whose faces were various shades of purple and red, began to stir, they groaned and then yelped in anger as they discovered their wrists bound behind them with duct tape.

"Don't tell me," said Detective Wang to the approaching police officer. "Methuselah, here, kicked the asses of these three innocents, trying to steal their varsity jackets."

"Hardly that, sir. But up to a point, the situation seems pretty clear."

Detective Wang sighed. Every few months, there was an incident such as this. Kids from the tonier neighbourhoods of Hillsborough and Menlo Park would come into the City for the purpose of proving their "manhood" by beating up old homeless people. This dingy, urine-stained alleyway was the perfect place for such entertainment. A gleaming BMW was parked around the corner, and the boys were, indeed, wearing leather varsity jackets, although the jackets, like the boys, were somewhat the worse for wear.

"So, who is the victim?"

"From what we can make out, the *intended* victim is Old Billy here."

Old Billy was known to the police. A surprisingly large percentage of the homeless were known to the police and tracked in an informal way. Billy had been left largely to his own devices, as he caused no trouble at all, and was a relatively clean customer, spending the little money he earned from recycling aluminum cans and bottles on the odd splurge: a bottle of Glen Garioch. Detective Wang felt a certain respect for Billy. Although Glen Garioch was a relatively inexpensive Lowland malt, it was a single malt, just the same. Not Night Train.

"Is he conscious?"

"Oh, yes. Quite lucid, in fact. Although you won't believe his version of the events."

Detective Wang went over to the gurney and knelt by the old man.

"Jimmy! Good to see you, man. What a mess, eh?" said Billy. His eyes were bright. It seemed that his only wound was a cut and bruise on his forehead. He reeked, however, of whisky.

"Billy. You've been drinking."

"Not a jot, your Honor. I had just taken it out of the bag when all hell broke loose."

"Well, if you don't mind my saying so, you reek to high heaven."

"They grabbed the bottle out of my hands and poured the stuff all over me. What a waste... It was when they flicked their lighters that I thought to myself, 'I'm completely fucked.' I mean, what a way to go, eh?"

"So how did they end up on the wrong end of the equation?"

"The most amazing thing. They had pushed me against the wall and thrown the bottle at me – hence the gash on my forehead here – and were starting to flick their Bics, as it were, when there was an incredible yell. He came at them on his bicycle. Flattened one of them right off by plowing right through him. I'll be surprised if that poor boy still has his testicles in the same place he packed them this morning."

"Who came at them on a bicycle?"

"The Masked Avenger. You've heard of the Masked

Avenger, certainly."

"No, I haven't. Don't tell me. He then swung between the buildings using his spider webbing. Billy, you *have* been drinking, and you've had a nasty smack on the head."

"Don't patronize me, Jimmy. I'm telling the story as clearly as I can. And I haven't been drinking. I told you that."

"Well, then what happened?"

"Before the other two could figure out what hit them, he was off his bike, and swinging this chain. He busted both of them in the face and chest with it. Knocked them out cold, he did. They'll need some dental work from what I can see, and they won't be playing football anytime soon, that's for sure."

"No, not, at least, until their parents' lawyers get them out of jail. Battery with lethal intent is not a light charge, but with no real harm done to you, they'll get off fairly easy. At least we'll get some community service out of them. They'll look cute in orange vests shoveling garbage down in China Basin. So, what happened next?"

"He trussed them up with that tape there, around their wrists and ankles. Fine job of it, don't you think? After making sure I was still breathing, he hopped on his bike and took off. I was just able to flag down one of your cars before my legs gave out from under me. Post-traumatic stress, I suspect. But I'm fine now, honest. Do I still have to go to the hospital?"

"Of course, you do. They just want to make sure that knock on your head isn't more serious. Come on, Billy, a chance for a shower and a night in clean sheets. You can't turn that down."

"But they'll take my clothes!"

"Your clothes are a mess. You'll get new ones."

"A shame about that whisky."

"Yes, well, we'll see what we can do about that. Now go get some rest, will you?"

"Aye, aye, cap'n."

"Wait. What does the 'Masked Avenger' look like?"

"Well, it all happened so fast, and it was dark. I know of him by reputation, more than by sight."

"By reputation…"

"You know, 'word on the street,' and all."

"Right."

"But the cape and the chain and the bicycle… I knew it was him. He's big – and a bit overweight, actually. Other than that, with the mask and all, and with the blood and whisky in my eyes, I'm not sure I could spot him in a line-up, if that's what you're asking."

"Thanks, Billy. Maybe our young friends can be more helpful."

Billy was loaded onto the ambulance, which pulled away with a little burp of its siren, and Jimmy Wang turned his attention to the three bedraggled teenagers. Before the duct tape had been removed, their wrists had been bound with plastic straps. One boy turned to Jimmy and spat blood. As he spoke, several teeth were missing.

"I hope you find the motherfucker that did this. Jesus, my teeth!"

"Rest assured we'll put our finest men on the case. But first, I think we have some questions for you and your friends back at the station."

"Why are *we* going to the station? What have *we* done? We haven't done anything; we were the ones who were attacked by that asshole."

"You mean Old Billy?"

"No, the fat Black guy with the plastic bag over his head. Assault with a deadly weapon!"

"Why do you think he attacked you, do you suppose?"

"No idea. We just stopped to ask for directions."

"I'm sure. That's why your car was parked so nicely, and all three of you were here in the alley. Listen, we'll sort all of this out, back at the station."

"Well, I'd better call someone. Where's my cell phone?"

"You'll get it back once we've sorted things out."

"What about my car?"

"That's yours, is it? Or your dad's. No, I take it back, it's probably yours. We'll look after it for you, don't you worry."

"If I find one scratch on that…"

"Just *shut the fuck up* before I take you over my knee. You have no idea how much trouble you're in, do you?"

"You have no idea who my father is. You're the one in trouble, asshole."

"I like my chances. You, meanwhile, had better behave yourself, or I might just lock you in the same cell as the Masked Avenger. Looks like the Atherton High football team will be a few logs shy of a load this season."

Jimmy Wang called over to the remaining police officers. "Take these panty-waists back to the station. In separate cars and hold them in separate rooms. I'll be there in an hour. And they don't get their cell phones until I say so. They get to make their one call collect."

Jimmy Wang was annoyed with himself. He prided himself on his ability to remain "above the fray," and rarely, if ever, lost his cool, no matter the provocation. But the sense of entitlement and the sheer audacity of these kids pissed him off. Having grown up within the respectable Chinese enclave in Nob Hill, he understood privilege. But he also understood his place within the greater scheme of things, and his obligations to honor and family. These punks understood nothing but video games and their own oversized egos inflated by years of being raised by parents who worried way too much about their babies.

As the teenagers were shoved, perhaps a little too roughly, thought Jimmy – but fuck those guys – into the waiting police cars, he took his old friend Damian Johnson aside.

"Have you ever heard of the Masked Avenger?" he asked.

"Not by name," said Damian. "'Masked Avenger' – it's sort of fantastic. I mean I *have* heard mention of a guy with a garbage bag cape, who cruises the Tenderloin on a bicycle, but I've never heard anything but that he was harmless."

"Well, as much as I admire his sense of fair play - and it seems pretty certain he saved Billy from a horrible burn, if not his life - I'm not entirely sure what to make of vigilantes, however much their hearts might be in the right place."

Damian laughed. "This is just like one of those conversations in one of those Batman movies. Where the well-meaning cop still feels an obligation to stop Batman, even though Batman is trying to save Gotham City."

Jimmy Wang sighed. He thought it sounded like one of those hackneyed scenes himself. He pulled out his wallet.

"Here's eighty bucks," he said. "Go pick up a bottle of something good for Billy... some Highland Park."

It really was a shame about that whisky.

XI

He was still breathing heavily.

Damn it. I've got to lose some weight.

But his sense of timing remained impeccable. Another minute and that poor gentleman would have been horribly burned. Killed even.

What a world, he thought. When decent people were prey to such brigandage. Again, those he was sworn to protect remained vulnerable. The police would never put themselves out to serve justice as he had just done. That gentleman would be too far below the view from their mountaintop.

He was heartened to think that he still made a difference.

He had plunked himself down to catch his breath behind the Museum of Asian Antiquities, near the service entry and the trash storage. It occurred to him that he was hungry. The museum café was excellent, and the garbage had not yet been picked up by the collectors. He had earned a meal of substance after his heroics, so he started to pull up the latch to the dumpster enclosure in order to peruse his dining options. He had just pulled the enclosure door ajar when he was startled by the bang of the service entry door being bumped open from within. Fearing discovery by the security guards, he slid into the enclosure and pulled the door shut behind him, leaving it ajar enough for him to survey the scene.

"Careful with that, for God's sake."

The voice was not that of a security guard.

A well-dressed man with silver hair had backed out of the service entrance carrying one end of a large crate. Incongruously, on the other end of the crate was a little Asian woman in a very elegant suit and high heels. They hauled their burden to the back door of a black Lexus SUV, which was gleaming in the dark space under a burned-out streetlamp. After a certain amount of grunting, the man and the woman shoved the crate into the back of the Lexus. Both took a moment to straighten their outfits.

"Glad I dressed for the occasion," said the woman with more than just a little annoyance in her voice.

"What. You would rather be in a black and white striped sweater, jeans, sneakers, with a bag marked SWAG? I'm sure no one would have remarked on *that* ensemble during the cocktail party."

"Listen, next shipment, we get one of my sons to help."

"I think not. The fewer people who know about this the better, don't you think?"

"I'm talking about my thirteen-year-old, who is, for all intents and purposes, clueless. If I can ever pull his head out from one of those games of his, he's strong enough."

"Let's just see how tomorrow goes."

"Five o'clock at the Mandarin, Room 4605. I'll meet you in the parking garage. How about you bring a hand truck?"

The man snorted. The woman climbed up into the driver's seat. She fired up the Lexus and peeled away, tearing down Hyde Street towards the south. The man took a quick look around, pulled out his keys, and, running his fingers through his silver mane of hair, strolled over to a black Mercedes sedan parked across the street. A clock chimed eleven as the car pulled away and moved slowly into the night.

Awfully late for deliveries, thought the Masked Avenger as he turned his attention back to the task of pulling together a late-night snack for himself and for Robin.

As he pulled out some half-eaten vegetable spring rolls, he thought to himself,

Perhaps I need to be near the Mandarin by five o'clock tomorrow.

XII

As the black sedan pulled away, Lucky Jerry thought to himself, Damn, I'm lucky.

He held in his hands a party platter of sandwiches. The man in the sedan had told him that they were leftovers from a party he had attended. Rather than take them home, he thought Lucky Jerry might make better use of them.

It's more than I can eat all by myself, he thought. He would be quite popular at the camp tonight. Jerry was part of a loose tribe of about ten homeless people that gathered around the fountain at UN Plaza. The platter contained about twenty half-sandwiches, so enough for everyone. This was definitely barter for some cigarettes, and maybe even a drink.

How great to be able to go to bed with some food in my stomach, he thought.

And good food, too. Looked like pesto chicken, seared tuna with garlic aioli, and grilled eggplant and bell-pepper wraps.

Why would any homeless person live anywhere but San Francisco? he laughed to himself. No one would begrudge me having first dibs.

And so, he selected the tuna sandwich, licked the aioli off the edges, and took a healthy bite.

XIII

Maddy couldn't sleep. It was a warm evening. Almost no one in San Francisco had air-conditioning – ninety-nine nights out of a hundred the evening air was cool, even cold. The Indian Summer evenings of late September, however, could be still and sultry, and it was one of the worst of those nights. The lack of movement in the air amplified the city soundscape, especially those idiosyncratic to San Francisco. The sea lions down at Fisherman's Wharf reacted as any annoyed animal would: they were barking incessantly. Anyone living in Russian Hill, with their windows open, had to endure angry sea lions telling the world to turn down the heat. This along with the usual sirens and cable car rings made sleep impossible.

And her roommate, bless her heart, was something of a screamer... At least *someone* is getting some tonight, Maddy thought.

And she felt that she was on to something.

She picked up her phone and called Carlos.

"Can't sleep?" asked Carlos.

"No. I didn't wake you, did I?" asked Maddy, sheepishly.

"Are you kidding? I'm a gay man in San Francisco. We never sleep."

"Um, if you're not doing anything, care to go on an adventure?"

"More adventurous than our day at the Island? My white blossom is opening up! Please tell me you want to visit the Power Exchange."

"Oh, Carlos, for Pete's sake. I just want to reconnoiter the Orpheum area. I somehow want to prove to myself that the Masked Avenger is real."

"He really had an effect on you."

"He did, but don't you think he might make an interesting story? I mean, there's something going on there. It wouldn't just be your basic feature on the plight of the homeless anymore. Instead, we could open up the inner workings of a would-be superhero. I want to find him and talk to him."

"But it's too dangerous for a pretty young white girl from Newport Beach to be skulking around the back alleys of the Tenderloin by herself, is that it?"

Maddy was more than a little annoyed with herself, but had to admit that this was, indeed, the case.

"I haven't yet graduated to Barbara Walters. I guess I need to toughen up a little, but not today. Please come with me!"

"Just give me a few minutes to put on the appropriate urban guerrilla-wear, and I'll be ready for anything."

"Oh, thank you, Carlos! I'll call you as I pull up in front of your house, and we can drive there."

"You're too much. You want to park that Beetle downtown on the streets?"

"Shut *up*. It's bright yellow. You can't stand next to it without giving yourself away. This will be faster. And if we don't find anything, I'll take you to Globe for a late bite."

"Now you're talking. See you in a few."

Maddy jumped up out of bed and got dressed quickly. She felt a new sensation coursing through her.

The thrill of the hunt.

XIV

Although the drive from her apartment to Carlos' Victorian in the Castro was just over three miles, even at midnight it took half an hour for Maddy to pull up to his front door. Carlos was waiting on the steps, wearing khaki fatigues, Timberlands, a black t-shirt, and a bandana.

"All you need is the AK-47," joked Maddy, as Carlos climbed into the passenger seat.

"Hey, I just want to be ready for anything. We're after some crazed vigilante maniac, for all I know."

"And you can run in those?"

"No. But I look as if I can kick the shit out of anyone, don't you think?"

Maddy couldn't help giggling. Carlos gave her his best Clint Eastwood, but it didn't help. Maddy was in jeans, a t-shirt, tennis shoes, and had her black zip-up fleece tied around her waist. As warm as the evening was, she also knew that if it was a long night, it would eventually cool off by the wee hours, and she wanted to be prepared. A stakeout could be long and tedious, or at least that was the way it was always presented on TV.

"I can't imagine you kicking the shit out of anyone. I'm prepared to let discretion be the better part of valor and run away if things get weird. And it's not going to get weird – we're just looking around, trying to get a feel for the area."

The "area," as she put it, was pretty bleak. As she parked her car across from City Hall, she surveyed the landscape. A great place for large public gatherings, but barely a tree in sight. A wasteland, actually, of concrete and asphalt, lit with sodium vapor lights. The public buildings all looked cold and dark. San Francisco, far from being the "wide open" town that lived in most people's imaginations, rolled up its sidewalks early, particularly in the Civic Center. If someone were moving around down here in the open, he would be easy to spot. It was the alleys, where the light barely penetrated, that was most likely home to denizens of the area. Maddy was very glad that she wasn't alone.

*   *   *

There was something about the way Lucky Jerry was lying there that put the Masked Avenger immediately on his guard. He didn't look as if he was sleeping. With his hands clutching at his throat, and his legs splayed as if trying to kick someone or something off of him, Lucky Jerry looked as if he had just lost the fight of his life. With the kitten purring in his pocket, the man in black and gray took in his surroundings quickly, and then approached the prone figure.

Lucky Jerry's eyes looked as if they were about to pop out of their sockets. Knowing better than to disturb the body, the Masked Avenger chose, however hard it was to look at them, not to shut the eyelids. He circumnavigated the body slowly, moving in tighter and tighter circles, assessing the situation as carefully as he could. Perhaps it was a heart-attack, he thought. That would explain much, certainly the look of terror on Jerry's face. But the hands clutching at the throat implied something else, something far more sinister. He knelt down, and leaned in towards Jerry's face, with its scraggly beard, and oily hair.

As he got closer, a squeak came from his pocket. Robin scrabbled out and headed straight for the few remaining pieces of a sandwich that lay on the ground near Lucky Jerry's feet.

"Robin, no!" called out the Masked Avenger, and his big hand shot out and scooped the kitten into the air.

45

Robin protested with another squeak and dug her claws into the Masked Avenger's glove.

Thank God for the gloves, thought the Masked Avenger, as he placed Robin firmly back into his pocket.

He had not noticed the sandwich until Robin had made her dash. Picking the pieces up carefully, he sniffed at the remains.

"Tuna," he said to the kitten grimly. "No wonder you got so excited."

He pulled a baggie from his other pocket, the one filled with little bags of soy sauce and mustard, and placed the remains of the sandwich inside.

*   *   *

"Do you see that?" whispered Maddy.

"See what?" hissed Carlos.

"Over there – just by that planter. Oh. My. God. It's him! And he looks like he's leaning over that man."

"That man isn't moving. Shit. He looks like he's dead! Fuck, your Masked Avenger just killed that guy!"

After a moment's wild-eyed hesitation – after all, they'd been there for only a few minutes and not the hours-long stakeout that she'd imagined – Maddy whispered back.

"No, no he didn't. Watch him, the way he's moving. He's inspecting the ground around him. Wait, what's that?"

"That... that would be a kitten," said Carlos in disbelief.

"What kind of crazed killer keeps a kitten in his pocket?"

"Shit, I don't know. If you stop to think about it, that would make him *really* crazy. I am *so* creeped out."

"Shut *up*. Let's go talk to him."

"Are you nuts?" whined Carlos.

"No, at least I don't think so. Something in my gut tells me that he's okay. And Beth said he was a good man. C'mon, let's go!"

With that, Maddy started to run over to the man in black and gray. Carlos put his hands on his hips for a moment in exasperation, then, grumbling under his breath, he lumbered after her.

These boots suck, he thought to himself. And they make way too much noise.

Certainly enough noise for the Masked Avenger to hear him. Maddy was almost on top of the man in black and gray and had just whipped her cell phone out of her pocket to snap a photo, when the Masked Avenger started up. Maddy's phone went "ca-chink," digitally imitating the sound of an old 35mm camera, capturing the look of surprise in the eyes of the caped crusader.

"Freeze!"

The plaza was ablaze all of a sudden. Three police cars had pulled up onto the curb in a series of screeches, with sirens blaring. Their searchlights intersected right where Maddy, Carlos and the Masked Avenger were gathered over the body of Lucky Jerry.

Great, thought Carlos. Nothing like being the Hispanic guy standing next to a dead body. This will not be any fun at all.

My dad is going to kill me, thought Maddy.

In a split second she could already see her father's face filled with disappointment as he bailed her out, after having driven all the way up from the OC in the middle of the night.

I must become one with the shadows, thought the Masked Avenger. Too much relies on my ability to fight another day.

With a nimbleness that completely belied his bulk, he spun and flipped his garbage bag cape over his face and bolted into an alleyway.

The next moment was one of those that separates the men from the boys. Carlos completely froze with his hands in the air. Maddy, watching the Masked Avenger dart into the shadows, did something she never would have thought she would do: she followed him.

She looked over her shoulder as Carlos was knocked to the ground by a couple of policemen. "I'm sorry, Carlos," she called back. She hoped he would understand. She was on the trail of a truly great story. Any *real* journalist would do the same.

As soon as she gained the darkness of the alley, she had to pause for a moment to let her eyes adjust. She blinked twice, then saw a glint of moonlight on plastic at the end of the alley, about ten feet above the ground. She ran towards a fire escape with its ladder pulled down and started clambering up. She could hear the thudding of the Doc Martens on the latticed metalwork above and gave chase.

Jeez, these buildings are old, she thought. I mean, a real fire escape. Something out of *West Side Story*.

From the sounds above her, she knew she was gaining on the black and gray-clad figure. From the sounds of his breathing, she thought to herself – almost in concern - he must not be in very good shape. She kept clambering up the fire escape, grateful for her regimen of running up and down Filbert Street every other day. Another couple of floors brought her to the roof of the building. Just as she crested the roofline, she thought she heard the sound of his footsteps as he crunched across the gravel that coated the rooftop. She stopped and listened, trying to discern which way he had gone.

It really was a noisy city. With the heat, most of the air-conditioners that were mounted to the outside of the windows of the downtown boutique hotels were running. If he stops moving, I'm never going to hear him, she thought. She scanned the rooftop. At least the moon was out, its light gleaming on the white stones. I should be able to see him…

In that instant, she heard a tiny squeak. From the ledge of the next building over, which was one storey higher than the roof on which she stood, she saw a little head pop up, with two little, pointy ears. A big paw of a gloved hand reached up and grabbed the kitten by the scruff of its neck. The kitten disappeared, with a loud squeak of annoyance. Maddy bounded across the rooftop and flung herself up the little ladder that joined the two buildings. She plopped down onto the next rooftop with a thud and a skid on the loose stones. She saw the glint off the plastic cape as it slithered around the edge of the enclosure of the roof deck stairs. Rather than run across this rooftop, making so much noise across the stones, Maddy moved stealthily around the perimeter, where the parapet met the rooftop at a slight curve. Here, there were no stones. She slowly approached the enclosure, but from the opposite side from where the Masked Avenger had gone. As she reached the corner of the enclosure, she could hear his heavy breathing, finally, over the hum of the air conditioners. She could also hear the complaining meow of the kitten.

"Shush, Robin," she heard a deep, raspy voice whisper.

At this Maddy couldn't help but giggle.

"Robin?" she said as she came around the corner. "How cute is that?"

The Masked Avenger turned quickly to face her – he had been watching and waiting for an assailant from the other direction and had been caught completely by surprise. He clutched the plunger in his hand, and waved it back and forth like a sabre, as he slowly backed away. He was about to clamber off again when Maddy said, "Please don't! It's okay. I'm not here to hurt you."

The Masked Avenger calculated his situation quickly, and then, with a huge sigh, he lowered the plunger and sank into a hunch over his heels. The kitten popped out of his sweatshirt pocket and hissed at Maddy as she approached.

"It's okay, sweetie," Maddy said gently. The kitten still arched its back, protecting its master as best as it could. The Masked Avenger took the kitten once again in his gloved hand and petted it. The kitten began to calm down.

"Are you okay?" Maddy asked the heavily breathing man.

"I'm... I'm so tired," said the Masked Avenger. "Just give me a moment to catch my breath." He looked embarrassed, Maddy thought.

"I'm sorry," said Maddy. "That was a sticky situation back there. I'm sure we're both in a lot of trouble with the police."

"Those fools!" spat the Masked Avenger. "They have no idea what they're doing."

"Um, do you?" asked Maddy.

The Masked Avenger looked at her sadly.

"No," he said, after a moment. His sigh almost broke her heart. "No, I don't. But I do give a damn."

"I'm sure you do. I've heard people speak well of you."

"What people?"

"People on the street."

A flicker of pride passed over the man's face. "Do they really?" he asked, with more than a little hope.

"Oh, yes," said Maddy, although, in truth, she had only heard this from Beth earlier that day. "They call you the Masked Avenger, and that you protect them from bad things. Are you the Masked Avenger?"

"None other," he replied, standing up to his full, towering height. He held the kitten up. "And this is Robin."

"Every superhero needs his side-kick," said Maddy.

"Exactly. Except I am not a superhero."

More lucidity than I expected, thought Maddy. At least he's not trying to fly.

"I'm really just a simple man," continued the Masked Avenger. "I am not gifted with superpowers. Hence my costume – it frightens the criminal element."

"I... I can see that," said Maddy. Now that she had found the Masked Avenger, she wasn't sure what to do

next. She felt a little like the dog chasing the car
– no idea what it would do if it actually caught
the car.

"Do you think we eluded them?" asked the Masked
Avenger.

There was a lot of noise on the street, but no sounds
of climbing on fire escapes. Carlos was running solid
interference. Good old Carlos.

"I think we did. But what should we do now? And
what happened back there in the first place?"

"Lucky Jerry. He didn't die by accident, from what I
could tell."

"What do you mean?"

"His face was contorted, and he had chunks of tuna
in his teeth. And it looks as if he dropped this." He held
up the remains of the sandwich in the plastic bag.

"Could it have been a heart attack? Or an overdose?"
asked Maddy.

"Lucky Jerry was clean. It could have been a heart
attack, but there was something about it that just didn't
look right." He sighed sadly. "I've seen heart attacks
before."

"We should take the rest of the sandwich to the
police. Perhaps they could have it analyzed."

"No, I cannot approach them," said the Masked
Avenger. "They have not chosen to accept my offers of
help in the past."

"Then how can we find out what happened? I could
go to them, but I had better have some sort of idea of
what's going on before I do."

"There is someone who could help us," said the
Masked Avenger, rubbing his chin.

"We should take this to the Man Without a Face."

XV

She had been walking for hours, without any real sense of direction. The grief Mary felt over the loss of Jack was profound, almost crippling, and she needed to keep moving to keep from curling into a ball of despair. No johns tonight – she simply couldn't muster the dispassion it would take. But her feet were starting to hurt – the heels she wore to compensate for her diminutive stature were starting give her blisters.

Where am I? she thought.

She looked around for the first time, and saw herself at the edge of a small, poorly lit parking lot. The dreary orange light of a few sodium vapor lamps mounted to the back of the large industrial building caused more shadows than illumination. A few blocks away was the 280 freeway. Trucks rumbled on the elevated intersection as they made the choice between heading into downtown or moving on east over the Bay Bridge.

I've walked all the way down to Dogpatch, she thought. Crap. And now I'm hungry.

She headed over towards a dumpster at the edge of one of the loading docks. She wanted to take off her shoes, but the parking lot was littered with broken glass mixed into the gravel. She had just passed into a shadowy spot between the lights when she was startled by the sound of a car that skidded into the lot, crunching over the garbage and gravel.

Nice car, Mary thought.

The black Hummer gleamed in the light of the sodium vapor lamps, its mammoth engine purring. A few seconds later another car, an old, but cherry BMW, pulled up next to it. At the arrival of the second car, the door of the Hummer opened, and a large man climbed down from the driver's seat. From the second car another large man climbed out. The two men faced each other, completely unaware of Mary's presence in the shadows just a few feet away.

"Nice car," said the man from the BMW. "Did you just pick that up?"

"Yeah, just yesterday. Nothing else seems to fit any more."

"Well, *yeah*. The way you've bulked up over the last couple of years. You know, no one's fooled anymore. You can talk about going to the gym twice a day all you want, but no one's buying it."

"That's not true, and you know it. The fans here will never see what they don't want to see. Especially with a championship on the line."

"You gonna get me some seats to the Series?"

"Fuck you. My girlfriend's family already has dibs."

"How's your wife feel about that?" sneered the man from the BMW.

"Look, let's just do this." The man from the Hummer pulled out a wad of bills from his sweatpants pocket. The man from the BMW pulled a black leather pouch out of his passenger seat and handed it to the other man. The money was exchanged.

"Buy yourself a new car."

"Nah. Chicks dig this one. And I'm one of those guys who funnels his profits back into his business."

The owner of the Hummer laughed, then opened the pouch to inspect its contents. Mary could see the glint of glass vials, and she knew a syringe when she saw one.

"What have we got?"

"A couple doses. According to the calendar, you'll need to refuel in a week."

"Yeah, well now that we're going into October. It's Showtime – no time to let up now."

"Then we should hook up at the end of the week. And hey, good luck with that record."

"Thanks, man. You have no idea how hard it is to

find a second's privacy with all that shit going on."

"What did you tell people you were doing now?"

"Going to the gym," laughed the first man.

"At midnight?"

"This body didn't happen by accident, dude," said the first man with a smirk as he climbed back into his Hummer.

As the cars pulled away, Mary couldn't shake that the feeling she had seen the one man before. Just as she was about to move on from this feeling without coming to a resolution, the billboard by the overpass caught her eye. Gleaming white against the night was a giant baseball, arcing out from the bat of the Goliath's superstar, Benny Cashman.

XVI

A nice evening, thought Peter Kohler as he sat on the veranda of his penthouse apartment, sipping his glass of Tokai. He lived in Russian Hill, in a Victorian that he had converted into an Italianate villa. He had a management company deal with renting out the flats on the lower two floors and the basement, which had been converted into a studio apartment. There was a nice older couple on the first floor, and, in the apartment just below his, two cute girls – one a Stanford graduate (for whom he had a grudging respect, he was a Berkeley man, after all), and one truly hot French girl. She's enough to make me turn straight, he thought. And Jesus, is she getting it on tonight.

I'm like a kid in a candy store, he thought to himself as he gazed at the sacred object. He had to unwrap it and look at it one last time.

I know how to handle this, he thought, and smiled.

The initial asking price had been $650,000. But, upon further examination and reflection, this was a $825,000 piece of Tibetan culture, at least as far as Peter Kohler was concerned. The client would be told as much – it's one thing to see an object in photographs, it was another to give it a clear, unbiased inspection once it was in hand. Should the client balk at this change in price, which was unlikely, Peter Kohler was comfortable in the knowledge that there was a waiting list. This is like printing money, he thought. All it takes is the connections.

Was he being greedy? As he looked out over the Bay, with the flash from the Alcatraz searchlight reminding him deliciously that he had a bridge-to-bridge view, he thought not. Even though his board of directors was willing to pay him "top dollar" - which sounded to him like he was a star quarterback or something - every time the Clarion published the "Who Was Making What" annual arts survey, he was embarrassed that he was still behind that goof who ran the Symphony. I have better hair, he thought. And there is a standard of living that I hope to achieve. It was a challenge sometimes to be so educated and cultured. One's needs were commensurately more advanced. His days of being a wage slave were blissfully limited, however. This was only the first of many pieces – the tip of the proverbial iceberg.

XVII

As Detective Wang left the interview room, he shook his head. I wasn't prepared for that, he thought. The stupid boy was right – his father was an extremely powerful and wealthy man. He was one of the richest men in America, and founder of one of the largest software companies in the world. Detective Wang did feel a pit at the bottom of his stomach when he was introduced, but then he was pleasantly surprised. He had heard stories about how ferocious the founder of Delphi software could be – relentless in both the boardroom and at the helm of his multi-million-dollar yacht. Jimmy Wang thought he was going to lose his job, after all.

Instead, the boy's father looked like he was going to tear his son a new asshole. James Wang almost felt sorry for the kid – almost – because he knew that the boy, in spite of being spoiled, was also in for some serious trouble when he got home.

At the very least, he might have his BMW taken away from him, thought Detective Wang with a sigh. That might actually hit the little asshole where he lived. The boy would have to return to enter a plea, but for now, he was released into his father's custody. God help him. Nothing like some negative PR to drive the price of Delphi stock down. That should piss *somebody* off.

"Hey, Jimmy. You might want to join us in IR3," said Damian, jogging down the hall after him.

"Why, what's up?"

"You're not going to believe it, that's all."

"Look, I've got more than a little paperwork to do..."

"Two words. Masked Avenger."

"You've got him?" Jimmy perked up.

"No, but we've got more of a line on him."

"Who's in Room 3?"

"Some kid – we found him standing next to a dead body near UN Plaza. He was seen with the Masked Avenger."

"Yeah, and what happened to the Masked Avenger?"

"Apparently he *can* swing between the buildings on his spider webbing."

"No shit."

"No, not really, but according to both the kid, and the guys who found them at the scene, that fat guy can really haul ass. And there was a girl with them, too."

"Let's see this guy."

They entered the room adjacent to Interrogation Room Number 3, the one on the dark side of the two-way mirror. As they looked into the brightly lit interrogation room, Detective Wang could see immediately that the boy in the chair was no criminal. The poor kid was as queer as a two-dollar bill and wearing all the wrong clothes. How do I know he's queer? thought Jimmy. He's too well groomed, for one, he thought, as he looked down at his own well-manicured fingernails. And he's just too pretty. And... ah, just forget it, he decided.

The detective on the other side of the glass decided it was time to take a break. Jimmy caught him in the hall. "Mind if I chat with him a bit?" he asked.

"Suit yourself," replied Detective Chen. "From what I can make out, he was just in the wrong place at the wrong time. I'll be back in a couple - just taking a smoke break."

"Poor guy looks like he could use a smoke, too. Anything on him?"

"Not much. His cell phone."

"Thanks."

Jimmy Wang entered the room, and Carlos looked

up.

"Hey," said Jimmy.

"Hey," said Carlos, more than a little glum.

"Not how you intended to spend the evening, right?"

"You could say that."

"What were your plans for tonight?" asked Jimmy.

"Seriously?"

"Seriously."

"Shit, you wouldn't believe me if I told you."

"You were out looking for the Masked Avenger," said Jimmy.

"You've heard of him?" asked Carlos, somewhat surprised.

"Never met him, but I've seen his work. So, what was the plan?"

Carlos sighed. "As I said to the other detective, I'm an intern at the Clarion. The other intern saw this guy first thing this morning, and we heard more about him during the day."

"During the day?"

"Yeah, we were assigned to research the various places where homeless people hang out and lay the groundwork for more in-depth interviewing by real reporters. We met some people down at this place called the Island, and they knew about this... Masked Avenger. That's what they called him."

"Okay, so why were you standing next to poor Lucky Jerry?"

"Well, Maddy had this idea..."

"Who's Maddy?"

Shit, thought Carlos. Now I've gotten Maddy into trouble. He had tried so far to be as circumspect as possible about Maddy.

"It's alright, just talk to me and it will be okay. I promise."

"That's not what the other guy said. You must be the good cop. According to the other guy, I was in a whole heap of trouble."

Jimmy sat down in the chair on the other side of the table, looked around the room conspiratorially, leaned in and whispered, "Detective Chen can be something of an asshole."

Carlos laughed.

"So Maddy had this idea..." prompted Jimmy.

"So Maddy had this idea that we might actually see the Masked Avenger for ourselves if we hung out where people had said he was sometimes spotted. I figured that it would be a bust and we would just go out for a late dinner. We had just gotten there when we saw this guy wearing a black plastic bag over his head leaning over this homeless guy. Next thing I knew, Maddy was running over to take his picture. I just ran after her."

"So, what did this Masked Avenger look like?"

"He's Black. And big. Really big, sort of fat, and wearing what looked like dirty sweatpants with basketball shorts. And the cape, of course."

Jimmy did his best not to laugh. "Of course. Anything else?"

"Well, the weirdest thing was he had this kitten."

"A kitten?"

"Yeah, this little kitten. It sort of creeped me out."

"Huh. And what happened to... Maddy?"

"I have no idea. She just took off after the guy when he split. I was knocked down by one of SF's Finest, so I completely lost track of her."

Jimmy thought for a moment, and said, "I'll be right back."

He left, and after just a few seconds, returned. He had Carlos' cell phone in his hand.

"Give her a call."

"What do I tell her?"

"Tell her she's in a whole heap of trouble, and she had better get over here as fast as she can." Jimmy looked at Carlos sternly for a second, then winked. "Tell her whatever you need to get her to come over here.

Again, you'll have to take my word for it that it will be okay."

Carlos reached over and took the phone.

XVIII

The Man Without a Face.

Maddy's friends from the OC who went to Berkeley had whispered about this mythical person. Someone who was rarely seen, but once seen was never forgotten. No one knew what his deal was, just that he was strange and horrible. Something about an accident.

Great. This has already been a full day, thought Maddy. The Island, the Masked Avenger - and Robin. A dead guy.

Now, as she hurtled across the Bay Bridge in her yellow Beetle with the Masked Avenger – and Robin – in the seat beside her, she thought to herself, when the going gets tough, the tough get weirder.

She was both excited and miserable. Excited because... it really *had* been a full day. Couldn't get better than this in the intrepid reporter department. But she was miserable because in the crucial moments, she felt herself lacking. Here she was, with the object of her research In. Her. Car. And she was completely tongue-tied.

It didn't help that he stank to high heaven.

She was so nervous navigating her way to Berkeley that she just didn't have the extra... whatever... to pepper the Masked Avenger with questions. All she knew was that the Man Without a Face was in Berkeley, and that it wouldn't be an issue hunting him down after midnight.

They had determined pretty quickly that the only way to get to where they were going was to take her Beetle. The Bay Area Rapid Transit – BART - was closed. Maddy thought to herself that she could never understand how a city as great as San Francisco could have a mass transit system that closed at midnight. Shouldn't that be when things got interesting in a town like this? If tonight was any indication, then BART should be running 24/7.

She and the Masked Avenger had waited until the last squad car had peeled away from the crime scene and poor Lucky Jerry had been zipped up in the body bag. They then clambered down from their rooftop perch and circled around to her car. The Masked Avenger had given her the vague direction of the Chemical Sciences building at UC Berkeley, and off they went.

This is hard, thought Maddy. Even natives of the Bay Area got confused dealing with the interchanges that wove their way across the Bay in the form of the Bay Bridge. One wrong lane and one ended up on Treasure Island, Yerba Buena Island or West Oakland. All of them difficult to get out of. But she caught the right sequence of exits, and eventually found herself cruising up University Avenue. It was along this long stretch of surface street between the freeway and the university that she finally got the nerve to question the huge man next to her.

"The Man Without a Face," she said. "He sounds more than a little ominous. A little like the Wizard of Oz. Why are we going to see him?"

"Because I need a heart," said the Masked Avenger.

Maddy had no idea what to say to that. The Masked Avenger then smiled. Sadly.

I will never get a bead on this guy, thought Maddy. Just when I'm sure he's insane, he says something ironic or incredibly true. Or just funny.

"I'm sorry. I couldn't help it. But there *is* something wrong with my heart, I think."

"Oh. Maybe you should see a doctor."

"No, I mean, my heart aches all the time. So much sadness." He looked out the window at the closed Indian shops and restaurants along University Avenue. "Have you ever heard the term Acedia?"

"Um, no."

"It's a condition in which your soul is so weary of the world, that you can do almost nothing."

"You seem to be doing a lot."

"It takes every ounce of strength I have to overcome this world weariness. I'm not sure I can sustain it for much longer."

Maddy thought to herself that she had felt something like that once or twice after finals, or after Justin broke up with her during her senior year. But the man's voice carried a weight and depth to it that made her think that her life could never be considered hard.

"But people need you," she said, trying to find that perky place inside her. "You're doing good things."

The man in black and gray sighed and pulled Robin out of his pocket and stroked the kitten absent-mindedly. That kitten can purr, thought Maddy. Robin was louder than her VW.

They rode on without speaking - the dual purring of the car's engine and the kitten filling the silence – for a few more blocks, finally arriving at where University Avenue dead-ends with the campus. A few blocks of going back and forth on one-way streets in an effort to work their way up towards the center of campus, and they found the rarest of rarities, a parking space in Berkeley.

They pulled up in front of the Chemical Sciences building. As Maddy climbed out of the car, her cell phone rang.

I have got to change that ring tone, she thought ruefully. "Music of the Night" from *Phantom of the Opera* revealed her to be the biggest musical theatre geek on the planet.

"Carlos! Oh my God! Are you okay?"

"After two hours in detention, I guess I'm okay. Look, you have to come in."

"Come in? What does that mean?"

"To quote Detective Wang, it means you're in a

whole heap of trouble. You've got to get over here to the station on Vallejo Street as fast as possible."

Maddy's stomach flipped over. Trouble with the police. Crap. She could really imagine the phone call to her dad now.

"I'll be over as soon as I can. What kind of trouble could I really be in?"

"Heaps and heaps." Maddy could hear the vaguest hint of sarcasm. Carlos wasn't very good at acting – his inner voice came out much too often. She was mildly relieved.

"Listen, I'm following the lead of a lifetime. I'm in Berkeley but will be there as soon as I can. At this time of night, I should be able to get back there within an hour."

"An hour? At this time of night, it should only take you twenty minutes. What have you got going on?"

"The Man Without a Face," she whispered ominously into the phone. "I'll tell you everything when I get there. You going to be okay?"

"Sure, I've got nothing else to do this evening. At least the Detective is super cute."

"So not a complete waste of your time? Jesus, you're incorrigible." With that, she hung up. She looked over to where the Masked Avenger should have been by her car, then at the entrance to the building. He wasn't in either place. She scanned the immediate area, then spotted a concrete bunker with masses of steam coming out of it. It was the ventilation shaft for the complex. On top of it, with his cape billowing around him, was the Masked Avenger. Maddy got chills up her spine. Where was the film crew when you needed them? she thought. For that moment, he really did look like Batman, with the steam roiling around him and with his cape dancing in the updraft.

He was fussing at something – the lock of the grate. Suddenly it opened. He looked up at Maddy and waved her over.

"Where are we going?" she puffed as she clambered up onto the bunker. "I thought we were going to the Chemical Sciences Building. It's right over there."

"We're going *under* the Chemical Sciences Building," said the Masked Avenger. "I'll go first."

With that, he clambered down the ladder into the mist-enshrouded darkness.

Crap, thought Maddy. This is really going to screw up my hair. At least I'll have one hell of a story to tell. She climbed down the ladder after him. A voice called up from the deep, "Shut the grate behind you." She climbed back up, took a quick look around her, then pulled the grate shut.

This is deeper than it looks, she thought as she worked her way down the ladder. After what seemed like five minutes, she hit bottom, or what must be bottom. She wasn't sure – she was standing on a mushy pile. With disgust she realized she was standing on a mound of cigarette butts, gum wrappers, leaves – all the stuff that made its way through the grate. This, obviously, hadn't been cleaned in years. It made her reflect on what she was breathing inside any large building. Ew.

She looked around her. To one side was a tunnel, with hundreds of pipes and conduit runs strapped to the walls, illuminated by dim bare bulbs in wire cages every thirty feet or so. The Masked Avenger beckoned to her through the mist. If he was saying anything to her, it was hard to hear. The whole place had a hum to it. Big old building breathing.

The tunnel was cleaner, thank God. Painted in that famous industrial green paint. The three of them – Robin had jumped out and was trotting alongside her master – moved deep into the rumbling bowels of the building. After making a right turn, they came to a steel door. The Masked Avenger pounded on the door with his gloved fist. After a moment, Maddy heard a shuffling from the other side of the door. Suddenly, the door flew open, revealing one of the most disturbing images Maddy had seen so far in her young life.

He truly had no face. There were holes in the right places, but only just holes. One eye was really just a pinhole. Where the nose should have been there were two small flaps around the nostrils, and the mouth was more of a scar than a lipped opening. It took every ounce of self-control for Maddy not to scream.

"What do you want?" rasped the Man Without a Face, the mouth hole just sucking air in and out to make the sounds. "Oh. It's you. Come in."

"We need your help," replied the Masked Avenger.

"We. Who is this?" asked the Man Without a Face, gesturing at Maddy. Maddy noticed that he was missing three fingers on his hand. He just had a thumb and a forefinger.

"She is an ally," said the Masked Avenger.

"An ally. Does she have a name?"

It had never come up. Maddy steeled herself and stepped forward, to help the Masked Avenger through the awkward moment. "My name is Maddy Stevenson. Good to meet you. Thank you for your help." Reflexively she started to put her hand out to shake, then hesitated. Without any hesitation, the Man Without a Face grabbed her hand in his thumb and forefinger. Chills ran down Maddy's spine.

"Good to meet you," said the Man Without a Face. Despite the strangeness of his voice, Maddy could hear sincerity and gentleness. Something inside her let go a bit, and she smiled.

He released her hand and gestured at them to come into the room. Maddy, who had, up to this point, been unable to take her eyes off the Man Without a Face, finally looked around. It was enormous, this room. And it was filled with all sorts of laboratory equipment, much of which was humming away. Several tables were filled with beakers, test tubes and Bunsen burners. Everything was burbling. In the far corner of the room was what looked like a monk's cell: a single bed, with a small bedside table and table lamp. A little bookcase with neatly arranged books. Next to that was a small table with a single seat beside a stove and refrigerator. At first, Maddy was thrilled to be in such a unique and mysterious underground world. She felt she was standing in a combination of Frankenstein's laboratory, Sherlock Holmes' living room and the lair of the Phantom of the Opera. All it needed was candles rising out of the floor. Then a wave of sadness washed over her. She wondered what such a life, lived mostly underground out of sight of the rest of the world, would be like.

"I don't get many visitors down here. Sorry the place is such a mess. Can I get you anything? Some wine? I just opened a nice Cotes du Rhone."

"I'm afraid time is of the essence, and we have work elsewhere. I'm sorry we can't stay," said the Masked Avenger.

"How can I help?" asked the Man Without a Face. His loneliness was palpable. Maddy felt for a moment that she was sad they couldn't stay.

The Masked Avenger pulled out the plastic bag with the remains of the sandwich.

"I think this is poisoned. I think this killed a man this evening. Can you help us identify what's in it?"

The Man Without a Face took the bag and set it down on one of his tables. He took a moment. Maddy thought that it would be terribly hard to read any expression. Was he sad? Was he angry? Was he thinking about his own dinner? When he spoke, though, she really could sense his emotions clearly. Kind of like the Elephant Man, she thought.

"Yes. There is enough left over to do the analysis." Maddy could hear clearly that he wanted to help, but that he was tired. "When do you need the results?"

"People's lives depend on our efforts, so please do

the best you can," said the Masked Avenger.

"Of course. Come back tomorrow," sighed the Man Without a Face. "It's not as if the beauty sleep would do me any good."

*   *   *

Driving back down University Avenue, Maddy was quietly devastated. She was wrestling with more than a new etiquette. It was a whole new world view. She had met more people with more disadvantages in one day than she had in her entire life. She had been brought up not to "notice" differences in people – which was weird because she grew up in a place where differences were measured in shades of blonde. "Differences" had all been theoretical. Never put to the test as it was today. And yet when confronted with the obvious, everyone she had met throughout the day had shared their disadvantages in the most direct way. No self-pity, nothing maudlin. So, quietly, she just put it out there:

"Was he born that way?"

"No. I've been told he was once quite handsome. And an incredibly promising graduate student in chemistry at UC Berkeley in the early 70's. He was also one of the early animal rights activists, and a would-be maker of bombs for a radical wing of that cause."

"Oh. My. God."

"He never hurt anyone but himself." The Masked Avenger paused, then looked out the window across the Bay as they approached the Bay Bridge. "There are some mistakes that..." His voice trailed off. "Once the surgeries were complete and he had taken time to heal, he was taken in by his old department because of his abilities, but, of course, it was understood that he could never teach. Besides, no one could bring themselves to look at him. So, he does research. Mostly for the Army, ironically enough. He brings in enough grant money that the University lets him have his own lab, as you saw."

"How did you meet him?"

"We both spend a lot of time in the shadows. You meet all sorts of people out of the light."

That's for darn sure, thought Maddy.

"Sounds like the Justice League," she chirped. "You know, the comic books."

When the Masked Avenger sighed and continued to look out of the window in silence, Maddy thought that she would make it a goal to get him to laugh. Maybe not tonight, though.

*   *   *

As she pulled up to the corner of Hyde and Ellis to drop him off, the Masked Avenger turned to her. "How much will you tell them?" he asked.

"As much of the truth as possible."

"They will not believe you..."

"That will be their problem. How can I find you? I mean, there's more work to do."

"Call me."

"Call you? On what?"

"My cell phone, of course."

"You have a cell phone?!"

"Who doesn't?" he asked matter-of-factly as he pulled out an old Samsung.

This was a tremendous revelation to Maddy. Homeless people have cell phones... She was suddenly reminded that many of them had bank accounts with ATM cards – she had seen people who were obviously homeless withdrawing cash from ATMs at the Bank of America at the cable car turnaround. Many of them had the things that anyone else would have in their lives. Just not a home.

"Give me your number," he said.

After reflecting ruefully for an instant that it had been a long time since she had given a man her phone number, she gave it to the Masked Avenger, and he punched it into his phone. He then pressed Send and "Music of the Night" started to jingle on her phone. Again.

"Catchy tune, that," he said. "Now you know where to reach me."

"What name should I punch in for you? You do have a name, don't you?"

"No," he said simply, and got out of the car. "Not anymore."

And he was gone.

XIX

It was 2:30 in the morning when Maddy walked into the station on Vallejo Street. She went up to the night desk and asked for Detective Wang. After sitting and waiting for a few minutes, she looked up to see a tall Asian man, about 30 years old, with a nice suit and crisp, short hair walking towards her.

"Hi, I'm here to see Detective Wang. My friend is here and…"

"*I'm* Detective Wang. You must be Maddy."

He smiled. Maddy was *so* not ready for this. He was killer cute. And he wasn't even blond.

"Um, yes. Maddy Stevenson. I understand I'm in a 'heap of trouble.' Look, it's all my fault. Carlos didn't do anything. I can explain everything, and I think I can even help." She was rambling.

"Come with me," he said, with a delicate mix of politeness, firmness and, could it be? a sense of humor, that made Maddy get a little weak in the knees. Confidence without arrogance, she thought. Nice.

They walked down a corridor and entered a room. Carlos had been lazily flipping through the station's back issues of People and Us magazines. The look of relief on Carlos' face was a sight to behold.

"Chica! Come and give me a hug."

They embraced, then Detective Wang coughed theatrically, and they pulled apart and looked around. Detective Wang motioned to the second chair for Maddy to sit down. As she hesitated, Detective Wang reassured her. "I'm okay standing," he said. "They don't call us flatfoots for nothing."

After Maddy had taken her seat, Detective Wang stood in front of her, and his smile turned into an expression of deep concern. "Fleeing a scene of a crime doesn't look very good."

"Yes, sir," said Maddy sheepishly. "But..."

"But it was for a good cause, I'm sure."

"Yes, sir, it was, sir."

"Um, it makes me feel a little uncomfortable to be called 'sir'. That's what we call my dad. My name's Jimmy."

"Okay, yes, sir."

Jimmy Wang rolled his eyes. Despite his professionalism, and in spite of the tiredness of Maddy's face and the state of her hair, he couldn't help thinking, She's a pretty girl. And not a malicious bone in her body.

"So, the good cause..." he prompted.

"I'm quite sure you won't believe me. There are caped crusaders and subterranean laboratories involved."

"Try me. I may know a thing or two about the caped crusaders, at least."

So Maddy told him about how she and Carlos had staked out the Masked Avenger, and how she had taken his picture, and then, when he ran, she just ran after him.

"Let me see that picture, please."

She handed him her cell phone. He saw a large Black man covered in black plastic, with his eyes large, looking straight at the camera. A pretty clear image. He could post this for the benefit of the whole SFPD. It wouldn't be hard to catch the Masked Avenger with this.

"I'll need to borrow your phone for a few minutes."

"What are you going to do with it?" asked Maddy. "I mean, this is my big scoop! And besides, he didn't do anything!"

Jimmy Wang looked at Maddy for a moment, then at the photo. "What's this in his hand?"

"That's a half-eaten sandwich. It's evidence."

"You bet it's evidence, and it's not in police custody. That's very serious. You should know that. Tampering with evidence is something you could be arrested for. So, what happened to it?" He had still not returned the phone.

Maddy then proceeded to tell Jimmy and Carlos the rest of her story, including the Man Without a Face, and how he was also just trying to help. Jimmy Wang did everything he could not to show either his wonder at the tale, or his increasing frustration. I hate this, he thought. I am about to sound like my dad.

"Listen, I know you think this guy is doing all he can to save the world, but I know that he is capable of some serious damage. I had three boys in here earlier who were beaten pretty savagely by this 'Masked Avenger,' or someone matching his description. To say he has become a 'person of interest' would be an understatement. Running around with him could be more than a little hazardous to your health. To compound all of this, he was at the scene of an apparent homicide, and absconded with crucial evidence. It doesn't matter that the evidence was delivered to someone you believe is capable of analyzing it – if everyone behaved with as much disregard for the law as you and your masked friend have done, my job would be impossible. As it is, you've just made it really, really hard."

There. That sounded just like his dad. And he could tell that he just lost Maddy with that one. Shit.

"Sorry to be such a tough guy," he said with a gentle smile, in an attempt to salvage the situation. "It's just that you seem to be involved in something you don't know enough about, and I can tell you are a nice person wanting to do the right thing. I would hate for you to get hurt."

That helped, thought Maddy. Only just a bit, though. A little patronizing. But her allegiance had been set. After only two hours with the Masked Avenger, as deluded as he might be, she still saw a person who really *did* give a damn. And who, despite his world-weariness, lived his life on his own terms and as fully as possible.

She felt like she was just a stupid, sheltered kid who had had much of her life handed to her on a silver platter, and she found herself respecting him profoundly.

"Do you know how to find him?" she heard Detective Wang ask.

"No. Um, really, I don't."

He looked at her for a moment, not sure what to say. This is where I get into trouble, he thought. With a sigh, he played his best card. He slid her cell phone back to her across the table.

"Don't you need to pull that image off of there?"

"No. This is where we start to do some trust-building. I am going to trust that you *do* know what you're doing, Nancy Drew, and I'm going to trust that when the time comes, you will call me, and help make my job a little less hard." He set his card on top of Maddy's phone.

Jimmy and Maddy looked at each other, and there was that heartbeat-skip moment. Carlos, who had been starting to nod off, suddenly got very *not* sleepy. His antennae were suddenly quivering. Before he could say anything smart, however, Detective Wang turned and opened the door, gesturing for him and Maddy to leave.

"I think it's time for you interns to get to bed," Detective Wang said. "Me, I have an autopsy to go to. Unless you want to come along," he added with a wicked smile.

"Who is it?"

"Lucky Jerry. The guy at the Plaza."

"Um, no thanks. He was creepy enough the first time."

"Yeah," added Carlos. "Besides, two hours of sleep is better than none."

*   *   *

The sky was turning the purple, bruised color that

signals the approach of dawn as the little Beetle pulled up outside Carlos' house. Both Maddy and Carlos were exhausted, but excited. Maddy wasn't sure if she would ever fall asleep, not that she would have more than a couple of hours before she had to head back to work, anyway. She didn't really want to say anything, not to Carlos who would never let her live it down, but she had to let it out of her system.

"That guy was *so* cute. For a..."

"For a gook?" said Carlos.

Maddy was suddenly flushed with embarrassment. She had just committed one of those silent, almost invisible acts of racism that "enlightened" white people commit almost daily. It was like John McCain saying Barack Obama wasn't a Muslim, he was too nice.

"I wasn't going to say that!" she retorted, although she was going to say, 'for an Asian.' "I was going to say for a cop."

"Right. And I'm Che Guevara. But you're right. He *was* cute."

"Oh, shit. Oh Carlos. I'm never going to get my gaydar up and running. Now that you mention it, he was too well groomed..."

"Calm down, Chica. He's straight."

"And you would know because..."

"Because what you lack in gaydar, I've got in... whatever the opposite is."

Maddy almost laughed out loud. It was the woman's curse in San Francisco – you assumed the guy was gay until he proved otherwise. She had never worn the shoe on the other foot. How often was a gay man's heart broken by the guy who really *was* straight?

It was a tough town.

*   *   *

"Oh, I'm sorry!"

Maddy had just walked into her bathroom to see

Jean-Michel climbing out of the shower.

"Bon jour!" he said breezily. "It is I who am sorry – jet lag, you know. I couldn't sleep so I took an early run. I will be out of your way as soon as possible."

Gosh, he is beautiful, thought Maddy, after she turned away to let him wrap himself in a towel. Having encountered Beth, Little Mary and the Man Without a Face during the last twenty-four hours, she was deeply affected now by how beautiful a thing a handsome, healthy young man was.

Maddy was desperate to go to sleep, but she wanted even more desperately to take a shower. Running across rooftops and crawling through ventilation shafts left her feeling grungy. That, and riding in her car with the Masked Avenger. Whew, *he* needs a shower, she thought. Once Jean-Michel had cleared the bathroom, she peeled off her clothes, turned on the shower and stood under the hot jet of water, letting the day, and the night, wash off her. She remembered the Calvin and Hobbes cartoon that she had cut out and put on her refrigerator, where Calvin comes home with grass stains on his knees, twigs in his hair, sap on his hands, sand in his shoes. Hobbes, his tiger friend, pumps his fist and says, "I would consider this day seized!"

Tomorrow we seize the day and throttle it, thought Maddy, as she started to fall asleep standing up.

XX

"I don't want to create an uncomfortable work environment for you guys with hard language and all, but you two look like *crap*. No other way to describe it. Do I have to send you home?"

"No ma'am," said Maddy. She and Carlos were standing in Carey Portman's office, debriefing from yesterday, and planning their day's work. The two of them had decided, for the moment, to keep the previous day's adventures limited to their field trip to the Island. It was too soon to be laying the Masked Avenger on Carey's desk, and the guy who wrote the police blotter was already dealing with Lucky Jerry – the police currently describing his death as a possible overdose.

They all decided that Dogpatch was their destination for the day, being one of the nodes and all. It was easy to get to - just take the tram down Third Street, past the ballpark.

Maddy, though, wanted to take a detour, much to Carlos' displeasure. "It will only take about fifteen minutes," she scowled at him. "I just need to do this."

At the Island, she found Beth and Mary getting ready for their late morning nap. Maddy had brought a grocery bag full of leftovers from her dinner with Angelique and Jean-Michel: pate, a loaf of bread, some roast chicken, Camembert and some pastries.

"All we need is the Beaujolais," said Beth with a big smile. "How are you chicks doing today?"

Both Maddy and Carlos said they were fine, but Beth teased them. "Partying late? You kids – remember, Just Say No. And you," turning to Carlos, "you're using condoms, right?" Then she turned serious. "Some bad shit at the Plaza. Lucky Jerry... doesn't make sense.

People are saying the place has got some bad
juju, that they're thinking of making their camp
somewhere else."

"What happened?" asked Maddy, feigning
ignorance.

"People are saying that Jerry was murdered. Police
are all over the place. And a bunch of people are sick
down there."

"Have any of them gone to the hospital?"

"Are you nuts? What good would that do? It's not
like any of us are on Blue Shield. But it's bad there."

"Maybe we should go to the Plaza instead of
Dogpatch," said Maddy.

"Not many people left."

"Where would they go?"

"Anywhere else. What's hard is that if they're
feeling bad, they'll just go to ground. Out to the Park, for
a lot of them. That way they can just sleep in the bushes,
and no one bugs them."

Little Mary, who was tearing into the pate, stopped
as if she suddenly remembered something.

"You're reporters, right?" she asked.

"Well, we're working on it," said Carlos.

"I think I know something important."

"*News* important or *police* important?" asked Carlos.

"I don't know. All I know is that I saw something
that didn't make any sense last night."

"What? Where?" asked Maddy.

"It was down off Third Street. Dogpatch. I don't
know how I ended up there, but I was in this parking lot,
behind this big industrial building, looking for
something to eat. I don't think they saw me."

"Who?" We're going to have to work on our
interview skills, thought Maddy. What. Where. Who.
Jeez.

"You know, the baseball player. The guy who's
always in the Sporting Green."

"Um, you mean Benny Cashman?" asked Carlos.

Not that he followed baseball or anything, but it was hard to ignore Benny Cashman. He was the face of the Goliaths. They couldn't print enough different shots of him launching homers into the Bay on the front page of the sports section.

"Yeah. I'm sure it was him."

"Well, so?"

"It was late at night, and I thought, why would he be hanging out in an abandoned parking lot at that hour?"

Good question, thought Maddy.

"And he met this other guy... they were both really big..."

Maddy could only imagine how huge someone like Benny Cashman would look to Little Mary.

"So, what did they do?" asked Carlos. "Make out?"

"You're funny," said Little Mary with a sparkle of a laugh. "No, this Benny guy paid this other guy a lot of money, and the other guy gave this Benny guy a couple of little bottles and some syringes. It was just a little weird, you know?"

"That *is* weird," said Maddy.

Not really, she thought. She, too, had heard all the speculation about how, over the last few years, Benny Cashman had gotten so big. And how he was hitting home runs at an astonishing clip – not that the fans minded. This didn't sound weird at all. But it did sound like there might finally be evidence out there to substantiate the speculation.

"News *and* police important," she said. "What did they say?"

"That there was enough of whatever the stuff was to get him through the week."

"Did they say when they would be meeting again?"

"No, just that he would need more before the... what is it? Oh, the playoffs."

I'm going to have to start reading the Sporting Green, thought Maddy, At least enough to know when the Goliaths start the post-season. Then - she rolled her eyes as she thought about it - another stakeout. She got tired just thinking about it, but no rest for the wicked.

"So, are you going to tell anybody?"

"Not yet," said Maddy. "We will look into it, though."

XXI

The stadium was a roiling mass of humanity around him. Faces painted in black and silver, contorted with emotion. He felt the grass crunching under his feet as he walked in slow motion towards the center of the field. He was searching for something... couldn't remember, though, what it was. The sound of the crowd grew in his ears, a thunderous roar...

He was awakened by the sound of water being sprayed under high pressure. It sounded like a jet engine, and Robin was equally startled – digging her claws reflexively into his arm. Outside, off the alley, several men were high-pressure washing the sidewalks and plaza around the Orpheum.

No rest for the wicked, he thought. Two hours were better than none...

He could sense that things were moving around him, that changes were coming. That he would have to move.

That's too bad. I liked this alley.

He liked it not just because it afforded him shelter, but because he felt connected to something... artistic? Beautiful? Shows came and went, and he liked the energy associated with the theatre: load-ins, load-outs, dancers, stagehands. But there was something about the music. On nights when he wasn't out on his rounds - which was rare - he would sit up on the fire escape and lean his head against the wall of the auditorium. The music would rumble through the concrete and mesmerize him. He had particularly enjoyed the most recent show, a revival of *South Pacific*. He thought the music sublime.

But there was something about the energy of what was coming that he couldn't put a finger on. Something that was less about art, or music, and more about... money. There were too many men in suits about. It made him feel even more tired than he already was.

When am I going to get some rest?

He looked out of the alley. Sure enough, there was a man in a suit, directing the other men with the high-pressure hose. The Masked Avenger took stock of the man in the suit: balding, definitely well paid – one could tell by the fleshiness of his face and the quality of his clothes – but nervous and intense. He's scared, thought the Masked Avenger. And his eyes are small and dark – he's looking at every angle.

I don't like him.

*   *   *

John Sanders looked around. The high-pressure cleaning was going well – the building and surrounding area glistening and shiny. There were several police officers milling about, but otherwise the sidewalks were empty. It occurred to him that without homeless people, San Francisco could look very empty. He consoled himself with the thought that within a week the sidewalks in front of the Orpheum would be crowded with families – lots of children – coming to enjoy *The Leopard Prince*. By then, he was sure, there would be plenty of panhandlers taking advantage of the boost in the middle to upper-middle class patrons to make the area "colorful" again, but by then it would be too late. The deal would be done, Niederman Productions would be making its profits, and he would be sitting on a pretty healthy bonus, without having to do much work. Once *The Leopard Prince* was ensconced at the Orpheum, it would "sit down" there for two years, with an option for a third. Plenty of time to negotiate the next production – most likely another MagicLand Theatrical release. The template would already be established – again, lots of money for not much real effort. It's time to book that cruise, he thought.

As the high-pressure cleaners erased the chalk outline that had indicated the final resting place of Lucky Jerry, John Sanders felt a twinge of... what was that feeling? Couldn't be remorse, he thought. Nah, no one had shed a tear for Lucky Jerry or his band of scumbag friends. He was in a better place, and the rest had run for cover.

He opened his cell phone and called his driver. In a few minutes the black sedan pulled up to take him back to his office downtown.

XXII

Nancy Drew. Grrrr. He got away with that one, Maddy thought ruefully as they rode on the Third Street Light Rail down towards China Basin and Dogpatch. The nerve of that guy. She thought that Sherlock Holmes would have been more appropriate. She felt that she was developing her own band of Baker Street Irregulars. Little Mary decided to come with her and Carlos, and she was fussing with her makeup in her seat at the back of the tram. Her little legs were dangling, swaying to the jerky movements of the tram as it made its way across the bridge by TBD Park. As Maddy watched her, she remembered reading what Sherlock Holmes once told Watson about his Irregulars – street urchins that were in Holmes' employ: "They can go anywhere, see anything, and yet remain invisible." This, in a town like San Francisco, was almost true about the street people. "Normal" people had learned, out of emotional self-defense, to ignore them, to pretend to not see them. Imagine if they chose to be unseen. They knew the hidden byways of the City, and if they paid any attention at all, could see and overhear much.

Little Mary had volunteered to show Maddy and Carlos the lot where she had witnessed the exchange. She had friends down there anyway, she said, and she would introduce Maddy and Carlos to them. She felt that it was the least she could do for the delicious lunch that Maddy provided.

"I think it was here," Little Mary said, and they got off the tram at 20th Street. They stood in front of a four-storey industrial building that covered a full city block. They walked down the street along the side of the building towards the back. Behind the building was a large parking area, covered in gravel. Being eleven in the morning, though, rather than being the empty lot that Little Mary remembered, it was packed with cars. The difference confused her a bit, but she then recovered.

"I was over there," she pointed to a sequence of dumpsters along the wall. "And they were over there."

Maddy went over to the dumpsters, which smelled horrible, and surveyed the scene. She couldn't help thinking about the level of desperation that would lead someone to seek food within such containers of refuse, reeking as they did of decayed fast food, stale beer, barf, chemical and industrial waste. It almost made her sick. After blocking the smell out of her mind, she settled down and took a sequence of photographs in a panorama. Could come in handy later, she thought. Another bleak place – the buildings surrounding the area were vacant. They were brick, with tall windows of mostly broken glass. Through the gaps between the buildings, Maddy could catch glimpses of the cranes that, at one time, off-loaded containers for delivery up and down the West Coast. Now, the Port of Oakland was the port of entry for most of the goods that arrived into Northern California, leaving the Port of San Francisco home to a few cruise ship docks, farther north along the Embarcadero, and little else. Huge flocks of seagulls swept up into the air from the empty field that was across from the parking area, and swept back down again, creating a cacophony of squawks and calls.

"What time was it that this happened?" she asked Mary.

"I'm not sure. I know the stadium lights were still on..."

Of course. The Goliaths had played a game at home last night, so the meeting must have taken place after the game was over, and after Cashman had hit the showers, gotten dressed and headed home. If the lights were still on - and even down here in Dogpatch one would have seen the glow up against the mist of the San Francisco night – that meant the encounter would have happened between about 10:30 and midnight. Not so bad as stake outs went – a tight time frame.

"C'mon," said Little Mary. "Let's see if my friends are home."

She started hobbling on her heels towards the far end of the lot, past the field, and towards a bombed-out looking building close to the abandoned waterfront. Through the tall, broken windows, Maddy could see that most of the roof of the building was gone – big gaping holes through which she could see the sky. Mary led them down a small set of steps at the back of the building. She knocked on a faded green metal door, which had a safety glass window. She paused for a bit, then pushed the door open.

"Anybody home? It's Mary! ...It's okay!"

There was the sound of shuffling from somewhere beneath them, followed by the sound of a can clinking across a floor. As Mary, Maddy and Carlos moved into the building, Maddy could see that they were standing on a large catwalk that circumnavigated the interior of the space, with metal stairs leading down several flights below street level. The place was enormous, with large turbine looking things rising out of the darkness below.

"Mary? What's up, girl?"

Out of the darkness, a misshapen clump of dirty sweat-clothes clambered up the stairs. A woman was inside them, judging from the sound of her voice, but it would have been hard to tell from looking at her. Her dirty face was covered by a hoodie that was trying to hold in a tangled mass of dreadlocks. And the quantity of clothing she wore made it impossible to determine how big or small she was inside them. As she got to the top step, though, she pulled her hoodie back, letting her dreadlocks free, allowing her face to be revealed.

She is beautiful, thought Maddy.

"Nothin'" replied Mary. "Just showing my friends around."

"Your friends?" the dreadlocked woman asked, more than a little incredulously after taking in Maddy and Carlos.

"Yeah. They're real nice. They've given me and Beth a chunk of food, and they're just trying to learn more about the way we live."

"Now why would they want to do that?"

Maddy had grown considerably braver over the last twenty-four hours or so, so she stepped forward and introduced herself.

"Hi. I'm Maddy, and this is Carlos. We work for the Clarion, and, well, we've learned that all of your stories are so interesting that we want to meet more of you and hear more of them."

"You want to learn all about losers, is that right?" The woman looked at them for a tough second, then turned on a megawatt smile. "You've come to the right place! I'm Jasmine. Come on in!" She motioned for the newcomers to start down the stairs with her. "You want some tea?"

As Carlos was about to decline, certainly concerned about the level of hygiene that he was about to encounter, Maddy briskly said, "Yes, we'd love some." She quickly shot a glance at Carlos.

"Cool," said Jasmine. "I was just about to put the kettle on."

As they started down the stairs, Maddy whispered to Carlos, "When in Rome…"

Carlos rolled his eyes.

As they reached the bottom of the stairs after several flights, Maddy's eyes adjusted to the gloom. The place was weirdly magical. There were lit candles in niches in the walls, giving the cavernous sub-basement space a feeling like a shrine or a chapel. Several old mattresses were strewn about the floor, with makeshift drapes hung between them turning each sleeping area into a cabana. In the center of the space a small ring of bricks contained a little fire over which a makeshift grill was suspended.

"Where is everybody?" asked Mary.

"Marcus found a twenty on the sidewalk, so he's gone to get some groceries. He took Charelle with him. Abe is across the way. He cashed in his cans and went over to the Dogpatch for the five-dollar martini and free lasagna."

"Free lasagna? That's cool," said Carlos. He could only imagine how it might taste being for free and all, although it was pretty hard to screw up lasagna. Sounded like a good deal.

"I love your place," said Maddy.

"Thanks," said Jasmine. "But it gets real cold, especially in the morning. And it's pretty dark down here."

"What was this place?" asked Carlos.

"I think it was some sort of small power station – not really sure, though. These giant old machines are cool, aren't they?"

They were. There was an aura of energy surrounding the huge turbine housings – faint echoes of deep humming power. Maddy found this underground world compelling.

"How did you end up here?" she asked, as Jasmine poured her, Carlos, and Little Mary their cups of tea. Nice china, she thought.

"You really want to know?"

"Sure, unless it's, like, really embarrassing or deeply personal. I guess we're trying to find the balance between an informal survey and a real interview. So, you don't have to tell us if you don't want to. Of course."

"I'm here, because I like it."

"You like it?" asked Carlos, incredulously.

"Yeah, I like it," affirmed Jasmine. "It's a real free way to live, you know?"

"It seems hard," said Maddy.

"It is, but no one tells us what to do, we have no bills to pay, no real obligations to anybody, except maybe each other."

"Where did you grow up?" asked Maddy, completely surprised by Jasmine's perspective.

"I'm from LA. You know, Brentwood."

"Brentwood?!" Carlos nearly spat his tea.

"I know. Pretty nice place. But my parents, you know, they were so tapped into this completely false lifestyle that I just couldn't take it. And my dad, he was something of an asshole. Just really intense, you know? Being a TV producer is really demanding, I guess."

"TV producer... what show did he produce?"

"A show for the MagicLand Channel. You know, about this girl who's a teenage rock star."

"You don't mean Haley Idaho?" asked Maddy.

"Yeah. Haley Idaho."

Maddy was blown away. She was too old to be a fan, but her little sister was a member of the Haley Idaho cult, as Maddy used to tease her. The amount of money surrounding Haley was purported to be staggering.

"So, your family – it's pretty well off, then... if you don't mind my saying so."

"But totally fucked up, you know?"

"So fucked up that you chose a life as a homeless person?" Maddy was starting to get a little angry but tried her best to hide it. After the stories she heard from Beth and Little Mary, she didn't know what to make of someone posing as homeless. She looked over at Carlos, who also was showing signs of incomprehension. Carlos, after all, was the first member of his family to make it past high school, his parents one generation removed from illegal immigrants. The notion that there was something glamorous about homelessness was completely outside the realm of his experience.

"Yeah. It's cool, though. I don't have to do this forever, you know?"

Right, thought Maddy. When you get tired of pretending that you're down and out, you can just phone home.

"So how do you live?"

"My mom sends me money – an allowance. It's not much. I text her every once in a while. It's her money – I would never take it from my dad."

"Do they know where you are?"

"No. They don't really care. It would take way too much of their energy to find me, and I prefer that they leave me alone."

But you'll take their money, thought Maddy.

"What about the others who live here? Are they also runaways?"

"We're a pretty mixed bunch. Different reasons for not wanting to live a normal life, but we take care of each other."

At that moment, there was the sound of several sets of feet working their way down the stairs.

"A party! Cool."

A young man came bounding in, followed by a slender little Asian girl in torn up leggings, a bright pink mini-skirt and white high heels. The young man was tall and good looking, if in a somewhat nerdy way, and he was wearing a sweater under a vest, under a worn corduroy jacket. He wore Elvis Costello glasses and a porkpie hat. Very beatnik. The little Asian girl looked incredibly frail and cold.

Any second now, we're all going to break into "Five Hundred Twenty-five Thousand Six Hundred Minutes," thought Maddy. It was as if she had stumbled on a site-specific production of *Rent*.

Carlos was eyeing the Asian girl with real interest. That's funny, thought Maddy. She doesn't seem his type.

"Who have we here?" asked the young man, setting down a bag of groceries. As Maddy stood up, she could tell that he was surprised to see two relatively normal people.

"I'm Maddy," she said and shook his hand. She took the hand of the girl, and the shake was returned daintily.

Maddy couldn't say why, but there was something about her hands.

"I'm Marcus," said the young man. "This is Charelle."

"Hey, I'm Carlos," said Carlos. "Good to meet you. You know Mary, here, don't you?"

"She's family. She's cool." Marcus gave Little Mary a hug. "What brings you to our crazy dive?"

"They're with the Clarion," said Jasmine.

"Reporters? Um, I'm not ready for my close-up," whispered Charelle, as she hunched down on her heels before the fire.

"No, we're working on becoming reporters," said Maddy. "Just cubs, I'm afraid."

"Got to start somewhere," said Marcus. "Well, cool. Hang with us if you want. Don't have much to eat. A twenty doesn't go that far, especially in this town." He pulled out some packages of Top Ramen, a bottle of ketchup, some Wonder Bread, peanut butter, and a bottle of Charles Shaw Cabernet – "Two Buck Chuck".

"Oh, that's okay," said Carlos. "We're not hungry."

Marcus started to make himself a sandwich with the bread, peanut butter, and some jam from the little jam packets that you get at any diner.

"So why would 'cub' reporters be wandering around this dump?" he asked.

Maddy and Carlos took turns explaining their assignment. Marcus looked bemused.

"And that leads us to asking what your story is," finished Maddy.

"*My* story?" asked Marcus. "I'm an artist. A poet. Figured you can't write real poetry until you've seen all sides of the equation. Lived in the trenches. Suffered for the art. You know."

"And what were the other sides of the equation?" asked Maddy. "I mean, the other sides than this?"

"Grew up on Vashon Island, near Seattle. Do you know it?"

"Yes," said Maddy. Of course, she knew it.

It seemed that half of her fellow students at Stanford came from Vashon Island. Another tight enclave of the wealthy and well-educated. "Did you go to college?"

"Yeah."

"Where?"

"Leland Stanford Junior University," said Marcus, with an undertone of irony.

"Really? What year?" asked Maddy, somewhat knocked back.

"14. Why?"

"19. We just missed each other."

"Huh." Marcus rubbed his chin.

"Don't tell me," said Maddy, narrowing her eyes. "Drama Department."

"Close. English Lit. Real love was music, though."

"So, you reject the material world, too?" asked Maddy. She couldn't stand it.

"Trying to decide, still," replied Marcus. "I know that much of what everyone else thinks is the right way to live is full of soullessness and pain. Not much happiness is bought with money."

"I'm sorry," said Maddy. "I'm trying to understand your point of view. I mean, I've met people on the streets in the last few days with some serious issues. Not one of them wants to live like this, certainly not if they could help it. You seem to be bright, and healthy, with all the advantages. It seems to me that you're just glamorizing poverty. You're just posing. Would it hurt you to get a real job?"

"You seem pretty self-righteous," smirked Marcus. "Ever hear of Siddhartha? He rejected the material, and instead searched for a greater self-awareness. What about St. Francis?"

"Wow. How full of yourself would you have to be to put yourself in the same company as Buddha and St. Francis?" Maddy lost any remaining professional composure and couldn't hide her contempt any longer. "And where's the risk for you? What are your stakes? If you don't find what you're looking for, do you just access your trust fund and move on, like Jasmine, here? I mean, what good are you doing anybody? If you want to see real suffering, you could still join the Peace Corp or something."

Carlos stood up and was looking to leave.

"Um, thanks for the tea and all, sorry but we have to be going..."

"He looks after me," whispered Charelle.

"What?"

"He looks after me. He takes care of me. Keeps me going."

"Look, I'm sorry," said Maddy. "I'm in no position to judge anybody. I'm really tired – long night last night." Turning to Charelle, attempting to make a joke of it, "Are you also a refugee from too much privilege?"

"No," said Charelle, quietly. "I'm a refugee from my family."

"Oh, I'm sorry," said Maddy, her heart softening a bit. "What happened?"

"My parents named me Charles," said Charelle. "I grew up in the Central Valley, in a little town called Wasco. My parents had come over from the Philippines. Farmers. But I knew, in my heart, for as long as I could ever feel these things, that I wasn't Charles. I was... Charelle." Her face turned up, and she stuck her chin out with something like defiance. "When I first started wearing makeup, my father beat me up. My mother was terrified of him, so she just watched him do it. When he found me in a skirt and heels, he picked me up by my hair and threw me out of the house. I came to San Francisco because it was the one place where I might be accepted for who I am. I'm still trying to figure out how to afford the operation..."

"Oh." Maddy was speechless.

"I came here and worked the streets for a bit." She

smiled ruefully. "Some boys think I'm pretty."

Better legs than mine, thought Maddy.

"But, well, I got sick, you know? No one wants to use a condom. I was stupid." She started to cry. "Jasmine and Marcus help me pay for my medicine."

Maddy looked at Marcus. "I'm really sorry. I was such an asshole right now."

"Don't mention it. As I said, I'm still undecided. It's hard out here, but I've seen things and met people. Maybe I'll write something that matters." He handed a sandwich to Charelle, who picked at it between sniffs.

"I hope you do. I bet you will," said Maddy.

*   *   *

On the tram ride back to the Clarion, Maddy dozed on Carlos' shoulder. He's a better man than me, she thought drowsily, as Carlos stayed awake to make sure they got off at the right stop.

XXIII

He rode through the alleyways – the smallest, narrowest alleyways. The ones that almost looked like there was no passage at all. He was concerned about the police. He had almost thought of walking, to reduce his visibility, but decided that with his bicycle he had maximum maneuverability and could more readily avoid capture.

It was 3:30 in the afternoon, and the Masked Avenger was working his way to the corner of Sansome and Pine. He wasn't sure what he would do when he arrived at the Mandarin Oriental Hotel, he just knew that there was something amiss, and his instincts were infallible.

His head was splitting, however. He'd had so little sleep in the last few days – nothing was helping, not the Advil – nothing. He sensed that his peripheral vision was tightening…

Argh.

He hadn't noticed the piece of pipe that had rolled away from a pile of construction debris in the middle of the alley. He hit it with his front tire and his wheel jerked in the wrong direction. He flew over the handlebars and landed with a thud. Blackness.

*　　　　　*　　　　　*

He had fought demons his whole life. He had wrestled with anger and violence since he was a boy. The roar of the crowds fuelled it, as did the screaming of the men he trusted to guide him towards victory. And he had been in pain for as long as he could remember. He had always been big, always been pushed to get bigger, always straining, always being beaten and shaped, until he had, at one point, been hammered into human steel.

He found release from the pain on the field of honor. The anger was channeled, the violence allowed to be unleashed. At the first collision - at the first crushing of muscle and bone against muscle and bone - he felt the outside world - the world where he could barely function - melt away in the roar of tens of thousands of people...

*　　　　　*　　　　　*

As his eyes began to focus, he thought to himself, Thank God I left Robin in the crate. What time is it? He pulled out his cell phone and saw that it was only 3:35. He had been out for only a few minutes. This hurts, he thought. Nothing broken, though. Only bruised. Big scrape on his knee. A flesh wound.

His bike, however, was in much worse shape – the front tire completely flat and the rim twisted. I'm walking from here, he thought ruefully. As he lurched forward down the alleyway, he thought that maybe it was time that he asked for help. He looked back down at his cell phone and thought for a moment.

An ally.

XXIV

Back at the Clarion, Maddy and Carlos were sitting in their respective cubicles checking their email. Crap, I need a nap, thought Maddy. Once I punch out, I'm going straight home to bed.

At that moment, "Music of the Night" made her look over at her cell phone.

"You crack me up with that," said Carlos, absent-mindedly.

Maddy, meanwhile, just froze. The number that appeared on the little screen on the back of her phone was the one that she had programmed the night before. She wasn't sure what to do.

"You gonna answer that?"

She flipped open the phone and almost climbed under her desk. "Hello?" she whispered, trying to be as quiet as possible.

"Meet me in the stairwell of the parking garage at the Mandarin Oriental Hotel. Come as quickly as you can. I'm on the P2 level. I need your help."

"My help? For what?"

"Just come... I need you."

"Can I bring a friend?" asked Maddy.

A hesitation. "Yes." Then Maddy could almost hear a smile in his voice. "The more the merrier."

Then he hung up.

I'm not made for this, thought Maddy. I could not be more tired. Gotta take some serious kind of vitamins at this rate.

"Carlos! Let's go."

"Say what? I'm about to pass out. Unless you're talking a Starbucks break..."

"I'm talking the Masked Avenger," she hissed

conspiratorially. He was, after all, still their secret.

"No way!"

"Way!"

"You mean, that was him on the phone just now? He has your cell phone number?"

"Yeah, he does," said Maddy.

"Homeless people have cell phones?" Carlos shook his head. "You totally lied to that police detective."

"Don't think I haven't lost sleep over it," sighed Maddy.

"So, what's the plan?"

"We're needed over at the Mandarin Oriental, stat. What's the best way to get there?"

"Shoot. From here? Probably just to run."

So, they logged out, and started running. Because of the way Market Street cuts through the middle of the City, there was no good method of public transportation that would get them from A to B without time-consuming transfers. And by the time Maddy got her car out of the garage, tried to hack her way through late afternoon traffic, and deal with parking at $24 an hour at the Mandarin, she thought the exercise was worth it.

In fifteen minutes, they were running down Pine Street towards the Mandarin. Wow, thought Maddy. That is one nice hotel. They ran into the stairwell at the side of the garage and pounded their way down to the level below street level – P2. Upon arriving at the appointed spot, they were disappointed to find no one there. At that moment, Maddy's cell phone pinged, indicating the arrival of a new text message.

It read, "P1-105 QUIET"

"What the heck does that mean?"

"Is it a room number? Room 105?"

They entered the garage, looking for a way into the hotel. Suddenly it hit Maddy as she looked at the stenciled numbers at each parking space.

"It's on the first level of the parking garage – space

105!"

"Shush," hissed Carlos.

"What?" asked Maddy.

"The text said QUIET."

"Right," she whispered back.

They tip-toed their way back up to the street level garage, gently opening the door and peering in. Based on the lower floor layout, which Maddy had quickly figured out, space 105 would be to their right as they came through the door, down at the end of the line. Sure enough, as she poked her head down towards the end of the row of cars on her right, she saw the Masked Avenger hunched down behind an Escalade – good cover, she thought. He spotted her and made that hand gesture from his eyes to the location under surveillance that made him look as if he was in the Navy SEALs or the Rangers.

What is going on? thought Maddy. She made the same gesture to Carlos, who thought it was funny, even though he was also apprehensive about coming into such close proximity to the Masked Avenger. They crept their way behind the cars, moving slowly towards the end of the row. As they got adjacent to the Masked Avenger, he put his finger to his lips and pointed over towards a black Lexus SUV. A well-dressed man with flowing silver hair was approaching, chirping the alarm of his just-parked Mercedes. A small Chinese woman in high heels climbed out of the Lexus.

That's Peter Kohler, thought Maddy. She had seen his picture more than a few times recently, due to all the press the Museum of Asian Antiquities had received. What does he have to do with the Masked Avenger?

"Did you bring a hand truck?" asked the Chinese woman.

Peter Kohler rolled his eyes. He had forgotten. "I'm the director of a world-famous museum," he said petulantly. "What would I be doing with a hand truck? Just wait a sec." With that he jogged over to the entrance to the hotel lobby, which opened off the parking garage at that level. He passed into the lobby and returned a few minutes later with a bellhop, rolling a luggage cart.

"Here we go," he said, and Madeleine Chang chirped open the back of the Lexus. The two men pulled the crate out of the car and set it on the cart.

"Checking in?" asked the bellhop.

"No just visiting one of your guests," said Peter Kohler.

"Do you know the room number?"

"4605."

"Thank you, sir, I'll see that this is brought up to you."

"Not a chance. This thing doesn't leave my sight. Let's head straight up if you don't mind. I'll make it worth your while."

After they had gone, Maddy went over to the Masked Avenger, with Carlos lurking a safe distance behind.

"How are you?" she asked.

"A little banged up, but otherwise okay."

"What happened?"

"A mishap. Nothing of consequence," said the Masked Avenger, in that way he had that made Maddy think of a medieval knight.

"This is my friend Carlos," said Maddy.

"Welcome to the fight," said the Masked Avenger, taking Carlos' hand firmly in his giant, gloved hand.

"Good to meet you, sir," stammered Carlos. "Mind if I ask what's going on?"

"I'm not sure. But every instinct tells me that something isn't right."

"Okay..."

"I know that that man and that woman took that crate from a side entrance of the Museum of Asian Antiquities at eleven o'clock last night. It didn't make sense."

"I don't know," said Carlos. "It doesn't seem all that weird."

"It does, though," said Maddy. "Anything leaving the museum should have gone out through a loading dock, and most likely carried by trained art transportation people, not the Director of the Museum."

"The Director of the Museum? Is that who that was?"

"None other. I don't know who the woman is, but that guy – no one has better hair than that guy. He's famous."

"Did you catch what room they were going to?" Carlos asked.

"4605," said the Masked Avenger and Maddy simultaneously.

"We must find out what is going on in that room," said the Masked Avenger.

"There's no way," said Maddy in frustration.

"I have an idea," said Carlos, who turned to Maddy. "Do you have your credit card?"

"Yeah...," said Maddy, not quite understanding.

"Look, go to the front desk and ask them for the room service menu. Find a good bottle of champagne, go to a house phone, and order it sent to Room 4605."

"What?"

"Trust me. Just don't call room service until I text you first."

"What are you going to do?"

"I'm going to turn invisible."

With that, Carlos headed for the service entrance. Once he got there, he turned and winked.

XXV

What a beautiful city, thought Robert Grant as he stared out at the incredible view afforded him by his 46th floor suite. He could see Coit Tower from where he stood, with the Bay beyond. At five o'clock in the afternoon, the glancing light caused the art deco tower at the top of Telegraph Hill to glow almost iridescently gold against the rich blue of the water behind. Breathtaking.

He sighed with contentment. He was full of contentment these days. At one point in his career, he was the hot young stud in the Hollywood firmament. Now, having grayed so beautifully, he was still a leading man, but in that genre of films that appealed to younger baby boomer women – the ones that read More Magazine. These were the middle-aged weepies – chick flicks. He loved the work - all he had to do was show up and look good. No need to channel the angst of a troubled young man anymore. He could channel his passions and energies in other directions.

His greatest passion was Tibet.

He had discovered the Kingdom at the Top of the World and its spiritual allure in his early thirties, when he was trying to make sense of his enormous fame and all that went with it. The pressures of Hollywood on a young, successful actor were so great that he sought release through meditation and the Buddhist faith. A meeting with the Dalai Lama cemented his fervor. From that time, he served as an advocate for the Tibetan freedom movement, and he used his celebrity to aid in raising public awareness and funding for their cause.

He also found the artwork and cultural history of the Tibetan people compelling. When he learned that he had the opportunity to acquire a large golden figure of Manjuvajra, dating from the 18th Century and larger than any previously available in the West – he knew he had to make the leap. Money was not an object. And no questions would be asked. He knew that it would occupy a special niche within his master bedroom suite. He alone would enjoy it, or even know of its existence.

There was a knock on the door. He went to open it and found Peter Kohler at the threshold with a forty-something Chinese woman, a bellhop and a large crate on a luggage cart.

"Come in, come in," he said. "I've been waiting for this moment for some time."

"The honor and pleasure are all mine," replied Peter Kohler. "Please, this is Madeleine Chang."

"I know you hear this all the time," she said, "but I'm such a huge fan of yours."

He took her hand and brushed it with his lips. She melted, as they always did.

Pleasantries exchanged, it was time for Peter Kohler to tap into his enormous reserves of both charm and firmness. One doesn't become the Director of a world-class museum without both, he thought to himself, and his abilities as a fund-raiser, more than his abilities as a curator, had led to his appointment. He worked his magic.

It started even before the crate was opened, so that by the time Robert Grant gazed upon the glistening, intricate sculpture before him he felt that even the revised asking price was a bargain.

"To whom do I write the check?"

"The Samos Foundation," replied Peter Kohler smoothly.

"That's an interesting name – isn't that a Greek island?"

"It is..." Peter Kohler coughed, then rapidly changed the subject. "Look at how the light is catching the statue!"

The sunset light was streaming through the floor-to-ceiling windows onto the golden figure, creating patterns of reflection that filled the room. Gold on gold. The effect was dazzling.

All three were startled out of their reverie by a knock on the door. Surprised, Robert Grant went to the door. A young man from room service stood outside with a bottle of champagne in an ice bucket.

"Compliments of the hotel," said the boy.

"How propitious," said Robert Grant. "Perfect timing."

The young man from room service wheeled the service cart into the room. "May I open this for you, sir?"

"By all means, by all means."

The cork was deftly popped, and champagne poured all around. "Can I get you anything else, sir?" the young man asked.

"Thank you, this is perfect," said Robert Grant, slipping a tip into the young man's hand.

"Thank you, sir, I'll let myself out."

As the three celebrants turned to toast one another, they failed to notice the young man from room service deftly take a quick snapshot with his cell phone, which he carefully secreted within his vest pocket as the door closed behind him.

*　　　*　　　*

He had paid his way through Columbia by working as a waiter in the lobby lounge of the Soho Grand. Popping champagne corks was second nature to him. Carlos had winked at Maddy, gone through the service entrance, and headed straight to the locker rooms. A well-groomed young man of Hispanic heritage would instantly turn invisible within the small city that was a large, world-class hotel. He checked out his uniform - he was new to the guy working the counter, but charm made all the difference - and he changed quickly, tucking his cell phone into his pocket. He then proceeded to the kitchen and the room service desk. He sent a quick text as he walked down the corridor, and as he approached the desk the call came in: a bottle of Veuve Clicqot to Room 4605. The expeditor handed him the ticket, he grabbed the ice bucket, filled it, and took the ticket to the service bar. Within twenty minutes he was standing in the forty-sixth-floor corridor and knocking on the door of a VIP suite.

At the Soho Grand, Carlos had served more than a few celebrities. But it took every ounce of self-control for Carlos not to squeal like a tween at a Justin Bieber concert as soon as the door opened. No one knew for sure for which team Robert Grant played, but there had certainly been rumors. The gerbil thing was one of the great urban myths. But for many gay men, Robert Grant was still an object of fascination and fantasy – Carlos no exception. If he was to be kept by an older man, thought Carlos, Robert Grant would be that man.

But the scene inside the room was startling. The entire suite was filled with a golden light playing off the walls, momentarily dazzling Carlos. At the center of the light was a remarkable statue – obviously ancient and obviously Asian. The multiple contorted limbs and the complexity of the composition made Carlos think immediately of China or India. The magic was cut through, however, by the angry and suspicious gaze from the silver-haired museum man. It gave Carlos the instant impression that he had something to hide. The look vanished in an instant, however, and was replaced by smiles and nods as soon as Robert Grant turned to him. And the champagne worked brilliantly. When I tell her what I saw, thought Carlos, I hope Maddy thinks it was worth the hundred bucks.

*   *   *

Maddy squealed like a tween at a Justin Bieber

concert when she saw the photo.

"Oh. My. God! That's Robert Grant!"

"What do you think was going on in that room?" asked the Masked Avenger. "What do a Hollywood movie star, a museum director and a golden statue have in common?"

"Maybe it's a fund-raising thing?" asked Maddy, doubtfully.

"I don't know for sure," said Carlos turning to the Masked Avenger, "but I think you're right – the room reeked of intrigue. And your museum director was really put out that I was there at first. Nice call on the champagne, though, Maddy. Some serious high-roller shit. That caused everybody to dial it down."

"So, what do we do now?" asked Maddy.

"We need to know more about that statue and where it came from," said the Masked Avenger.

"It's from China or Nepal or something," said Carlos.

"An Asian antiquity," mused Maddy. "Wait. I know someone we could call..."

XXVI

"Nancy Drew!" said Jimmy Wang into his phone. "Have you cracked the 'Problem of the Poisoned Panhandler'?"

"Not yet," answered Maddy. "And hey, please don't call me that." After a moment, "Sorry. It just sort of bugs me, and this is already awkward. Look, this is pretty humiliating, and I apologize for any sort of apparent racial insensitivity, but, well, you're… you're…"

"Chinese. Yes, can't help it, I'm afraid," he said with a laugh. Poor girl was adorable but totally clueless. "How can I help you?"

"Well, we need to figure out what this golden Asian statue is, and I was wondering if you knew somebody who could help us."

"Being Chinese and all."

"Yeah… look, I'm sorry if I offended you, but, well, I didn't know who else to ask."

"Well at least we're talking. It's a start. So… a golden statue. Sounds like another mystery. The 'Adventure of the Asian Antiquity.'"

"Well, that's just it. We think it came from the museum. The Museum of Asian Antiquities. But we can't know for sure."

"But it's not in the museum now."

"No, it's in a hotel room at the Mandarin Oriental."

"How appropriate."

"And wait until you hear whose hotel room it was!" After Maddy told him, he whistled.

"I'm not sure I want to know how you found that out. Okay, describe it," said Jimmy, intrigued.

"It's some sort of dancing figure with many arms…"

"A bodhisattva," said Jimmy.

"We have a picture of it."

"You kids and your cell phones. Can you send the image to my phone? I can download it and enhance it and print it out. I don't know much about art or antiquities, but you're right - I know someone who does."

"That's awesome. Thanks!"

"Listen, can you come by the station – no, I'm not going to throw you in jail… it's just that it's a fairly short walk from here to the person who can help us."

"Um, okay," said Maddy. "See you in about fifteen minutes."

"Hey. You haven't seen the Masked Avenger, have you?"

"No, not today."

She's still lying about that, thought Detective Wang as he hung up the phone. Still got some work to do there.

*   *   *

"You must go on alone," said the Masked Avenger. "I can't come with you. They don't understand what it is I do."

"But we'll let you know what we find out. What are you going to do?"

"Try to sleep during the remaining hours before it gets dark."

"And then?"

"And then we must return to the Man Without a Face to learn what he has discovered."

"Right," said Maddy. "Sounds like another full evening."

"You don't have to come if you don't want to."

"Wouldn't miss it for the world. Don't worry about me."

"Can I come?" asked Carlos.

"Of course. You did good work just now - you make a solid member of the team. But we must part for the

109

moment."

"When and where should we meet?" asked Maddy.

"May we take your car again?"

"Um, sure."

"Then pick me up at the corner of Embarcadero and Folsom. Ten o'clock. We can get onto the Bridge easily from there."

"Hey, whatever happened to your bike?" asked Maddy.

"It... is damaged," sighed the Masked Avenger.

"Oh, that's too bad..."

"What kind of bike was it?" asked Carlos.

"An old cruiser."

"Dude, I've got one in my basement. It's black with flames painted on the fenders. The guy who lived in my house before me left it. I'm not using it – you can borrow it."

Maddy was so proud of Carlos she almost burst.

"Thank you," said the Masked Avenger. "That is most kind." Then with a swirl of his cape, he bounded towards the staircase. "See you at ten," he called out behind him.

"Vaya con Dios!" called Carlos after him.

"Carlos! You were so cool just now. Thank you!"

"Are you kidding, Chica? This is so much more fun than they promised in the internship application. Alright, let's hook up with that hot detective."

Maddy wrinkled her nose and poked Carlos in the stomach, causing him to giggle like the Pillsbury Doughboy.

XXVII

As they walked down Grant Avenue, Maddy and Jimmy compared notes – Carlos drifting a discreet distance behind them. There was still no cause of death determined for Lucky Jerry – the forensic lab at the Coroner's Office was stacked up, dealing with not only Lucky Jerry, but a drunk tourist who fell off the end of Pier 39, and a potentially scandalous apparent double suicide at an address up in Pacific Heights. The test results would take another day or so. Lucky Jerry was at the bottom rung in death, as well as in life.

"What did the autopsy reveal?" asked Maddy.

"Mostly that Lucky Jerry had almost nothing in his stomach when he died. Trace amounts of bread and tuna, some vegetable matter, but almost nothing else."

"So, whatever caused his death must have acted pretty quickly," mused Maddy.

"Well, with so little in his stomach, it wouldn't take much."

"I wonder where he got that food?" wondered Maddy.

"And if there was any more of it," said Jimmy.

"I hadn't thought of that. All the Masked Avenger found was the remainder of the sandwich on the ground. I was talking with some friends of mine this morning, and they said most of the tribe that hung around UN Plaza went to ground, a bunch of them were sick. Maybe they had some, too, but weren't as weak or empty as Lucky Jerry."

"Wait. Who were you talking with?"

"Beth and Little Mary," replied Maddy. "They live down at Homeless Island."

"These are friends of yours…"

"Well, yeah, they've sort of become so. I met them yesterday and brought them some food today. They're cool, in a really sad kind of way."

"And they told you about the rest of Lucky Jerry's group?"

"They did, and... I can see where this is leading. Okay, I'll call you next time. I'm sorry – it just didn't make any sense at the time, it didn't seem that important."

"And what would Sherlock Holmes say about that?"

"'Let me be the judge of what is important and what isn't.'"

"Well done. You like Sherlock Holmes?"

"Much better than Nancy Drew.... and anyway, we got distracted by this other thing."

"What other thing? 'The Adventure of the Asian Antiquity?'"

Maddy rolled her eyes. "Well, if you want to play that game, this would be called 'The Mystery of the Beefy Ballplayer.'"

"Wait. How many mysteries are you unraveling?"

"Three. At least today."

"And how long have you been at this?"

"Thirty hours. And counting."

Jimmy Wang was more than a little impressed.

"I want to hear more about this one." An impulsive moment. "Over a drink - later?"

Maddy got flustered. "Sure. No. Wait. Um..."

Carlos couldn't help himself. "She's already booked this evening."

If Maddy could've poked him, she would have.

"I'm sorry, I was being impertinent," said Jimmy. "But it sounds like another good story, that's all."

"Well, I've got this appointment. Should be done by eleven..."

"Tell you what. I know a place that serves late, if you're up for a nightcap after a full day of sleuthing."

Maddy flipped a loose lock of hair behind her ear.

God. She hadn't done that in front of a boy in, like, for*ever*.

"Can I call you when I wrap up my appointment?" she asked.

"Sure. I don't mind working late – it's not like I don't have a mountain of paperwork to catch up on. Here we are."

They had arrived at a giant antique shop. They were just a block and a half from the Chinatown gate. The window of the shop was crammed with little Buddhas and fu dogs and jade chess sets, with racks of I Left My Heart In San Francisco t-shirts along the walls.

"Is this the place?" asked Maddy. She was more than a little dubious, because this was the sort of shop that catered to the casual tourist, not any aficionados of Asian art.

"No, *this* is the place," replied Jimmy. He had disappeared down a little alley that would have been almost invisible to anyone not paying attention. The alley was dark – it looked almost as if it were a tunnel in the side of the building. Jimmy pressed a button at the side of a small door which was set in the middle of a wall of peeling paint and cracked plaster. After a moment, the door buzzed, and they went in.

They climbed a flight of stairs, turned a corner, went through a beaded curtain, and entered one of the most remarkable rooms Maddy had ever seen.

Unlike the shop downstairs, which was crammed with a factory's worth of tchochkis, the room they entered was spare and elegantly furnished. Black leather chairs were arranged on a white marble floor around an exquisitely carved teak table. The juxtaposition of early 20th Century German minimalist furnishings with the gorgeously rendered, and obviously antique table spoke volumes about the taste of the proprietor. One wall was lined with floor to ceiling shelves, internally lit, with beautifully carved statuettes in ivory and jade. On the wall opposite were hung what appeared to be window shutters and doors, intricately carved in exotic woods, with a rich patina of age. The room reeked of sophistication and discreet wealth.

Carlos whistled.

"Mom?" called out Jimmy.

Carlos and Maddy looked at each other with wide eyes. Mom? they both wondered simultaneously.

At the far end of the room was a large door, the most elegant and intricate of the collection. It opened, and out came a tiny Chinese woman with short white hair, impeccably dressed in a severe black suit. Her face lit up when she saw Jimmy and she trotted up to him in her heels. Jimmy towered over her, but she didn't seem to notice. He gave her a hug and pecked her on the cheek, which she raised expectantly and automatically. He then turned to Maddy and Carlos.

"Mom, I'd like you to meet my colleagues, Maddy Stevenson and Carlos Rodriguez. Maddy, Carlos, this is my mother, Mrs. Wang."

"Please call me Pearl," she said brightly. Turning to her son, a little severely, "Your father was disappointed that you didn't come for dinner on Sunday. Of course, I was disappointed, too, but well…. We hardly see you, and you work just down the street."

"I know, Mom – you, of all people, should know that when duty calls…"

"Yes, yes, I know." Turning to Maddy and Carlos, "Forty years married to a policeman, I should know." She clucked at her son for a moment, then asked, "So, to what do I owe the pleasure?"

"We're working on a case together, and we thought you might be able to help us identify something."

"You're working on a case together?" she asked, gesturing at Maddy and Carlos. She arched an eyebrow, which remained frozen in that position as she returned her gaze back to Jimmy. Jimmy looked a little uncomfortable.

"Yes, ma'am," interjected Maddy. "Although we're

not sure it's a case, just a problem. We work for the Clarion and we're just doing some research on something we found. We asked Detective Wang if he knew someone who knew anything about Asian antiquities, and, well, it sure looks like we came to the right place."

"My mother deals in some very rare artifacts. A very select and private clientele."

"You would need to know that this place even existed," said Carlos. "Not much street traffic, I suppose."

"None. We prefer to be discreet," said Pearl. "So, what have you got?"

Jimmy pulled out the photograph of the golden statue. He had thought it best to crop out the persons around the relic, and to enhance the photograph up to full page size. He had placed it into a plastic protector.

Pearl took the image, placed the pince-nez that hung around her neck onto her nose, and looked at it hard. The expression on her face revealed her surprise at what she saw.

"You found this? I should be extremely interested to know where."

Maddy looked at Carlos, uncertain what to say. Finally, she said, "We know it came from the Museum of Asian Antiquities. Well, that's not entirely true... We know it passed through there."

"That would surprise me immensely," said Pearl. "I know their collection intimately, and they have nothing like this. This is Tibetan, and its like has not been seen in the United States to my knowledge - or at least not since the forties."

"Is it valuable?" asked Maddy.

"It is almost priceless. And it is most likely illegal. I know of no legal means by which such an object could leave Tibet."

Maddy looked at Carlos, who was making a face well known to her by now – he was chewing on his lower lip the way he did when he knew he was in over his head.

"So, someone would have had to smuggle this into the US," asked Maddy.

"Or made some deal with the People's Republic of China," replied Pearl. "Which *has* been known to happen."

Jimmy Wang sighed. This was going to be politically very sticky. He hated that. And he was going to have to talk with his dad, which he hated even more. He couldn't hide the sour look on his face.

"How's Dad?" he asked his mother.

"The same. More so." She turned to Maddy and Carlos. "He's been a bear ever since he retired. All he does is play chess down at the park. Thank God for the tai chi in the mornings, otherwise I would have killed him by now." She shrugged.

"Tell him I'll come and see him tomorrow," said Jimmy. "Mom, thanks for the help." She raised her cheek to him expectantly and he gave her another peck.

"Good luck to you two," she said with a smile. She arched her eyebrow at her son again. This time it was comical. Jimmy rolled his eyes.

"And we *will* see you for dinner on Sunday. Bring your friends."

"Yes, Mom. Will do."

As they climbed back down the stairs, Maddy thought to herself that nothing makes a person more human than being seen with their mom.

XXVIII

"Everything's ready for tomorrow," said John Sanders.

"It had better be," replied Cheryl Niederman, applying a delicate amount of wasabi to her soy sauce with her ceramic chop sticks. "Mark Eichler is one of those executives who doesn't fuck around."

One of the perks of working for Cheryl Niederman was she had extremely expensive and sophisticated tastes. Dinner meetings were always at one of several select restaurants within the City. The price paid for such a perk, however, was that one rarely had much stomach for the meal, thought John Sanders ruefully. One tough boss.

Tonight, they were dining at one of Cheryl Niederman's favorite places, Tadao. The dark paneled walls of the elegant sushi bar, the atmospheric lighting and the bulk of the clientele were distinctly masculine. Perfectly suited for Cheryl Niederman. The view of the Bay Bridge was outstanding, and as it basked in the last rays of the setting sun it gleamed. A magical moment: the necklace of lights that dotted the curved suspension cables just turned on. John Sanders was transported, even if just for a second.

"Try the blowfish, it's excellent," prompted his boss.

John Sanders almost spat his sake. "Um, not for me, thanks," he mumbled into his plate.

"Don't be a pussy," growled Cheryl Niederman.

"No, it just doesn't do it for me. I prefer spicy tuna."

"Mmmmm. When prepared properly, it gives your lips such a tingle."

"That would be the toxins. Blowfish is the second most poisonous vertebrate in the world."

"Thank you, Mister Discovery Channel. What's the first?"

"Some frog."

Cheryl Niederman looked at him witheringly for a moment. "Anyway, it's good – the chef here prepares it perfectly. Live large. Live dangerously. Go Big or Go Home."

As John Sanders dipped his spicy tuna into his soy sauce he thought,

Living dangerously doesn't begin to describe it.

XXIX

He slept fitfully, as was most often the case these days. The kitten had crawled up next to his face, purring for all she was worth. It was as if she was trying to comfort her giant, troubled master. But his limbs twitched so violently that she retreated to safe distance.

So much noise. A constant roar. It would sometimes subside into a soft whooshing in his head, but it never completely left him. As he approached the days on which he would do battle, it would build into a scream so loud that it was as if a jet was taking off between his ears. It was the stress, the pressure. The greater the pressure, the greater the noise. He wished he had hands inside his head so that he could cover his ears from the inside.

His dreams were filled with a tremendous sense of anxiety and longing. Always he was lost, searching for something, something that had slipped through his fingers or something he had forgotten to do. There was always something that he had forgotten to do.

Tonight, he was in a bar. No, a cantina with colorful walls, and colorful bottles everywhere. Music pulsed through the roar in his brain. The cantina was packed with revellers, but they slipped in and out of focus. When they became momentarily clear he found himself alarmed by them. Strange, grotesque faces in vivid colors, eyes bulging, mouths agape. They pushed him, clapped him on the back, and kept filling the large glass that floated strangely in front of him. Was he holding it? It seemed to pour itself over and over into his mouth, without any conscious effort on his part.

There were floating faces all around him. Men in suits talking, talking, talking. What were they talking about? Something important. Something... something he had forgotten to do. Some place he needed to be.

He was suddenly flooded with a sense of shame. He was filled with longing. His heart was breaking…

XXX

By the time they picked up Maddy's car, it was almost eight o'clock. They decided that it would be easiest if they just went to Maddy's to regroup. They could take a nap – Carlos was more than content with her sofa – and shower before heading out for the next part of what was looking to be another long day. Maddy was exhausted, but she was also keyed up. Like Alice falling down the rabbit hole, she was on an adventure that, at each step, caused her to rethink her definition of reality. She rubbed her forehead, aching from constantly having to re-tool the brain behind it. At least I'm not bored, she thought. And God. I'm finally going on something of a date. With a real man. She was excited but nervous. It had been a while since she had been out with anyone remotely interesting, good looking or professional. Sure, she had been hit on at every bar she ever visited, but with Angelique as her wing man, she always ended up stuck with the third-tier boys. And, truth be told, even the first tier were pretty shallow and self-involved. Being twenty-something, I'm sure, has something to do with it, she thought.

But a police detective. I bet he has some stories to tell, she mused to herself as she lay on her bed staring at the ceiling. And what a mystery both his mother and father are! She looked over at her alarm clock and realized it was only fifteen minutes before she had to jump in the shower. She sighed. She would never fall asleep.

The alarm caused her to bolt upright in complete disorientation. Nothing like five minutes of sleep to make you feel on top of your game, she grumbled to herself as she climbed into the shower. The hot water worked its charm, however, and her perk started to return. She remembered the adage that a shower was worth three hours of sleep and reflected that that could be true. She was feeling pretty good, all things considered. Only after she toweled off, surrendered the bathroom to Carlos, and went to her room, was Maddy hit with the devastating complexity of the problem: What. To. Wear?

This goes way beyond the usual day to night transition that many working women wrestle with, she thought as she rummaged through her closet. Not many women would be climbing through ventilation shafts and scrambling through back alleys before going out on a first date. Thank God for casual chic. Jeans, tennis shoes and a red silk t-shirt were covered with a sweatshirt. Knowing she would be wandering around Berkeley made her grateful that the Stanford logo was pretty discreet. After she dropped Carlos off later, the shoes would be replaced with heels, and the sweatshirt with her black leather motorcycle jacket – the only remaining vestige of her relationship with Justin. Should work. Even the wind-tunnel effect of the ventilation shaft on her hair might work to her advantage, too.

Okay. Let's go.

Except Carlos took more time in the bathroom than any girl she knew. When he finally emerged, he looked and smelled… marvelous.

"Going on a date?" she asked as they headed out the door.

"Maaaaaybe…" wiggled Carlos. "I intend to be ready for anything."

As they passed through the lobby of her apartment building, they met Angelique and Jean-Michel returning from a dinner out.

"Heading out – at this hour?" asked Angelique in some surprise. To the best of her knowledge, Maddy had always been a "bed by ten" kind of girl.

"Yeah," sang Maddy as they passed each other.

"Don't wait up!"

*   *   *

As they drove down the Embarcadero, they slowed on approaching Folsom Street. They were both gazing at the giant Cupid's bow and arrow by Claes Oldenburg – symbolizing where Tony Bennett had left his heart – when a flash of light swept through the windshield.

"The Bat Signal," joked Carlos.

Maddy started to pull over to the side of the road. A flashlight waved to them from behind a column at Hills Plaza on the inland side of the Embarcadero. Maddy moved forward towards the flashing light. She was still rolling to a stop when in an instant, the large Black man threw himself into the back seat, nearly crushing Carlos in the front seat as he did so. The whole bug creaked from his added weight. "Drive," he said.

"Are you okay?" asked Maddy in concern. "Is someone after you?"

"There is always someone after me," said the Masked Avenger in a whisper. There was something in the way he said it that made Maddy suspect that paranoid schizophrenia might be part of whatever disorder it was that he wrestled with.

Maddy pulled away from the curb, drove down to Harrison Street, turned right and on to the Bay Bridge. They hit the bridge just in time – the fireworks were being launched over TBD Park, signifying the end of the game and the flooding of fifty-thousand people into the streets. In fifteen minutes, traffic on the Bridge would be slowed to a crawl.

The ride to Berkeley was a little more conversationally lively than the night before – if only just a little. Carlos had fewer qualms than Maddy had, and Maddy, having made the navigation once already, felt more confident. Carlos jumped right in.

"How did you become the Masked Avenger?" he

asked, twisting in the front seat to look back at the man in black and gray.

Maddy almost swerved into the next lane on that one.

"The origins of the Masked Avenger must remain forever shrouded in mystery," said the large man in the back seat. Again, with the voice of a knight of old.

"Huh. Well, can you tell me why you do what you do?"

"Because someone must. Because no one else does. Because... because..." The Masked Avenger's voice trailed away. Maddy looked over at Carlos. She thought that perhaps the Masked Avenger had just grown thoughtful. She saw a look of concern in Carlos' eyes.

"What?" she whispered.

Before Carlos could answer, her question was resolved. The car was filled with the sound of snoring.

"What should we do?" whispered Carlos. "Should we wake him? Jesus what a racket!"

"No. Let him sleep. You think *you're* tired. I can't imagine how tired he must be."

"I could take a peek under his mask..."

"Don't you dare. Let him be. He'll tell us his deal in one way or another at the right time. If we want him to trust us, then we have to show him that we deserve his trust."

They drove on for a few minutes in silence, save for the sound of the ragged breathing of the Masked Avenger. Every once in a while, he would stop snoring - stop breathing altogether.

"Sleep apnea," whispered Maddy. "That's so bad for you. It's like stopping your heart every few minutes. Jeez, no wonder the poor guy is so tired."

"He could stand to lose some weight," whispered Carlos. He had been scrutinizing the slumbering giant most of the ride across the bridge. "He really is a big guy." He then turned to Maddy, taking only a sideways glance at the Masked Avenger to reassure himself that he was sleeping. "You have his cell phone number, right?"

"Yeah, why? You want it?"

"I do."

"What for?" asked Maddy, just a little suspicious.

"I'm a member of the team, aren't I?" replied Carlos.

"Yes, but what are you going to do with that number?"

"Look, if you've got a cell phone, you've got a name, right? I mean, Verizon Wireless has to be sending the bill to somebody."

"Yeah, so?"

"Well, I have a friend who works for Verizon. In accounting. He could pull up the name and billing address."

"I don't like it. It feels like violating a trust."

"It would be if he told us who he was, and we then told other people. But he hasn't and we won't."

"I don't know…"

"What if he's missing? What if someone who loves him is looking for him?"

"Remember Beth? Perhaps he doesn't want to be found."

"Look," said Carlos, still glancing over his shoulder at the sleeping hero, "you want to write a story? Then you had better be willing to do some investigating. This guy is amazing. But we need to know where he comes from. I don't think he will ever tell us himself." As Maddy drove on without responding, Carlos made one last plea. "We've placed a lot of trust in this guy. If we know who we're dealing with, then we'll know how to respond. All I'm saying is that we can learn who he is, and then we can decide what we want to do about it. And that can be nothing at all."

Maddy bit her lower lip, sighed, and passed her phone over to Carlos. "It's under M. Of course."

XXXI

"Tetrodotoxin. One of the most powerful poisons known."

This time Maddy had accepted the glass of Cotes du Rhone from the Man Without a Face. She had felt the need to both offer some level of social interaction with the man, and she had also admitted to herself that a little "Dutch courage" would go a long way towards getting her through the evening. As much as one could tell that a face so disfigured could smile, Maddy could feel him do so. He had poured a glass for himself, into which he placed a straw. He sucked the wine and sighed with contentment.

Carlos was stirring on the little bed in the corner. He had simply passed out from shock when the Man Without a Face opened the door. The Masked Avenger had scooped him up and laid him on the bed, saying to his friend, simply, "He has been pushing himself too hard."

Maddy had tried to warn Carlos, to no avail. He had been determined to meet the Man Without a Face and had protested that nothing could shock him. Maybe now he'll listen to me once in a while, thought Maddy.

Once Carlos was upright, and had some Cotes du Rhone himself, the Man Without a Face went on.

"The toxin will cause the muscles of the diaphragm to be paralyzed. Death would be not unlike drowning. The poisoned person would suffocate."

"How horrible," said Maddy, in almost a whisper. "It certainly looked like Lucky Jerry had struggled terribly."

"What a way to go," said Carlos with a grimace.

"We must find the person who committed this

atrocious act," growled the Masked Avenger.

"Where do you get this tetra...?" asked Maddy.

"Tetrodotoxin. From the liver of a Blowfish, or Pufferfish. Certain high-end sushi restaurants prepare the meat of the Blowfish as a delicacy."

"Who would want to eat something that poisonous?" asked Maddy.

"When prepared properly, the toxic organs are removed. Trace amounts are in the meat, which causes a tingling sensation on the mouth and tongue."

"Sounds dangerous," said Maddy.

"Sounds cool," said Carlos. "A little oral stimulation..."

Maddy poked him. He was incorrigible. And obviously feeling better.

"So, whoever did this had access to Blowfish livers," said the Masked Avenger. "That would be a very select group of people."

"It's certainly a lead. We could find out which sushi restaurants in town serve Blowfish. We could even try to find out who had reservations the few nights before, and the night of, the murder," added Carlos.

"What if it's a walk-in?" asked Maddy.

"It would be a regular, regardless," said the Masked Avenger. "How else would they have developed the relationship with the sushi chef to get the toxin?"

"Checking the reservation lists would be a start - the trick would be knowing what or who to look for," sighed Carlos. "We don't have anything to cross-reference against."

"Unless someone saw something strange that night down at UN Plaza. Saw someone give the sandwiches to Lucky Jerry," replied Maddy.

"How could we find them?" asked Carlos.

"There was a tribe that lived in the area," said the Masked Avenger. "According to you," he turned to Maddy, "most of them left – some with symptoms of illness. They would have gone out to the Park."

"So, we need to go out there and see if we can find anyone who might have seen anything. That sounds hard."

"I know a few people," replied the Masked Avenger. "We'll work the network." He turned to the Man Without a Face. "Thank you, my friend. Your aid has been invaluable."

The Man Without a Face raised his glass in salute. "It's the least I can do." He looked thoughtful for a moment – again as much as one could tell that he looked thoughtful. "Were there any events last night in the City? Where did the sandwiches come from? The piece you gave me looked like the sort of sandwich that comes from a catered affair."

Carlos had an inspiration. "Of course. The intern who works with the Society editor – I can hit him up for a listing."

"And this way we triangulate," added Maddy excited. "Diners at high end sushi restaurants, possible sighting of sandwich delivery, and people who might have been at an event where the sandwiches were available."

"A shitload of work," said Carlos.

"Serious detection often is," said the Masked Avenger. "It is time for us to go."

*   *   *

By the time they had crossed through the toll plaza and onto the Bay Bridge back to the City, they had divided up the work. Carlos would dig up the City's social calendar, Maddy would generate the list of high-end sushi restaurants where Blowfish was served, and the Masked Avenger would put out feelers regarding sightings of strange goings on at UN Plaza before everyone got sick. Once they had compared notes, Carlos would follow up with the restaurants, and

Maddy would accompany the Masked Avenger out to Golden Gate Park in order to do follow up interviews.

"Where do you want us to drop you?" asked Maddy as they approached the Fremont Street exit off the Bridge.

"Where you picked me up, but around the corner," replied the Masked Avenger.

They wrapped around off the Bridge and approached Hills Plaza. They then drove down the Embarcadero and turned again on Harrison, as before. This was the "back" side of the Plaza. As they pulled up to the curb, the Masked Avenger leapt out of the back seat. "'til tomorrow," he called. "God bless you both." Maddy and Carlos watched as he disappeared into the loading dock, his plastic cape snapping behind him.

"The Bat Cave," said Carlos, shaking his head.

"And you? Where do you want me to drop you?"

"I know you've got a hot date, so just drop me up at Market. I can take the trolley home."

"Home? I thought *you* had a hot date."

"Nah, I just said that to keep you guessing. My sweet Mexican ass is whipped. I need a straight eight."

I do, too, thought Maddy. But she wasn't going to take a rain check. She dropped Carlos at Market, and then called Detective Wang.

"Are you still working?" she asked as he picked up.

"Just shoving the big pile on the left side of my desk over to the right. I should be done in a few minutes. I can meet you in front of the station."

"I'll be there. Where are we going?" she asked. It was eleven-thirty on a Tuesday night. Most of San Francisco would be closed by now.

"A secret little spot. Only the true locals know about it. I'll give you directions when you get here."

Maddy pulled over by Jackson Square to do her quick make-over. As she applied some lipstick and checked herself in her vanity mirror, she thought that she suddenly didn't look like a twenty-three-year-old girl anymore. Was it a new level of social sophistication? Was it the wind-swept hair?

No. It was the newly developed bags under her eyes. Great.

XXXII

He was still lounging in front of his lockers in his giant Barcalounger, sipping a beer. Everyone else had gone home, and the media circus had finally died down. This was his favorite time. The locker room, which was his throne room, had finally gone quiet, and he could collect his thoughts. He had started to notice how much he appreciated the quiet as he got older – there was so much noise in his life. The crowds, the media, his family, his mistress, and his entourage of trainers, doctors, and gym buddies. As much as he knew he needed their adulation, he also found himself wishing they would all just go fuck off.

It should have been a good time to be Benny Cashman.

Another home run. One to tie, one to be the greatest home run hitter in the history of baseball. Six more games to reach the hallowed achievement. He was averaging almost a home run every other game – an unheard-of clip - so he might actually break the record and have a couple to spare. At this point in the season, with the Goliaths' place in the playoffs secure, no opposing coach was willing to be seen as such a chicken-shit that he would pitch around him anymore. He was getting honest at-bats now, instead of free passes to first base. His legacy was virtually assured.

To be the greatest. He had dreamed of this his entire life. He recalled the moment in the film *The Natural* when Roy Hobbes, played by Robert Redford, had told the Woman in Black that he wanted, as he walked down the street, to have people say, "there goes Roy Hobbes, the best there ever was." Benny Cashman. The Best There Ever Was. It would be true, at last.

As he popped open his third beer, he mused that he had paid a high price for it. The estrangement of his family, the whisperings of the media, the torture his body endured. And, although he was the second highest paid player in baseball, he felt as if he had no money of his own. The entourage exacted its toll - as did his wife, who was willing to swallow her pride regarding his mistress and keep her silence as long as she received an enormous percentage of his income. And his mistress. She was so no longer worth the trouble, he thought. She had become greedy. She wanted a new house. First class travel to every city the Goliaths played on the road. And, because she had given up a lucrative career of her own to be on call, she demanded a level of financial maintenance that left him breathless.

I'm going to have to have her killed, he thought. Joking. Just a joke, he reminded himself. But his jaw set and his brow furrowed. He crushed the can, tossed it over his shoulder and popped a fourth beer.

And the tax lawyers. Jesus. Fucking barracudas. His taxes, with so much income, so much real estate, and so many mouths to feed, were Byzantine. And his agent. What an asshole. He claimed fifteen percent, off the top, for doing almost nothing but keep the Goliaths' management in a constant state of groveling. Which was satisfying in its way... But he was incapable of landing any new endorsement deals, and the contract with Nike had come and gone. It seemed that no one wanted an outspoken and controversial athlete on the cover of their boxes of Wheaties anymore, even if he was breaking records and selling tickets like crazy.

As he did his mental calculations, Benny Cashman reflected that twenty million dollars a year didn't go as far as one might think.

*   *   *

Paul MacDougall had entered the locker room

quietly. As he had walked down the corridors under the stadium, he reflected sadly that, even though he owned the Goliaths and was responsible for paying his star an astronomical salary, he was profoundly afraid of Benny Cashman. MacDougall was the boss. He had fired managers, built a state-of-the-art ballpark, and he was on the boards of ten Fortune 500 companies. He should command the utmost respect of his employees. But there was something about Cashman. He was a surly, arrogant, horrible human being who didn't give a damn about any of that. There was something almost quaint about Cashman's attitude towards "The Man," thought MacDougall with a rueful smile. There was nothing any person of authority could tell him that he wouldn't resent. Any exchange with him was sure to be unpleasant, although he had a way with the media that made him an object of fascination to them. Cashman's wit was sharp and made good news. You just didn't want to be on the receiving end of it.

Paul MacDougall did not look forward to this conversation at all.

"Good game," he said as he stood at the end of the bank of lockers.

"What do you want?" growled Cashman. "A man can't get a moment's peace."

"Nice to see you, too, Benny," MacDougall replied evenly. He was going to keep his cool, he had decided, no matter what. "I thought we might have a little bit of a heart to heart."

"That should be interesting, since you don't have one," replied Cashman.

"Then let's call it a meeting of the minds, although I'm not sure *you* have a brain in thick skull of yours."

Cashman glowered. He looked for a moment as if he might actually rise up out of his chair. Instead, he just crushed the can in his hand and tossed it over his shoulder without looking where it landed.

"We dodged a bullet yesterday," continued

MacDougall.

"We. Really. Listen, there's almost nothing *we* need to talk about that shouldn't include my agent in the room."

"No, Benny, I think this is one thing we need to talk about, just the two of us." The coolness of Paul MacDougall's voice registered with Benny Cashman. He looked up at his boss with an expression of surprise. "You see, I know."

"Know what?" asked Cashman.

"I know that you can be stupid enough to pee into a cup and do so within a week of taking some kind of steroid. The results from the lab were pretty conclusive."

Benny Cashman opened his mouth to speak, then thought better of it.

"So, what should we do?" asked MacDougall rhetorically. "The way I see it, this time you were lucky - I was able to divert the evidence. Not something I'm willing to do on a regular basis, though – it gets expensive."

"You diverted the evidence?"

"I took some precautions. The test results that will end up in the Commissioner's office aren't from your urine."

"That's cool. So, I continue to make you a shitload of money. What's the problem?"

"The problem is that you're an asshole. And the good will of this city and its fans will last only as long as you don't screw up. It's only a matter of time until someone has definitive evidence of your doping. I don't want you on my team when that happens."

"What are you saying? I have another year on my contract."

"You have another year at *our* option," replied MacDougall. "An option we have no intention of picking up."

This time Benny Cashman stood up. Paul MacDougall did his best not to cower.

"What the fuck are you talking about?" demanded Cashman.

"You're done here, Benny. We both benefit from your pursuit of the record, no question about that, and I can protect you through the playoffs. But when this season is over, you're retiring."

"Fuck that," snarled Cashman. "I got bills to pay."

"I'm sorry, but that's the deal."

"I can always play for another team."

"Somehow I don't think so. I can't imagine any other team putting up with your bullshit. What's the term? 'A cancer in the locker room?' And there's this thing called an Owners' Meeting. If you don't retire, leaving your legacy and records, as well as the hundred-year tradition of the Goliaths intact, then, well, it would be a shame if those test results were discreetly presented to the other twenty-nine owners during the cocktail hour."

Benny Cashman, whose body fat was a very tight six percent, started to show veins bulging in his neck and on his temples.

"Just play a couple of weeks of good, clean ball," continued Paul MacDougall. "We'll take care of you." He turned and walked out of the locker room.

Paul MacDougall thought that replacing the locker room chairs that were being thrown in a rage behind him was a small price to pay for winning just one argument with Benny Cashman.

XXXIII

There had been no sign on the door, no awning, no marquee. Maddy would never have thought that there was a restaurant in the building. It looked like they were entering someone's Cow Hollow first floor flat.

"It's called the Brazen Head," said Jimmy. "The kitchen is open until 1 AM. Are you hungry?"

Maddy was starving. Thinking back on it, she had had nothing to eat since breakfast.

"Yes. Yes, I am. Very," she replied.

"The food's not bad here, although by this hour, almost anything would be delicious."

"How did you find out about this place? It looks a little like it doesn't want to be found."

"In my line of work, you seek out any place that serves late. And serves a decent cocktail. What are you having?"

Maddy ordered a glass of red wine, Jimmy ordered a martini. They both acknowledged how good it felt to just sit down. Once their drinks arrived, and they ordered two cheeseburgers, Jimmy raised his glass in a toast.

"To crime," he said. Maddy laughed.

"To crime!"

They clinked their glasses. Jimmy smiled contentedly.

"So, is it Madeleine?"

"Madison," said Maddy wrinkling her nose. "My parents are of a generation which thought it best to give their children gender neutral names."

"Any siblings?"

"A younger sister. Austin."

"Not only gender neutral, but state capitols, as

well."

"Yes," Maddy replied, rolling her eyes. "So, I prefer Maddy. And you? Any siblings?"

"I bear the awesome responsibility of being an only son."

"Oh."

"I had four sisters, but we threw them down the well."

Maddy almost choked on her wine. Politically incorrect humor regarding his heritage was something she would have to get used to.

"Kidding," he laughed. "I do have four sisters, though. I'm the youngest, the baby brother. The others are all doctors and lawyers."

"So, you're the only policeman in the family. Other than your father, of course."

"Yes. I tried not to be, but... my father, well, he's a force of nature. If he had a son, he was going to be a policeman."

"Your mom is fantastic," said Maddy.

"She, too, is a force of nature. He's the ocean. Deep, stormy, relentless. She's the earth - big heart, expansive, but hard as a rock. I've never met such a couple who embodied so well the concept of Yin and Yang."

"So, you didn't want to be a policeman?"

"No, but I've made peace with it. Actually, I've grown to like it. I like the puzzles. The paperwork, that's another matter, but you can't have everything in life. You want to be a journalist?"

"I think so," said Maddy, swirling her wine glass around on the table thoughtfully. "I wanted to be an Olympic swimmer, but you reach a point in your life where you just know that you don't have what it takes. I like puzzles, too, but I didn't think Maddy Stevenson, Private Eye, was the answer. So, journalism."

"I'm not so sure – you said you had three cases going on."

"Three pieces of investigative journalism, if you

don't mind."

"Right."

At that moment the burgers arrived. They had both agreed that by midnight one either had Chinese food or a cheeseburger. Maybe breakfast with eggs and bacon. But anything legitimately healthy was out of the question. Maddy was starting to think that she had found someone with whom she could really relate. It was a great feeling, and she was enjoying herself.

After a couple of truly satisfying bites and contented sighs, Jimmy returned to the subject at hand.

"Three pieces of investigative journalism. Let me see if I can keep them straight."

"Okay."

"First, we have the Adventure of the Asian Antiquity. What's our position on that?"

"Well, we have an extremely rare Tibetan artifact that shouldn't be anywhere outside of Tibet or a museum. It is seen, instead, in the hotel room of a famous Hollywood actor, with the director of the Museum of Asian Antiquities present. The same director was spotted the night before removing the artifact..."

"Spotted removing a crate. There's no evidence that the crate contained the artifact."

"True," said Maddy.

"And spotted by whom? The Masked Avenger, who's credibility is still open to doubt."

"When you put it like that, I guess we don't have much," said Maddy, somewhat deflated.

"Look, there's plenty of circumstantial evidence. You know that Robert Grant has displayed a passion for things Tibetan."

"I didn't know that – how did you know?"

"Generational difference," teased Jimmy.

Maddy wasn't so sure she liked being teased about that.

"Do we know anything about the woman who was in the room?" continued Jimmy. "And who, according to the Masked Avenger, was also at the Museum late last night?"

"No, not at all."

"It might have been a mistake to crop her out of the picture when I showed it to my mom. As someone who knows many of the players within the art scene, maybe my mom knows her. Perhaps she could give us the clue we need."

"But the Museum director. Carlos was quite convinced that he had something to hide."

"Again, circumstantial at best."

"Then what do we do?" asked Maddy.

"What are your thoughts?" prompted Jimmy. "What plan of action would you advise?"

"Well, first we identify the woman in the photo, if we can."

"Good, I can show it to my mother. What else?"

"We tail Peter Kohler?"

"Who's got that kind of time? We certainly have no resources on my end to do that."

"What about the Robert Grant angle? Couldn't we interrogate him?"

"If he's still at the Mandarin tomorrow, I could stop by. But I wouldn't have a warrant, and he would be within his rights to turn me away at the door. It's not much to go on."

"We stake out the Museum," said Maddy a little desperately.

"Same problem with manpower, and we don't know if this is a one-time deal, or if there is a pattern developing. A stake-out could last weeks."

"Then I'm going to have to get back to you on this." Maddy paused for a moment. "We could do some biographical research on Peter Kohler. If he's up to no good, there may be something in his past that is driving him to it."

"Excellent. A true detective. Follow the leads you can, let go for the time being the leads you can't. Okay.

You mentioned the Beefy Ballplayer. Can you share that with me?"

Maddy told him about what Little Mary had witnessed. Jimmy shook his head.

"Not much to go on there. Unlike the issue with Peter Kohler, this is all hearsay. And even if Benny Cashman is cheating with steroids or some such, I'm not sure it's illegal. There's no crime there."

"Just a violation of a trust. And I never said it was a crime, just a mystery."

"Investigative journalism. If you did get the goods on that guy, it would be huge. Do you have a plan?"

"This would be a legitimate stake-out. We have isolated the few days that an exchange might take place, and we have isolated the time of night when it would happen, too."

"Based on the word of a homeless girl."

"Based on the word of a homeless girl," replied Maddy a little defensively. "She's homeless, not stupid."

"Fair enough," said Jimmy putting his hands up in surrender. "So, a stake-out. And you're going to…"

"I guess we'll take photos of the exchange."

Jimmy sighed. "The stakes for these guys are enormous. Millions of dollars hinge on this. It could be profoundly dangerous. I can't pretend that I like this."

Maddy was starting to feel like this date wasn't going so well, after all.

"Detective Wang, I respect your opinion, but I'm not asking you to like it, and unless you think I'm doing something illegal, then maybe we just let this one alone."

"As you wish," he replied, conceding the point. He found he really hated it that she just called him Detective Wang. With a gentle smile, he asked, "Is the Problem of the Poisoned Panhandler off the table as well?"

Maddy knew this would be hard. She wanted to protect her sources, but she knew that this was a case of murder, and legitimately within the province of the SFPD.

"No. I have information that might aid in your investigation."

Jimmy Wang arched an eyebrow. He was about to say something, but that hadn't worked so well so far. He chose to let Maddy come forward on her own.

"We have determined that the poison in the sandwich is Tetrodotoxin. It causes paralysis. The muscles of Lucky Jerry's diaphragm stopped working, causing him to suffocate."

Jimmy whistled. "This is the assessment of the Man Without a Face?"

"Yes," said Maddy.

"I suppose we can confirm that through our lab. When they can finally get to it," he added sourly. "And what is your plan of investigation on this one?"

"Tetrodotoxin is found in the livers of Blowfish, a delicacy in Japan, and served in very exclusive sushi bars. We thought we would identify the restaurants in town that served Blowfish and try to get their reservation lists for the days leading up to the murder."

Jimmy shrugged in grudging admiration. "How would you do that?"

"The restaurants should be easy... I think. Just an internet search and checking the menus online."

"And the reservation lists?"

"That would be Carlos' undertaking. He has... a 'way' with wait staff."

Jimmy pursed his lips. He really didn't like this at all.

"Alright, you have the lists. But what are you looking for?"

"We figured on two other points of triangulation." Maddy was starting to get excited again. "The sandwich was a catered sandwich. You can tell by the cut on the diagonal bias and the size of the portion. We have access at the Clarion to listings of all the social events that took place in the City last night – certainly any event that might have been catered. It was a Monday night, so we're hoping that there weren't too many, and we can identify the event and possibly the participants."

"And the third point of the triangle?"

"Checking to see if anyone might have seen anything down at UN Plaza during the hours preceding Lucky Jerry's death."

"That place is a graveyard at that hour. How would you do that?"

Maddy hesitated. "We… have a line on a group of people who may have seen something, that no one else would look to ask."

"Who's that?"

"The people who live there but remain invisible to most of us."

"How will you find them?" This time Jimmy paused. "The Masked Avenger?"

Maddy looked down at her plate. "What if I said, yes?"

"Part of me wants to say that you are getting in way over your head. That your involvement in a murder investigation will hamper police inquiries, and that you run dangerously close to obstructing justice." He was sounding more and more like his dad, and he knew it, and he hated it, but he kept on going. "These are people's lives we're talking about, you are fresh out of college, and your Masked Avenger is, for all we know, a crazy old homeless guy. Which he must be to run around in that outfit."

Maddy opened her purse, took out enough cash to cover her dinner, and started to get up. Jimmy gently put his hand on hers. "Please don't do that. That's what only one part of me wants to say."

She sat back down.

"The other part wants to say that you're a pretty remarkable young woman. I learned from my father that, after being relentless, a cop's greatest attribute is his instinct. I'm relying on it now, and I'm respecting yours. You have good instincts."

Maddy chewed on her lower lip. "So which part of you am I giving a ride home tonight?"

Jimmy Wang laughed. "Both. Yin and Yang. Father's and mother's son. Thanks for the offer. I thought for a moment that I was walking home. Which isn't such a bad walk, just a couple of steep hills between here and there.'

Maddy smiled.

"Look. May we establish some ground rules?" he asked.

"Like what?" asked Maddy.

"Like we share what we find."

"I can agree to that."

"That you can follow your leads on Lucky Jerry, but if I find that there's any muddying the waters, I pull rank."

"Okay…"

"And that you call me if you're even within a mile of any trouble."

"I'll think about it."

"And, finally, most importantly, you let me pick up the tab."

"Done," said Maddy, shaking his hand.

*   *   *

As she pulled into the little cul-de-sac on Telegraph Hill where Jimmy told her he lived, Maddy felt the butterflies that come at the end of a first date. Do I kiss him? she asked herself. It felt like it had been forever since she kissed a boy, and she felt terribly self-conscious. Do I turn off the ignition? That was always a sure sign that a smooch was intended or expected, if not more…She decided that she would play it cool – professional – and leave the engine running. If he made his move, she would just go with her gut.

As she pulled to a stop in front of a small but elegant gate, Jimmy turned to her, put his hand on her arm and said, "Thank you, Maddy, for a wonderful evening. We've got a lot of work to do, but I'm looking forward to it." He looked at her intently for a moment. "Are we good?"

"We're good," she replied.

"Great," he said. He smiled broadly and then got out of the car. "See you soon. Good night."

"'night," said Maddy. She almost let the sigh escape from her lips. Cool, remember? she whispered to herself.

She put the Beetle into drive and made the turn around the end of the cul-de-sac. As she approached Jimmy's gate from the opposite direction, she was startled to see him approaching her, waving his badge in front of him.

"Stop the car," he said. As Maddy pulled to a stop and rolled down her window, he continued, "I'm going to have to ask you to step out of your vehicle, ma'am."

"Are you kidding?" Maddy couldn't figure out what was going on. Jesus, he's going to arrest me or something.

"Please step away from your vehicle," he repeated. Maddy, completely bewildered by now, put the car into park, put on the parking brake and climbed out of the car.

"What's going on?" she asked.

"You are under..." Suddenly, he started to sing like Frank Sinatra, and he grabbed her around her waist and swayed her to his rhythm. *"'under my skin. I've got you, deep in the heart of me...'"* He smiled. "I just wanted to say good night properly.' He put his hand to the side of her face, brushing her hair back. He then gently pulled her towards him and kissed her softly on the lips.

All cool went out the window. Maddy kissed him right back. She then put her head on his chest, which felt really good, she thought. After that, she pushed herself away a bit to get a good look at him. "Gosh, you're tall," she laughed. She just came up to his shoulder.

"For a Chinese guy," laughed Jimmy. Maddy

smacked him playfully on his chest. She would never win the political-correctness game.

"No, it's true," he continued. "My parents could never figure it out. I tried to tell them it was all the cheeseburgers I ate in high school. My parents were just not used to that level of protein consumption. I'm a foot taller than my dad, and you've seen my mom."

She shook her head. He was pretty unpredictable. She liked that. She kissed him one more time then broke away.

"Thank you," she said.

"For what?" he asked.

"For keeping me on my toes. But I've got to get some sleep. Full day tomorrow."

"Call me?"

"You bet," she replied. A little wave and then she was in her Beetle, pulling away down the street.

XXXIV

He pushed his way through the gate and walked down a little lane to the steps that led to his apartment. At one in the morning, the air was cold and moist – a relief after the last few days of heat. The Indian Summer had broken, and San Francisco was returning to its typical autumn evenings. Good football weather, he thought.

Jimmy's apartment was the bottom of four flats stacked on top of each other, hanging off the edge of Telegraph Hill. As he entered his front door, the view of the Bay, and Treasure Island sitting at the base of the Bay Bridge, opened before him through the sliding glass doors that went wall to wall across his living room. The place was small – a studio - but it felt enormous because of this view. At this hour the Bay was still magical, ringed by lights that sparkled in the distance and reflected off the water. Giant container ships, with their floodlights flickering as they rose up and down in the water, were anchored throughout the Bay in a random pattern. Rather than turn on the lights and break the spell, Jimmy negotiated his way through the apartment by the light that glowed onto the ceiling from the streetlights below. He moved into his small kitchen, pulled out a glass and poured himself two fingers of whisky. He then went to the sliding glass door, opened it, and stepped out onto his small balcony, taking a deep breath of the cool, soft air.

I love this city, he sighed.

He had been born here. He shook his head, thinking about how strange and lucky it was that his parents, two people from completely different social strata, managed to meet, fall in love, and have five children. He still couldn't imagine how it happened, especially now that he had grown used to them in their sixties. Yin and Yang is right, he smiled to himself as he sipped his whisky. Maybe that's why I'm such a mess.

His mom was of the oldest money in Chinatown. Her family had come over with the building of the railroad during the 1860's, and her great-great-grandfather, once he had survived his work as a basket man placing explosives into the sides of mountains in the Sierras, had started with a small curios shop on Stockton Street. The shop had grown in quality and influence over the years to the point where her father was wealthy enough to send his daughter to Princeton, and then on a Grand Tour of Europe upon her graduation. Jimmy smiled at the thought of it, having learned over the years of some less than savory activities by his mother's side of the family – especially during the Twenties and Thirties. Smuggling, bootlegging, even a speakeasy in the basement of the Stockton Street store. But any taint of criminal influence had been washed completely clean by his mother's generation, and she was the embodiment of well-heeled, well-bred grace and sophistication. An art history major in college, she had come home to San Francisco to study at the famous Art Institute. She had hoped to earn a master's degree in arts administration but got side-tracked before she got more than one semester into the program. Her father died suddenly, and she assumed management of the family business, which took a tremendous amount of her energy, but at which she was extremely successful. At this time, she also met Sergeant James Wang, a handsome and ambitious young policeman, at a San Francisco Policemen's Benevolent Fund Ball, and, with one dance, fell in love.

In the Sixties, no one fell for a man in uniform. Between the Vietnam War, Kent State, the Democratic Convention in Chicago, and campus protests all over the country, anyone seen defending the military-industrial complex was immediately suspect. But Sergeant James Wang pulled it off. He had grown up in Stockton, his family owning a small laundry. With little hope for anything more than a high-school education, he had managed to break away from the family business and escape to the San Francisco Police Academy. His drive and relentlessness catapulted him to the top of his class. A year into his career as a police officer he had been promoted to Sergeant. After his marriage to Pearl Fong, he continued his steady rise up the ranks. By the time he retired, he had reached the rank of Deputy Chief of Police.

How they raised four daughters and a son, I'll never understand, thought Jimmy. Well, he understood that his sisters looked after him mostly. And then, well, after a certain point, he looked after himself. Even though his family had settled into a quiet, dignified condominium building in Nob Hill, he spent most of his days after school bombing around the dirty streets of Chinatown or hanging at Rasputin Records - and the McDonald's across the street - down by Union Square.

His grades had always been good, though. Between the constant exposure to art, culture and intellectual curiosity from his mom, and the sheer terror of failing to live up to his dad's expectations, he developed into an A student. He took his good grades across the Bay to UC Berkeley, where he got most of the wildness out of his system. After four years of drinking and smoking at his fraternity, he had had enough of being stupid, and decided to make something of himself.

Or, if I'm really honest with myself, he reflected, my father just kicked me in the ass.

His father had been nicknamed the Dragon. Not that anyone called him that to his face, but he knew about it, and even kind of liked it. Jimmy learned this the hard way, entering the force just as his dad was retiring. He endured a mix of deference and resentment from the older officers, who were doubtful of his abilities and yet fearful of any repercussions from his father that might result from getting in Jimmy's way. It took several years of really hard work, late nights, and constant good humor for Jimmy to earn the respect and friendship of his colleagues in his own right. His blend of his father's relentlessness and pride in his work, with his mother's sensitivity and sophistication made him able to negotiate all the personalities that inhabited the force. That, and he had a good smile and a goofy sense of humor.

Crap, what time is it? He realized that he had been standing on the balcony for an hour and was chilled to the bone. His glass had long been empty. He sighed and climbed back into his apartment, shutting the sliding glass door behind him. As he sat on the edge of his bed and pulled off his shoes, his thoughts turned to Maddy.

That was a very nice kiss, he thought. She has soft lips. He laid his head down on the pillow, thinking he might just rest for a second before getting fully ready for bed.

As the rising sun poured through his windows several hours later, he cursed himself for still being fully dressed.

XXXV

The idea came to her, as most of her good ideas did, about five minutes into her shower.

Far from floating on a cloud by the time she got home, Maddy had sunk like a stone onto her bed. The overwhelming sensation she felt as she drifted off to sleep was one of deep contentment.

He smelled good.

She had awakened with a start, five minutes before the alarm was set to go off. There were some serious puzzles to solve, and she suddenly felt the apprehension that comes from heading into an exam without being prepared. The question of Peter Kohler nagged at her. Some coffee helped fuel the brain cells, then a long, hot shower. It frustrated her to realize that she hadn't gone running for several days, but she consoled herself with the muscle ache that came from all the pavement pounding she had done. She laughed recalling Carlos' imprecation that a real journalist had to "pound some pavement." Truer words were ne'er spoke.

At the five-minute mark - after the shampoo but before the conditioner - it hit her. Wait a frickin' minute. A stake-out didn't require significant manpower. This was the Twenty-first Century. She chided herself for her tendency to romanticize the art and craft of detection. She had seen too many movies and television shows growing up where the two cops hung out in an unmarked car drinking Dunkin' Donuts' coffee until the wee hours of the morning, confessing their past sins. There was now a better, cleaner way.

She knew the technology existed. After all, she would often check the Corona del Mar State Beach webcam to see if the fog had burned off before committing to spending an afternoon down at the beach. All she needed was a camera, a good vantage point in which to place it, and, of course, someone who knew what they were doing. The first was just a trip to Radio Shack. The second - she had an idea for a site. For the third, well, she knew who to call, it was just going to be emotionally fraught.

Justin.

He had been an electrical engineering major, but he spent most of his time at Stanford working as a master electrician and lighting designer for the various campus theatre groups. He was a theatre junkie, and he and Maddy had found common ground over their love of musicals. By his sophomore year he was supplementing his work-study money by taking over-hire calls with the stagehands' union in the City. He was smart, knew what he was doing, and had quickly become a favorite of the Local's business agent. By the time he had finished his degree, he had his union card and was filling in as a back-up light board operator at the Orpheum. Upon graduation, he sat down and weighed the offers he had received from local engineering firms against the income he could make as a full-time union stagehand, and he realized that he was better off as a stagehand. With overtime he could easily make six figures and have one of the best benefits packages anywhere. The lifestyle suited him better, too.

This had been the bone of contention between him and Maddy. Part of the lifestyle that Justin enjoyed was hanging out with the performers after a show. He was a tall, good-looking dark-haired boy with blue eyes, and he enjoyed being one of the few straight guys backstage. With all of those dancers, stage managers and even the occasional diva, the world was his oyster. Maddy felt she could never compete with all those glamorous girls and had burned herself up over his dalliances. But she had been too much of a chicken-shit to break up with him. Instead, she had just gotten so frustrated and bitchy that he finally told her that they would be better off without each other. She knew he was right, but it didn't make her feel any better – especially having him be the dumper, leaving her as the dumpee. She had cried and stayed in bed for days.

Six months had gone by, though, and she realized that she really didn't care anymore. She felt that there was now enough emotional distance to give him a call. And confidence. And she had a new boyfriend, she smiled to herself. Nyah, nyah, nyah.

"Hey, Maddy," he said sleepily as he answered the phone. "What's up?"

She took some pride in knowing that he must still have her number programmed into his phone.

"Sorry to be calling you so early. Late night?"

"Yeah. Loading out South Pacific. For a national tour, these guys had more trucks than Jesus. We got out of there about four in the morning."

"Ouch. I can call you back later…"

"It's cool. What's up with you? It's good to hear your voice."

"I hate to bother you, but I need a favor. A big one. And you're uniquely qualified for the job."

"Um, sure. What do you need?"

She told him that she was working on a story for the Clarion and needed to do some clandestine ops.

"A little Nancy Drew action, eh?"

"Justin? One more favor. *Please* don't call me that."

"Oh. Okay." She could tell he was rolling his eyes recalling their last few months together. She regrouped.

"Hey, no biggie. It's just you're not the only one who has teased me about this, and it just, I don't know, rubs me the wrong way. I'm sorry."

"No worries, girlfriend. So, what do we need to do?"

"I need to mount a webcam to the roof of the Orpheum."

"Shit, really?"

"Yeah. How hard would that be?"

"Well, once we move past the potential legal issues – which I assume we're disregarding - it would be super easy."

"Really?"

"Yeah. Funny thing is, there are cameras on the roof already. The VP of Operations had them installed a while back. But since they didn't generate the results they hoped for, no one pays attention to them anymore. As long as nobody notices, we could refocus one of them and take the feed and stream it onto my laptop in the booth. I could then have the video posted on my website – I can set up a secure area that's password protected that you could go to. The video would be date/time stamped. Is that what you need?"

"That is more than super awesome. That's sheer genius." She wasn't just appealing to his vanity, she really meant it.

"The only problem is that I only have the capacity on my site to store maybe a few hours of video at a time."

"I think that's okay. I really only need to catch from about 11 pm to 1 am each day."

"That should work – I can set it up to automatically upload at 1 am. You would just need to review it before, say, 10 pm the next evening. At that point, the site would be set to overwrite the files with the next upload. Does that work for you?"

"That totally works!" Maddy remembered why she fell in love with him back in the day. Super-cute super-geek.

"What are we focusing on?" he asked.

"I'll show you when we set this up. Are you going in today?"

"Yeah. We have to be back by ten. We have to make the place super squeaky clean for the MagicLand people. The word backstage is that Mark Eichler himself is coming this afternoon."

"Wow. What's up with that?"

"We're supposed to be the staging theatre for the

national tour of *The Leopard Prince*. From load-in through opening it will be an insane amount of hours. I could almost make six month's salary in the next two weeks. Makes me tired to think about, though."

"God, I love *The Leopard Prince*,' sighed Maddy. "That opening scene with all the animals and drums – sends chills up my spine."

"I'll see if I can score you some tickets to the invited dress on Sunday."

"That would be amazing. How could I ever thank you?"

"Don't worry about it. Just paying a karmic debt… So, when do you want to come over?"

"What works for you?"

"Come by the stage door at two. We'll be taking our lunch then, and I'll sneak you up to the roof. We have to be out of the way then anyway. That's when the suits are doing their tour."

"I'll make it happen. Thank you!" She hesitated for a second. "Hey. I'm really sorry about… about all…"

"Oh, Maddy. It's cool. It was all my fault, anyway. I know that. Don't worry about it. As I said, I'm paying a karmic debt." He paused. "You okay – I mean, everything good in your life?"

"Yeah. Great, actually."

"Seeing anybody?"

"I am. At least I think so. It's pretty new."

She was struck by the note of regret in his voice. "That's cool. It will be good to see you."

"It will be good to see you, too. Thanks again."

As she hung up the phone, she felt better about being prepared for her exam. Now to pass the second test of the day.

Carey Portman.

XXXVI

He had spent the rest of the night after Maddy dropped him off putting out feelers. People were upset and scared by what had happened down at UN Plaza, and wanted something done. Word on the street was that the Masked Avenger was on the case and that made people feel better.

I still matter, he had sighed as he wedged himself behind a dumpster in the back of the loading dock of Hills Plaza. It was four in the morning, and it had been a long night. By the time he had taken his refuge he knew that he had only a couple of hours before the garbage collectors would be pulling in to empty the dumpsters.

This town wakes up too damn early.

His inquiries had taken him to Golden Gate Park. Old Benji was still recovering from the bite of the sandwich he had eaten. According to him, he figured that Lucky Jerry had just had a heart attack, and it would have been a shame to waste all that food. He had seen Jerry's body at about 12:30. No reason to hang around, he had figured. It had looked like it was going to be too hot a scene, so he had grabbed the tray and vamoosed. Marissa and Rodney had also started to chew on some sandwiches, and they had all known within a few bites that something was wrong.

"Rodney was real bad. He was shaking and shit and could barely breathe. We bundled him into his blankets and headed out to the park. He's still sleeping." The Masked Avenger had learned that they had scored a large pizza from the dumpster behind Patxi's Pizza only an hour before. Deep dish, Chicago-style. The heavy food in their stomachs had probably saved their lives.

"I'll be back tomorrow evening," he said. "With

help."

"That's cool," said Old Benji. "Maybe my lips won't feel so funny by then."

"In the meantime, can you ask around and see if anyone saw where Lucky Jerry got those sandwiches?"

"I'll ask, but you know, most people don't pay much attention to shit, and even if they do, a lot of us have poor short-term memory, you know?"

The Masked Avenger knew. When one was devoting so much energy to eking out an existence, there wasn't much left for anything else.

He had made his way out to the park on the MUNI train – the N Judah. It was in such a time as this, when he was without his bicycle, that he had to resort to traveling in disguise. The Masked Avenger didn't just ride MUNI – it would cause to much interest, too much distraction. The citizens of his City would be surprised and perhaps even awed. He had shifted into some baggy trousers with an old trench coat. He had taken off his mask but diverted attention from his facial characteristics by means of an old pair of glasses. No one would recognize him – or, even better, no one would look twice in his direction.

The art of misdirection. In his years of training to reach his capabilities as the Masked Avenger he had learned that simple trick. He had learned so many simple tricks over the years. It was good to be well trained and skilled. It compensated, as well he knew, for the ravages time had wreaked on his body.

Age and treachery will always defeat youth and enthusiasm, he chuckled to himself.

His training had been hard. It had been intense. No one becomes the defender of the weak - the champion of the defenseless - without years of committed subjugation to the Way. He had thrown his body and his soul into learning the various techniques necessary to cloud men's minds and to move invisibly through their lives. He thought about the question Carlos had put to him earlier in the evening. Why did he do it? Because he had to.

XXXVII

"So, what have you got?"

Carey Portman was looking over her glasses at Maddy and Carlos in a way that made Maddy think of the mean old schoolteacher of legend. Maddy and Carlos had compared notes hurriedly first thing that morning and had agreed to keep the three mysteries off the table for as long as possible. It wasn't as if they hadn't covered ground, found some nodes, and made connections. They flipped through their notebooks and laid it out for Carey.

"We made contact with some people at Homeless Island, as you suggested, and they gave us leads on tribes at UN Plaza and down in Dogpatch. We're out to Golden Gate Park later today to follow up on the next round of leads," said Maddy.

"Anything of note?" asked Carey.

"A few things," said Carlos. "We've got a lot of buzz about this one guy who died down at UN Plaza, just behind the Orpheum. The street people are saying it wasn't natural causes – possible murder, although they are also saying the police aren't helping." He and Maddy, as part of their strategy with Carey, agreed that telling as much of the truth as possible would go a long way.

"It's not like the police don't have better things to do," said Carey. "No, I didn't say that. A possible angle there. How the police prioritize their caseload, homeless versus privileged, something like that." Maddy enjoyed watching the way Carey's mind worked. Always looking for the way into a story.

"And the leader of the tribe down at Homeless Island also died just two nights ago. In his case the cause was also pretty intense – tissue necrosis."

"I told you kids to be careful out there." Carey took off her glasses and used them as a pointer. "Are you guys okay? Death is a big part of life on the streets. Can you handle this?"

Maddy forced a smile. "It's been an education to be sure, ma'am, but we're okay. We're both learning a lot about a whole new side of life."

"Good. I told you this wouldn't just be filing and typing. So, what else?"

"We met this interesting group of young people down in Dogpatch. Homeless by choice, not necessity," continued Carlos.

"Those kids make me so mad," said Carey. "Get a fucking job. But there might be an angle there, too – compare and contrast the bohemians with the real down-and-out. Something to think about. You have names?"

"Yes, although no one will give us their full name, just their street name."

"But you could find them again?"

"Yes, ma'am."

"This is all good. So, the plan for the Park?"

"We've been told that we should visit the people out there after dark," said Maddy, "so we thought we would head out just as the sun was going down – try to catch them as they prepare for their rounds."

Carey raised an eyebrow.

"It's okay, really," said Maddy. "I've got Carlos to protect me."

Everyone in the room knew that Carlos wouldn't scare anybody. Carey drummed her fingers on her desk.

"Don't know that I like it, but this is where we separate the men from the boys, isn't it? I'm going on record as telling you not to be out there after dark, but what you do on your own initiative is up to you."

Maddy knew that Carey had also started young, but in places like Beirut and Moscow. No wimps, no whining. If Maddy was going to get somewhere, she had to acknowledge the subtext of Carey's message.

"No problem," she replied evenly.

"Now go to work," said Carey, placing her glasses back on her nose and turning towards her keyboard.

"Excuse me, ma'am," said Maddy. "Since I'll be working late this evening, may I take a long lunch?"

"Take whatever time you need. It's all about production here, not hours. But I want all of your notes typed up and emailed to me before you go, all right?"

"Yes, ma'am. Thanks!"

As Carey returned to her computer, she smiled to herself. Age and treachery would always beat youth and enthusiasm, she chuckled, but she had to love Maddy's enthusiasm. The girl was all right.

XXXVIII

The morning flew by. Not only had Maddy finished her notes, but she had found the time to Google-search all the restaurants in San Francisco which might serve Blowfish. The list could never be considered comprehensive, she thought. She knew that most really high-end restaurants had "secret" menus. Blowfish was not something that would normally be found on the menus that were posted on-line. But even so, there were really only a handful of sushi bars in town that had both three stars and three dollar signs in the Clarion reviews. These would be a place to start.

In the meantime, Carlos had pumped the intern over at the Society desk for a listing of social events on Monday night. As they had suspected, Monday was something of a quiet night for such gatherings, Tuesdays and Wednesdays being more popular.

"There were only three events that night that made the paper," he said as he and Maddy exchanged research. "A cocktail party at the Museum of Asian Antiquities – look, here's a photo of Peter Kohler himself… Jesus, what hair; a pre-opening gala out at the new Science and Technology Center in Golden Gate Park; and a 'Night with the Stars' – a fund-raiser hosted by Cheryl Niederman for the Children's Cancer wing at the hospital – with the cast of *South Pacific*, which would make sense, since Monday would be their 'dark' night. See, there she is. Look at all that jewelry! And look how tight her cheeks are – some serious work done there."

"And the guest lists?"

"Got 'em right here." There were several hundred people at each event.

"Holy crap," said Maddy. How do we sort through

that?"

"It's not as hard as it looks." He spun his monitor around and showed Maddy that he had already entered the names into an Excel spreadsheet and had organized them alphabetically by event.

"Nice!" whispered Maddy. She then gave him the list of restaurants. There were only eight that qualified. Certainly, there were hundreds of sushi places, but only eight that were of such a level of exclusivity that they might serve an entrée which, if prepared incorrectly, might kill somebody.

"Mmmm, mmmm!" said Carlos, smacking his lips. "If only I could afford to eat at these places."

"Where are you going to start?" asked Maddy. "I mean, this could take days."

"No, not really," replied Carlos, studying the list. "Most of them are clustered within a few blocks of each other. Something about seafood and Bay views. They go hand in hand. I'll just start at the southern end of the line and work northward."

"How are you going to get the reservation lists?"

"Leave that to me. It will be a case-by-case thing."

"Okay, but when will you have time to do it? Can you go tonight?"

"I'm supposed to be protecting you out at the Park, remember?"

"I'll be okay – I've got the Masked Avenger looking out for me. It's too important – we have to divide and conquer."

"Who's tougher than you?" asked Carlos, teasing.

"Carey Portman," replied Maddy, seriously.

"No shit," said Carlos, suddenly serious himself.

Maddy looked at her watch and realized that she had to scramble. It was coming up on quarter to two, and she had a date to keep.

"Hey, remember that bike you were talking about?"

"The one in my basement?"

"Yeah. What time are you punching out today?"

"Five."

"I'll meet you at your place at 5:30. I've got a bike rack. I can deliver the bike this evening."

"That works – I was going to go home and change, anyway. If I'm working five-star restaurants, I've got to look fine."

"Great. See you then!"

"Good luck, Chica. And hey, don't let that old boyfriend get under your skin."

Like I needed to make my life more complicated, Maddy thought with a sigh as she headed to the elevators.

XXXIX

Maddy ran up to the stage door of the Orpheum right at two o'clock. Justin was leaning against the wall by the door, chatting with another stagehand – a cute girl in army fatigues who looked quite buff and tough with her cropped hair, tattoos, and pierced eyebrow. He was smoking a cigarette. Another habit he picked up backstage, and one Maddy hated.

He looked pretty cool, though, she had to admit.

As Maddy approached, he stubbed out his cigarette and waved to the tough girl who started off down the street after blowing him a kiss. He opened his arms for Maddy to give him a hug. She gave him the "buddy hug" and smiled at him.

He's doing me a big favor, she reminded herself.

They entered the stage door. Justin vouched for Maddy to the Stage Doorman who had her fill in her name and time of entrance in his log. He then gave her a stick-on visitor's badge and waved them through. They proceeded to a staircase and headed up several flights. They then passed down a corridor and entered the mezzanine lobby of the theatre.

Maddy had been a frequent visitor to the Orpheum when she was in school going to the Best of Broadway series, but she was struck anew by the baroque excess of the décor. It was rich with detail in some sort of pastiche of the arabesque style – wild patterns throughout the ceilings, curlicued and spiraled columns, strange creatures carved into the corners. She loved it. It made going to the theatre feel like stepping into a magical, exotic world. Perfect for transporting children and preparing them for such romantic and theatrical fare as *The Leopard Prince*.

They crossed the lobby and went up the grand staircase to the balcony level. It was a little weird, thought Maddy, to be in the lobby when it was so quiet. The thick carpeting muffled their footsteps, causing Maddy to feel like they were ghosts or something. They crossed this lobby and entered a small door marked "Staff Only." Passing through this, they climbed up a steep ship's ladder to the booth, which was at the back of the second balcony.

Wow, the stage is far away from here, thought Maddy, as she looked through the windows over the auditorium. She could see that the stage floor was gleaming with a new coat of black paint, and that all of the theatre's ladders and lift equipment were neatly stacked against the back wall. She had never seen a stage so empty, clean, and so waiting for a new production to fill it.

The booth was home to the lighting consoles and the follow spots, four of which were standing quietly like cannons waiting to be loaded. The lighting consoles were exotic in their own right, with sliders and buttons and multiple monitors. The room felt lived in and close, the way the bridge of a submarine might feel. Maddy could smell years of men working in there. A clubby, dark smell.

"Come this way," said Justin. They crossed the booth to a ladder that went up towards a trap door in the ceiling. He climbed up, slammed his hand against a lever, and popped open the trap door. The dimness of the booth was pierced by a shaft of brilliant sunshine. Justin clambered through and Maddy followed.

She climbed out onto the graveled roof of the Orpheum. The Civic Center and UN Plaza splayed out before her. The dome of City Hall rose majestically a block away. It *is* a beautiful building, Maddy thought. Feels like a nation's capital building, not just a city hall. Justin had crossed over to the ledge overlooking UN Plaza, and was hunched down next to a long, rectangular object.

A camera.

There were two such cameras on the roof. They were encased in large steel weather-proof boxes, positioned on the two corners facing the backside of the theatre – UN Plaza.

"You sure that no one is monitoring these?" asked Maddy.

"Pretty sure. Besides, what are you planning on focusing on? If we're just tilting or panning the camera a little bit one way or another, I'm sure no one would notice – at least not for several days. At that point, they would just send a maintenance guy to make the adjustment back. No big deal. So, what's our target?"

Maddy pointed to the back side of the Museum of Asian Antiquities just down the street.

"Towards that door in the side of that building," she said.

"Huh. Casing the joint?"

Maddy could only shrug. "Sort of. Just checking for 'irregularities.'"

"Right," said Justin. He pulled out his Leatherman, flipped open the Philips screwdriver attachment, and started to loosen the screw on the side of the stanchion supporting the camera. He sighted along the top of the camera as he tilted it, but after a moment seemed satisfied and tightened the screw back down. "Just a small tilt up the street – about one degree's difference. Now downstairs to the patch bay to see if we can route the signal to the booth."

As they were getting ready to head back towards the trap door, Maddy saw a cluster of men in dark suits surrounding a little woman in a red suit down in the Plaza below. "Is that who I think it is?" she asked Justin.

"The tall, balding guy. Yeah, that's Mark Eichler."

"And who's the lady?"

"That's Cheryl Niederman. She owns the place."

"Wow, she looks so tiny next to Eichler."

It was true. Mark Eichler was quite tall, and Cheryl Niederman was quite little. But there was something in their body language that made an observer reflect that Cheryl Niederman never noticed the difference.

*   *   *

"The place looks great, Cheryl. Just great."

"Thanks, Mark. The old lady cleans up nice, doesn't she?"

Cheryl Niederman was impressed herself. The cleaning crews had done an excellent job. The glorious fall weather and the exquisite lunch at Jardiniere didn't hurt anyone's impression of the place, either. She was excited and she knew she was charming the pants off Mark Eichler. She felt the thrill of finalizing a deal.

"And the Plaza – looking good. I haven't seen a vagrant yet. What's up with that?"

Without missing a beat, Cheryl Niederman said, "We made them an offer they couldn't refuse." She smiled at Mark Eichler. The look in her eye, however, made him stop for a moment.

She's fucking serious, he thought. I'll bet she did.

But he laughed. "Cheryl, you're one tough lady. But a pleasure to do business with."

"Come on. I still have to show you the guts of the place." She took Mark Eichler by the arm and led him towards the stage door. As she did so, she looked back at John Sanders, who was lagging the proper four paces behind with the MagicLand executives of his rank. She gave him a wink that said, Good Job.

John Sanders just gave a small nod, as if to say, All in a day's work. Think nothing of it, ma'am.

*   *   *

They were standing in the A/V room. One thing's

for sure, thought Maddy, they run a tight ship. The room was clean and painted battleship gray. Thick ropes of wires came into a patch bay through various openings in the walls and ceiling, but they were bundled neatly and labeled clearly.

"Union guys do good work," said Justin, as if reading her thoughts. "That makes this part easy."

They had decided that, rather than simply hijack the feed, they would just patch a second line from the router. The computer server that contained the security video would still document everything from that camera, but the feed would also run to Justin's laptop in the booth. This way, no one would really be the wiser, even if they cared enough to review the security videos in the first place.

"How long does that computer store the security video?" Maddy asked.

"I don't know," Justin replied. "Why?"

"Just curious."

"It would be easy to find out." He turned on a monitor that was built into the Audio/Visual rack and slid out a keyboard that was stored just underneath. He manipulated a mouse next to the keyboard and clicked his way through the file structure. "The files are a week old. They must be erased from the memory every seven days to make room for new stuff. It's just like the system we're setting up, just bigger."

They clambered back up to the booth, Maddy once again grateful for spending the bulk of her youth on swim teams. Once she stopped to think about it, it was a six-story climb from the basement to the booth. A good work out.

After about fifteen minutes they had what they were looking for. A clear view of the rear of the Museum of Asian Antiquities.

"The resolution is pretty good," said Maddy.

"Camera technology is getting better all the time. It's necessary if anyone's going to actually identify anyone.

Now all I need is your email address."

"It hasn't changed, at least my personal one hasn't."

"Cool. I'll send you the link and the password later this evening."

"When do you have to go back to work?" asked Maddy, realizing that it was just past three.

"I should be back now," said Justin looking at his watch.

"I'm sorry – I totally monopolized your lunch break. I was going to take you out as a small thank you…"

"I'm good. I knew this would take a while, so I asked one of my crew to pick something up for me."

"The girl at the stage door?" asked Maddy, trying not to sound too interested.

"Cate. Yeah," said Justin, just as nonchalantly. "I'll take a rain-check, though."

"Sure. I totally owe you."

Maddy signed out at the stage door and gave Justin another hug – slightly less "buddy" and more genuine. As she turned around, she saw Cate standing there with a couple of brown bags. Cate smiled tightly at Maddy, who smiled back just as tightly and headed out the door.

Much too complicated, Maddy thought.

*   *   *

She was going to grab her Beetle and head home when the thought struck her. She didn't know what it meant that her good ideas came at her totally sideways, when she was least expecting them, but she was grateful that they came at all. So instead of heading into the parking garage, she ran into the Clarion building and headed for Carlos' cubicle.

"How'd it go?" he asked as she threw her bag down and pulled her chair over towards his.

"We are so dialed in. If anything goes in or out of that museum at some odd hour, we'll know it."

"Awesome. I didn't think I would see you 'til later. What's up?"

"I just wanted to take another look at those photos from the Society page. Something's been bugging me."

Carlos pulled the paper out of his trash can and opened it up to the page.

"Look at the photo of Peter Kohler with those guests," said Maddy. "See anybody you know?"

"You know me, I can't tell one Asian from another," he said with a wicked smile.

Maddy poked him. "Don't be such an asshole." He giggled and then looked at the photo more seriously.

"Holy crap!" said Carlos. "That's the woman from the Mandarin."

She was off to the side of the main group that had been photographed with Kohler. She stood in profile, slightly in the background, holding a champagne glass. But it was her, no doubt about it.

"That means she's involved with the Museum in some way," said Maddy.

"Sounds like a good excuse to call your boyfriend."

Maddy stuck out her tongue. Why did he make her feel like she was twelve? "I'll see you at five-thirty," she said and spun on her heel.

"Hey!" he called after her.

"What?"

Carlos pulled out the front page of the Sporting Green and waved it at Maddy. It had an enormous photo of Benny Cashman splashed across it with the number 754 in huge type underneath.

"Couldn't find a bigger news story on the planet, right now. Are we going after it?" he asked.

"It's on the pile. Although it's pretty intimidating." Maddy reflected on what Jimmy had said the night before. "If what Little Mary says is true, then we can catch him cheating. And if he's caught cheating, then millions of dollars are going to go up in smoke."

"Some serious shit."

"Some serious shit, indeed. Look, I've got to get going if I'm going to make it home and back in time." She grabbed her bag and started, once more, towards the elevators.

"Hey Chica," he called, this time in a sing-song voice. "I've got one more present for you."

"Can it wait?" she called back.

"Remember what I said about my friend at Verizon?"

Maddy froze.

"Well, I've got a name and an address."

Maddy slowly turned and walked back to his cubicle. Carlos handed her a piece of paper.

"Clarice Bryant," she read. "He certainly doesn't look like a Clarice."

"Unless she had a sex change. Which could explain a lot."

"I don't think so. Dork. The address is in Oakland."

"West Oakland. I looked it up."

"So, what do we do?" asked Maddy.

"I don't know. We could go out there..."

"And get shot? Not today, thank you," said Maddy. She knew that West Oakland was several square miles of crime scene. More people were killed in drive-by shootings in West Oakland in any given year than in all of Los Angeles. "Look, we'll figure it out. Right now, I've got to get ready for this evening. See you in a couple of hours."

"You got it," called Carlos as Maddy, once again, headed towards the elevators, and out onto the streets.

XL

"Hey, how are you?"

Jimmy Wang was glad to hear her voice. At four in the afternoon, he was still feeling creaky from the night before, but a steady dose of coffee had him moving in the right direction. He had had a full day, with some interesting developments. He put his feet on his desk and kicked back in his chair, cradling the phone with his shoulder.

"I'm okay – a little beat, to be honest," replied Maddy – she was driving home and grinding her way up Larkin Avenue. "It's only Wednesday and it feels like Friday afternoon."

"Roger that," laughed Jimmy. "So, what's up?"

"I've got a couple of pieces of news that I thought might be helpful."

"Lay it on me. I've got some odds and ends myself, but since I'm talking with the press, this has got to be strictly off the record."

"How does that work when I'm talking with the police?" asked Maddy. "Can I be off the record, too?"

"Deals can be struck," said Jimmy, smiling. "Let's say that as long as no one is in imminent danger, then we can set all this off to the side. I still get to make the final call as to whether or not we need to jump into action."

"Okay, but I don't think there's any jumping that you need to do – at least not yet."

"Okay, cool. So, what have you got?"

"Peter Kohler. He was at a cocktail party at the Museum of Asian Antiquities the evening he was spotted removing that crate."

"How do you know that?"

"Connections within the Clarion. Society column."

"Nice."

"Anyway, there's a photo in today's Clarion of Peter Kohler at this party Monday night, with a bunch of donors, and the woman who was in the room with the golden statue is in the background. She must be connected with the Museum somehow."

"Good. That's good," said Jimmy. "I'll let my mom know – I was just about to head down to see her. I can pull that photo and add it to the one we've got from the room. What else?"

"I've managed to figure out how to stake out the museum without actually being there."

"How are you going to do that?"

"Let's just say I've got an eye in the sky."

"Nothing illegal? I mean, I'm just asking."

"No, don't think so. Just taking advantage of some technical expertise offered by an old friend. If something comes up of any substance, you'll be the first to know."

"Fair enough. Anything on our Poisoned Panhandler?"

"News at eleven."

"Seriously?" asked Jimmy.

"Well, pretty seriously. We've identified a handful of restaurants that might be capable of providing the Blowfish toxin. Carlos is going to work his way through them, starting tonight."

"Keep me posted on that – remember our deal. It's not as if he's a trained professional..."

"Have you ever waited tables?" asked Maddy.

"Um, no, why?"

"He has. So, he's got some street cred. Just give it a chance."

"Point taken. I will. And you?"

"I'm heading out to the Park to do some interviews."

"In your capacity as intern at the Clarion, or as Maddy Stevenson, Private Eye?"

"Both."

"Are you going by yourself? You shouldn't be out there after dark. That's when the crazies come out."

"I'll be fine. Really."

Jimmy sighed. Why couldn't he find some quiet Chinese girl who wouldn't give him a stomach-ache? Well, there's still time, he thought.

"Where in the Park are you headed?"

"Um, can't tell you?"

"Hey, now."

"No, it's because I don't know yet for sure. I'll know more in a bit."

"Call me when you do. Please."

"I'll try. I'm guessing it will be another full evening. You said you had some news."

"Just following up on a few things. First, you'll be pleased to know that your faceless friend's diagnosis has been confirmed. The report just came back from the lab."

"That's excellent! That means we haven't been wasting our time, and we've even got a jump on the case."

"It does. Points to you, and your Masked Avenger."

"Jeez. Thanks!"

"On a less satisfying note, I stopped by the Mandarin and poked around. Robert Grant had checked out. I did get a positive ID, though, from a bellhop who helped Peter Kohler with a crate up to the forty-sixth floor, and from another bellhop who helped Robert Grant with what sounded like the same crate down to his car first thing this morning."

"Does that help us in any way?"

"Only if we find other, more successful, avenues of investigation. These are the pieces - albeit small pieces - of the puzzle should we decide to attempt some sort of charge against Kohler. We just stack up enough evidence, however circumstantial, until we can persuade a judge to give us a warrant to search the Museum, or his home. Or Robert Grant's home, if it comes to that, although that's rife with political implications. One wouldn't want to be the cop to screw that one up."

"You said his home. Where does he live?"

"In Russian Hill. On Lombard Street."

"Where on Lombard Street?"

"I'm not sure I can give out that information..."

"I live on Lombard Street!"

"What's your address, then?"

"999C."

"Huh. How many flats in your building?"

"Four. We're on the floor just below the penthouse."

"Well, Peter Kohler, according to this, must live right above you."

"No shit!"

"Language..."

"Sorry. I mean, how incredible is that? I've only been there for just over a month. I moved in over Labor Day weekend. I've never seen him coming or going..."

"You probably keep different hours."

Maddy's brain was working furiously. "I never made the connection, but I've seen that black Mercedes in my garage. The one we saw at the Mandarin. Holy crap. This changes things."

"How so?"

"Well, if we can clock him leaving the Museum with some new crate, and I can clock him coming home with it - although I'm not sure yet how to do that - then we've got him."

"And what do we do with him once we've got him?"

"I don't know," said Maddy. "Isn't that your department?"

"Well, this is what is known in the common parlance as a 'hot potato' - he's a powerful civic figure. The City has already suffered a major black eye over Burritogate. We'd have to really want to bring him down."

"Oh. Real world stuff," said Maddy dejectedly. "I forgot about that."

"Don't get down about it – and don't lose the enthusiasm. I just don't want you to bank on a home run on this one, that's all."

"Thanks… Anything else? I'm just pulling into my garage now. I've got to get myself together and head back out again."

"Any black Mercedes in the garage?"

"Nope. Okay – got to go."

"Call me once you know where you're meeting out at the Park."

"Right. Thanks. 'Bye." Maddy switched off her Bluetooth earpiece. She felt herself more than a little frustrated as she turned off the ignition. She had just spent the last day and a half laying down some serious groundwork in an investigation, and she had only just been made to realize how fraught and complex the results of such an investigation might be.

Screw it, she thought. The Masked Avenger was right. She was going to keep pounding away at it anyway.

Because she had to.

XLI

"Have you ever seen this guy?"

Angelique looked at the society column photo from the Clarion that Maddy had just placed in front of her.

"Bien sur. He lives upstairs."

"How did I not know that?"

"I don't know. You've only been here for four weeks. He's been my landlord for a couple of years."

Maddy had never really thought about the question of a landlord. She had found Angelique through a mutual friend. Angelique had been looking for a new roommate, her old one having gotten married and moved out. It had been a pretty uncomplicated deal as far as Maddy was concerned, especially for San Francisco. Angelique didn't have a car, so she was willing to sublet both the other room in the flat and her parking space in the building to Maddy. Maddy just wrote her a check every month, and that was the end of it.

"What do you know about him?"

"Not much, other than he has really nice hair. He's never really given me the time of day."

Jeez, he must be gay, thought Maddy. Angelique was making something delicious in the kitchen and was wearing a white apron over her short black dress. Killer French maid look, thought Maddy wistfully. Her roommate could pull that off, and what was super sexy about it was that she didn't even realize it. Just came naturally. Maddy would feel self-conscious in a second.

Sigh.

She looked at the clock on the wall and realized she had to keep moving quickly. She left Angelique to her Coq au Vin, or whatever, and ran into her room. She climbed out of her slacks and blouse and threw on some black jeans, a T-shirt, a sweater, and her sneakers. She then grabbed her heavy windbreaker - the one she would wear sailing with her dad on cold, blustery days - and headed back down to the garage.

She grabbed her bike rack and mounted it to the top of her Beetle. She was just about to climb into her car when the call came in.

"Meet me at the corner of Lincoln and 25th," came the deep, gravelly voice.

"Okay. What time?"

"The sun sets a little before seven. Meet me at 6:30."

"How will I find you?"

"I know your car. I'll signal you, just as before."

"All right, I'll be there – and I'm bringing a present."

"Thank you. My friend."

He hung up. The way he said "My friend" made Maddy feel... strangely proud. It was like she belonged to some secret society, striving to save the world. Cool.

*   *   *

As she pulled up in front of Carlos' house, Maddy saw Carlos in the front with a rag and a tire pump. He was just putting the finishing touches on a detailing of the bike, buffing the black finish to a shine.

"It looks like it was made for him," said Maddy.

"It does, with the flames on it, and all. Bat-out-of-hell kind of thing."

"Thank you for doing this."

"Hey, just doing my small part to save the world, you know?"

"It does feel like that, doesn't it," said Maddy.

"You just gotta believe," replied Carlos. "Here, let's get this thing up there."

They strapped the bike onto the roof rack, and Maddy cinched it tight. "Good luck tonight," she said giving Carlos a hug.

"Good luck to you, too. Be careful."

"I'll be fine – I've got that grizzly bear of a crusading defender of the meek looking out for me. I actually feel pretty safe."

"Damn. What you call safe." Carlos shook his head. "Call me when you're done, okay?"

"10-4," shouted Maddy as she pulled away and headed north towards the Park.

As she sat at the intersection of Castro and Market, Maddy debated whether or not to call Jimmy. There was a feeling in the pit of her stomach that made her hesitate, but she talked herself into doing the honorable thing. They had a deal, and she would do her best to keep her end of the bargain.

* * *

His phone was vibrating on his desk as he returned from the restroom. A message.

"I'm meeting them at the corner of Lincoln and 25th. 'Bye!"

Jimmy Wang scratched his head, unsure of what to do. Maddy had, for a small woman, a relatively low voice – an alto – but her voice rose in pitch as she got excited. Very Southern Californian. There was something about her voice in her message, though, that sounded strained. He had learned, during special training sessions, that the voice did certain things when the speaker was under stress. The same sessions brought the latest in physio-psychological research to the police. Observations of subconscious eye and mouth movements when people lied, felt guilty, were evading. For instance, a person almost always looked down and to the left when lying. This was incredibly helpful to police during such stressful moments as roadside confrontations.

She's stressed about something, he thought. Question is, is it me?

He walked over to the giant map of the City which hung on his wall. Just inside the Park from Lincoln and 25th was Elk Lake. A pretty heavily wooded area. Perfect refuge for a tribe of homeless people.

After a moment's hesitation, he picked up his radio.

"Damian, what you up to? Over."

"Just hangin' at the Starbucks out on Clement with a rookie. Soon as we fuel up, we're just going for a drive. I'm giving him the lay of the land."

"Got time for a little cross-country?"

"Shit. What's up with that?"

"Golden Gate Park. Elk Lake. Could be Masked Avenger lurking in the trees."

"What do you want me to do?" sighed Damian. No one liked hiking around in the bushes after dark.

"Just take a look around. A little bird told me the Masked Avenger might be out there this evening."

"Little bird my ass. More like that little chippy from the Clarion."

"Hey, just do me a favor. More exciting for your new recruit than riding around listening to your stories."

"Man, my stories are great," said Damian trying his best to sound indignant.

"Fifteen minutes, that's all I ask."

"All right. We'll see what we can find. You owe me."

"I know. It's a tall tab."

As he hung up, Jimmy had a funny feeling in the pit of his stomach.

XLII

Carlos adopted the look of the young Financial District type, dark suit with tie. This, he felt, would give him some latitude. He could stroll into any of the restaurants without question. At the very least, he could pretend to be the assistant of someone really important.

He had changed his mind, deciding to start at the north end of the Embarcadero and work his way south. This way, by the time he got to the last restaurant, he would be near the top of Market, and could grab a MUNI tram straight home.

The first stop was up by Fisherman's Wharf. It was a discreet, little place off Bay Street that had a commanding view of Alcatraz over the top of Ghirardelli Square. As he entered, he was greeted by a pretty, young Japanese girl.

"Welcome, sir," she said. "Do you have a reservation?"

"No, I don't," replied Carlos. "I'm interested in setting up a dinner reservation for my boss. He's hosting some very important clients from Japan. May I see your menu?"

"Certainly, sir, although, if it is an important meeting, I would recommend the Chef's Choice."

"What is that?" asked Carlos.

"It is a seven-course meal that is designed by the Chef, created completely through his inspiration on the night."

"Sounds fantastic. Does he take requests?"

"With some advance notice, he might make special arrangements."

"Wonderful. My boss wants very much to impress his clients and is interested in Blowfish. Does your chef prepare this?"

The girl pursed her lips. "I will have to ask. Please, it will only take a moment."

"Thank you, I'll wait," said Carlos. As the girl headed off to the kitchen, Carlos quickly took stock of the situation. It was a very small room, seating maybe thirty guests. The sort of place that didn't require a computerized reservation system. Sure enough, as he looked over the reception desk, he saw an old-school reservation book. With one eye on the kitchen door, he pulled open the book by the ribbon that served as the bookmark. He quickly flipped back two days to Monday and saw only ten entries. He pulled out his camera and quickly photographed the page. The girl had not yet returned, so he photographed the pages on either side, just to be sure. On any given page, there were no more than a dozen entries. A pretty exclusive place – one that could sustain itself with only twenty to thirty patrons a night. He was just adjusting the reservation book back into its original position when the door to the kitchen opened and the girl returned.

"Our chef is licensed to prepare the dish, but it is a special-order item, and would require the signing of a waiver. I hope this would not present any difficulties," the girl said deferentially.

"None at all. As you can probably tell, my boss likes to live dangerously."

"I understand," replied the girl. "Many powerful men do. Which night are you interested in?"

Carlos pulled a date out of his head for the following week, for a party of eight. For a phone number he gave out his old boyfriend's – the one who dumped him unceremoniously just before he moved to San Francisco. It would be a tiny annoyance when they called him to confirm the reservation – a small bit of revenge.

His next stop was a much newer and sleeker place. This was inside one of the warehouse buildings at the base of one of the piers along the Embarcadero.

Developers had started to take the old buildings and turn them into cool office spaces for architects and marketing firms, or, in this instance, an ultra-modern, ultra-chic seafood restaurant. It was a big, loft-like space with a second level that looked out through the tall warehouse windows onto the Bay. The main floor was the bar and restaurant. The upper level was the sushi bar, which turned into an ultra-lounge after eleven PM. There was a glass elevator which carried patrons from the first to the second floor.

Nice, thought Carlos.

The place was just starting to pick up. Not many diners at 6:30, but the bar was doing brisk business. Carlos could see that a couple of guests had already been seated at the sushi bar upstairs.

"May I help you?" asked a young Asian man, who was dressed similarly to Carlos. Dark suit and tie. Very well groomed. Very cute. He had separated himself from a team of receptionists at the front desk, the other two young women in dark suits, as well. Carlos decided to try a different angle. He pulled out a card. He had "borrowed" it off the desk of the assistant arts editor at the Clarion.

"Yes. I'm with the Clarion, and we're looking to do a spread on the best designed restaurants in the City. I'd like to set up a time to do a photo shoot of your place. It's really striking. One of the best-looking new restaurants I've seen."

"Thank you," said the host. "It was done by a famous local architect, although I don't remember his name. I could look it up."

"That's okay, there'll be follow up. I'm just scouting. May I take a look around?"

"Of course. Here, let me take you on a tour."

"Thank you, but you look busy. I can just stroll around."

"No, it would be my pleasure. Here." The way the young man put his hand on Carlos' shoulder and smiled at him made Carlos think that he had made something of a conquest. He smiled back. "My name is Robert," the young man went on. Carlos was about to say his name was Carlos, when he remembered that he had used Ramon Gonzalez's card.

"I'm Ramon," he said. "Good to meet you."

They walked through the space, Carlos pretending to frame potential shots, and taking notes on his pad.

"This is my second favorite part," said Robert, as he hit the up button on the glass elevator.

"Seems a little much to go up one flight of stairs," said Carlos.

"I know, but it makes it easier to manage entry to the lounge. And for some reason, people think it's cool."

"What's your favorite part," asked Carlos.

"To be honest, the restrooms," replied Robert. "They're super cool."

"I'll check them out. You can always tell how classy a place is by the restrooms."

They finished their tour, with Carlos being escorted into the Men's room by Robert. It *was* nice. The sink was a giant slab of broken concrete with a trough carved into it. Instead of faucets, water flowed like a waterfall the entire length of the sink when one placed one's hands underneath the motion sensor. The whole room was lit with candles that had been placed in niches carved into the brick and concrete. It was a religious experience.

"Wow," said Carlos.

"I could just move in here," said Robert. Then, a little abruptly, "I get off at one."

Carlos looked at him. He was flattered and said so.

"Tonight is tough, though. I've got an early day tomorrow."

Robert nodded understandingly. Rejected, his face said.

"But can I call you?" asked Carlos.

Robert's face brightened. "That would be great. Here, let's go back to the front desk – I'll write my number on a card."

The front desk was what Carlos really wanted. It had a monitor built into it. He could tell by the logo floating on the screen that it was an up-to-the minute restaurant management system.

"I used to work one of those. Not nearly as cool, though."

"It tracks everything. Reservations, orders, wait stations, inventory. Automatically updates from our online reservation system."

"How long does it store reservations for? I mean, does it track previous patrons?"

"Yes. We just punch in their phone number when they call, and it pulls up everything about them. We've only been open for about six months, but if, for instance, someone was celebrating a birthday a year ago, it would track that. We could then send them a card to invite them back with a special birthday offer."

"Nice. Can I play with it?"

"Sure, just don't cancel anybody's reservation! I'll be right back."

Robert greeted an incoming couple who wanted to go upstairs. He took them to the elevator and rode up with them. The two girls were escorting other diners, so, once again, Carlos was alone at a reception desk. A young couple, some rock star and his girlfriend, entered. "Someone will be with you in a moment to escort you," said Carlos smoothly. He tapped the screen and accessed the reservation list. It was quite intuitive. It would have to be, given the transient nature of restaurant staff, he thought. In two seconds, he had pulled up the reservation lists for the last week. He hit print and pulled the printout out of the printer under the counter just as Robert was returning.

"I've got to get going," said Carlos.

"Here's my number. Call me. Please," said Robert.

Carlos put his hand on Robert's. "I'll call you tomorrow. We'll get together. Thanks for everything.

Can I have your manager's card? I'll call him to set up the shoot."

Robert gave him the card, and Carlos headed out into the evening. It was seven o'clock. He still had six more restaurants to cover.

XLIII

"Mom? Are you home?"

Jimmy knocked as he opened the door to his parents' home and peered in. He still had a key – their apartment was always open to him – and it helped when they were traveling for him to stop by to check on the cat. They traveled more and more these days – they had four daughters spread across the United States and Canada, with a multitude of grandchildren to visit. And Pearl still made trips to Hong Kong on a regular basis to meet with her agents there.

"I'm in the kitchen!" she called out.

As if he couldn't tell. It smelled fantastic. But not what you would think. The smell of basil pesto filled the apartment. Garlic, toasted pine nuts, as well as the heady aroma of roast chicken made him instantly hungry.

He entered the kitchen as his mother put the finishing touches on a salad of roast beets and gorgonzola. A risotto was burbling on the stove. Jimmy shook his head. Pearl was the best Italian cook he knew. Satisfied with the arrangements on the plates, she wiped her hands on her apron and turned to her son, offering her cheek for him to kiss.

"I thought you were your father," she said. "He should be home any minute. Can you stay for dinner? I've made more than enough."

He hesitated. Dinner with his father was always fraught, but the food looked and smelled fantastic.

"I'm on call this evening, so, you know, if anything comes up, I'll have to run. But sure. Where's Dad?"

"Down at the park, as usual. He's like you were when you were nine – I have to call him in when it gets dark for dinner." She took stock of where things were and seemed satisfied. "Everything's about ready. Why don't you set the table, and we can chat while we wait for your father to get here."

Jimmy pulled the plates down from the cupboard, which was too high for Pearl to reach without a step stool and organized the table. Once everything was settled, he sat down with his mom in the living room. Ming, the big black Persian, came over to Jimmy and jumped in his lap. He settled there imperiously, purring furiously.

"He's missed you," Pearl clucked, gesturing at the cat. "You need to come around more often. So, what's up?"

"I've got some more photos for you, Mom. When we showed you the bodhisattva, we felt it best to just concentrate on the object, to keep things simple. We've since learned things are far from simple. Here's the complete photo. Recognize anybody?"

"Is that Robert Grant? Such a handsome man... I love his movies, although I can't get your father to watch them. I've sold him a piece or two over the years."

"I'm impressed, Mom. Your clientele *is* pretty select."

"Oh, well, you know. Word of mouth..." She looked back at the photo. "Now that's Peter Kohler. I'd recognize that hair anywhere." She pulled off her pince-nez and looked at Jimmy. "This is a pretty incriminating photograph. Nothing about this looks right."

"As I said, things are far from simple. The woman. Do you know her?"

Pearl squinted at the photograph. As she did so, Jimmy observed his mother. For sixty-five, her skin was still smooth, with only a few laugh lines around her eyes. Her face was round and open, but full of animation. She could convey more meaning in a raised eyebrow or a frown than anyone he knew. Her hair was white-white, and Jimmy was secretly proud that his mom had such a sense of personal style that she could wear it in such a sharp, short, and distinctive cut. Her hands were tiny with slender fingers, and they shook only just a little as she held the photograph. She's still very beautiful, thought Jimmy. But she *is* getting old. He would worry more about her if he didn't know how tough she was.

"The light isn't good – it's mostly coming from behind her. It's hard to say."

Jimmy pulled out the second photo from the Clarion social column. This time the woman was in profile.

"That's Madeleine Chang. I'd know those cheekbones and that boob job anywhere."

Jimmy was a little shocked.

"Mom!"

"Well, Chinese girls aren't built like that naturally. Just aren't."

"If you say so, Mom. Jeez. With four older sisters, I guess I learned not to notice. So, who's Madeleine Chang?"

"She's on the board at the Museum. Her husband's one of the founders of YooHoo! She might even be the chair of the Museum board by now. Pretty high cotton."

Jimmy was stumped. "Why would a woman with that kind of money and prestige be involved in what looks like a smuggling operation?"

"Who knows? For that matter, why would someone like Peter Kohler? He gets paid as well as anyone in the City. Maybe this isn't what it seems."

Jimmy had been worried about that. A lot of enthusiasm and fuss, but nothing yet in the way of facts. Just a very suspicious set of circumstances.

"The Prodigal Son returns," said a rich baritone behind him. Ming jumped off Jimmy's lap and ran towards the voice.

"Hey, Dad," said Jimmy standing up.

James Wang, Sr. entered the living room. He was six inches shorter than his son but had a presence that made him seem six inches taller. For a man almost seventy, he still stood ramrod straight, and had a handshake that could make you wince. His hair was short, almost a military cut, and the color of steel. His eyes were clear and bright, but they had an intensity that was hard to withstand. Only Pearl could look at him without any trepidation.

"Son," said James Wang, extending his hand. The two men shook hands, with a slight bow from each. An extremely formal greeting.

"I was getting worried about you," said Pearl.

"Tai Chi at sunset." Turning to Jimmy he added, "I keep trying to get your mother to join me."

"You have your therapy, I have mine," she said primly.

"I could smell it in the lobby. I'm hungry as a bear."

"Bear is right," said Pearl as she headed into the kitchen to gather up the meal. This was the moment that Jimmy dreaded – alone with his father.

"Can I pour you a whisky, or are you working?"

"Working, but I told Mom I could stop for a bite."

"How are things at the office?" James Wang went over to the sideboard and pulled out a bottle of Laphroig. He poured himself a neat finger.

"Good. Good. Busy."

"How's Chen?"

"Still an asshole."

James Wang almost smiled. But he did his best to hide it and turned to his son with a frown instead. "He works hard. He can't help it if he isn't all that bright. He makes up for it with shoe leather. I respect that."

"Sure, Dad. I was only joking."

"Catch anybody lately?"

"Working on it."

"Well, see that you catch somebody soon. Promotion in police work is all about results. No one gives a rat's ass about your paperwork. People want photos of criminals in cuffs."

"Trust me, I know how paperwork can get in the

way…" Jimmy stared at his shoes.

James Wang sized up his son. He was proud of him. He had heard that Jimmy worked hard and put in long hours, but he could never let Jimmy know that. James Wang had a role to play in the growth of his only son. He was the one who could never be satisfied – who had to instill in Jimmy the drive he didn't have by nature. A goofy boy, but a good heart, thought James. He needs to be tougher to be a good policeman. Perhaps time will make the difference.

"Are you drinking whisky?" asked Pearl as she set down the risotto.

"A man can have a whisky," growled James Wang.

"As long as it's only one. Otherwise, you're sleeping on the couch. Besides, how you can taste anything after you drink that stuff, I don't know. I'm having a Sangiovese, you should, too. Doctor Elson says it'd be good for your heart."

James Wang rolled his eyes. Jimmy pretended not to notice.

He loved his parents.

XLIV

As Madeleine Chang sat in her Lexus, waiting for her son to finish his swimming lesson, she burst into tears.

Great, she thought. I can't go to the board meeting with mascara all over my face.

She pulled out a Kleenex, but before she could put it to its intended use, she found herself wracked with sobs. She ended up blowing her nose with it.

Just breathe, she reminded herself. Just breathe and you can get through this.

The stress had just been too great. After fifteen years of marriage, it was all falling apart. Her husband, who had built a fortune through one of the most sophisticated search engines on the 'net, had decided he wanted to become a Hollywood player. Rather than continue to spend time at their home in Woodside, he had bought himself a palace in Malibu, and had started working his way through a succession of starlets and American Idol runners-up. It had been humiliating for Madeleine, who tried her best to keep the impending dissolution of her marriage from her sons and from her friends. And most certainly from the board. But pretending had taken its toll.

Even worse were the financial implications of a divorce. Fifteen years ago, YooHoo! had been a small start-up, but Bobby Chang was smart enough to insist on a prenuptial agreement, and he already had the lawyers in place to make it decidedly in his favor. Madeleine had actually been in love, and felt, again fifteen years ago, that a potential settlement of a couple hundred thousand dollars a year would leave her more than comfortable should the worst happen. Which it never would. Love is eternal.

She sobbed again.

YooHoo!, of course, had seen its value skyrocket. Even with dot-com bubbles bursting and the most recent recession, Bobby Chang was a billionaire. And Madeleine had come to assume the level of lifestyle that came with that. She could play on some level of sympathy, and even guilt, but she didn't expect much more than the house in Woodside, the agreed upon settlement and some sort of allowance for the children. The clout she had within the City's social scene would evaporate. The opera galas, the museum openings, the summers in East Hampton, the winters at St. Moritz, the lodge outside of Sundance - all gone. At one point, she thought ruefully, she was going to have to resign from the board at the Museum and get a real job. For which she had no skills whatsoever.

But when things had seemed their darkest, she had found a way to provide for herself. The offer had fallen into her lap one night, over drinks after the monthly board meeting. She had confessed her troubles to Peter Kohler who had been profoundly sympathetic. He understood. Several hundred thousand a year simply didn't go as far it used to. After embarrassing herself by weeping at him in a dark booth at the back of the Bambuddha Lounge, she was grateful that instead of looking at her with disdain, he took her into his confidence.

Peter Kohler had needed an ally, and she was perfect. Beautiful, sophisticated, and fluent in Mandarin, with social and business connections on both sides of the Pacific, she would be the grease that smoothed the wheels of his negotiations with the Chinese. She would also provide the necessary status to aid in the air of propriety that his endeavor required. They would split the profits equally, which were not in the billion-dollar range, most certainly, but in the millions. The quality of the product was great, and between Madeleine's and

Peter Kohler's connections, they had a built-in client list. Plenty of movie stars, casino owners and precocious video game company CEOs who wanted to own an ancient piece of cultural history - and feel the energy that came from an artifact of religious significance.

Who needed some stupid husband, anyway? she sniffed.

A tap on the window woke her from her reverie. It was her son, Michael, ready to head home.

"Hi, Sweetie," she said, pulling herself together.

"Hey, Mom," said Michael.

Before she could ask him how swimming went, his phone pinged, and he started texting furiously.

It was just as well, thought Madeleine Chang. He would never notice his mother's red eyes.

XLV

He had made it out to the Park incognito, once again adopting the guise of a seedy, old professor riding the N Judah train. He had carried his costume and tools in a garbage bag. No one seemed to notice or care about the plunger that he had tucked under his arm. Robin had attracted some attention from a couple of schoolgirls when she stuck her head out of his jacket pocket, but they had stopped short of attempting to pet her when they got close enough to smell him. He had thought that once his evening's work was done, he might see if he could break into the locker room under Kezar Stadium and take a shower. He hadn't been sure what to do about getting his costume cleaned, though. That really smelled.

Riding on the train had been hard. Harder today than yesterday, he thought. His head was throbbing. Not enough sleep. Never enough sleep. And the crowds had made him tense. He had had to close his eyes in an effort to not feel crushed by the weight of all those faces, all those voices. Periodically, the faces would distort, become strange and ferocious. Frightening. The voices had also slipped in and out of... what? Reality? What was that? He only knew that they sounded like monsters, not human.

Now he was crouching in the bushes at the 25th Avenue entrance to the Park, having changed into his sweat suit, basketball shorts and cowl. He was armed to the teeth, plunger at his side, spatulas at the ready. He held his flashlight in his hand, ready to signal his location to his friend once she arrived. Robin was poking around amongst the leaves, chasing bugs. The Masked Avenger picked her up and held her before his eyes.

"We don't have time for that now. We must stay alert."

He almost missed her. He was momentarily confused by the bike rack and bicycle. But he saw the car slow down, as if the driver was unsure what to do, and he recognized Maddy's blonde hair. He flashed his light at her, and she pulled over. He leapt from the bushes, and before she had a chance to come to a complete stop, he jumped into the passenger seat, causing the Beetle to sag and groan.

"Drive into the Park a bit," he said gruffly. "We can find a place to pull over farther along."

"Nice to see you, too," said Maddy. She looked over to see the Masked Avenger looking this way and that, making sure he hadn't been followed.

They came to a fork in the road. "Turn right," said the Masked Avenger. Maddy did so. After a few hundred yards, the Masked Avenger asked her to pull over to the side of the road, onto the gravel that bounded it.

It was just before sunset, the stretch of road they were on already in shadow from the woods around them. The tops of the trees were turning gold with the last rays of the sun. With the night turning cool, and the light fading, the Park had emptied. Or at least appeared to be empty, thought Maddy.

They climbed out of the car; the Masked Avenger having first ascertained that they were not being observed.

"What do you think?" asked Maddy, gesturing towards the bike.

The Masked Avenger looked at it in wonder. "It is beautiful. I shall strive to be worthy of it."

"Help me get it down," said Maddy. Once they had placed it on the ground, Maddy said, "Take it for a spin."

The Masked Avenger took Robin from his pocket and handed her to Maddy. "Please hold her. She gets frightened on the bicycle."

He then climbed onto the bike and started peddling down the road. His cape snapped behind him in the evening breeze, and for a moment he regained the magnificence that Maddy had seen on Monday morning.

"The flames on the fenders really make it," she said clapping her hands as the Masked Avenger pulled up.

"They do," said the Masked Avenger simply.

"So where do we go from here?"

The Masked Avenger gestured over towards a small lake.

"They're in the woods on the other side. Come with me."

He dismounted from the bicycle and walked with it across the road. Maddy followed. As they approached the woods, the Masked Avenger picked up the bicycle and carried it on his shoulder.

It was getting dark. Maddy looked up and realized that the last rays of the sun were getting obliterated by the wall of fog that was approaching from the west. The wind was picking up and the tops of the trees were beginning to sway. She was glad she brought her heavy jacket – it was going to get really cold.

They reached the edge of the lake and moved around it to the right. The lake glowed light blue from the reflection of the graying sky, while the trees were turning black in the twilight. Giant fingers of fog were reaching through the branches.

This could be the setting for a horror movie, thought Maddy. It didn't help that there was an enormous black-clad figure moving through the mist in front of her. She suddenly wished that she wasn't out in the woods without back-up. She hoped Carlos was doing okay, but didn't want to call him, feeling that talking on her cell phone would somehow violate the almost cathedral-like atmosphere within the grove of pines. But she thought it might not be a bad idea to send him a quick text. Give him her 20.

After a few minutes, a response came through. "2 down 6 2 go got date." Got date? Sheesh.

Suddenly the hulking figure in front of her stopped. "There they are."

Maddy could see the glow of a small fire. In the mist around the fire hunched three or four shadows. Maddy didn't know if more people made her feel safer or not, but she steeled herself and moved forward until she and the Masked Avenger entered the small campsite.

At the sight of the large man cloaked in black, several of the campers staggered to their feet in alarm.

"Do not be afraid," said the Masked Avenger. "We're here to help."

"Oh, it's you," said an old Black man with a salt-and-pepper beard. Gesturing at Maddy, "This your help?"

"Yes. She, too, is a defender of justice."

"Well, good to meet you. I'm Benji."

"I'm Maddy Stevenson," said Maddy stepping forward. She took the proffered hand. It was rough and calloused. The grip was weak, though.

"Not feeling too good," said Benji. "As I told the Masked Avenger, I ate some bad sandwich. Feel better than yesterday, though."

"That's a good sign. Means you'll probably be okay." She knew that if someone who had ingested Blowfish toxin made it through the first couple of days, they would most likely recover fully. "You should be drinking tons of water. Try to flush that stuff out of your system."

"Water's hard to come by. That lake water is too sketchy."

"I can run to the store when we're done and get some big jugs. Would that help?"

Benji looked at the Masked Avenger. "Girl's all right, man." To Maddy, "That would be a great kindness. Thank you. Please come sit by the fire. It's going to be cold tonight."

"Do you have enough blankets?" asked Maddy.

A woman who had been watching all of this with heavy-lidded eyes spoke up. "Man, there's never enough blankets. They weigh so much; you can only carry so many."

"Hi. I'm Maddy."

"Marissa." She just waved listlessly.

She doesn't look too good, thought Maddy. The woman could be white, but Maddy couldn't tell for sure. She was so filthy that only the small slits of her eyes could be made out in the dark. Marissa was slowly rocking back and forth, clutching her knees against her chest. A thought occurred to Maddy. "I've got a couple of space blankets in my car. They're real light weight, but they keep the heat in when it's cold and the heat out when it's hot. I can go get them for you." It was true. Her dad had given them to her a while back. He was fussy about being prepared for the worst. Always keep some blankets in your car, he would admonish her. You never know where you'll be if your car breaks down. She was now glad for his advice.

"We can get them in a few minutes," said the Masked Avenger. "How is Rodney?"

"Man, he's barely breathing. I'm not sure he's going to make it," said Benji. He gestured over to a lump of blankets. Maddy could just make out a dark face through all the layers of swaddling.

"We need to get him to a hospital," she said. Turning to the Masked Avenger, "Can you carry him to my car?"

"No, no hospital!" said Benji. "He wants to stay here."

"But he's dying! We could maybe save him," cried Maddy.

"Save me for what?" came a thin, ragged voice.

"Damn. That's the first words come out of him in days," said Benji.

"Save me for what? I'm ready," choked Rodney. "I

don't need this shit anymore. They'd just stick me up with tubes, keep me hanging on, then they'd just dump me out on the streets again. I don't need that bullshit. Just let me die here, under the stars."

No one said a word.

The Masked Avenger went over to him. The black Doc Martens crunched in the leaves and gravel as he hunched down. He cradled Rodney in his huge arms.

"As you wish, my friend. As you wish."

"A black car."

"What?" asked Maddy, startled. Rodney's voice was so weak.

"A black car. A limo." Rodney wheezed. Drool was rolling down his chin. "It caught my eye because it pulled over. No one stops along that stretch at that time of night."

"Did you see anyone in the car?" asked Maddy.

"No. Tinted windows. I just saw Lucky Jerry go over to it. I figured the guy in the car was asking for directions or something. I went back to foraging. Didn't think much of it."

The voice was a whisper at this point. It was as if the life was being squeezed out of him with each word.

"Sleepy. Got to…" Rodney's eyes closed. There was suddenly a sharp intake of breath, a jerk and then his body went limp.

No one moved for a moment. Then the Masked Avenger took off his glove and placed his fingers on Rodney's neck.

"Is he…" Maddy couldn't form the rest of the words.

"He is dead," said the Masked Avenger.

Maddy had never seen anyone die before in real life. She was frozen with dread.

What do we do now?

Marissa started keening. Benji bowed his head. "Our Father, who art in heaven…" he began to intone.

The Masked Avenger gathered Rodney up in his arms. With a grunt he stood up.

"What do we do with him?" asked Maddy in a whisper. "Should we call the police?"

"We will lay him beside the road. Someone will find him in the morning. It is the only way."

Maddy shivered. What a horrible, lonely thing.

The Masked Avenger began to move slowly away from the fire and into the mist-enshrouded trees, with the limp body cradled in his arms. As Maddy turned to follow him, a shaft of light pierced the fog, causing the Masked Avenger to be silhouetted by the luminous mist.

"Freeze, motherfucker!"

Oh crap, thought Maddy.

XLVI

All things considered, it had been a pleasant dinner. Jimmy had managed to steer the conversation towards catching up on his sisters' lives. He didn't talk with any of them much. Different time zones, different schedules, different concerns. He was closest to the youngest sister, Helen. She was three years older and had done the bulk of looking after him when he was little. She called him once a week to check in on him, and to get his assessment of the state of the health of their parents. She checked in with Pearl, too, but always wanted to corroborate with Jimmy. Pearl would usually underplay any health issues, but Jimmy, who saw his parents regularly, could give her a more unbiased opinion.

But Pearl had all the news and loved to share it. She had embraced the latest communication technologies with great fervor. Not a day went by without her downloading and posting photos of grandchildren on her Instagram account, and texting and even instant messaging her daughters. She was a very solid virtual grandmother.

She had waved Jimmy off when he offered to help clear the table. This had left room for James to launch into his favorite topic: Baseball.

"Goliaths are playing some great ball," he said. "I don't see anyone stopping them, especially the way Cashman is smacking it around. He's a machine."

"Sure is, Dad," nodded Jimmy. No joke there, he thought. A well-oiled machine.

"And what a great thing for baseball, and this city," his father went on. "A pennant, a home run record. Very exciting. Good time to be a Goliaths fan. I can score some tickets for the playoffs if you want. Still have some connections. Want to go?"

"Sure. That would be great." Jimmy wasn't really into baseball – the game bored him. But he knew that it would be a Good Thing To Do.

He was just starting to get up from the table – he had been there for longer than he had intended - when his BlackBerry started jumping around next to him on the table, vibrating furiously.

"Sorry, Dad." He cut the vibration off. As he looked at the screen, he froze. Imprinted on the glowing background was the code no policeman wanted to see: 10-108.

Officer down.

XLVII

It was like a battle zone, thought Jimmy, as he arrived at the scene. The fog was now thick, and it caused the flashers atop the squad cars to look like explosions as they swept and strobed. The silhouettes of the trees danced with the rhythm of the lights. There were four police cars, three ambulances, two stretchers with paramedics gathered around, and a third stretcher with a body bag on it. Dark shapes moved in and out of the mist.

What the fuck happened?

As soon as he had learned the location of the incident, his heart had plummeted to the bottom of his stomach. He tried calling Maddy, but she didn't pick up. Now that he was on the scene, he was even more anxious – her yellow Beetle was still parked by the side of the road, and she was nowhere to be seen.

He approached one of the stretchers. Damian was flat on his back, his eyes puffy and his nose bloody. Jimmy looked over at the other stretcher and saw a young man with an oxygen mask over his face. He wasn't in uniform, but his hair was wet. His skin looked almost blue. His stretcher was loaded into one of the ambulances and its doors were slammed shut behind him. The siren began to whir up to speed as the ambulance pulled away, rising to a howl as it disappeared through the windswept and fog-enshrouded trees.

"Damian, are you alright?"

"What do *you* think?" wheezed Damian. "Just fifteen minutes my ass. Last time I'm doing you any favors."

Jimmy shook his head. Damian would be fine. He just looked like hell.

"What happened?"

"Fuck, man, I don't know for sure. It all happened too fast. Cats and bats and shit. Never seen anything like it."

"Like what?"

"Like the Masked Avenger. He's big, and he's fast."

"And the cats? What's up with that?"

At that moment, a paramedic came up to the stretcher to start to move Damian towards the ambulance.

"Can I have two minutes with him, please?" asked Jimmy.

"You get a minute and a half. We've got to get him to Emergency and fast. He could have one hell of a concussion."

"All right, a minute and a half. Go Damian."

"So, we drove into the Park, like you asked, and saw this Volkswagen pulled over to the side of the road. It was already pretty foggy. We ran the plates, and it came up Madison Stevenson – figured it must be this Maddy you were talking about."

"Any sign of her?"

"Not after the cat took off."

"What cat? Dude, you're not making any sense at all."

"It was a kitten. I think. The girl was holding it."

"Now back up, which girl?"

"Just shut up and let me tell it. Jesus. So, we started looking around. We heard some voices over by the lake. Kind of creepy, you know, the way voices carry in the fog... so we worked our way through the trees. We got near this clearing and could see these people gathered around a fire. Just as we approached, we saw this giant guy in black pick up this dead guy and start walking towards us. Man, it was straight out of Evil Dead or something."

"The Masked Avenger."

"Well, in the fog he looked fucking monstrous. He's

big. So, we told him to freeze, guns out. Suddenly this girl screams, and this kitten shoots right at us. Fuckin' rookie jumps and starts shooting into the fog. Next thing I know, I've got a dead body on top of me, pinning me down. I look over and see this Masked Avenger guy grab Bobby..."

"The rookie..."

"Yeah, and twist his arm near clear out of its socket, making him drop the gun. Bobby was screaming, but this monster just picks him up like he was a rag doll and hurls him into the middle of the lake. Fuckin' threw him twenty feet. Lucky the lake is only about four feet deep or Bobby'd be dead by now."

"Jesus Christ."

"I finally get this dead guy off me, grab for my gun, and next thing I know, I'm looking at the wrong end of a piece of chain. Whipped that thing right into my face, knocked me flat. Fuckin' broke my nose. When I came to, there was no one to be seen, except for Bobby almost drowned, lying at the edge of the lake coughing water, and this dead guy. I was able to haul Bobby out – dude couldn't swim with his arm all busted up like that."

"Time's up, man," said the paramedic. He and another paramedic grabbed the stretcher and popped it up onto its legs, rolling it towards the second waiting ambulance.

"Where you taking him?" called Jimmy.

"Saint Mary's."

"I'll be there as soon as I can, Damian. I'm sorry."

"Take your time," said Damian. "Can you call my wife, though? Just try to get her to not freak out."

"I will."

Damian was trundled up and into the ambulance. It, too, wailed into the night. Things were a little calmer now that two of the ambulances were gone. Only the third waited there, not in any hurry. No rush for a dead man.

Jimmy approached the policeman who was

standing guard next to the stretcher and flashed his badge. "Who's the officer in charge?" he asked.

"Detective Wilson, over there." The policeman gestured towards the lake. Jimmy could see a group of men standing in a circle next to a dying campfire. He worked his way towards them.

"Hey, Jimmy. What a mess, eh?" Bob Wilson waved him over. He was sipping on a cup of Starbucks, with a sour look on his face. It was cold and damp and one could tell from everyone's demeanor that they wished they were somewhere else.

"At least. That poor rookie," commiserated Jimmy as he shook Bob Wilson's hand. "Any idea what happened?"

"Well, the kid couldn't tell us anything. He's still got half that lake in his lungs. And I couldn't make head nor tail out of what Damian was going on about. Just looks like they stumbled onto a group of crazies, and got their asses whipped. Wish I knew what they were doing out here."

Jimmy was about to say something then thought better of it.

They were out here because of me, he thought. This is my fault.

"Anything I can do to help?" he said, instead.

"Nah. Pretty much got this buttoned up. We've ID'ed the Beetle. Belongs to some girl, address over on Lombard. We'll send someone by her place to check that out."

"I can do that," said Jimmy as evenly as possible. "It's on my way home."

"Really? That would be great. I could maybe get home to watch the end of the game. Maybe tonight he ties the record." Bob Wilson slurped the last of his coffee. "Jesus, it's cold. Man, I don't know how the Goliaths can play on these foggy nights."

"Gives 'em home field advantage. They're used to

it," chimed in one of the policemen. "I remember going to games out at Candlestick. *That* was an icebox. From the right field bleachers some nights you couldn't even see home plate it was so foggy."

Jimmy pointed to the stretcher with the body bag. "Who's that?"

"Far as we can make out, just a vagrant. He was all wrapped up in blankets, like a mummy. No apparent cause of death. Could have just died, you know?"

"And Damian, what did he tell you?"

"Just a lot of wild-ass shit about some guy in a mask and a cat. He took a nasty hit, so no wonder he wasn't making any sense."

"Yeah, sure. I'll stop in and see him in a bit. What are you going to do with the car?"

"Nothing. It's not parked illegally, the owner's record is clean, and there's nothing to connect the car with all of this anyway. For all we know, she's just gone for a night run."

Yes, she has, thought Jimmy. Yes, she has.

XLVIII

"Robin, no!"

When the lights hit them, Robin had leapt out of Maddy's arms, digging her claws in as she bolted towards her master. Maddy was lucky that her windbreaker was as thick as it was, otherwise, she would have had some deep scars.

The sound of the gun had been deafening, and the flash from the barrel had filled the foggy night with what looked like lightning. What happened next, Maddy could not fully make out. Just a blur of shadows and light, some screams, splashes. With the explosions of gunfire, she had done what any sensible person would do and had run as fast as possible in the opposite direction. She had plowed into the woods - not looking back until she had put a great distance between her and the campsite.

She had never been shot at before. She had never been so scared in her entire life. She wanted to know what had happened, but she also wanted to stay alive and to stay out of trouble.

Jesus, am I in a lot of trouble.

She had dropped down behind a fallen tree to catch her breath. Now she was lying there, trying to control her breathing enough so that she could listen for anyone approaching. She knew she couldn't go back to her car, at least not right away.

Suddenly, from somewhere in the fog came the "Music of the Night." Maddy felt in her pockets but couldn't find her phone. Crap, it must have fallen out. It's out there, ringing. She had to get to it before it gave her away. She crawled commando style in the direction of the music. After a few yards, she could see the glow from the phone as it tweedled away. She grabbed it, silencing the ring. She had just missed the call. It was Jimmy.

Not a good time to talk.

As she lay there on her belly looking at the phone, she felt a pressure on her back. She was just about to scream when she heard the purring.

"You are one stupid kitten," she whispered as she rolled over. "You could have gotten us all killed."

Robin was rubbing up against her thigh as Maddy sat there. Robin seemed relieved to have found her. The purring was growing louder and louder.

"Shush! You'll give us away." Maddy picked up the kitten and looked it in the face. It didn't help. Purr, purr, purr. "Okay, you asked for it." Maddy unzipped a pocket on the side of her jacket, shoved the kitten into it and zipped it back up. "Now calm down!"

It was then the hand came around her head and clamped her mouth shut. Maddy could barely get a muffled scream out before she passed out.

XLIX

The creatures in his dreams. Sometimes they had horns. Sometimes they had wings on their heads. Some had bolts of lightning. They were colorful. They were huge. They were always trying to stop him.

Somehow, though, he could always defeat them.

In this dream, the creatures had come out of the mist, bristling with weapons. At the sound of the explosion, he had been overwhelmed with rage. A rage that came coursing through him like high octane fuel into a high-performance car. He had catapulted into action with a speed and ruthless efficiency that came naturally to him – from some place deep inside him, from years of training.

He had known instinctually what to do.

The creature with the gun – it had to be stopped first. Within a second, he had thrown it to the ground, forcing it to drop its weapon. It was nothing to hurl the creature into the water. It was only a phantom.

The other phantom was bigger, but slower. He had used his fallen comrade in a most undignified manner against it. There was a vague discomfort in this, but his friend was past caring. Before the bigger phantom could recover, he had whipped off his chain and sent the creature reeling.

With both of his enemies defeated, he stood over the larger one, reared his head back, threw his arms open and roared.

The ever-present crowd in his head roared back. Then there was blackness.

*　　　*　　　*

When he awoke, it took him a few seconds to figure out where he was. His head was pounding, and he was gasping for breath.

Damn it, getting old sucks.

What had happened? The dream had been more vivid than most. As the layers of mental fog began to disperse, he became aware of a thrashing in the lake behind him. Someone was drowning. The Masked Avenger jumped into the water without hesitation. The drowning man flailed at him, but the Masked Avenger was able to grab him around the neck and haul him to the shore. He dumped the man onto the ground, retching and coughing water, and only then did the Masked Avenger see the badge, and the uniform that had turned black from being soaked through.

The police. Trouble.

Another man was stirring over at the edge of the woods – also a policeman.

I must flee, thought the Masked Avenger. I cannot be found here.

In the distance, off to his left, he suddenly heard music. Music he recognized. Follow the music, he thought. The music is my salvation. He grabbed the bicycle that was leaning against a tree, threw it over his shoulder and worked his way quickly into the woods. The camp site had been abandoned. Benji and Marissa had vanished.

And Rodney. He is in a better place, his troubles now over.

As he moved towards where he had heard the music, he heard a voice behind him. The policeman was talking on his radio.

Must work quickly.

The music had stopped. He paused and listened intently. The fog was still thick and there was very little light. What light there was came from the clouds overhead, a muddy glow that was the reflection of the distant city lights below. He heard a heavy breathing just yards in front of him.

Then he heard her voice. She was whispering. To whom? She must be quiet – she will give us away.

L

When Maddy came to, she had a moment of sheer terror. A large, Black face was staring at her intently, its outline distorted by a glistening black plastic cowl.

"Jesus, you scared the shit out of me!"

"We must move quickly. The place will be overrun with police in minutes."

"What happened?"

"I do not know."

"What do you mean you 'do not know?' You were there."

The Masked Avenger looked uncomfortable. "I..." He hesitated, then sighed. "I am unsure of what happened. I was hoping that it was just a dream."

"What happened to the policemen? Are they okay?"

"They are both alive."

Holy crap, thought Maddy. That means that they're probably not much better than that.

"As I said, we must move quickly."

"To where?"

"Anywhere but here. There will be many policemen here shortly."

"I can't go back to my car. At least I don't think so. Not right now. Jesus. We're in a lot of trouble."

"Yes," said the Masked Avenger. Maddy was suddenly intrigued by how he quickly he could move from hyperbolic speech to simple, restrained responses.

"How do we get to where we're going?" asked Maddy.

"The bicycle."

Maddy realized that they were right next to a little maintenance road. She and the Masked Avenger stepped up onto the asphalt.

"Um…"

"Put your arms around my neck. Hold on tight." The Masked Avenger hunched down a bit so Maddy could do so. He was a foot and a half taller than she was.

"I've got a kitten in my pocket," said Maddy as she adjusted her windbreaker so that Robin was off to the side.

"Good," replied the Masked Avenger. "Best place for her right now."

Maddy put her arms around his neck – Jesus, he needs a shower – and the Masked Avenger rose up, lifting her off the ground. He then mounted the bicycle, which groaned under the combined weight of the three of them. Maddy wrapped her legs around his waist, and they took off into the foggy night.

LI

As he rounded the bases slowly, the stadium was a blur of camera flashes – fifty thousand people capturing the event. The stands were almost obliterated by the strobing white flashes, the roar of the crowd deafening. Fireworks were launched into the air, splash cannons erupted. An historic moment.

Ah, when you've done anything 755 times, it should look easy, Cashman thought.

As he touched first base, he expected a handshake, or at least a high five, from the first baseman, but nothing came. The same at second base. Rafael just stood there. No one on the field made a move to congratulate him. Stupid, jealous assholes.

And where's the Commissioner?

As he headed for home, the Goliaths' bench cleared, the whole team waiting for him. At least these guys know their meal ticket. As he stomped on home plate, he gestured to the one person who might understand his greatness. God.

Not that he was a religious person. Hardly. Just that in the pantheon, there was God, Bono, and himself. Mental note. Go out for a drink with the other two guys. Compare notes. Breathe some rarefied air.

His teammates all shook his hand. None smiled. His coach mustered a "good job," and patted him on the back. There was something about all of their demeanors that said, well, this is going to go on for a while. There would be the stopping of the game for a pre-recorded announcement from some baseball dignitaries, the obligatory curtain call, blah, blah, blah. It would be worse when he actually broke the record.

But the fans were going nuts. They didn't have to

share a locker room with Cashman or play against him. They just loved that he was a winner and was bringing a pennant to San Francisco.

And I'm in it for the fans, he reminded himself with an interior smirk. I'm in it for the fans.

LII

There comes a point in almost every project when it becomes apparent that what looked good on paper isn't, and what would be fun won't be. Carlos was at that point. It was now nine-thirty, and the five restaurants he had visited since he left the second restaurant at the wharf had all been washouts. He had gotten cocky after the first two, but at the subsequent stops it had been too difficult to access the information he needed without giving the game away. Over-officious maître d's, the evening rush of patrons clogging the entries, outmoded reservation systems – they all conspired to make his initial supposition that this would be a piece of cake fall apart.

This may be a job for the police, after all, he thought as he kicked his way down the Embarcadero towards his last stop. Then it hit him that maybe he was going about this backwards. He was talking to the wrong people.

He cut in a block and then turned down Steuart Street. As he made the turn, he heard an enormous roar come from somewhere in the near distance. Suddenly, the sound of explosions filled the air. Carlos stood for a moment in confusion until he realized what was happening. He was about five blocks from TBD Park, its presence apparent by the intense glow onto the foggy night sky above from the stadium lights. Someone had probably hit an historic home run.

Looking into the sky, he realized how foggy it was becoming. He became aware of the call and response from the fog horns of the container ships moored out in the Bay. The combination of the mournful, soulful keening of the ships with the distant pulse of some heavy metal music from the ballpark made him feel

217

strange, disjointed. He shivered, then thought about how cold it must be out at the Park. Poor Maddy. I hope she dressed for the occasion.

Half a block down the street he came to the giant, intricately carved wooden doors that marked the entrance to Tadao. Rather than enter, he walked past, down towards the alley that provided the service entrance to the building. Carlos had given up smoking, deciding it had been nothing more than a really stupid and health damaging affectation, but he still partook on occasion – when it became socially expedient to do so. Now, he realized, it would be professionally expedient to do so.

He lurked around the edge of the alley, trying not to look too much like some sort of male hooker. After a few minutes, the service door opened down the alley, and a young Japanese man in kitchen whites and black checked pants came out. He pulled out a packet of cigarettes and shook out a smoke. As he lit his cigarette, Carlos approached with one in his hand.

"Got a light?"

The young Japanese chef nodded and held out his lighter. "Thanks, man," said Carlos. After the cigarette was lit, they both took a moment to inhale deeply, savor the flavor, and exhale. In that ritual, all cigarette smokers bond.

"My boss doesn't want to see me smoking," continued Carlos, by way of explaining why he was not closer to the front entrance. "I've been trying to give up, so I didn't have my lighter on me."

The Japanese chef nodded again, knowingly. When he spoke, his English was heavily accented. "Your boss dining tonight?"

"Yeah. She's a fan of the place." Carlos had no idea why he said 'she.' Perhaps because Carey was his real boss...

"Really? Not many women here. Mostly men. Sushi man's food."

Carlos had never thought about that.

"Salty," continued the chef. "And pieces too big."

"Dangerous?" prompted Carlos.

"No. Only the Fugu – how you say… Blowfish. And that not really dangerous – prepared properly."

"You serve Blowfish?"

"A few times night. Not much. Most people afraid."

"Who prepares it?"

"I am one of two chefs who prepare."

Carlos nodded, impressed.

"You get a special license?"

"Yes."

"How long you been preparing sushi?"

"Long time. Eight years. Learned from father in Japan."

"Why you here?"

"Girlfriend. At school."

So much for that angle, thought Carlos. He decided to play it straight.

"What do you do with the stuff you take out of the Blowfish?"

"Why?"

"Just wondering. I've heard it's poisonous."

"Yes. We just throw it out. No big deal. Just throw it out."

"Huh. I would have thought you'd have to do something special with it."

"People throw out paint and lots of poisonous stuff all the time. No big deal."

There was a pause. Both men were finishing their cigarettes. Then the Japanese chef flicked his cigarette down the alley. As he was about to head back in from his break, he stopped.

"Funny thing. Some guy offered to buy the Blowfish guts from me."

Carlos almost swallowed his cigarette but regained his composure quickly. "Really. Did you sell it to him?"

"No. It seemed a stupid thing to do. I said no."

"You don't know who he was?" asked Carlos. It would be too good to be true.

"No. But he comes every few weeks. Always with same woman. She is rare woman who likes sushi, like your boss. Blowfish, too."

"Any idea who she is?"

"No. Sorry. Got to go."

"Thanks for the light."

"No problem."

And the chef went back into the building.

Carlos pumped his fist. He had nailed it. Now to call Maddy.

LIII

"Just how crazy are you?" whispered Maddy once she had caught her breath.

They were hunched under the bleachers at Kezar Stadium, having felt it a good idea to let things cool down a bit before venturing out of the Park. The old football field was dark and deserted, and the passageways under the stands were damp and echoey. The foggy mist was condensing on the pipes overhead, and as the water dripped off and fell into pools, the sound reverberated throughout the concrete corridors.

The Masked Avenger had been petting Robin, who had just been released from Maddy's windbreaker pocket. She had not been wild at all, which is what Maddy would have expected, having been cooped up for almost an hour. Robin had somehow resolved herself that all was good – she knew her master was nearby, and she had been warm and cozy next to Maddy. She came out of the pocket as meek, well, as meek as a kitten.

The Masked Avenger paused in his rubbing of Robin's cheek. A sense of tremendous inner strain exuded from him. Maddy was suddenly quite frightened that she had been so blunt in her question and began to wish somehow that she could withdraw it. But she had, after all, just seen someone die in front of her, and she had been shot at, and she was cold, and her hair was dripping with damp. In for a penny, in for a pound, she thought. She had little left to lose.

After a deep sigh, the Masked Avenger spoke slowly, his voice a deep whisper which sounded almost ghostly in the dark.

"I don't know. It has been a long time since I've seen a doctor."

"So you used to get... treatment?... for...?" Maddy had no idea how to form the question.

"Yes. I received treatment. I could not continue with it."

"Why?"

"Because I couldn't." It seemed like that would be the end of it, but after a moment he continued.

"I had to stop. There was an... interruption in the treatment, and I was unable to continue. Reduced circumstances." He looked so embarrassed, Maddy's heart went out to him.

"And it was humiliating. To be so dependent on... medication. I am better than that. Stronger." His deep sigh, however, belied his conviction.

"Almost everybody needs some kind of help," said Maddy. "I've had all sorts of friends who needed to take Ritalin or Prozac. There's no shame in that."

The Masked Avenger looked away.

"What do – did - you take the medication for?" she continued.

"To keep the demons at bay."

This was the sort of response that made Maddy wonder if he was crazy at all. Almost everybody has demons, she thought. Few people recognized it or admitted it.

"So do you see demons now?"

"They are everywhere. It is a constant struggle."

Maddy wondered what it would be like to live so apprehensively. No wonder he's exhausted.

"You need some rest," she said. "Is there any place you can go? Do you have any family at all?"

"No. I am alone. Except, of course, for Robin."

"I would offer my sofa, but I'm pretty sure that my apartment isn't safe for you right now."

"Why is that?"

"My car was at the scene. I'm sure that the police will follow up on that." She screwed up her face. "How badly did you hurt those policemen?"

"I'm afraid that they will both need hospitalization. I think."

"Putting policemen in the hospital will get you into real trouble. They'll be looking for you pretty hard. And this will be in the news." And she should be writing the story, she thought ruefully. Talk about being embedded. "You need a place to hide for a while. And you need a shower and some clean clothes."

"I cannot part with my costume," he said defensively.

"We could get you a new one," Maddy said. "Look, I have an idea. Can you wait here for a couple of hours?"

"If I must."

"It's just that I can't use my car right now. I'm sure someone is watching it, to see if I come back for it. I'll deal with it in the morning, but for now, we need some alternate mode of transportation. It'll take me a bit to get something. And I think I know a place you can stay. I just need to pull some things together."

"How will you do that?"

Maddy waved her credit card. "With this," she said. "You okay here?"

"Yes."

Maddy stood up from her crouch, her whole body aching all of a sudden. She looked around. "This is a really cool place. I've never been out here. Does anyone play here anymore?"

"I don't know."

"I remember reading that this was the original home of the Oakland Knights. The football team."

At this the Masked Avenger suddenly let out a howl. A deep, heart-wrenching cry of pain. Robin bolted out of his arms to a safe distance. The cavernous concrete bunker in which they had taken refuge rang with the echoes of his cry. He then collapsed into a fit of sobbing.

Jeez, I hope nobody heard that, thought Maddy, who, herself, had pulled away to a safe distance. But as the Masked Avenger wept, she was overcome with the instinct to comfort, and approached him slowly.

"It's okay," she whispered. "It's okay. It will all be okay." She knelt beside the sobbing giant – slowly, like sidling up to a bear – and gently put her arms around him and gave him a hug. "It's okay, it's okay," she cooed over and over. Eventually the Masked Avenger began to calm down. After what seemed like an eternity, his body slumped and his breathing became regular, albeit ragged.

He had fallen asleep.

Thank God for that, thought Maddy as she gently pulled herself away. Robin had returned and had climbed up and into her master's lap. She was purring in that furious way that she had. The sound was soothing. This is how she helps him, thought Maddy. Her purring soothes the savage breast.

"I'll be back soon, sweetie," Maddy whispered to Robin. Robin just slowly blinked her eyes, as if she understood.

LIV

Jimmy Wang pressed the buzzer at the entrance to Maddy's building. He looked around as he waited for someone to answer. Nice place, he thought. A little bit of a view of the Bay – a commanding view from the roof. Before he had entered the building's vestibule, he had looked up and seen that the windows of the penthouse apartment were dark. Peter Kohler must be out.

What a night, he thought. It was ten o'clock. He had stopped briefly at St. Mary's to make sure that Damian was okay. Damian's wife had already arrived, and she had been fussing at him. He had been due to have his nose reset, it having been thoroughly broken.

"You gonna get the guy that did this," she had sternly told Jimmy. Jimmy thought that he had better, if he knew what was good for him. No one wanted to mess with Mrs. Johnson.

A voice crackled through the intercom. "Allo?" An accent.

"Hi. I'm here to see Maddy."

"She is not here," replied the voice. "Who are you?"

"I'm a friend. And I'm with the San Francisco Police Department. May I speak with you? I think Maddy may be in some danger."

There was a pause. Jimmy looked up and into the security camera that was mounted in the corner of the vestibule ceiling. He smiled as disarmingly as possible, then held up his badge. After a moment the door buzzed, and he went in.

The door to the apartment opened as he reached the landing of the next floor. A beautiful, young, dark-haired woman with the longest legs he had ever seen stood in the doorway. Her gaze, as she took him in, was frankly appraising. Usually, when making such a call, Jimmy felt confident, armed, if nothing else, with his badge. But he had never been dissected so thoroughly by such an attractive woman before. He felt profoundly self-conscious, all of a sudden.

"Come in," said the woman, after her scan was complete. "I am Angelique. Maddy's room-mate."

Toss me in the middle, thought Jimmy, then blotted the thought from his brain. Totally unprofessional.

"Hi, thank you for seeing me." He stepped into the apartment. On the sofa sat a young man, who was watching a soccer game. He muted the TV and stood up as Jimmy approached.

"This is Jean-Michel, my boyfriend," said Angelique. "He is just visiting from Paris for a week."

Jimmy offered his hand, and Jean-Michel shook it. "Good to meet you," he said. Jimmy was impressed. A really beautiful young man.

"So, are you Maddy's new boyfriend?" asked Angelique bluntly.

"Um, well, we're just friends. We've been helping each other out."

"I see. I thought, since she's been out late every night this week, that maybe, well, you know."

"No, just professional acquaintances, really."

"Hmmm." Angelique was obviously dialed in to the whole male/female dynamic. A woman of the world, thought Jimmy. He wasn't fooling anyone.

"You said she was in danger," continued Angelique. "What has happened?"

"We ID'd her car out at Golden Gate Park, but she's nowhere to be found. Have you heard from her this evening?"

"No. I saw her around five, but she headed out. She was dressed as if she was going camping."

"Did she say where she was going, or if she was meeting anyone?"

"No."

"What did you talk about?"

"I could tell you that it was personal, but it wasn't. She was curious about our landlord. Peter Kohler."

"Yes. I see. Anything else you can think of?"

"No. I don't think so. As I said, she's been out late every night, but she has always come home, so I am not yet too worried. She's sweet, but she's tough."

That she is, thought Jimmy.

"Who knows. Maybe she has some other boyfriend," continued Angelique.

"Yes, well, that would explain it," said Jimmy. He found himself annoyed at the idea. "Here. Please take my card. I would be grateful if you called me if you hear anything. My cell is on there – you can call anytime, day or night."

"D'accord. Will do."

He was heading down the stairs back to the lobby when the door from the garage opened. A tall, striking looking older man with a mane of silver hair entered the lobby. In his arms he carried a small box, wrapped in plain brown paper.

"Congratulations on the new museum," said Jimmy.

"Thank you," replied Peter Kohler. "Do I know you? I'm sorry, but I meet so many people these days…"

"No. I'm just a friend of the girls upstairs."

"Lucky devil," said Peter Kohler with an arched eyebrow.

"I've seen your picture in the papers."

"Right. Well, good to meet you." Peter Kohler was obviously in a hurry but was trying his best to be polite. The men passed each other on the stairs.

"Been shopping?" asked Jimmy casually, gesturing towards the box.

"A small gift for a friend," replied Peter Kohler, just as casually, giving the box a jaunty wave.

"Good for you," said Jimmy. "Good night." Peter Kohler vanished up the stairs.

Jimmy would have given almost anything to know what was in that box.

LV

Maddy was coming up out of the MUNI station at Powell Street when her cell phone pinged. Service was spotty in the MUNI train tunnels, and her phone had just caught a strong signal again. Two new text messages. The first was from Carlos. "Home run. Call." The second was from Jimmy. "Where r u? Need u. Call."

Damn, I'm popular, thought Maddy.

As she hiked up Powell Street towards O'Farrell, she decided to start with Carlos.

"Hey Chica. You okay?"

"I've been better, but alive to tell the tale."

"No shit. I just got home and it's already on the news."

"Don't tell me. 'Phantom Superman Attacks Police in Park.'"

"Somebody must have been talking with somebody, but they're calling him the Masked Avenger, already. He's become famous. We'd better fess up to Carey, otherwise we're going to get scooped."

Crap, thought Maddy. Things are moving way too fast.

"We'll sit down with her in the morning. How'd you do? What's this about a home run?"

"I found the restaurant where the poison came from, or at least I'm pretty certain."

"Great work! Did you get the reservation lists?"

"No," sighed Carlos. "Not for all of them. It was a bit of a mess. But I know that some man tried to buy the poison from one of the chefs, and the guy is a regular. He comes every couple of weeks with the same woman."

"Did the chef say he sold it to him?"

"No, but he's one of two chefs at the restaurant. I'm

almost certain that the guy just made the same offer to the other chef."

"So how do we find out who he is?" asked Maddy.

"I'm thinking that we're going to need your boyfriend to follow up. He could get the list. It's time we got the police on board on this, anyway."

"Yeah. Another guy died from the toxin, out at the Park."

"No shit."

"I saw him, Carlos. I've never seen anyone die before." Her voice began to quiver. She pulled herself together.

"But he gave us a clue. He saw a black limo pull up and Lucky Jerry go over. So now we have a ring of clues – the restaurant, a man and a woman, a limo, the social register. I know we can pull this together… Wait. I have an idea. I know where to look for the next piece of the puzzle."

"Where?"

"I need to do some research first."

"Alright. But be careful."

"Oh, this one's easy," said Maddy.

"Famous last words," said Carlos. "Hey, so what's up with the Masked Avenger? Did he get away?"

"I have him under observation."

"What does that mean?"

"It means he fell asleep. I'm going to try to find him a better place to hide."

"This is serious shit, Maddy. You're aiding and abetting a guy who just clobbered two policemen. There's no way this is going to play well."

"History is written by the victors," said Maddy. "If we play this right, it'll be okay. At least I hope so."

"Do you need help?"

"I think I'm okay. And *you* don't want to be 'aiding and abetting.' You get some sleep. Let's meet for coffee before we go in tomorrow so we can get our stories straight."

"Alright. I've got my phone right by my bed. Call me if you need anything."

"Will do. Good night."

She wasn't sure what to do about Jimmy. As she replayed the evening in her mind, she got more angry by the minute.

I'll let him stew a bit, she thought.

She arrived at her destination. The downtown rental car agency on Mason, between O'Farrell and Geary. This place was open 24 hours. She knew about it, only because Lori's Diner was across the street, and it was one of the few places in town that was also open 24 hours. Within fifteen minutes she was driving out of the garage, in the most non-descript Ford sedan possible, and heading back towards the Park. It was going to be another long night.

LVI

He was standing in the throne room, alone in the center. The other knights were standing on either side of the hall, forming a corridor of steel. As he approached the throne, he felt a sensation that he had never felt before. Mortal dread. The man on the throne was old, but his eyes were keen, and in his gaze was something worse than anger. It was disdain. To the side of the throne were the advisors, men of knowledge and power. They, too, gazed down on him as if he were less than human. With each step towards the dais on which the king sat, the knights on the sides stomped their feet. The sound was thunderous, filling the throne room with echoes of doom. As he reached the foot of the dais, the thunderous stomping ceased suddenly.

"On your knees," said the chief advisor.

He fell to his knees.

The chief advisor then approached him with a knife. He grabbed him by his surcoat and cut the emblem of his order right off his breast. The chief advisor returned to the king and handed him the torn fabric.

"Surrender your sword," said the king.

Not that. Anything but that, he thought.

But he did as he was told, slowly unsheathing the sword from his scabbard. A small man came over from the side and took it from him. The small man was hunchbacked and strange. The armorer.

"Throw his sword back into the fire," said the king.

"As you wish, my lord," said the armorer, who bowed and left with the sword.

"You come before us disgraced," said the king. "You have betrayed the honor of your fellow knights, and the oath that you swore. What is worse, your actions have caused us to lose the fight for which we all live."

He fell to the floor, sobbing with grief and shame.
"Get up," said the king with disgust.
He slowly stood up.
"Now get out. You are banished from the realm. Never set
foot in our kingdom again, on peril of your life."
With that, two of the knights grabbed him by the arms.
His legs gave way beneath him, and he was dragged to the
giant doors of the great hall. The doors swung open, and he
was hurled face first into the rain and mud. He lay there
drowning in sorrow.

*   *   *

"Mister Avenger? Mister Avenger..."

Maddy had realized she didn't know what to call him to his face. Mister Avenger sounded respectful enough, she thought.

The Masked Avenger awoke with a start. He had fallen forward in his sleep and was drooling on the cold, damp concrete floor. He did his best to collect himself, although he was rattled by his dream.

"I have a place for you to stay for a day or two, so you can get some rest. At least I think it will be okay. Certainly safe."

"Thank you, my friend," said the Masked Avenger as he rose to his feet. "You have done so much for me."

"It's okay. My small part." She helped steady him. "The car is on the corner. We'll have to make a run for it."

"What about the bicycle?" asked the Masked Avenger with deep concern.

"I think we'll have to leave it chained to the fence for overnight. I'm hoping that it's too cold and foggy for anyone to steal it. I can bring it to you tomorrow."

The Masked Avenger hesitated for a moment, then undid one of his chains. After the bike was locked securely, Maddy jogged over to the car to start up the engine. Once the coast was clear, the Masked Avenger

233

ran over to the car and leapt into the passenger seat, as was his wont.

"Where are you taking me?" he asked.

"I know some people down in Dogpatch. I'm going to make them put their money where their mouths are. They should help us, if their philosophy holds together. The place is really out of the way, so if you stay there for a day or two, no one should find you."

"But I have work to do," insisted the Masked Avenger.

"Living to fight another day, is how I look at it," replied Maddy, as she pointed the car southward down Stanyan Street.

*   *   *

"Take these," said Maddy, handing him two pink pills. They were Ambien. She kept them in a little pill box in her purse. She had 'borrowed' them from her mother and used them occasionally when she was too stressed to sleep, or when she flew back East to visit her friends. She figured that he would need at least two to set him down and keep him down for a while.

"I know these," he replied evenly. He took them in his giant hand and swallowed them. He then curled up on the stack of cardboard that had been arranged for him in the corner. Within a few minutes he was deep asleep, with Robin watching over him.

Maddy had found Jasmine, Marcus, Charelle and Abe gathered around their little fire in the sub-basement. Maddy had put the case to them, asking for aid for another damaged soul, whose efforts on behalf of the homeless had left him in trouble with the authorities. Marcus was all for helping, Maddy quite sure the Masked Avenger being a remarkable new case study for him. Charelle's maternal instincts came right to the fore, and she had been the one who had set about making the bed of cardboard. She had found someone she could take care of, instead of being the only invalid, and she was happy. At first Jasmine had been fearful, but Abe reassured her.

"I've heard of the Masked Avenger," he said. "A good man. Looks out for people like me. I was over at the Dogpatch, and I heard how he saved old Billy's life the other night. We can take him in." Abe was an old guy, looked to be a former sailor or dock worker. His grizzled face and the tattoos on his arms bespoke a life lived near the water. He was carving a piece of wood delicately, making a piece of scrimshaw. Maddy came to understand that although Marcus was the leader of the group, Abe was their shaman – their tribal elder who bore with him the wisdom of the streets.

What a group, thought Maddy. Families are made in all shapes and sizes.

"Thank you, guys – so much," she said as she made to depart. "He really needs, like, two days of sleep. And here's some money – if you're going to the store, Robin might need some tuna."

They wouldn't hear of taking any money. They had some cans of tuna, already.

"I'll be back sometime tomorrow. I'll bring him some clean clothes and some food." She paused for a moment, not sure how to phrase the next question. "How do you guys get by for showers or baths and stuff?"

"Showers are over-rated," grumbled Abe.

"There are several options," said Marcus. "There's a shelter up the street, and one can take a shower there." He smiled wryly. "Although I'm not sure that would work for someone with a secret identity. Sometimes, though, I just stand on the loading docks of some of the buildings down here."

"What? What do you mean?" asked Maddy.

"The refurbished buildings have installed sprinkler systems on the loading docks. They go off throughout the night. It's meant to discourage people like us from camping out on the docks overnight, but if you can handle a cold shower, it's pretty convenient. And kind of sexy, in a way – you know, open air bathing. You just can't be too shy."

It was one thing to rinse off down at the beach at one of the cold-water showers in your swimsuit, it would be another to be au naturel standing on a loading dock, thought Maddy. I'm sure not cut out for a life on the streets. I'll take my showers hot, thank you.

She bid her goodbyes and headed back out into the night. It was midnight.

I'm tired, but I don't think I could sleep a wink, she thought.

As she put the key into the ignition, her phone went off. It was Jimmy. This time she answered.

"Thank God you're alright," he said when she picked up.

"No thanks to you, dick-head," she said.

"Hey, now! I… Listen, we need to talk. Can you come down to the station?"

"No way. If we're meeting, then it's neutral territory. I've got a lot of information for you, but I'm going to need some real promises."

"Tough girl."

"Damn straight." Maddy thought she suddenly sounded like one of those wise-cracking dames from some film noir movie. Where did this new voice come from?

"Where do you want to meet?" Jimmy asked.

"There are some benches along the Embarcadero just north of the Ferry Building. See you there in an hour and a half. Alone, please."

"An hour and a half? What do you still have to do?"

"I've got one more stop to make – some good stuff, I hope."

"You keep some late hours, but I'll be there."

"See ya." She hung up. She kind of liked being a tough girl.

LVII

She knew she'd find him there. Justin was just getting warmed up. The gang was hanging at the Chieftain bar, home away from home for most of the stagehands in the City. One wasn't allowed to smoke anymore in any of the bars or restaurants in San Francisco, but this was the kind of place that felt like a smoke-filled room, anyway.

"Maddy, what's up?" asked Justin. He had a large Black and Tan in front of him. So did Cate, who looked a little too cozy on the stool next to him. Maddy was in just enough of a mood to deck her if she said anything stupid, but she reminded herself that she was both emotionally disengaged and had bigger fish to fry.

"Can we talk?"

"Sure. Pull up. Want a beer?"

"Could we talk outside for a minute?"

"Sure. That's cool. I could use a smoke. Baby, do you mind?"

Cate did her best to look like, sure, no problem, but she was obviously annoyed.

"Sure, no problem."

"I'll be right back." He put his hand reassuringly on her shoulder then followed Maddy out of the pub. As they hit the cold night air, he lit up a cigarette and inhaled deeply.

"So, what's up? I thought you were a bed-by-ten kind of girl."

"New job. Got me pulling a few all-nighters."

"That's cool." He looked at her closely. "You look really different. It's good. You look good, all windswept and everything. Kind of wild."

Maddy thought that she looked like a wreck, but

then, with boys, you never could tell for sure what turned them on.

"Thanks. Look, I need your help again. Can we get back into the Orpheum?"

"When? Right now? Shit, well, yeah, I suppose so, but..."

"Awesome. Look, if it makes her feel any better, Cate can come too."

Justin looked at her for a moment and arched his eyebrow. "Sounds complicated," he said as he blew out some smoke.

"Shut *up*. I don't mean to break up any party, but this is time sensitive. If you don't want her to come, then just tell her you'll be back in half an hour."

Justin shrugged. "Alright, give me a sec." He went into the pub and returned a few minutes later with his leather jacket on.

"How'd she take it?"

"She'll be alright. Adds spice to the relationship." He smiled wickedly.

Maddy knew all about that.

*   *   *

The theatre was quiet, but it had an energy just the same. The Orpheum was over a hundred years old – plenty of ghosts inhabiting the fly galleries and the back halls. As much as she was in a hurry, Maddy asked Justin for one more small favor.

She wanted to stand center stage.

"This place is amazing," she whispered in awe as she stood in front of the empty auditorium. Twenty-five hundred seats stared back at her in the dim glow of the "ghost light" that had been left on stage. "What do you think, does this thing work?" she asked gesturing at the bare bulb on a stand.

"I think so. I've never seen any ghosts *on*stage when it's on. But there is a ghost here – I know. I've seen it up

238

in the catwalks."

"Really? What did it look like?"

"It was hard to make out. The lighting up there is pretty terrible. It was like this big, black shadow. I heard the breathing - that's what made me look up. I just caught a glimpse of it. What I remember most were the eyes. They glowed out of the shadows."

"Wow. That's creepy."

"I know. It really startled me. I stood up too fast and smacked my head on a duct. Hurt like shit. When I pulled myself together, it was gone."

Maddy shivered.

"The Phaaaaaaantom of the Opera is there..." sang Justin melodramatically.

Maddy giggled nervously, then gave him a poke. "Let's get going. You've got a warm girl waiting for you."

Justin smiled. "She'll keep. So, what's the plan?"

"You remember the server with the video stored on it from the surveillance cameras?"

"Yeah."

"Well, I need to see the video from this last Monday night."

"But that was before we refocused the camera."

"I know. That's the point. On Monday night it was pointed down at the entrance of UN Plaza. I think there's something on that video that might open up an investigation I'm working on."

"Okay, let's take a look."

They climbed down into the basement to the A/V room. Justin once again clicked his way through the server until he found Monday's video.

"What time are you looking for?"

"It would be sometime around midnight, plus or minus a half hour. I was in UN Plaza that night at around 12:30, and the crime had already been committed."

"Crime? What crime?"

"A homeless man was murdered," said Maddy, not wanting to give too much away. The fewer people who were involved in this case, the better.

"No shit! What did he look like?"

"Skinny old man with stringy gray hair. Last seen wearing an old Goliaths baseball cap."

"I know that guy. He was cool, unlike some of the other cats that lurk around the Plaza. That blows. You're trying to figure out who did it?"

"Yeah."

"Some internship. Sounds pretty intense. I thought interns did photocopying and went for coffee."

"So did I. Got more than I bargained for."

Justin started scanning the video at high speed. The resolution was pretty good. It was crazy, though, watching the traffic burp by in such a herky-jerky fashion. Maddy was thinking that it would be easier to scan in real time, but she didn't want to hang out for an hour.

"Wait – stop!"

The angle of the camera made all the cars look like they were falling from the top of the screen out the bottom. A long black car had just fallen off the screen having paused for a blip of moment. Justin scanned back in double time. The cars were now crawling back up the screen. The long black car worked its way back. A black blob connected with it from the side, then broke away again.

"Stop. Play that forward. Can you do it in slow motion?"

"I can do it a frame at a time. Here."

They clicked their way through. The black car crept down from above and pulled over to the side of the road. What had been a black blob was now clearly a person coming in from the right side of the screen – Lucky Jerry, thought Maddy. Lucky Jerry had paused on his way towards the car, then continued towards the rear window. The window was down, and suddenly a round object was passed out and into Lucky Jerry's hands. Lucky Jerry made a gesture – was it a wave of thanks? – and then moved back and off the right of the screen. The black car then moved forward, dropping out of the bottom of the screen.

"Back it up a couple of frames," said Maddy. "There. See how there's suddenly more light on the front of the car?" At that moment, the car was lit up. It was from the headlights of a passing car. "I wonder if we can make out the license plate." The time stamp was 00:12:16.

"You'd need some pretty serious enhancement. No way we can do that," said Justin.

"Yes, but I know some people who can. Can I get this on a CD or something?"

"I've got a thumb-drive, but it's up in the booth." Maddy looked at him, pleadingly. "All right, all right. It'll just take me about fifteen minutes to get up there and back."

"Thank you so much. I can't tell you how much this means to me."

"Well, if it helps to catch a murderer, then I guess it's the least I can do. Wait here."

As she waited for Justin, Maddy slowly clicked her way forwards and backwards on the video. It was weird, watching the phantoms on the screen - watching a murderer and his victim go through their motions. Maddy shivered. And she was tired. Maybe some sleep in an hour or so, but she realized that she was afraid of what she might dream about.

LVIII

This is a terrible place to meet, she thought as she plopped down on the bench. The fog had made everything damp. The idea had come to her out of another one of her romantic notions about detective work. Clandestine meetings on park benches, information exchanged by two people staring off into the distance. Just forgot how cold it was, that's all. At least this will keep things brisk.

Jimmy was right on time. Maddy could hear the sound of his shoes clicking along the sidewalk. She turned to see him approaching in a very elegant trench coat. He cut a rather dashing figure, emerging out of the fog, she thought.

"Don't you have a car?" she asked.

"Yeah, but I live so close to everything, I prefer to walk. Beats trying to find a place to park."

"I thought policemen could park anywhere."

"They can, except, even then, there's almost always some car in the way, so it's still a hassle. Besides, I really like walking around this town. Keeps me grounded and gives me time to think."

"So, what did you think on the way over here?"

"I was thinking that this was a really cold place to meet."

"Yeah, well, my bad."

"No, it's good. It's like a spy movie or something. Back at the station, this would all be really official, and, well, I think we'd both be really apprehensive. Here, at least, it's just the two of us and we can work some stuff out."

"Like the pervasive mistrust?" asked Maddy, more than a little bitterly.

242

"Look, we both have our positions on what we did and what happened. The trick is for us to understand the root causes."

"Like you sending in the fucking army, and having your guys start shooting at us? What's to understand? I knew I shouldn't have told you where I was going." Maddy got up from the bench and went over to the railing and looked out at the lights blinking in and out of the fog.

"Let's try some role reversal," replied Jimmy as he approached the railing. "Imagine someone you cared about was doing something dangerous. Imagine that no matter how much you might trust that person and their judgment, you've seen too much trouble in your life not to want to offer protection. Imagine you have a certain life experience that the other person doesn't have, and you know what's possible in a way that she might not. What would you do?"

"I get all that, but you make me sound like a child. You can be so patronizing; do you know that?"

"I get that from my dad. The worry, I get from my mom. I care for you, and I did what I thought was best. I'm sorry that there was an inexperienced cop. But try this on for size, imagine yourself in *his* shoes. Your Masked Avenger looks pretty dangerous carrying a dead body through the fog, and Damian, at least, has seen what he can do to a person. If you didn't know what was going on, wouldn't you have assumed the worst?"

"That's just it. I did know what was going on. I was fine."

"Hanging with a psychotic and delusional homeless guy who's big enough and strong enough to hurl policemen into the lake and beat the crap out of someone as big as Damian?"

"When you put it like that it doesn't sound good, I can see that, but yeah. He may be a psychotic and delusional homeless guy, but he's *my* psychotic and delusional homeless guy. He won't hurt me, I know this."

"How can you know this?"

"How can you know that you care for me?"

Jimmy looked at Maddy in frustration. His answer would be hers. He gave it, anyway.

"Because I just know."

"So, do I. There. Now can we move on from this circular argument?"

Jimmy scrunched up his face. After a moment, he asked, "Would you like a drink?"

"What you got?"

Jimmy reached into his trench coat and pulled out a bottle wrapped in a brown paper bag.

"Whisky."

Maddy had never had whisky – she could never get past the smell. But she was cold, and it sounded good. She reached out her hand and took the bottle. She unscrewed the top and took a sniff. Smelled like old cigars, leather, and the sea. Whew. She took a swig, anyway. It burned going down her throat, and she gave a small cough. "How can you drink this shit?" she asked passing the bottle back. Jimmy just smiled. But in the next second she felt warm all over.

Jimmy took a swig. "Where's the Masked Avenger now?"

"Why, are you going to arrest him?"

"Assaulting police officers would require something like that."

"Then I can't tell you."

"Aiding and abetting…"

"I know all about that. But I'm also aiding and abetting you. Look, I've got some good information, some of it courtesy of the Masked Avenger, and I'm happy to give it to you, but I'm not giving up my friend."

"Your friend? How's that?"

"I don't know, but we've adopted each other. There's something about him. A lost-ness. A deep, deep sadness. But he cares deeply for people, and wants to do right by them, and to protect them from harm."

"I know. Old Billy owes him his life."

"And I respect his mission. He has a gentle soul. He's a good person. He just needs help, that's all. And yeah. A friend."

"Don Quixote. Tilting at windmills."

"Yeah," said Maddy. "Tilting at windmills. And I'm his Sancho Panza." She reached out her hand for the bottle again. Jimmy passed it over. She took another swig. "I can see how someone could get to like this, after all." She made a face. "In spite of the smell and the taste."

"It's amazing what people can get used to." He paused. "Do you think I could ever meet the Masked Avenger?"

"I don't know – I don't think so. It would be hard. You would have to scrub all the cop off of you. You can understand how he might be suspicious."

"So, then what should I do? I've got the entire department gunning for this guy now, not to mention Mrs. Johnson. Maybe I can find some way to protect him."

"Take him off the streets? Put him in a prison? Or a hospital? He doesn't want that. I think that would kill him. He's doing some sort of, I don't know, some sort of penance. You can't deny someone that. He would never be at peace."

"There wouldn't be some proprietary angle here, would there? You're not trying to save him for yourself and a good story?"

Maddy still had the bottle and she made to throw it out into the Bay. "Don't make me toss this."

"Hey, now! That's good stuff. I didn't mean what I said – but I had to ask." Maddy looked at him. He gestured to her pleadingly. "May I have that back, please?"

"What's this stuff called, anyway?" She looked at the label. There was no way she was going to be able to pronounce it. Bunnahabhain.

"It's pronounced Boon-a-havn," said Jimmy. She took one more drink, then passed it back. Maddy looked out at the Bay. The drink was affecting her a little, and she was growing philosophical, wistful.

"I grew up in a place where I didn't have to worry about a thing," she said softly. "The extent of my hardship was what to wear on any given day. I had parents who were too busy, too tired, or too disconnected to give me any of their time and energy – or to get in my way, for that matter. Most of my friends were shallow and self-involved. No one had any passion for anything, except shopping, dope, or their iPods. Maybe putting on a musical. Now I've met someone who gives his heart and soul for something bigger than himself, and I need to support him. I'm sorry that there was an accident out at the Park. He didn't mean to hurt anyone. He was just helping Rodney to his... final resting place."

"Rodney?"

"The dead guy. He died of the same Tetrodotoxin that killed Lucky Jerry. There were three people out there who all ate the sandwiches. Rodney gave a description of the car driven by the person who gave Lucky Jerry the sandwiches just before he died."

"He died right there? In front of you?"

"Yeah. So, sorry I'm in such a bad mood."

"I'm... I'm so sorry, Maddy. I really am."

Suddenly, Maddy burst into tears. Between the fatigue, the cold, the whisky, the stress of seeing someone die, of being shot at, of being close to solving a great puzzle and close to connecting with, and maybe saving, a lost soul, it all just came out in a flood.

Not much of a tough girl now.

She moved completely on instinct and buried her face in Jimmy's chest and cried and cried and cried. Jimmy was momentarily overwhelmed and held his arms apart as if in surrender, but he eventually decided to throw what remained of his professionalism out the window and wrapped his arms around her tight. He didn't say anything, just stood there, taking the full brunt of Maddy's emotional release. There's no other way to play this, he thought. Just be there for her.

After several minutes, Maddy started to pull herself together.

"Sorry about your shirt," she said, wiping her nose on her sleeve. "There's snot and mascara all over it."

"This old thing? Don't worry about it."

Maddy laughed, surprisingly. "Jeez, so much for keeping it cool and professional. What do we do now?"

"I could take you home..."

Maddy almost crumpled. "I think sleeping with a policeman would be more than my poor little heart could handle right now."

Jimmy shuffled his feet. "That's not what I meant. You're not in much shape to drive. I should take you to your place. You need some rest."

"Oh."

That was awkward.

"But some other time, okay?" he added.

Well, no way to retreat from that, thought Maddy. "Okay." She smiled sheepishly and tucked a loose strand of hair behind her ear. "It would be nice if you drove me home. Thanks." She handed him the keys to the rental car. He held out his arm and she took it.

As they strolled to where she had parked – illegally, but she had figured that she was in a whole heap of trouble anyway, so why bother – Jimmy asked, "So you have a description of the car that the sandwiches came from?"

"Better than that, I have a video of the car and the transaction taking place."

Jimmy stopped and looked at her in wonder. "How in God's name did you pull that off?"

"You just have to know where to look, and who to talk to," she said smugly.

"Not revealing your sources again, right?"

Maddy debated whether or not to remain coy. She decided not. "No. It's from one of the video cameras on the roof of the Orpheum. My boyfriend... I mean my ex-boyfriend," – a flash of relief played across Jimmy's face – "is one of the electricians there. He helped me pull up the video. With Rodney's description of the car, I knew what to look for, and we knew approximately the time of the incident from my initial encounter with the Masked Avenger Monday night."

She handed Jimmy the thumb drive as they sat down in the car. He pocketed it and started the engine. They headed north, wending their way towards Columbus Avenue, the most direct route to Lombard Street.

"The Masked Avenger. So put yourself in my place," Jimmy said. "What would you do about your vigilante friend? He's going around town busting people up, whether or not it's for his idea of good, right or justice. He might not be dangerous to you, but he's certainly dangerous if you get on his wrong side. I know he can be canny and helpful, but he would be the walking embodiment of a 'loose cannon.' I'm a public servant entrusted with protecting the citizens of this city. Where does my duty lie here?"

Maddy was thoughtful for a moment. "Let him be, at least for a few more days. I give you my word of honor that I will do everything I can to prevent him from hurting anyone again, but if he does, then I will help you do your job. I will help you find him and bring him in, if only so that he might get some help, and to save him from himself."

Jimmy was silent for the rest of the drive. As he pulled up in front of her building he sighed. "I'm in a profoundly tough spot. There's going to be an investigation as to what happened out at the Park, and you're a material witness. The longer I sit on this the more my job is on the line. If I'm discovered to be covering for you and for the Masked Avenger, then not even my dad will be able to save me."

"I understand. Please give it another day or two. Just not tonight, okay?"

"Okay."

There was that awkward moment again. Two people looking at each other, not sure if they should acknowledge their feelings with a kiss. Maddy decided it was her turn to put it out there and leaned in. She suddenly stopped, remembering there was more Jimmy should know.

"Carlos found the restaurant!"

"What?"

"The restaurant where the blowfish came from. And he's pretty sure he knows which chef gave the poison out. Between the reservation list, a description from the chef, cross-referencing the social register and possibly pulling up the plates of the car from the video, we should have our killer."

"Does he have the reservation list?"

"No, he couldn't get that one – he got others, though. Besides, we thought it might be better for the police to do the follow up."

Jimmy laughed. "Finally letting us in on the case! Thanks, Sherlock."

"Oh, shut *up!*"

She finally kissed him.

LIX

"Let me get this straight."

Carey Portman was squeezing the bridge of her nose trying as hard as possible to fight back the enormous headache that had just hit her like a Benny Cashman line drive. She had not been prepared for this.

Carey had come in on Thursday morning thinking that, all things considered, it had been a pretty slow news week. Her thoughts, as she had read through her emails and made her phone calls, had been dominated by her upcoming weekend getaway to the Russian River Valley with her husband. This had been planned for months, since it was high season in the wine country. Early October was the most gorgeous time of year to be up in the lush, heavily wooded countryside, dotted with some of the most excellent wineries on earth. A half day on Friday, and then off up the winding roads for two nights and three days of excellent restaurants, wine tasting, sleeping in, catching up on a good book and most importantly spending some quality time with her husband. He was a partner at one of the more prestigious law firms in the city, so his time was as precious as hers. It was hard to get away, just the two of them.

But now, looking across her desk at the two interns, she didn't know what to do.

I might be going to jail, she thought.

Right after I kill them.

For Maddy, it had already been a very long day, and it was not even lunchtime. She had been up since 5:30. She had taken the dreaded Number 30 bus straight through Chinatown, past the dead pigs and chickens stacked up in the back of the open trucks making their morning deliveries to the restaurants along Stockton Street. The bus had been packed tight with every layer of San Francisco's social strata at that hour: young bankers and secretaries headed to the Financial District, Chinese grandmothers off to do their shopping, graveyard-shift restaurant workers headed to their homes deep in the East Bay, the girlfriends who were over-dressed – or underdressed, rather - from the night before who had slept over and were hoping to get home to change before going to work, and the homeless lady dozing in the back seat, snoring loudly.

There had even been a chicken on that bus.

But this time, Maddy had taken it all in with a new appreciation for the richness of the human experience. She had found herself applying no judgments at all – something she had never really done before. She resolved that she would take the bus more often.

People were cool.

From the bus she had taken the MUNI train out to the Park, retracing her steps from the night before. Her car was still there, much to her relief. Even more to her relief was that the bicycle was still chained to the fence next to the stadium. Luckily, she had remembered to get the key to the lock from the Masked Avenger as soon as they had locked it up. It had been a strain to hump the big cruiser onto the bike rack by herself, but she had somehow found the will.

Next had been picking up Carlos. She had explained that she had some errands to run, so they would grab their coffees and talk in the car. At Starbuck's they had bought out the entire case of sandwiches and juices, much to the dismay of the baristas, and the annoyance of the people in line behind them. They next made it to the Target in Daly City right when it opened, picking up a pair of gray sweatpants and a sweatshirt, along with some underwear and crew socks, all in XXXL. There were even some black basketball shorts, which they added to their haul. A box of heavy-duty black plastic garbage bags, along with some towels, body wash and deodorant completed their purchase there. Across the parking lot was the DSW shoe store. It hadn't opened yet, but Maddy banged on the door and the salesgirl who was setting up let her in.

"We're not open yet," said the salesgirl.

"It's an emergency," said Maddy.

"Girlfriend, I know all about shoe emergencies," said the salesgirl with a roll of her eyes.

"We'll be quick, promise," said Maddy.

"Take your time. As long as you behave yourselves, the place is yours. Just grab me when you're ready."

"Thanks!" And they had taken off towards the men's section. "Jeez. How big do you think his feet are?" Maddy asked Carlos, suddenly worried.

"Well, they only have sizes up to 16." Carlos had pulled out a pair of Doc Martens that were as big as two battleships and set them on the floor next to him. After a moment of appraisal, Maddy grabbed them and ran towards the check-out counter.

"That's some shoe emergency for real," said the salesgirl as she rang up the purchase. "You gonna live in those? Both of you?"

Driving down Army Street towards Dogpatch, Carlos looked at his watch. "We are in So. Much. Trouble."

"You're writing this all down, aren't you?"

"Not even a fucking Pulitzer Prize is going to save us from Carey."

"Well, if we live to tell the tale, someone will hire us."

"Yeah. I'll be writing obituaries for the Modesto Bee."

They had hauled their treasures down into the basement. Charelle was there, looking tired from staying up watching over the Masked Avenger all night. She could not believe her eyes when she saw the panoply of sandwiches and muffins. "Wow! What a feast! Mmm,

mmm. I just love those Pesto Chicken Wraps."

"Help yourself," said Maddy. "Although we need to save a lot of this for the Masked Avenger. I can't imagine how hungry he'll be."

"He hasn't waked up, yet. He thrashed about something fierce during the night, but he's finally calmed down."

"How about you?" asked Maddy. "Did you get any sleep? You look tired."

"Oh, I'm fine. I'll be better after some breakfast. Everyone else is out foraging – won't they be surprised when they get back."

"We have to run, but we'll be back later this afternoon – early evening," said Maddy. "Let him sleep. And don't let him go out – the police are looking all over for him. I need to talk with him before he goes anywhere. And his bike's upstairs. I chained it to the railing by the door. If he wakes up before we get back, tell him I'll give him the key when I get here."

"Will do. Thank you." Charelle had given them both big hugs – as big as she could with her tiny, frail frame, anyway.

"Thank you. Take care, now," Maddy chirped as she and Carlos ran back up the stairs.

As they bombed down Third Street towards downtown, Maddy turned to Carlos.

"Brace yourself."

*   *   *

"Let me get this straight."

Carey finished squeezing the bridge of her nose and looked at Maddy and Carlos.

"The wires are lit up with all sorts of speculation about this character, this Masked Avenger, who trashed two police officers last night in some epic fashion, and you've been running around with him for the last three nights without telling anyone? And you were there when it all went down?"

"Well, I missed the actual 'trashing'..."

"Hang on, I'm not finished. And you have several leads involving the murder - no, double murder - of two homeless people, and are coordinating with the police, despite your involvement in the brutal mugging of two of San Francisco's finest?"

"Well, I wasn't really involved..."

"I'm not done. And you have evidence of some malfeasance on the part of the Director of the brand, spanking new Museum of Asian Antiquities, involving Hollywood megastars?"

"We have the photo..." said Carlos.

"Shut. Up. And to top it all off, you have it on 'good authority' that Benny Cashman, the pride of the Goliaths who is leading a world-class professional sports franchise on a championship run and is the darling of our city, has been seen exchanging cash money for drugs?"

At this point neither Maddy nor Carlos dared say a word.

Carey Portman slowly and methodically placed her reading glasses in front of her on her desk, arranging them just so. She looked to the heavens for a moment in a gesture of gathering strength from above. She then returned her gaze to Maddy and Carlos.

"Are you out of your fucking *minds*?" Both interns jumped in their seats. Neither of them knew what to do. We're *so* toast, thought Maddy.

"Never, I mean *never*, pull stupid stunts like this..." Carey, at this point, was standing and pounding her fists on the desk, "without keeping me completely informed. This is what the BlackBerry was invented for. This is *news*, people, and you've got it, and if I don't see some serious-ass writing on my desk before the day is out, then you will not walk out of this building alive. You hear me?"

Maddy was so bewildered she could only stutter.

"You... you... mean that we're supposed to keep up our investigations?"

"Damn straight. Just don't fucking get shot. You've managed to get this far on your own – keep going."

"Yes, Ma'am! And what should we do with the Masked Avenger?"

"Don't let anyone else near him. He's ours. Reminds me of the time in Afghanistan, I had managed to get an exclusive with one of the Afghan warlords. I damn well wasn't going to share his location with anyone else. Didn't matter whose side he was on. So, we keep him under wraps. Understand me?"

"Yes, Ma'am."

"I need timelines, players, strategies, the works. On. My. Desk. 5pm. Now get going."

Maddy and Carlos could not get out of her office fast enough. They ran down the hall towards the open plan office and their cubicles. Once they got there, they collapsed on the floor, giggling with relief. More than a few eyebrows were raised by the occupants of the nearby desks. Maddy crawled under her desk, and Carlos followed. It was as if they had climbed up into the tree house of their secret club and were making plans and creating codes.

"I thought we were dead," whispered Maddy.

"I thought we were worse than dead. I thought she was going to crucify us. Leave us hanging upside-down by our toenails for the crows to eat. That was scary."

"So how are we going to pull this off?" asked Maddy. "It's almost noon."

"You concentrate on the murders – you know more about those than I do. We can attach the various lists as appendixes or addenda or something. I'll tackle the museum stuff, since I was in the room."

"What about Benny Cashman?" asked Maddy.

"I don't know... wait. How many games left in the season?" They grabbed a Sporting Green. "Holy crap! He tied the record last night. That must have been what

I heard last night – the roar from the stadium was unbelievable. What's today?"

"Thursday, so there are only two games left – tonight and tomorrow."

"That means he should be getting his next round of doses any time over the next few nights. Little Mary said the last 'meet' was after a game. So that would mean either tonight, or more likely, tomorrow night. We should be in position by ten o'clock."

"When am I going to get any sleep?" whined Maddy.

"You can sleep when you're dead," said Carlos as he climbed out from under the desk. "Now get to work!"

*   *   *

Before they set about their separate tasks, they went to the weblink that Justin had emailed Maddy. When she saw that it worked, and they had video of the service door to the Museum, Maddy squealed with delight. Carlos was very impressed.

"Your boyfriend's cool."

"He's not my boyfriend. He's my ex-boyfriend."

"Whatever. You are so Nineties. Why not have more than one boyfriend?"

"Hate to break it to you, but I don't have any boyfriends right now. Jeez."

"I thought you and Mr. Detective were an item."

"We've had, like, one date. Hardly makes him my boyfriend."

"As I said before, whatever."

They turned their attention to the video. It revealed nothing but a stream of cars rolling down Hyde Street. It was almost identical to the images Maddy had seen the night before, just further up the street. At least they could scan through the video at high speed. Certainly beats hanging out in Dogpatch in a dumpster in the cold, thought Maddy.

*   *   *

Fueled by a steady stream of coffee, they made it through the afternoon. At 4:30 they passed each other's reports back and forth, redlining as they went. They arrived at Carey's office at 4:55.

"You both get to live," said Carey, looking over her glasses. Funny thing about Carey was that you couldn't tell if she was joking. Probably wasn't. "What's the agenda for the next few days? And I want real answers."

"To be honest, we're in a bit of a holding pattern," said Maddy. "We have to wait for the police to interview the staff at Tadao to see if there's any identification of the patron who bought the blowfish toxin, and to get the reservation list for the days around last Monday. We're also waiting for the police to see if they can enhance and trace the license plate of the sedan car that stopped by UN Plaza to deliver the poisoned sandwiches."

"How did you know the poison came from the sandwiches, again?"

"We didn't say. We weren't sure if we should include that in our report – you won't believe it."

"It's all pretty unbelievable, but then, hey, this is San Francisco. Try me." Carey settled back in her chair and crossed her arms.

"The Man Without a Face," said Maddy and Carlos in unison.

Carey just looked at them, with the glazed look of a cow staring at a passing train. After a moment, she returned to the notes in front of her. "Right," was all she could say. It was obvious she had reached her saturation point.

"Who's your liaison at SFPD?" Carey asked, after she had glanced over her notes.

Carlos looked at Maddy, who made a face.

"Detective James Wang," said Maddy.

"Old James Wang? I thought he retired," said Carey.

"His son," said Maddy. "Detective James Wang, Jr."

"Well, stay liaised," said Carey.

"Yes, Ma'am," said Maddy, as Carlos snorted. Maddy gave him the evil eye.

"And the Museum?"

"Also in a holding pattern. We have the initial irregularity, and the photo-documentation of what appears to be the transaction at the Mandarin, and the statement of an expert on Asian antiquities and artifacts that the piece in question should not be for sale, but we're trying to develop additional evidence. To that end, we're virtually staking out the Museum, and we're following the lead on the woman who was seen with Peter Kohler. Her photo is attached to our report."

Carey flipped through the pages and looked at the photo. "Well, I could have saved you a lot of trouble. That's Madeleine Chang. Her husband owns YooHoo!" Carey looked at her interns. "Now this is serious. Between Peter Kohler, Madeleine Chang, YooHoo! and Robert Grant, we've got to have our shit correct before we say or do anything."

"Which is why we are close-circuit monitoring the service entrance to the Museum."

"How are you doing that?"

Maddy felt like she was airing all her dirty laundry in public. She told Carey about her connection with Justin and her access to the camera feed. Carey nodded, impressed. "Good. Resourceful. And I don't see any real legal ramifications from this, at least not yet. Let me know if anything happens. Meanwhile, let me have a word with the Financial Editor. Maybe there's something going on with YooHoo! that would cause an otherwise perfectly respectable Silicon Valley mogul's wife to try to sell stolen Tibetan artifacts."

"Thank you, Ma'am, that would be great."

"It would be outstanding if we could catch Grant in this, even if he's just an unwitting participant. Talk about ratings. Any angle on that?"

"No. Right now, this is all too hot, and too circumstantial for the police, but their interest is increasing. Again, that's why we need more before they're willing to move."

"I don't blame them." Carey took off her glasses and leaned back in her chair. "Let's talk about the Masked Avenger. What do you know about him? You've spent the last three nights crusading around town with him."

"He's a complete enigma," said Maddy. "It's as if he had no past and has no name. We can get almost nothing out of him."

"He must be somebody or have been somebody before he became the Masked Avenger. We need to know who he is. This could be a huge human-interest story."

"That's what I thought when I first saw him," said Maddy. "What could drive a person to do what he does? He has some skills. He is sort of canny in his way. But there's something troubling him. He's not completely deranged or psychotic – there is a weight that he carries that is very human. We just don't know what it is."

"Well, keep chipping away at it. These other stories are potentially huge, sensational, but our crazy, local vigilante will be the story that makes you a journalist." Carey started to organize the papers on her desk. The meeting was wrapping up. She stopped and looked at her interns closely again. "Cashman. What are your plans there? Your witness doesn't sound all that credible."

"We couldn't think of anything better than staking out the drop area over the next few nights. Our witness is okay, she's as lucid as anyone we've met over the last few days, and she showed us the location. There are photos of the lot."

"Looks bleak enough," said Carey as she scanned the panorama of shots that Maddy had taken. "When do you start?"

"We were going to go out there tonight..." said

Carlos.

"I haven't been on a stakeout in years. What time do we meet?" asked Carey. Maddy and Carlos weren't sure what to make of this. Carey then grinned wide, like the Cheshire Cat.

Great, thought Maddy. I get to hang out in Dogpatch in a dumpster in the cold.

With Carey.

LX

Jimmy Wang was dragging. Oh, to be twenty-three again, he thought. I'm too old for this shit. It occurred to him in that moment that everyone was almost always too old for something, even twenty-three-year-olds. This realization didn't make him feel any better.

His day had also started very early. He had gotten up and returned the rental car for Maddy. He had then given himself a treat and taken the cable car back up over the hill and down into North Beach, walking a few blocks to his office at the station. After downloading the contents of Maddy's thumb drive and reviewing the video over a cup of hot coffee, he had emailed the still-frame of the sedan to Jose down in forensics. Jose had all of the software necessary to climb into a photograph and pull out whatever could be pulled out. It was amazing what could be dug out of a photograph. If we can identify a license plate from space, thought Jimmy, we should be able to do it from the top of the Orpheum. He was hopeful.

Rodney was also being processed. He got swifter attention than Lucky Jerry, now that there was a trend developing. Results would be back later in the afternoon, although he knew what they would be.

Jimmy had then gotten into his car and had driven over to St. Mary's. When he got there, Damian was already being wheeled down the hall towards the exit. He was dressed in sweatpants and tennis shoes with his Oakland Knights sweatshirt on. His wife must have brought that for him to wear home. Jimmy shook his head. The Knights were the baddest team in football, attracting the craziest of fans. He couldn't imagine Damian painting his face and screaming from the stands, but then again, one never knew.

"I don't understand why they won't just let me walk out the door," said Damian, testily. "I'm fine, dammit."

He didn't look all that fine. His dark face was all mottled and bruised, with a big white bandage on his nose, lots of white tape crisscrossing around his eyes and a plastic mask.

"Now you shush," said Georgia, his wife, who was walking beside him. The orderly struggled a little with the wheelchair – Damian was a pretty big guy. "Last thing they want is you slipping on the way out and suing their asses. Just enjoy the ride."

"Everything okay?" asked Jimmy. "Other than the obvious, of course."

"My nose is going to look more Roman," said Damian, proudly displaying his profile.

"Mild concussion," said Georgia. "But he passed his tests, so he gets to go home. Any word on the jerk that did this?"

Jimmy faltered for a moment, then recovered. "We're all over it, Georgia. Truth of the matter is that I'm not sure it was anyone's fault. Just a bad sequence of events."

Damian shook his head. "You can say that again. Wrong place, wrong time. For everybody."

"Alright, Baby, let's get you home," said Georgia. They had reached the entrance and the automatic doors slid open. The car had been pulled up. Damian climbed out of the wheelchair with a grunt and gave Jimmy a handshake and a hug.

"It's okay, man. Gives me a chance to hang around the house and watch some TV. Knights are on this weekend. Against Kansas City. That's always a good game."

"Don't rush this," said Jimmy. "Take your time and get some rest."

"Copy that. See you, man."

Jimmy had then gone down to Intensive Care.

Bobby Cochran was still sleeping. Jimmy had looked in on him and wasn't happy with what he saw. Poor kid had his whole left side in a cast, and he was hooked up to all sorts of tubes and wires. At least he wasn't blue anymore.

I wonder if he saw Maddy? thought Jimmy. I hope not.

He had returned to the office and hooked up with Detective Chen. They had compared notes on the deaths of Lucky Jerry, whose case Detective Chen was officially responsible for, and Rodney. They had decided to head on down to Tadao to see if Carlos' story checked out.

"Nice place," said Detective Chen as they passed through the ancient-looking, giant wooden doors. "Let's stay for lunch and see if we can get reimbursed for it."

"I've heard complaints about the food," said Jimmy wryly. They approached the hostess stand, and Jimmy pulled out his badge. "Good afternoon, ma'am," he said to a beautiful young Japanese woman in a kimono. "We'd like to ask you a few questions." It was two o'clock and the room was quiet. The lunch rush was over.

"Of course, sir. Should I get the manager?"

"Please do."

The woman shuffled away, returning shortly with a middle-aged and elegantly dressed Japanese man.

"Good afternoon, officers. How may I assist you?" he asked smoothly.

"May we review your reservation lists for two days prior to and including this past Monday?" asked Detective Chen.

"Of course. I can have them printed out for you if you like. May I inquire as to what this is about?"

"We're just corroborating the statement of a witness. You know, alibis and stuff. Times and places."

"No problem." The manager spoke quietly to the hostess who went off towards the back of the restaurant. "She will bring them to you, shortly. May I offer you gentlemen anything to drink while you wait?"

"No thank you," said Jimmy. "By the way, how many sushi chefs do you have on staff here?"

The manager paused for a second to consider. "Five. They rotate through. We have two a night."

"How many are licensed to prepare blowfish?"

The manager looked at Jimmy sharply. He pursed his lips and said, "Two. They alternate, mostly."

"Who was on last night?" asked Detective Chen.

"I would have to refer to the staff calendar. One moment, please."

The manager left for a few minutes, returning with the hostess. "Here are the reservation lists. And Hiro was working last night."

"Is he here now?" asked Jimmy.

"No. The other one, Hideo, is working."

"May we speak with him? Is there some place we could be alone?"

"I will ask him to join you in the private dining room. Excuse me, please. Lois, here, will show you the way."

The hostess took them to a small, extremely elegant room. She ushered them in and then slid the door shut. "Really nice place," said Chen, taking in the golden tapestries that covered the rich, dark, wood paneling. The view of the Bay Bridge was breathtaking.

After a minute the door slid open and a small, older Japanese man entered with the manager behind him. "This is Hideo. Would you like me present for the interview?"

"That will not be necessary," said Jimmy. "We'll only be a few minutes." The manager bowed and stepped out, leaving Hideo standing there nervously.

"Have a seat," said Jimmy. He noticed beads of sweat running down the man's face. Given that the room was heavily air-conditioned, that didn't speak well for the chef's composure, he thought.

"We know you sold the blowfish toxin," said Chen.

Subtle, thought Jimmy. It's pretty clear who the Bad Cop is.

But the blunt approach worked. Hideo breathed a deep sigh and then collapsed in his chair, completely deflated.

"Yes," he said simply. "I am sorry. I have regretted doing so ever since."

"To whom did you sell it," asked Jimmy, gently. Good Cop.

"I do not know his name. He is a regular customer, though."

"So, you would recognize him if you saw him again?"

"Yes. He is balding white man. Heavy set."

"Well, that's just about every businessman in America," said Chen, dismissively.

"His eyes are small and dark. How you say?"

"Beady."

"Yes, beady. Nervous man."

"Why'd you do it?" asked Chen.

"Wife is sick. We needed the money. We have no insurance."

"What night was this?"

"It was Monday afternoon. After lunch."

Well, that does it. Lunch reservation for Monday. Carlos gets a gold star, thought Jimmy.

"You'll lose your license," said Chen.

"I know," said Hideo simply. Jimmy's heart went out to him.

After names, addresses, contact info and statements were taken, Jimmy and Detective Chen headed back to the station. Hideo was not charged - not yet - but he was told to be on call. His manager, however, was apoplectic. The chef was fired on the spot, causing him to crumple even more, if that were possible.

Jimmy wondered what he would have done in the man's shoes.

LXI

"Are you okay?"

The voice came to him as if through a fog. It was soft and gentle. Compelling. "Are you okay? There's food if you're hungry."

His eyes began to focus. He felt both rested and as if he could continue sleeping for years. In front of him was a very pretty girl, looking at him with concern.

"I am okay. Thank you," he replied huskily. He had not slept like that for so long he couldn't remember. No dreams. He stood up stiffly. "What time is it?"

"It's six o'clock. You've slept for over eighteen hours. I was getting worried."

Such a pretty girl, he thought. He remembered meeting her briefly. "I'm sorry, ma'am, I was so tired, I did not register your name."

"Charelle. It's okay. You were pretty strung out. Do you want some food? Your friends dropped some by this morning. And some new clothes."

As he took in the display of sandwiches and juices, and the pile of new clothes, he was overcome with emotion. He was ashamed, but he could not help but shed a tear.

"I have not seen such kindness in a long time."

"Not much kindness in the world," said Charelle. "But there is some, just the same. Your friends are all right. Would you like to eat first, or would you like a bath?"

"A bath?"

"Yeah. They brought some towels and some soap. I heated up some water. It would be more like a sponge bath, but still. There's an old bathroom down that corridor. Everything still works pretty well, just not the hot water."

"Thank you, Miss Charelle. If I may, I should like to freshen up. Would you please then join me for dinner?" He took her hand.

"I should be delighted." She dipped slightly – almost a curtsy. Blanche DuBois.

His heart leapt. There was something about her. Something damaged and haunted, but still full of life. He bowed and kissed her hand. "Enchante," he said.

"Oh, I made you a new cape and mask. Here, take it with you." Charelle handed him the garbage bag ensemble. She had cut the eyeholes out and everything. He smiled and took it from her. As he stood there in wonder at the new friend he had found, he felt a soft, warm sensation at his ankles.

"Robin. How are you my little friend?" She was rubbing up against his legs. He scooped the kitten up and stroked her in his big hand. Robin purred furiously.

"She never left your side," said Charelle. "She's a cutie."

"You wouldn't have any tuna..."

"We do. Maybe now that you're up, she'll eat." Charelle handed him a can of tuna, which he set on the floor. He placed Robin next to it and stroked her as she dug into the can.

"I'll be right back," he reassured the kitten, who purred and blinked her eyes.

*   *   *

It was the best meal he could remember. The candles, the sandwiches, the company. He felt like a new man – clean, and his new costume was magnificent. Charelle was charming. She laughed and gasped as he told her stories of his adventures and his quests. The thought crept over him that perhaps it might be time to set aside his life as a lone crusader and settle down with a good woman.

No. There was still work to do.

But she was worthy of his admiration. Perhaps she might allow him to carry a token? Perhaps she might be his "disdainful lady?" Every knight needed his lady, who would spur him on in his quests and drive him to greater feats of daring. The thought pleased him.

For the first time in years, he was happy.

LXII

"Your boyfriend," mouthed Carlos to Maddy after he answered his phone. They were sitting at the counter at Carlos' favorite taqueria on Valencia Street. They figured that with a cold night ahead of them, they should fortify themselves as thoroughly as possible. A carne asada burrito should do the trick. As the burrito was placed in front of her, Maddy thought it was as big as her forearm.

This should hold me, she thought.

"Yes, sir. Will do, sir, first thing." Carlos set his phone down and took in the burrito in front of him. "It's like eating a baby," he said in wonder. "And yet, it's so good it finds a way to fit, somehow."

"That was a lot of 'yes, sir' on the phone just now."

"Detective Wang. Being brown-skinned, I learned early on that it was always better to say 'yes, sir,' 'no, sir,' to the police."

"Right. Cruising in Buttonwillow, I'm sure you were in trouble all the time," she said, teasingly. "So, what's up? I thought *I* had the direct line."

Carlos puffed himself up. "He called to say that my instincts proved correct – that the other chef was the one who sold the toxin. Now he wants the lists from the social register. I guess the case is officially being passed on to the police. I told him I would get him the lists right away."

"How are you going to do that? I thought they were on the machine at the office."

Carlos just waved his iPhone. He ran his fingers over it, tapped it and he said, "Done."

"Cool," said Maddy. That Carlos. Sharpest knife in the drawer. She turned back to her burrito.

The plan was this. A fueling stop at the Mission Taqeria, followed by checking in on the Dogpatch gang and the Masked Avenger. They had arranged to meet Carey on Tennessee Avenue a few blocks from the drop site at 9:30 and walk over. No need to have any extra cars in the lot that might give the game away. The Goliaths' game that evening started at 7:35, so it wouldn't come down until 10:00 at the earliest. This would give them plenty of time to reconnoiter and place themselves in position. Maddy had her camera with her – her good one, not her phone. She also wanted to be at the site early enough to play with the settings. The light would probably not be very good, so she wanted to be ready for that.

"You're right. This is the most amazing burrito I've ever eaten." She had to push away after eating half of it. If she ate the whole thing, she would either be sick to her stomach or fall into a food coma. Both bad.

Carlos managed to keep going, putting the entire thing into his stomach. Where does it go? thought Maddy. Carlos was slight of build but could eat like nobody's business. He's a fidgeter. That's how he does it.

They drove down Valencia all the way to Cesar Chavez and then headed towards the Bay. At seven o'clock the sky was a deep cobalt blue with lavender clouds. No fog. This meant that the night would be even colder than the night before.

They had been smart, though, and filled up a thermos with some coffee from the little Mexican coffee shop across the street from where they had dinner. It wouldn't be so bad – a little like camping out. And Carlos had the bright idea that they could get real-time game updates on his iPhone through ESPN.com. This way they would know when the game was finally over. They could not be more prepared.

As they climbed down the stairs to the basement of the turbine hall, they both stopped for a moment in wonder. The place had become even more magical than before. Candles were everywhere, more dramatic now that the sun had set and no longer entered from above. And there was laughing. Laughing!

The Masked Avenger sat before the fire, laughing with Charelle. Maddy just about fell over. When he saw Maddy and Carlos, he bounded up to them and scooped them both within his arms, almost crushing them with gratitude. "Well met, my friends!" he cried. "Well met!"

It just goes to show what sleep can do for a person, thought Maddy. And thank God he took a bath.

"It's good to see you, too," choked out Maddy. "Remember, though, that we're little and you're big."

"Yes. I'm sorry. It's just that you have treated me with such generosity." The Masked Avenger released them, Carlos expanding his chest and cricking his neck, Maddy able to put her feet on the floor again.

"You look good. Does everything fit? We were worried about the shoes..."

"Like a glove."

"Oh. We forgot new gloves..."

"It is fine. It would have been too much all at once."

Maddy turned to Charelle. "Thank you for taking such good care of him."

"It's been a pleasure. He's a very charming man. He has regaled me with stories."

Maddy and Carlos exchanged a glance. Charelle got more out of him in the last few hours than they had over the last four days. Huh.

"Here is the key to your bike lock. The bike is still chained to the railing upstairs. But you shouldn't go out yet. You should hang here at least one more night."

"There is work to do," said the Masked Avenger, rubbing his chin thoughtfully.

"It will be waiting for you when you return. The rest has obviously done you good. A little more and you could save the world. And besides, it's still pretty hot out there with the police."

The Masked Avenger looked troubled. But he glanced over at Charelle, and his demeanor softened.

Another evening here wouldn't be such a bad thing, he thought.

"I shall remain here, if I am still welcome."

"No problem," said Charelle with a smile.

"That's great," said Maddy. Taking Charelle by the arm, she took her aside. "What did he tell you? The stories…"

"Just funny stuff. He is so odd, but he's sweet. He told me about 'creatures he has slain,' about 'evil-doers he has brought to justice.' It's like talking to a medieval knight. None of it makes any sense, but he believes it. And the stories are cool, in a way."

"Nothing about himself – where he comes from, who he is, though?"

"No. I asked him his name and he wouldn't tell me."

"Thanks. I'll just have to figure this out on my own. Although if he ever does take you further into his confidence, please let me know."

"I guess, so. I don't know. Why would you want to know?" asked Charelle, her face showing concern.

"He's not well. He needs help. Maybe someone is looking for him," Maddy replied.

"If he doesn't want to be found, then that's his business. Sometimes people make a choice not to be found, or not to be taken into someone else's idea of 'care.' I would leave it alone."

"Maybe you're right," said Maddy thoughtfully. This is going to kill me, she thought. I'm sitting on this great story with no way to tell it.

"Ladies, please join us for a while," said the Masked Avenger. Carlos had obviously been trying to glean information from him on his own, and the Masked Avenger had grown wary, preferring to avoid the subject.

"Sorry, sir," said Maddy, and she and Charelle re-joined them. They sat down around the little fire.

"Mister Avenger, I need your help."

The Masked Avenger looked ready to bound into action. "Of course, my friend. In what way may I assist you?"

Maddy hesitated, not sure how to ask. Finally, she plunged ahead. "There's some serious stuff going on out in the real world because of what happened out at the Park. It's very tenuous, my relationship with the police, but I am in a position to try to help you. But I can't do that without knowing what you would want them to know about you. Is there anything you would want me to tell them? For that matter, there's a lot of stuff in the news about what happened, but it's all speculation. Rumors. That the Masked Avenger is someone to be feared and captured. Is there anything you would want the world to know? Can I help to set the record straight?" Carey Portman interviewing the Afghan warlord.

The Masked Avenger's bravado failed him suddenly. He became very quiet and the glint in his eye faded. There was the sense that he was cornered, captured, and maybe defeated. After a long pause, he said quietly, "Tell them that I meant no harm to anyone. My only goal is to help those who need help, and to protect those who need protection. Can you tell them that?"

"I'll try," said Maddy.

He sighed and continued. "And tell them that I only do what I must because no one else will. I have no ill will towards the police, but my charges are often beneath their notice, so I must work independently of them, and in many cases, around them. I regret that harm may have come to them by my hands, and I shall do all in my power to make amends."

Maddy thought that that would be the end of it, but the Masked Avenger was starting to build up steam. The glint returned to his eye, and his voice developed strength as he spoke.

"Please tell them that they misjudge me and my people. That circumstances, however reduced, do not define a man, but his actions do. That the difference between good people and bad people is not what is in their wallets, or in the cut of their clothes, but what is within their hearts. There is not much good in the world," at this he nodded towards Charelle, "but there is good just the same, and we must celebrate and nurture that good the way we would a child or a small tree. It is within all of us."

Maddy and Carlos looked at each other. "Wow," mouthed Carlos.

"And I know what it is to make mistakes – terrible mistakes – and what it means to repay great debts. My life's work is an embodiment of that knowledge, and I place myself at the feet of the greater good, the noble quest, and at the altar of hope." He paused, and then added quietly again, "Can you tell them that?"

"I would be proud to," said Maddy, moved. She saw tears running down Charelle's cheeks. Carlos cleared his throat, himself choked up a bit.

The Masked Avenger put out his hand. Maddy took it in hers and he grasped her hand firmly, looking deeply into her eyes. "Thank you, my friend. Thank you."

"You… you're welcome," said Maddy. She wanted to write it all down as fast as she could – but she then looked over at Carlos who just clicked off the small digital recorder that he had stashed in his pocket.

They took their leave of Charelle and the Masked Avenger. It was almost time to meet Carey, several blocks away. The sky was now dark, except for the faint glow from TBD Park about a mile up the street. And it was cold. Maddy thought how good that hot shower was going to feel when she finally got home.

LXIII

What did his father do without all this technology? thought Jimmy as he sipped his coffee and looked at the enhanced imaging that Jose had sent him. It occurred to Jimmy that with all of the tools at a policeman's disposal in the 21st Century, it was the rare criminal that could get away with anything – assuming that there was a policeman who took the time. In his father's day, crimes went unsolved all the time. Notorious cases like the Zodiac Killer were never closed, due to the inability to process the forensic evidence and to crunch the numbers in the way they could now. No wonder dad is so bitter, he thought. It must have felt every day as if evidence was sifting through his fingers – no way to pull the pieces together unless he got really lucky.

He returned his gaze to his computer screen. Only the first four characters of the black sedan's license plate were legible, due to glare off the license plate holder, but once that was input into the DMV database, along with the make and model of the vehicle, the 42,875 possible combinations of potential plates were distilled down to three – only one in the Bay Area. The car was registered to a limo service based in San Bruno, down by the airport south of San Francisco. He checked his watch. It was 9:30. He was at that breakpoint between going home or pushing on. A drive would be nice, though – get out of the office for a bit and still feel useful. If he headed south now, he would miss the traffic from the game. He threw on his jacket and headed out, pausing by the break room. The game was on. Not much scoring – it looked like a pitcher's duel – which meant that the game was going quickly. It was already the bottom of the seventh inning. The color commentator was remarking on the restlessness of the crowd, who had come to see some home run fireworks and the breaking of a record. Cashman hadn't connected with the ball all game, walking once, and striking out twice. Just not his night, it seemed.

Maybe I'll listen to the game on the radio, he thought. He smiled as he realized that he might just be starting to get into baseball, after all.

LXIV

"We should be selling this shit by the pound," puffed Madeleine Chang as she pushed her way through the service door on the back end of a large crate.

"It never works that way," said Peter Kohler, on the front end. "It's the little stuff that's really valuable."

"Then why are we hauling this big-ass statue around?"

"The request was specific. Mr. Lynn's VIP lounge at his new casino resort required a one-of-a-kind, signature piece. Of a certain size."

"Nothing like purchasing priceless Tibetan artifacts by the yard," sniffed Madeleine as they slid the crate into the back of her Lexus. "Maybe you should get a bigger car, so we don't always have to load these into mine."

"Wouldn't fit in my garage," replied Kohler, smugly.

"Excuse me! May I be of any assistance?" the voice called out from just behind them. Madeleine and Peter Kohler spun around, both caught completely by surprise. At ten o'clock at night they weren't expecting much of an audience. It was hard to see who was calling to them, blinded as they were by the headlights. A young Asian man stepped out of what was revealed to be an unmarked police car.

"I wasn't sure what was going on," said Jimmy Wang as he pulled out his badge. He had been driving down Hyde Street, being one of the most direct routes from North Beach through the City to the southbound freeway. And the route had the advantage of passing by both the back of the museum and the entrance to UN Plaza. Perhaps he might spot something. "It's rather late to be moving things out of a museum, isn't it?"

Peter Kohler had the odd feeling he had seen the young man before but couldn't put his finger on when or how. He quickly applied his smoothest demeanor, battle-tested more than once in board rooms and at media events.

"Thank you for stopping by, officer. I'm the Director Of The Museum." He said it in such a way that one could hear the capitals at the beginning of each word. "This is the Chair of the Museum Board. We're just taking this piece for a preliminary evaluation. You see, as much as I consider myself an expert on such artifacts, it is unclear to me the precise dating. We are transporting it to an independent analyst who might offer a second opinion." Kohler was obviously thinking that the more multi-syllabic words he used, the more he might impress his interrogator.

"I would have thought that professional museum movers would take care of that for you," said Jimmy.

"Some pieces require special handling," said Kohler with a shrug. "And, truth be told, in these difficult economic times, we do what we can to reduce costs."

"I see," said Jimmy. "I'm impressed by your efforts – long hours, it seems, running a museum. May I take a look at it?"

"Unfortunately, it is packaged in such a way as to minimize any potential damage in transportation. Easier said than done, I'm afraid."

"Of course. Well, if everything is alright, I'll be heading on. Sorry to trouble you," said Jimmy, sounding just like a policeman from an English detective story.

"No trouble at all, officer. Good to know that you're looking after us." Kohler gave a tight smile. Madeleine gave a little wave. They shut the back of the Lexus and headed off. As Jimmy climbed back into his car, he looked up at the top of the Orpheum. He could just make out the tiny, blinking red indicator light from the camera. Sitting in his car, he punched in the plates of the Black Lexus. Registered to Robert L. Chang, Woodside.

Jimmy whistled. Before he put the car into drive, he sent a text to Maddy.

"Kohler. Museum. 10pm. Black Lexus SUV. Check video."

He then pulled away from the curb and headed south, climbing on to the 101 Freeway towards San Bruno. The night was cold, but he rolled his window down. It felt good to feel the crisp, autumn air in his face. The lights glowing to his left from TBD Park reminded him that the game must still be going. He turned on the radio. Bottom of the ninth, one out, Goliaths down by one to their arch-rivals from Los Angeles. But Benito Juarez had just looped a single into left field. Davey Rayburn was coming up with Benny Cashman on deck. Jimmy could hear the crowd going nuts, and he could feel the adrenaline in his own blood. An exciting game. Could be decided in the final at-bat.

As he passed the dark and silent hulk that was Candlestick Park, he listened as Davey Rayburn drove a sharp ground ball to the LA shortstop. It should have been a double play, ending the inning and the game, but the shortstop bobbled the ball. He had no play at second, since Benito had a jump on the pitch, so he made the play at first. Two out, but the Goliaths had a runner in scoring position. Now the roar of the crowd threatened to destroy the speakers in the car radio.

Cashman was taking his position in the batter's box. Jimmy could see the lights of the San Francisco Airport up ahead, and knew his exit was approaching. Not going to miss this game, though, he thought. Might just keep driving all the way to San Jose. The play-by-play announcer was working every last detail of the duel between the opposing pitcher and Cashman. Jimmy was sure that all of San Francisco had stopped to watch and was holding its collective breath. Cashman was a formidable presence at the plate. He was 6'-2" and 230 pounds of fiercely articulated muscle. Jimmy wondered how any pitcher could face him without fear. The announcer reminded him, however, that the closer for Los Angeles was a leading candidate for the Cy Young Award. A clash of titans.

The first pitch was high and inside. High enough and inside enough that Cashman had to twist to avoid it. The fans and the players in the Goliaths' dugout screamed, knowing a brushback when they saw one. Cashman made a half-step towards the mound, but then thought better of it. The Commissioner of Baseball was in the stands for this game. Cashman had his sights set on a higher goal. The pitcher just looked as if butter wouldn't melt in his mouth.

Man, talk about the machismo it takes to be those guys, thought Jimmy. More than a little testosterone. He smiled.

The second pitch, clocked at 97 miles per hour, blew by Cashman. Strike. One and one. Cashman called time and stepped out of the box, adjusting every article of his clothing before climbing back in. Mind games. The third pitch just missed the strike zone – ball. Two and one. Pitch four also just missed. One had to admire Cashman's patience. He wasn't the best hitter in baseball for nothing.

With the next pitch, Cashman connected. The sound of bat hitting ball was explosive, and the ball screamed into the night air. It towered above the 50,000 fans who shouted as one. After a moment of suspension, the ball came crashing down into the stands – just outside the yellow foul pole. Foul ball, and a full count.

Jesus. It doesn't get much better than this for drama, thought Jimmy. He took the San Bruno exit, but then pulled off to the side of the road as soon as he could, so as to give his full attention to the game.

The next four pitches were all fouled off. The first was a rocket into the LA dugout, almost decapitating their manager. The second was fouled back into the backstop, the ball actually bursting through the netting. The third and fourth both made it into the upper decks, causing huge scrums of fans fighting for the souvenirs. This was now a ten pitch at-bat. The fans were getting their money's worth.

Then, suddenly, as if the crowd knew it was about to witness history, a hush fell upon the stadium. Jimmy almost turned up the volume of the radio, thinking something had gone wrong. It was as if everything shifted into slow motion – Cashman's adjusting of his elbow guard, the pitcher's walk around the mound before climbing back on top to scrutinize the catcher's signals. It was so weirdly quiet that when one voice called out 'Go Benny,' it was heard distinctly.

Finally, the pitcher went into his wind-up. A huge intake of breath from the crowd. The ball hurtled towards the plate, pegging the speed gun at close to 100 miles per hour. Benny Cashman took a huge step, putting all his might into crushing the ball into the stratosphere. Every person in the crowd could feel the air current caused by the enormous swing.

Which missed.

The mighty Benny Cashman had struck out.

LXV

Jimmy's text arrived just as they had settled into their positions. Carey had arrived right on time, very sensibly dressed in a sweater, windbreaker, and some well-worn hiking boots. For someone who was always impeccably dressed in the office, she sure could shift gears to outdoor and rugged, thought Maddy.

"It's been a few years, but what the heck. A bonding experience, if nothing else," said Carey. "Too bad about the stench from the dumpsters, though. At least it's cold. Imagine Islamabad in the summer. Once you've lived through that, you can handle just about any sensory experience."

They had been watching the progress of the game on Carlos' iPhone. Even with the slow rate of refreshing the play-by-play on the ESPN.com website, they all got more and more excited with each pitch.

"Helluva game," said Carey. She had brought some hot chocolate in a thermos, along with some blankets for them to sit on. It was kind of cozy. "It would be a remarkable story to really pin that guy. Everyone knows what's going on, but they don't *know* what's going on, you know what I mean?"

Then the text came through. Maddy jumped a little – she had her phone on vibrate and in her pocket. She had been playing with the various settings on her camera. She set it down by her side and pulled out her phone. When she saw the message, she gave a little gasp. She showed it to Carey and Carlos, who gave a thumbs up. Maddy then had an inspiration.

"Allo?"

"Angelique, it's me," whispered Maddy into her phone.

"Bien sur. I have a special ring tone for you."

Maddy wasn't sure she wanted to know what the ring tone was. "Listen," she said, "I need you to do me a really big favor."

"Sure. What do you need?"

"I need you to watch out the front window for Peter Kohler. I think he'll be showing up with a black Lexus SUV. If he hauls out a big crate and takes it upstairs, text me, okay?"

"Okay, I guess. How long should I wait?"

"Probably about ten minutes – they're coming from pretty much just down the street. Can you head there now?"

"I'm already in position. What's in the crate?"

"Something really valuable," said Maddy. "And most likely stolen."

"Nancy Drew!" laughed Angelique. "Okay, I'll let you know."

"Thank you, you're the best," said Maddy.

"By the way, what happens after he takes the crate upstairs?" asked Angelique.

"I don't know. Maybe I'll call the police."

"You should call that nice Chinese boy who stopped by last night," teased Angelique.

"He stopped by last night?" He hadn't mentioned that to Maddy. Shoot. Now he's seen my home, she thought. Now he knows what a slob I am.

"Yes. He was very nice. And good looking, too."

Great. And he's seen Angelique. So much for being the prettiest girl he knows.

"Wait!" Suddenly Angelique's voice dropped to a whisper. "The car. It is here."

Meanwhile, the count on Cashman was full. Carey and Carlos were squirming with excitement.

"Well?"

"It is pulled into the driveway. They're... yes, they're pulling out a big crate. Looks heavy. How strange – I can hear them now on the stairs. It is very valuable, this thing?"

"Very. God, Angelique, you're the best. Thanks!"

"No problem at all. That was easy. When are you coming home?"

"Don't know yet. Could be another late night."

"You be careful. You are working way too hard."

"Tell me about it," whispered Maddy. She didn't want Carey to hear that part. "Talk to you later."

As Maddy hung up, Carey and Carlos were hanging on the tenth pitch of the at-bat. Suddenly the screen on Carlos' iPod showed Final Score. LA had beaten SF. Cashman had struck out.

"Jeez, if he shows up tonight, he's going to be pissed," said Carlos. "Nothing like being the goat."

It was 10:05. Now the wait began in earnest.

LXVI

"Man, nothing like being the goat."

The guy in the dispatch office was still shaking his head over it as he sat down at his desk, having unlocked the door for Jimmy. The television in the background was muted, but it was obvious from the post-game demeanor of the talking heads that Cashman's strikeout was the news of the sporting day.

"The money that guy makes," continued the dispatcher. "All he needed was a single." The shrug of a man who was washing his hands of the whole mess. "What can I do for you, sir?" He was trying to be as pleasant as possible. It didn't do in the livery business to piss off the police.

"Just following up some leads. Nothing much. You've got a car with this license number?" Jimmy slid his notepad across the dispatcher's desk.

"Let me see." The dispatcher tapped his keyboard and looked at his screen. "Yes, officer, that license is one of ours. What do you think? Should I be calling the manager? Or our lawyer?"

"No. Just looking to see who booked that car on Monday night. You know how it is, just the legwork that I've got to do. Checking alibis and stuff."

"Got it. Columbo." The guy immediately dated himself. "Well, on Monday night, it was on call for NTP – Niederman Theatrical Productions. It wouldn't say who was the pick-up – we're on retainer with them."

"Retainer?"

"You know. We always have a car available for them. We're on call."

"Sounds expensive," said Jimmy.

"It's good money for us, that's for sure. But it can be

a pain in the ass. Theatre people. Work all sorts of hours."

"Can you find out who was driving?"

"You sure we're not in any trouble?"

"Not that I know of."

The dispatcher returned his gaze to his monitor. "Ernesto. Ernesto was driving on Monday night."

"Is he on call tonight?"

"No, he's off."

"Can I get a contact number for him, and an address?" asked Jimmy. The dispatcher looked at him over his glasses, sighed, and then gave him Ernesto's cell phone number and address. The address was in East Palo Alto. A crummy neighborhood.

"He'll probably be up. He works most nights, and I don't know how anybody could sleep anyway after that game."

Jimmy thanked him and climbed back into his car. He had to go down there. No one would talk to him over the phone – or at least give him any information that would be useful, and if he announced his arrival, there would be a good chance that Ernesto would take a powder. Jimmy looked at his watch. It was now 10:45. He could be at Ernesto's in about twenty minutes. His night just got longer. He sighed as he climbed back onto the 101 South.

What the heck. It was true. Who could sleep after that game?

LXVII

How long would a ballplayer take to get out of the stadium after a game? Most players were gracious enough to conduct the post-game interviews, however painful, however humiliating. It was part of the contract they made with the fans and with baseball. Most players felt the obligation – on most days they remembered how lucky they were to be playing in the big leagues and being paid small fortunes, and they owed something back. But not Cashman. He owed nothing to anybody, as far as he was concerned. He blew out of the stadium as quickly as possible, offering, at best, a grunt to a team-mate or to his manager, who was left to do damage control.

Benny being Benny. The price we all pay for greatness or genius. What can you do? The Goliath's manager, George Randolph, was an old hand – patient and philosophical. He had, in his forty years in baseball seen pretty much everything. Tomorrow was always another day, and every game offered the possibility of a victory.

*   *   *

Carey was telling Maddy and Carlos about being in Berlin when the wall came down. Within thirty seconds of starting her story, she realized that her interns weren't even alive during that historic event. They had no idea what the Iron Curtain was, or any sense of the Cold War. Carey sighed. It was a good story, though.

They were startled by the roar of a giant car and a dramatic spraying of gravel as it spun into the lot. The Hummer slid to a stop and idled there, the thumping of the bass from its stereo so powerful Maddy could feel it in her chest from yards away. All three observers shrank into the shadows. Carey was visibly excited. Nothing like a tip that panned out – the evening might come together for them. The car sat there, gleaming under the sodium vapor light. No one moved.

A second car, a vintage BMW, pulled into the lot. As its driver climbed out, the door to the Hummer flew open. The thumping of the music cut out. Maddy gasped as Benny Cashman jumped down from the driver's seat. She slowly reached for her camera, careful to not let the viewfinder cast a glow onto her face that would give her away.

"Man, sorry about that game," started Mr. BMW.

"Shut the fuck up," growled Cashman. "Can't fucking win them all."

"Dude, that was a disaster," said Mr. BMW, obviously not too afraid. "Everyone on the planet saw you choke. Nothing like being the goat."

There was a moment of terrible silence while Cashman stared at the other man with a vicious glint in his eye. Suddenly he grabbed the other man by the throat and slammed him up against his BMW. "Don't you ever talk to me like that again," he seethed. "I don't need your shit anymore."

"Hey, man, I'm sorry," gasped the other man. "Won't happen again. My bad, my bad."

Maddy was terrified. Mr. BMW was a big guy. Cashman was shaking him like a rag doll. Some serious testosterone-fuelled rage. The camera was shaking in her hand. She was still waiting for the right moment to take the photo – the exchange was what she wanted.

Cashman relaxed his grip and the other man slid down to the ground, giving a cough. "Let's do this," said Cashman. "I've got places to go."

Mr. BMW reached back into his car, pulling out a little black leather satchel. Cashman reached into his sweatpants pocket and pulled out a wad of bills. He started to hand it to the other man, but then pulled some bills off the top and put them back into his pants. "That's for being a fuck-up," he said. He handed the remainder of the wad to the other man and took the leather satchel.

"Now!" whispered Carey. Maddy pressed the button on the camera. The flash startled everyone.

Oops.

Rookie mistake. She kept her finger on the button, snapping away as fast as possible as Cashman and Mr. BMW stared at her and then started running towards them.

"Motherfucker!" shouted Cashman.

"Run!" shouted Carlos.

"Stop!" shouted Carey. She pulled out her Press badge. "I'm with the Clarion. Don't take another step."

"I don't give a fuck who you are," snarled Cashman. He blew through Carey, knocking her sideways. Her head hit the side of the dumpster and she slumped to the ground, unconscious. Cashman was unfazed by this. "Give me that fucking camera!" he screamed at Maddy. He lunged for her, but she avoided his grasp and she started running as fast as she could, the camera under her arm like a football. Carlos was right in front of her. They barreled out of the parking lot, running instinctively down Third Street towards where they had parked. "Get them!" Cashman shouted to Mr. BMW. Mr. BMW started pounding after them down the street. Cashman jumped into his Hummer and gunned the engine, peeling out of the lot, gravel flying.

Maddy and Carlos had never run so fast. Maddy, at least, was a trained athlete. Carlos was simply scared shitless, so he was able to maintain her pace, at least for the first hundred yards. But Mr. BMW was six foot plus of hard muscle and he was gaining on them. He was just feet from Carlos, who was starting to flag. Mr. BMW stretched out his arm, swiping at Carlos' jacket, just missing. Carlos, feeling the pressure behind him found a burst of adrenaline, and dodged the lunge.

Suddenly, out of a side alley, a shopping cart full of bottles and cans shot out, right in front of Mr. BMW. His momentum caused him to fly right into it and over it. The cart flipped over on top of him, bottles smashing into pieces all over the sidewalk. Mr. BMW slid for a few yards, broken glass slashing his face and arms. He came to an abrupt halt against the side of a fire hydrant, his nose crunching up against it. He jerked for a second and then went limp. As Maddy looked back over her shoulder, she saw old Abe step out of the alley and give her a thumb's up. At least they didn't have to worry about Mr. BMW for the moment.

But the roar of the Hummer on the other side of the median on Third Street served to remind them that they were far from danger. The giant truck, with its headlights glaring, plowed over the median and directly towards them. Maddy and Carlos froze for a moment, then Maddy screamed, "Split up!" She took off towards the Bay, Carlos running in the opposite direction. The Hummer kept after Maddy, she bearing the object of Cashman's desperate desire.

Maddy tore down the sidewalk of 23rd street, the Hummer whipping around the corner on only two wheels. The top-heavy car looked to topple over, but it righted itself, and screamed across the lane towards Maddy. Maddy was running alongside a large industrial building that took up the entire block. Suddenly, to her left, opened up a loading dock, with dumpsters arrayed near the opening, full of cardboard awaiting collection by the recycling company. She thought the dumpsters might block the car from getting to her and ran between them into the dock, but it plowed right through them. She ran out again, having gained a little time as the Hummer ground its way through the wreckage. She continued towards the Bay, looking for someplace to hide, or a route that was too small for the Hummer to negotiate. On her right a dark opening beckoned, and she dashed across the street as the Hummer bore down on her. It was an alley, and the opening was indeed too small for the Hummer. Maddy looked over her shoulder as the truck screeched to a halt, blocking the entrance to the alley. When she looked forward again, she realized that the alley was a dead-end, with a wall rising up in front of her.

Crap, she thought. She turned around to see Cashman leap out of the passenger side of the Hummer. His car was dented and deeply scratched from ramming its way through the dumpsters. That's *really* going to piss him off, thought Maddy. Cashman bounded down the alley. He was not as fast as Mr. BMW, his famously sore knees hampering his movements a bit. But only a bit. Maddy turned to the wall in front of her. It was maybe eight feet tall. Nothing to do but go for it, she thought. She ran as hard as she could and jumped for the top. Her face smacked up against the brick, but she was able to grab the top of the wall. She scrabbled with all her might, and she managed to swing her right foot up and onto the wall. As she pulled herself up, she felt the grip of a giant hand on her left ankle. It was as firm as a vise. In a heartbeat she was yanked off the wall, falling the eight feet to the asphalt below. Through all of this, she managed to shield the camera from harm, protecting it like a baby. She landed on her butt with a smack that knocked the wind out of her. Cashman's hand was crushing her ankle, causing her to cry out in pain.

"You fucked up my new car," he seethed. "Now give me the fucking camera before I kill you."

LXVIII

The little house was at the end of the street, a small bungalow dating from the Twenties. It sat in its yard, a little sad, and more than a little tired. It was just after 11:00. Jimmy wasn't sure if it was a good idea to disturb its occupants, but he then saw the steel blue flickering light of a television through the closed curtains. He climbed out of his car and approached the little gate in the fence that surrounded the little yard. As he lifted the latch, a big German Shepherd came running at him from around the side of the house. It barked, and then leapt up at Jimmy. Jimmy threw up his arms to block the attack, only to find himself receiving an adoring tongue bath.

"Hey, now," he said trying not to get licked to death. "That's a good dog." He found, though, that the dog was serving some sort of protective purpose, as he was unable to move forward towards the house.

"Beatrice! Down, girl!" The voice was firm but gentle. The dog quickly obeyed. "Come here and sit!" With only a backward glance at her new boyfriend, Beatrice jogged over to her master.

"Some watchdog," he continued. "How can I help you?"

It was only then that Jimmy saw the gun in the man's hand. He was holding a beer in the other. Welcome to East Palo Alto.

"I'm looking for Ernesto Gonzalez."

"And who are you?" asked the man. Beatrice had settled down at his feet at the top of the porch. The gun was still leveled at Jimmy.

"Police Detective James Wang, SFPD." Jimmy gestured towards his jacket pocket. With a wave of the gun, the man acceded to Jimmy's implied request. Jimmy slowly pulled out his badge, holding it out to catch the light from the streetlamp. The man squinted at it, then took Jimmy in with a steady gaze. After a moment, he tucked the gun into the back of his pants.

"You don't look like an asshole. Do you want a beer?"

"I would, actually," said Jimmy with some relief.

"Come on up. I'm Ernesto. This is Beatrice, but you've met already. She's the terror of the neighborhood, as you can doubtless tell." He gave the dog a thump on her shoulder, and she wagged her tail. Ernesto held the screen door open for Jimmy and they went into his house.

The living room was tiny. The whole place was tiny – Jimmy ducked as he entered out of an instinct of being too tall for the room. The TV was on in the corner opposite a shabby sofa, with a cooler of beer right at the arm of the sofa. Ernesto gestured towards an armchair, and Jimmy had a seat. Ernesto then pulled a Dos Equis out of the cooler and popped it open, handing it to Jimmy. He pulled out another, opened it, and sat down on the sofa, reaching for the remote to mute the TV.

He was a small dark-skinned man, with black hair, graying at the temples. His moustache was grayer. Although he was wearing jeans and a t-shirt, he was well-groomed and carried himself well. A chauffeur. "Did you see that game?" he asked Jimmy, gesturing towards the TV.

"No, but I listened to it on the radio."

"You should have seen it. Did you ever see the famous game with Kirk Gibson at the plate? Against the A's? That guy was dying, could barely walk, bottom of the ninth, two out, and he hit the winning home run. That's greatness. I don't know. Cashman, man... it's not right."

Jimmy tilted his beer in Ernesto's direction. The

toast, or salute, was returned. Two guys hanging out, talking baseball.

"Nice place," said Jimmy out of politeness.

"Used to be nicer," Ernesto stared into the middle distance. "Maria – she could keep a home."

Jimmy was smart enough to stay silent.

"We miss her, don't we, girl?" said Ernesto to Beatrice. Beatrice just rolled over onto her side. "I miss her every day. Cancer. She was so beautiful..." Ernesto took a moment. Jimmy became aware of the stack of empty bottles by the side of the cooler. After a few minutes, he asked gently:

"May I ask you a few questions about your work? I'm sorry to trouble you on your night off."

"It's okay," said Ernesto, stoically. "What do you want to know?"

"You were driving on Monday night, weren't you?"

"Yes. It was a late night."

"Who was your hire?"

"I was on call for Mrs. Niederman."

"Was she in the car when you stopped at UN Plaza?"

Ernesto suddenly got a spooked look in his eye. "How do you know that we stopped at UN Plaza?"

"We just know. It's funny about these things. Some things we know, other things we don't. So, who was in the car when you stopped at UN Plaza?"

"I dropped Mrs. Niederman at her home in Pacific Heights, first thing. It was Mr. John who was still in the car. He lives in Hillsborough, down the freeway a bit, so we went down Hyde Street."

"I know the route. Mr. John..."

"He's just Mr. John to me. I don't know his last name. In all this time, I never heard his last name. She always just calls him John."

"And he asked you to pull over?"

"Yes. He had some leftovers from the party. We, I mean they, were at an event. He wanted to give them away. It was nice of him, don't you think?"

"Yes. Very kind. What does Mr. John look like?"

"Round. Soft. Balding, with light brown hair. Pretty non-descript."

"Beady eyes?"

"How did you know?" Ernesto again looked spooked.

"We just know stuff, that's all. Listen, thanks for the beer. You look tired. I should say goodnight."

Ernesto looked a strange combination of relieved and sad. Jimmy thought about how lonely he must be. He was certainly relieved to not be in any trouble, but Jimmy could sense that he spent many nights alone. Thank God for Beatrice.

"Say, you're a long way from your beat. Drive safe, okay?"

"Okay. I'll let myself out." As Beatrice rose to poke him in the leg, he gave her a pat. As he pulled the screen door gently behind him, Jimmy watched as Ernesto closed his eyes. Beatrice went and curled herself up at his feet.

LXIX

"Give me the fucking camera before I kill you."

He still had her ankle, but she was kicking for all she was worth with the other leg, all the while shielding the camera from his outstretched arm. Damn, he was angry. She could see the veins in his neck bulging, and his mouth was foaming, causing him to look like a rabid dog. His eyes were wild with rage. He made one more lunge at the camera, then his eyes got even wider.

He gasped. Suddenly his grip on Maddy's ankle released. At that moment, Maddy saw a giant gloved hand clutching Cashman from behind and between his legs. Maddy winced – that's got to hurt, she thought. Another giant gloved hand had Cashman by the back of his neck.

Everyone knew Cashman's stats by this point. 6'-2," 230 pounds. Maddy stared in horrified fascination as he was lifted, by his crotch and his neck, straight up into the air. A perfect clean and jerk.

The Masked Avenger stood there, holding baseball's greatest home-run hitter up in the air over his head. Cashman's arms and legs flailed, but the grip was relentless. A stream of profanity flowed from Cashman's mouth, but he remained up on his back like an overturned tortoise. After taking a moment to stabilize himself, the Masked Avenger turned, and then carried his burden a few steps down the alley. He threw it at the Hummer. Cashman went head-first through the passenger door window.

Maddy was awestruck. Her one lucid thought was, thank God for safety glass.

There was a terrible moment when Maddy thought that the Masked Avenger had killed Cashman, but the groan emanating from the front seat of the car gave her some small reassurance. The Masked Avenger turned back to her and knelt down beside her.

"Are you all right, my friend?" he asked gently.

"I'm going to have a huge bruise on my butt, but otherwise, I think I'm okay," said Maddy. "Thank you for saving me... I think."

"He hurt you. His punishment is just. Here, let me help you."

The Masked Avenger's idea of helping Maddy was to scoop her up and carry her in his arms. "It's okay," she said. "I can walk, really. It's only going to hurt when I sit down." With that, he set her gently on her feet. "Now how are we going to get out of here? That Hummer is completely blocking the alley. And we better make sure Mr. Cashman isn't bleeding to death."

They went up to the car. Cashman was knocked out but was breathing. All things considered, he was going to be okay – just the biggest headache he ever had, and a few stitches on his face.

"I should call 911," Maddy said. "He's in no shape to drive."

"Call them once we are away from here." This was pretty good advice. If Maddy ever thought she was in trouble before this, she was in seriously deep shit now.

"Yes," she replied. "You have to get as far away from here as possible."

"I know," replied the Masked Avenger.

"No, I don't think you really do. I made a deal with the police." Maddy made a face. "They let me avoid telling them where you were as long as you didn't hurt anybody else. Now I have no choice but to help them find you." She sighed. "To say I'm conflicted would be an understatement."

"I understand. Do what you must. I'll be safe." With that, he grabbed the Hummer's roof rack and pulled himself up and on to the top of the car. For a moment, standing there on the roof of the Hummer like a hunter on top of his fallen elephant, with his plastic cape snapping in the late-night breeze, he again recalled in Maddy's mind a true caped crusader. A dark, haunted, heroic figure. She had the presence of mind to snap the photo. In the next instant, he bounded off the car and was gone.

*   *   *

To get out of the alley, Maddy found the easiest way around the Hummer was to go under it. The car was so jacked up on its wheels that there was plenty of clearance for her, although crawling along on her backside hurt like the dickens. As her head poked through the other side, she saw Carlos standing there in wonder. "Give me a hand," she called out, and Carlos quickly obliged.

"Jesus Christ," he said as he surveyed the scene. "Some serious-ass mayhem. Is he going to be alright?"

"I don't know. I've never seen a man thrown through a car window before. Especially a man that big."

"How does he do it?"

"Who? The Masked Avenger? I don't know. You read these stories about mothers picking up cars to save their children. Something must just happen to him in these moments, and he just tears things up. Some sort of instinct."

"Some instinct. So, what do we do now?"

"We better go find out if Carey's okay, and we'd better get the heck out of Dodge before the police show up."

"Roger that," said Carlos. They jogged down the street back towards the lot behind the warehouse. They came to the spot where Mr. BMW had come to rest. He was still unconscious. Abe was picking up the bottles and cans that were salvageable.

"He'll be okay," he said. "If he comes to, and threatens any trouble, I'll take care of him." Abe tapped an empty wine bottle in his hand. I'll bet you would, thought Maddy. Never underestimate an old sailor. "And he won't be chasing after anybody, either. Slashed his tires."

By the time they reached the parking lot, Carey was sitting up - Marcus, Charelle and Jasmine clustered around her. "She needs to get to the hospital," said Marcus. "She's got a nasty bump on her head."

"I need to get to the Clarion," said Carey, testily. "I'm fine. We've got news to get to print. Where's Cashman?"

When Maddy told Carey what had happened, Carey's eyes grew wide. "Cashman and the Masked Avenger? It doesn't get any better than this. Let's go."

Maddy ran the two blocks to her car and returned to pick up Carey and Carlos. Carey agreed that she shouldn't try to drive. She gave the keys to her car to Carlos, and they all headed back towards downtown, after thanking the Dogpatch gang for their intervention.

"Where's the Masked Avenger?" Charelle had asked.

"I don't know," said Maddy. "He had to make himself scarce."

"I hope he's okay. I liked him," Charelle said wistfully.

"I'll stay in touch," said Maddy, giving her a hug. "You okay?"

"I'll be fine. You take care now."

On the way back to the Clarion, Maddy made two calls. For the first, she stopped at the first payphone she spotted – maybe the last payphone in all of San Francisco, she thought as she pulled over. The call was to 911. She refused to give her name, and she stated simply that she had seen a man's legs sticking out of his car, as if there had been some sort of accident. This did not go over well with the dispatcher, who wanted more information. Maddy said that the neighborhood looked so unsafe she had been unwilling to investigate further.

On checking the cross-streets, the dispatcher said she understood. Maddy then climbed back into her car and made the second call to Jimmy who was on his way home from East Palo Alto. He insisted on meeting them at the Clarion. It was time to clear some air and to put some pieces of the puzzles together.

Another late night.

LXX

Midnight oil was being burned at the Clarion. The Editor-in-Chief, Paul Stone, who had returned to the office upon hearing the news, was already fielding the phone call from Cashman's lawyer.

"If you publish a single one of those photos, the Clarion will be sued for defamation of character," the lawyer insisted.

"Which character would that be?" replied Stone. "Everyone already knows he's an asshole, now everyone will know he's a cheat, as well." He slammed down the phone, with more than a little satisfaction. "That's why we keep good lawyers on retainer," he said, looking over at Carey. Her husband, one of said lawyers, was on his way.

Carey was torn. On one hand, she was part of one of the biggest local news stories in recent memory, on the other, it looked as if her weekend was going to be shot to hell. The price one pays for great journalism.

They all gathered in the conference room to compare notes and to strategize. Maddy's photos had been printed out, eliciting whistles from Carey and Paul Stone. The shots of Cashman with cash in hand in exchange for the pouch was incriminating enough - especially when the pouch in question had been gathered up by Marcus and placed into Carey's custody. But the shot of the Masked Avenger on top of Cashman's Hummer, with Cashman's legs dangling out of the front passenger window, was deemed sensational enough to make the front page.

"We won't make the morning edition," said Stone, "but we can get this out and online by the afternoon. Now who's going to write this thing?"

Carey's response was immediate and clear. "It's her story," she said gesturing towards Maddy, "she should write it."

"Her by-line?"

"Hers and Carlos'. Good work deserves its reward. I'll review prior to submission."

"Which had better be by this morning," replied Stone. "If we're going to make the afternoon, I need this on my desk by eight." Maddy and Carlos were so excited that they gave each other a fist pump. It was at that moment that Jimmy Wang entered the room.

"Sorry to crush your groove," he said, "but no one's writing anything until we get some answers." He had Detective Chen with him, along with a couple of cops in uniform.

"Our legal counsel is on his way," said Stone.

"That's fine, we'll wait," said Jimmy. "You guys got any coffee?"

*   *   *

They decided to round-table it. It was a full room: Jimmy, Detective Chen, Maddy, Carlos, Carey, Paul Stone and Carey's husband, Robert Portman. After getting each person's version of the events, Jimmy scratched his head.

"There was no one at the scene by the time the emergency team got there, so Cashman must have been able to drive away on his own. I understand you've already heard from his lawyer, so he's already made a few calls. He's got a serious Assault and Battery against your Masked Avenger – I hope the MA's got a good lawyer."

"And I've got some serious Assault and Battery against Cashman," said Maddy, pulling up the leg of her jeans to show a very nasty bruise on her ankle. "Don't make me show you my butt." Carlos snorted, causing everyone in the room to look at him sternly.

"And let's not forget my head," said Carey, whose face was turning more purple by the minute.

"So where do we stand?" asked Jimmy. "We can try to bring in Cashman for questioning, but he's currently inaccessible. And until we analyze the contents of the pouch, it is unclear, other than the alleged assault on Ms. Stevenson and Ms. Portman, that any other crime has been committed. What is the Clarion's intention?"

Paul Stone looked at his notes. "We still have a story here. The facts are still damning, regardless of chemical analysis. We're going to run it."

"Including the Masked Avenger," said Jimmy.

"He's as big a news story as Cashman. Maybe more so. San Francisco now has its own vigilante defender of justice."

Jimmy turned to Maddy. "We had an understanding. As much as he continues to be in the right place at the right time, and it's clear he saved you from some serious harm, he has still crossed a line. It's time for us to bring him in. Where is he?"

"I don't honestly know," said Maddy. "By the time I got out from the alley, he was long gone."

"And you have no way to locate him?"

Maddy looked at Carlos who was biting his lip.

"No," she replied, after a moment.

"May I have your phone, please?" Maddy was prepared for this and handed it over. Robert Portman objected, but Maddy said it was okay. Jimmy scrolled through the address book, and then the recent calls and found only the call to him. He sighed, as he put the phone down on the conference table.

"You deleted his number, didn't you?"

Maddy said nothing. She knew that Jimmy couldn't be sure that she had had the number. She would keep this secret.

"Do you have any idea where he might have gone to hide?" asked Jimmy as evenly as possible.

"He could be anywhere. I've met him at the Park, at Hills Plaza and around the Orpheum. I doubt he would return to any of those places."

"Right. Well, he's to be found. And I'm going to find him with or without your help."

"He's helped you in many ways, though," said Maddy. "He's helped you get close to finding out who killed Lucky Jerry, and he's also got us close to Peter Kohler. Doesn't that count for anything?"

"It could count for a lot. But he can't be on the streets anymore."

Meanwhile, Paul Stone was almost apoplectic. "Lucky Jerry? Peter Kohler? What the hell else is going on here?"

Another half hour went by, with Maddy, Carlos, Carey, and even Jimmy recounting the events as they knew them over the last four days. Paul Stone turned to Carey.

"How much are we paying these two?"

"Nothing. They're interns."

Paul Stone turned to Maddy and Carlos. "Story on my desk by eight. Then we meet with HR at nine. You two are now hired, full-time." He turned to Jimmy. "Any other questions, Detective?"

"Not at the moment, sir, although I would like a word with Ms. Stevenson alone."

"Before we break up, how long until we can receive a chemical analysis on the stuff in the bag?" asked Stone.

"It will take a few days," said Jimmy. "Our lab..." He stopped and made a face. Maddy, Carlos and even Carey all said in unison:

"The Man Without a Face."

Jimmy just sighed as he withdrew one of the vials from the leather pouch and slid it across the conference room table towards Maddy.

*   *   *

"Alright, Nancy Drew, let's go through it by the numbers." Jimmy had not forgotten that she hated being called that, but he was very frustrated with her. "We had a deal. We were to share everything. I'm sharing all I got with you, you're still holding out on me with the Masked Avenger. I know you know how to get a hold of him or know where he is."

"You're wrong. I really don't." She sighed. She was feeling stupidly tired by now, and she still had a front-page story to write. Photocopying and making coffee sounded more her speed at this moment. "But you're right to be upset. I'm sorry. I did have his phone number, but I deleted it. I didn't want to be in this position, and I felt the most honorable thing was to eliminate my ability to compromise him."

"He's a dangerous maniac."

"This is why I deleted his number. I know he isn't, but you'll never see it that way. Benny Cashman is a dangerous maniac. He's the one who shouldn't be on the street. Peter Kohler is a crook, and he's raping the history of a disenfranchised people. And there's still someone out there who murdered homeless people, and we haven't brought him to justice. I can't imagine the Masked Avenger belongs in their company."

"So, you don't know where he is?"

"I don't. He's canny in his way. Maybe it's because of the way he sees the world, but he sees opportunities that we don't. He could find a place to hide, and we'd probably never find him, if he wanted that. Right now, he knows he's in danger – I told him I was in this position. He understood. All he's ever done since I met him was to try to protect me, so to protect me now, he'll probably go into hiding."

"All I've ever done since I met you was to try to protect you, too," said Jimmy quietly.

Maddy looked down. She then slid her hand across the table and put it on top of Jimmy's. "I know. I'm sorry." She then gave him a sad smile. "We have three

305

other mysteries to solve, still. That's plenty for us to do. When the time comes, we'll both do our best to take care of the Masked Avenger."

Jimmy gave her hand a squeeze. "Alright," he said. "Let's go to work."

LXXI

The windows near Maddy's and Carlos' desks faced north. They took a break to watch the white stone on the building across from them change color from lavender to peach to gold to white as the sun rose, the slanting light from the east casting the facade in sharp relief. During the night there was a lot of comparing of notes, editing of text, and moments of sheer punch-drunkenness. But they got it done. They emailed it to Carey, who had been taken to the Emergency Room as a precaution and who was then put to bed – with her laptop. She emailed back her edits, and they then posted it onto the intranet at the Clarion. It was time for the other people in the chain of newspaper publishing to do their jobs. Maddy and Carlos were done with theirs.

For the night.

They then scanned the video from Justin's site, and clocked the moment when two figures hauled a large crate from the service entrance into the now famous black Lexus SUV. Maddy and Carlos laughed when they watched the confrontation with Jimmy. The video was downloaded and processed. One more brick in the wall, thought Maddy. At some point, this has got to add up to something.

Upon pressing the "Send" button, both Maddy and Carlos decided to head out for a well-deserved breakfast. They were willing to travel far, so they headed up to Lombard Street and the Home Plate. Apt name, thought Maddy. The diner was greasy, it was small, it was perfect. She hadn't eaten since the famous burrito more than twelve hours before, and she did some serious damage to a Denver omelette as Carlos climbed all over the Lumberjack Breakfast.

Lumberjack Breakfast. Maddy laughed out loud.

"Did you ever call that guy back?" she asked as she mopped up the grease on her plate with her sourdough toast.

"Which guy?"

"The guy at the restaurant. Robert."

"Oh, crap. We've been so busy, I totally forgot."

"So, you gonna call him? He sounded nice."

Carlos looked at his last piece of bacon. After a moment he scooped it up and finished it off. "I guess so. I'm sort of feeling out of practice. Dating, I mean."

"I know how you feel."

"Liar. You've got your dueling boyfriends."

"They're not my boyfriends!" She kicked him under the table. "Oh, Carlos. I'm so over Justin. He really is just an old boyfriend. But what am I going to do with Jimmy? I feel like every encounter with him is so fraught. I don't know. Maybe I'm just too high-strung."

"High maintenance, that's for sure. You could try letting him be right once in a while."

Maddy considered this.

"I'm joking," said Carlos. "I think it bodes well for the relationship. From what I can tell, you won't be bored, and I think he really likes you. I can see he wants to look out for you. Otherwise, you'd be in jail by now."

"Oh! Now that you mention it, how much trouble do you think we're going to be in once the news hits the stands?"

"Nothing that Carey's husband can't handle. We might have to go to court or something, but I can't see how we did anything wrong. He's the one who's got everything to lose if he comes after us. Talk about bad publicity."

"How much do you think they'll offer us, now that we're supposed to be on staff?"

"I have no idea," said Carlos. "You know, when I decided I wanted to pursue a career in journalism, I never even thought about what a journalist gets paid.

Isn't that funny?"

"No, I didn't even think about it either, until just now. That *is* funny. What does that say about us?"

"It means that we love what we do," said Carlos. "I think I would do this for free."

"We *were* doing it for free," said Maddy. "Well, at least I won't have to ask my dad to keep paying for my car. That will feel really good, you know?"

"I wouldn't know. My dad never gave me anything. I had to work for every penny. That doesn't mean that I wouldn't mind being somebody's 'kept boy.'"

"Well then you need to find a nice older man."

"I'm not wired that way," replied Carlos, ruefully. "I'm too much of a romantic. I'm marrying for love. Which means I'm just setting myself up for heartache, I'm sure."

"Hey, what time is it?" asked Maddy suddenly.

"Eight o'clock, why?"

"We're supposed to be at HR at nine. Let's order some French Toast to go."

"What for?" asked Carlos.

"We owe Little Mary a breakfast, at least."

"That we do," said Carlos, pushing back from the table and heading for the register.

"That we do."

LXXII

His sleep was disturbed by the beeping of a truck backing up. He was still groggy when he heard the giant loading dock door being ratcheted open. From his vantage point high above the auditorium, he could see the light pour onto the stage from the outside, catching the dozens of stagehands in the bright, gray light. The load-in was underway.

This will be hard staying out of sight with all of this going on, he thought. With a new production, there would be technicians all over the building, even possibly in the crawlspace in the ceiling above the catwalks, where he had found refuge. And the hours they kept would be long. At least there would be music. He hoped it would be good.

Robin was perched on a beam, fascinated by the activity a hundred feet beneath them. After a few minutes, she jumped down onto the catwalk below and then disappeared. The Masked Avenger was a little concerned by this, but then reflected that Robin was getting older, and had to learn, as they all did, how to fend for herself. She would be alright.

Sure enough, after about ten minutes, Robin was sitting at the edge of the stage, watching large boxes being rolled off the trucks and into positions against the back wall. Stagehands were pulling lighting equipment out of the boxes, trusses were being assembled, cables were being run. It was fascinating. After a while, one of the stagehands looked out towards the auditorium and noticed the kitten sitting there.

"Hey," he said. "We've got a theatre cat!"

Another stagehand stopped to look. "That's good luck. I wonder where she came from? We should take care of her."

Everyone stopped for a moment. Someone went and got a sandwich out of their lunch. "Do you think she'll eat tuna fish?"

"Dude, all cats eat tuna."

The tuna was placed at the edge of the proscenium, deemed the safest place on the stage for the time being. After a moment's hesitation, Robin trotted over, sniffed the tuna, and began to eat. The Masked Avenger watched and shrugged to himself. She'll be fine.

The first stagehand, a tall fellow with dark hair, went over and picked her up. "She can hang in the booth with me," he said. "What shall we name her?"

"What's the name of the girl leopard in the show?" someone asked.

"Sheba. Like the Queen of Sheba. We'll call her Sheba."

A voice rang out. "What the fuck is going on here?" Everyone froze as a heavy-set, balding man in a suit came onto the stage. "At forty bucks an hour, all of you get your asses in gear. We've got to get this up in two days. Jesus. And get that fucking cat out of here."

The tall stagehand scooped up the kitten and the food and vanished off into the wings. Everyone went back to work, the heavy-set, balding man moving downstage to observe the progress of the load-in.

Up in his perch, gazing through the empty hole that used to contain one of the house lights, the Masked Avenger watched. He knew that heavy-set, balding man. There was something about him that triggered a sixth sense within the man in black and gray.

I don't know why, but I hate that guy.

LXXIII

The French Toast was gratefully received, and Little Mary and Beth were fascinated by the story as it had unfolded. Little Mary couldn't help feeling responsible for all the mayhem that had ensued and was very concerned about the damage inflicted on Maddy. Maddy reassured her that she was fine, and that Mary had played a valuable part in getting the story off the ground.

Maddy and Carlos then said they had to get back to the Clarion.

"We're going to get real jobs," said Maddy with excitement.

"Good for you, duck," said Beth with a big smile, but in that moment Maddy realized what a schmuck she had just been. She had been so self-involved that she had forgotten that Beth's job was working the rush hour trade from her wheelchair, and Little Mary, well, Maddy didn't want to think about Little Mary's way of staying alive.

"I'm sorry," said Maddy. "I'm counting my chickens before they're actually hatched. I'll let you know if this turns out to be the real thing."

"We'll keep our fingers crossed," said Beth. "Now I've got to get a nap before this afternoon's rush. Come on, Mary. Same for you."

As they headed towards the Clarion, Carlos looked over at Maddy. "You're awfully thoughtful all of a sudden."

"I was so inconsiderate back there."

"What do you mean? They got some fine French Toast."

"I know. It's just that you'd think we could do more

than just give them food every once in a while."

"That's more than most people will ever do for them."

"But does that mean that it's enough?"

"Too much white guilt, Chica. You're doing the best you can."

"I wonder." She was quiet for the rest of the drive, which was really just circling around in the parking garage.

They arrived at the desk of the Human Resources Director of the Clarion. Madge Brighton shook their hands and then asked Maddy to wait outside her office while she talked with Carlos. As Maddy settled into an uncomfortable, modern leather chair, causing her to wince with the pain emanating from her rear end, her phone rang.

"Hi there, Nan... I mean, Maddy. How's your butt?"

Maddy laughed. Unpredictable? Incorrigible. "It hurts like shit if you really want to know. What's up?"

"I've got tickets to tonight's game. Final game of the season."

"No way."

"Way. My dad scored them for me. He's got a few connections, to say the least. Would you want to go?"

"I was going to sleep for twenty-four hours straight, but what the hey, I'm still standing, so sure."

"It should be pretty sensational, what with the news and all," said Jimmy. "I can't imagine that Cashman will show after last night's misadventure. Still, if the Goliaths win, they win the division. A lot at stake. So, you're up for it?"

"Wouldn't miss it," said Maddy as the door to Madge Brighton's office opened. "Hey, I've got to go."

"Meet you at the statue at seven – we'll just eat at the game."

"Cool. Bye!" Carlos came out, carrying a big file folder and gave Maddy a thumb's up. Madge held the door open and Maddy went in.

"Have a seat," said Madge.

"May I stand, please?" asked Maddy. As Madge looked at her over her glasses, Maddy explained. "I'm sorry. I was injured in the line of duty and it kind of hurts to sit down."

"I understand," said Madge Brighton. She probably couldn't, having much more padding than Maddy had, but she sounded sincere. She sat herself in her chair, adjusted her reading glasses and looked over her notes. "Mister Stone would like you to be full-time here at the Clarion. Congratulations."

"Thanks!" said Maddy. "It's something of a dream come true."

"Well, there's more than a little paperwork to fill out – you might change your mind," said Madge revealing a slight sense of humor. She pulled out a huge folder stuffed with forms.

"Do I fill them out now?" Maddy asked, her eyes getting large.

"You can take them to your desk. Let's see..." Madge reeled off a sequence of forms – waivers, disclaimers, personal contact info, medical history, insurance applications. Maddy felt more overwhelmed than she had in the clutches of Benny Cashman. This was, after all, her first real job.

Then Madge reached into a filing cabinet and pulled out The Sacred Object. It glowed with an inner light, and Maddy thought she heard angels singing. It was her Clarion press badge.

"It's a temp badge for now. Once we get all of the paperwork together, we'll get you set up properly – full photo ID."

Maddy felt terribly awkward all of a sudden. "May I ask how much I'm getting paid?"

"Oh. Right. I nearly forgot." Madge pulled out another folder, flipped through it and found Maddy's offer sheet. She slid it over to Maddy. "I hope this is okay – you know, times being what they are, no one is being paid enough. Look it over, and if you accept the offer, please initial here."

Maddy looked at the offer. She suddenly became aware that it could be more than that, but she was still grateful, all the same. She initialed the sheet and slid it back to Madge.

"Well, that's that, then," said Madge. "Just get those back to me as soon as you can. The sooner I get them, the sooner you get paid."

"That's an incentive," said Maddy. "I'll get them to you on Monday." She shook Madge's hand and turned towards the door. As she put her hand on the knob, she turned back to Madge. "Are there any openings at the Clarion for any other positions?"

"How do you mean?" asked Madge, pulling off her glasses.

"Like, I don't know. Secretarial, or custodial."

"Funny that you ask. I just posted two positions this morning. You can imagine, with this economy, how many resumes I've received and it's only ten o'clock."

"What are the positions?" asked Maddy.

"One is in accounts receivable, and the other is in the mail room."

"I know two people who could really use those jobs and could do them great."

Madge was looking at her computer screen. She wrinkled her nose. "I've got applications from people with law degrees. Here's one with a degree in Computer Science. Used to work for Delphi Software. I've got no shortage of over-qualified applicants."

"I'm sure, Ms. Brighton," said Maddy with her most sincere and pleading expression. "But the people I'm talking about really *need* those jobs. Like, it would help them get off the streets. And I know they'd be great. They wouldn't be able to post their resumes online or anything, but... Is there any way they could apply?"

Madge chewed her lower lip. "Can you get them in here for some interviews this afternoon? Before five?"

"I'll do my best. You'd be saving two lives."

"Well, I don't know about that... I'll see what I can do."

Maddy ran around Madge Brighton's desk and gave her a huge hug. It occurred to Maddy that it might have been a while since Madge last had a hug. It then occurred to Maddy that she needed to go home and take a shower. She had been going for almost thirty hours straight.

LXXIV

"Where's the Masked Avenger?" wheezed the Man Without a Face as he opened the door to his lair.

"He's had to go into hiding. I'm not sure where he is," said Maddy. "I hope I didn't wake you. I wasn't sure how early, I mean, how late…"

"It's okay. I don't sleep much. Come in."

Maddy had had a hard time finding him. It was noon, and she had felt more than a little awkward about climbing down a ventilation shaft in broad daylight. She had decided to go in through the front door and take an elevator down to a sub-basement. The trick was that the elevator required a key to get to that floor. She had been about to give up, when an old maintenance man pulled up next to her with his cart full of fluorescent lamps and tools.

"Where you headed, Sweetie?" he asked with a little bit of a leer.

"I'm trying to get to the sub-basement," replied Maddy. Ick, she thought.

"Now why would you want to do that, now?" asked the maintenance man suspiciously. "There are monsters down there that eat little girls like you."

"I'm sure. I think I can take them, though."

After sizing her up, the old man stroked his chin. "I'll bet you could. Alright, I'll give you a lift."

"Thank you," said Maddy civilly.

It had been a creepy ride down in the elevator, Maddy half afraid the maintenance man might try something. As soon as the doors had opened, Maddy had bolted out and down the hall. "Good luck with those monsters," the maintenance man had laughed after her.

It was a maze. After multiple wrong turns and

switchbacks, Maddy had finally found the steel door.

"Come in," repeated the Man Without a Face. "To what do I owe the honor?"

"Well, we need your help again. I've got something that needs chemical analysis, and, well, you're the best man for the job."

"Is this to help our friend?"

"No, this time it's for me."

The Man Without a Face hesitated.

"I work for the Clarion, and I've been authorized to compensate you for your efforts."

"No compensation necessary. I'm... I'm taken care of. It would be a pleasure. What have we got?"

Maddy pulled out the vial from her shoulder bag. "We think it's some sort of steroid or human growth hormone."

"Where did you get this?"

Maddy explained what had transpired. The Man Without a Face looked troubled. As much as his face could look troubled.

"That's too bad," he said. "I've been a Goliaths fan for a long time. As a lot, we've been willing to suspend our doubts in the hopes of a championship. And it's been exciting to follow the chase for a home run record." He sighed. "I hate cheaters. Now there'll always be an asterisk."

"Well, this is our proof, one way or another. The circumstantial evidence is pretty strong, but this would nail it."

"Why aren't the police handling this? This would be more their deal, wouldn't it?"

"That's just it. They're overbooked. And, to be honest, my paper wants to be on top of this story. You've shown that you're fast and you're an expert."

The Man Without a Face bowed theatrically. "I've got plenty of time to practice. I'm not going on any dates, or anything."

"When could you get the results back to me?"

"Sometime tomorrow."

"Is there any way I can get in touch with you?" asked Maddy. She enjoyed the "face time," but she also had many items still on her agenda and bouncing back and forth to Berkeley was time consuming.

"I'll send you an email. What's your address?"

Maddy was caught a little off guard. In the Masked Avenger's world, people didn't seem to have access to the Internet. She was embarrassed that she hadn't thought that a scientist of the Man Without a Face's stature would be online all the time. She wrote out her email address.

"Thank you,' said Maddy. She hesitated, then dove in, as she had become used to do over the last few days. "The Masked Avenger told me a bit about you. I'm terribly sorry for your accident."

"Accident? This wasn't an accident."

"Oh."

"I did this to myself. An atonement for a young life lived stupidly."

"But that's... that's terrible!" Maddy couldn't help herself. "How could you... disfigure yourself like this?"

The Man Without a Face sat down on his stool and sighed. "Have you ever heard the expression 'Suicide by Cop?' This was meant to be suicide by deliberate stupidity. Allowing myself to make a mistake that I would never have made unless I chose to make the mistake. Have you ever had a moment in your life when you have a choice to extricate yourself from something, or to allow yourself to be destroyed by it? I chose to let myself be destroyed."

"But why? The Masked Avenger said that you never hurt anybody."

"It depends on how you define 'anybody.' Animals are people, too – to use the oft quoted expression. I allowed myself to believe the leader of our animal rights group, and I came to believe that only through violent acts could we effect radical change. I set off a bomb at a research lab, hoping to destroy the facility. In the process I killed hundreds of animals that I had hoped to save. Monkeys, rabbits, pigs, dogs, and cats. I feel the weight of their souls, and I still hear their cries of pain, every day. The next bomb I set, I somehow chose to… linger too long. I had hoped to die."

"But you lived," said Maddy. She was profoundly moved by this confession.

"I did. And as I lay in my bed in the hospital, I faced another choice. To allow myself to die, or to take my talent – for I did have talent – and use it to save lives. I realized that giving up - choosing to die - was the most selfish thing I could do. And that a life lived with this disfigurement might just be penance enough."

"What do you do?"

"I mostly bring in grant money from the Army."

"You do work for the military?"

"Ironic, isn't it? But I help to develop anti-toxins. And I have developed topical medications to help burn victims – a personal interest, as I'm sure you can understand." He sighed. "I can't stop people from fighting each other, but I can help them from killing each other."

"Is there anything I can do for you?" asked Maddy, her voice just above a whisper.

"You're a kind person," said the Man Without a Face. "Stop by, every once in a while."

"I will." Maddy was thoughtful. "The Masked Avenger said to me, 'There are some mistakes that…' and he never finished the thought. It was in the context of our conversation about you, but I feel strongly that he was thinking of his own past. What do you know about him?"

"Not much, really," replied the Man Without a Face. "I've never known anyone so guarded about his past, or his name. But he carries a weight even deeper than mine."

"I know. I can feel that, too." Maddy turned to leave. "Thank you for all of your help. I'll come back to visit soon."

"Here. You'll need this." The Man Without a Face held something in his hand.

It was an elevator key.

LXXV

Maddy was weaving her way back across the Bay Bridge when Carlos called. "It's been posted on the website. It's getting a mind-boggling number of hits. We're famous. And there's going to be a press conference at TBD Park in fifteen minutes."

"I'm just coming into the City off the Bridge. Who's covering it? I can be there in minutes," replied Maddy.

"Sean Ostling, the lead sports columnist, is going. I'm sure he'd love to meet you."

Maddy saw her press badge poking out of her purse on the seat next to her. "I get to use my press badge for the first time. Yay! I'm on my way."

*   *   *

The media room at TBD Park was packed, and the atmosphere was electric. Paul MacDougall was just stepping onto the speaker's podium as Maddy squeezed herself into the back. For a hastily called press conference, anyone who was anyone was there. Maddy spotted Sean Ostling near the front of the crowd – she recognized him from the black and white line drawing portrait of him that accompanied his column, although he was a little older and a little heavier than his portrait.

Paul MacDougall looked profoundly uncomfortable. So did George Randolph, the Goliaths' manager, who stood behind him.

Paul MacDougall cleared his throat.

"I know there is a lot of speculation concerning the events of last night. It is the position of the Goliaths that until substantial evidence is presented that any criminal or unethical activities were engaged in by any of our players or personnel, we shall move forward towards the end of the season and into the playoffs with the players we have under contract expected to play."

"What sort of investigation is taking place into the allegations posted in the Clarion?" This from the Oakland Express.

"We are engaging in our own internal investigation, and we have received notification from the Commissioner's office that they are pursuing the matter, as well. We remind ourselves that this is America, and until there is concrete evidence of wrong-doing, all parties must be allowed to be presumed innocent, and to be allowed to continue their work."

"Does that mean Cashman will play tonight?" The question came from the sports newscaster from the local NBC affiliate.

"We are still evaluating the extent of his injuries sustained in what we believe was an unprovoked encounter with a crazed individual – the so-called Masked Avenger. Pending our evaluation, we will then leave it to Coach Randolph to make the game time decision."

Unprovoked my butt, thought Maddy. She started to work her way towards the front of the room. Being small had its advantages.

"Is there any explanation as to why Benny was in Dogpatch last night?" asked Sean Ostling.

"None, and we have not asked him that question. We respect the privacy of our players and personnel. Unless they blatantly violate any terms of our contractual agreements, we choose to let their private lives remain just that, private. There may be more details pending our internal investigation, but for now we feel an obligation to protect the rights of our personnel."

Maddy had made her way to the front. As the scrum of reporters waved their hands and called out for the next question, Maddy found her voice cutting through the din.

"Coach Randolph!" Everyone turned to see where the bell-like voice came from. Maddy felt incredibly self-conscious all of a sudden. "Maddy Stevenson from the Clarion." There was a collective gasp as everyone in the room realized who she was. Maddy was suddenly blinded by the flash of dozens of cameras aimed in her direction. It took every ounce of self-control for her to continue to focus on her question. "If the Goliaths win the pennant tonight, and Benny Cashman is found guilty of playing while enhanced by a banned substance, shouldn't there be some sort of disclaimer or... asterisk next to his, and your, achievement?"

George Randolph hesitated. "That's a question for the Commissioner." He sighed. "And for Cooperstown."

*   *   *

It took an hour after the news conference was over for Maddy to extricate herself from the press room. She had Sean Ostling to thank for the help. He ran very solid interference for her and helped keep the questioning from the other members of the press above board. Paul MacDougall and George Randolph had slunk from the room, leaving the media turning their attention to the new star in their firmament.

"Thanks for getting me out of there," she gasped as they walked quickly to the parking lot. "It was like a mosh pit."

"Don't let it go to your head, kid," said Ostling with a wink. "You did good in there, though. Very professional."

"Thanks. I couldn't have done it without you. I wasn't expecting to be there – just in the right place at the right time, I guess."

"That would be about 99% of reporting. Just managing to be in the right place at the right time. Do you need a lift?"

324

"No, thank you. I'm all set. Oh, my gosh!"

"What's the matter," asked Ostling, somewhat startled by Maddy's sudden outburst.

"I need to be somewhere, like, right now. I've got to run. Thanks again!"

"See you around campus," Ostling called back after her as she jumped into her Beetle. He shook his head in wonder.

Kids these days.

LXXVI

Jimmy needed to go for a walk. And he needed some coffee that was better than what was lurking in the coffee maker at the station. It was a beautiful fall afternoon in San Francisco, and he had been chained to his desk since first thing in the morning. He headed out and down Columbus Avenue towards North Beach. The sun was slanting through the buildings, clear and sharp for the few hours of the afternoon that it had to shine before the fog swept in. After stopping by Caffe Greco for a cappuccino to go, he continued north towards Washington Square Park.

He spotted his father at his usual spot, staring at a chess board in front of him. James Wang Sr. was as aggressive in retirement as he had been on the force. He was going to be a grandmaster in his old age if it killed him. Opposite James sat an old Black man smoking a cigar.

"Dude, you can look at it all day, if you want," said the man with the cigar, "but you're still not going to find your way out of this. Lay the king down, man, lay the king down." Jimmy recognized his father's opponent as one of the great park chess players. Jefferson Rollins *was* a grandmaster, and he sat out in the park from noon until it was too dark to see, playing and playing. Chess players were all crazy, thought Jimmy.

"Hey, Dad," he said as he approached the two players. James Wang looked up, then down at the board again. After making a face, he laid his king down on its side in defeat.

"You're getting better, though, old man," said Jefferson. "You just need to lighten up a bit. Let the game come to you – not force it so much." Jimmy did everything he could not to burst out laughing. That was some advice.

"Let's take a break," said James. "Set 'em up but give me a few minutes. What's up, son? Catch anybody lately?"

"Hey, Jefferson," said Jimmy. The two men shook hands, and Jimmy turned his attention back to his father. "No, but I'm hot on their tail. Do you have a minute, Dad?"

"Well, I can certainly take a break from getting my ass whipped. Again. So, what's on your mind?" Father and son walked out towards the middle of the park. A young man and two young women were playing Frisbee. Several people were lying out on towels, sunning and reading. The Number 30 bus pulled up and disgorged a noisy group of children who were on their way home from school. The park was perfect.

"It's the catching people part. I think I'm ready to do it, I think I have all the evidence I need, but I'm not sure I have the stomach for the politics behind it."

"What have you got?"

"I've got all sorts of bad guys that everyone looks up to – who will make all sorts of noise if I tackle them - and one good guy who needs help, but who took down a couple of my men, so I've got real pressure to catch him and put him away, but if I do, I know that I'll regret it. To say I'm conflicted would be an understatement."

"Are you making choices? About who to bring down and who not to bring down?"

"I'm trying not to, Dad."

"Don't. You can't. Your job is to uphold the law, not to decide whether or not the law applies. You bring 'em in, let the rest of the process take care of itself."

"I know that, Dad. It's just that the rest of the process... I'm finding I don't have much faith in it, anymore. Or in myself. You see every day that some guy rips off people who have trusted him for millions – billions – of dollars, and he gets the slap on the wrist. A few years in a minimum-security prison, or even just house arrest with a tracking device on his ankle. And he has ruined hundreds, maybe thousands, of lives. Someone else is just in the wrong place at the wrong time causing little to no harm to anyone but himself, and he ends up in prison for the rest of his life. Or some institution…" Here Jimmy squinted into the sun for a moment. "I'm just thinking that, isn't there a middle path that one can take? Maybe doing nothing is the best thing for everyone."

"Then what's the point of your job? To cruise around in a police car helping people think that they're safe? Saving kittens from trees and walking little old ladies across the street? Listen, son, you need to embrace what you do like a religion. Asking yourself too many questions about the meaning of what you do will only cause you pain, trust me, I know. Just *believe*. And *do*. And observe the faith."

Jimmy bit his lip. "I try, Dad. I really do. I'm just having a bit of a crisis of conscience. A crisis of faith."

James Wang looked at his son. This was one of the moments that many parents dread. On one hand he felt he needed to display the firmness and strength of character that his son might need to be successful, on the other, he longed to confide in Jimmy his own moments of doubt – to allow his son into his heart, and to confess that he, too, was human and frail. James sighed. He put his hand on his son's shoulder and said, "Maybe you should take old Jefferson's advice. Let the game come to you. Don't force it. Buddha might have said as much. It's advice I could have used myself all these years… I guess what I'm saying is that I trust you to do the right thing, and you should trust yourself to do the right thing. And you will know what the right thing is only as you do it."

In that moment it came to him.

I love my dad, thought Jimmy.

"Thanks, Dad. Thanks for the… for the vote of confidence." He suddenly, impulsively, gave his father a hug. He might have crossed a line there, but he couldn't help it.

His father, after a moment of surprise, hugged him back.

LXXVII

Peter Kohler rubbed his hands with glee. How much fun is this? he thought. Tonight, he got to meet a billionaire casino owner. The fact that Dave Lynn was flying in to get a personal look at his new acquisition caused Kohler no end of delight. This was the world which he was born to navigate. Hob-nobbing with the super-rich, powerful, and famous. Mr. Lynn's personal appearance also just upped the price for the statuette – he would consider it a waste of his time, thought Kohler, if he spent less than a million for the piece. Nice.

He debated for a while the most advantageous spot in his home to display the statuette, deciding, ultimately, that his veranda would be the most dramatic, with the Golden Gate Bridge glowing softly in the background. Mr. Lynn, a creature of Las Vegas, was a night owl. He was due to arrive at midnight. It's a Friday, thought Kohler. I can sleep in tomorrow. He laughed. Now to setting the scene.

He thought that placing the statuette on a pedestal, with a hundred candles arranged around its base, would provide the most drama. A hundred candles… he would just run down to Cost Plus World Market and buy them out of their votives. It would be a couple hundred bucks, but worth it. He knew also that Mr. Lynn was a scotch drinker. A trip to the high-end wine and liquor store was also in order. Kohler preferred his dry white wine, but he would accommodate his guest. It would have to be a rare and expensive scotch. This was a considerable investment, but Robert Grant's check had cleared that morning, so Kohler was feeling that he could sustain it. As he looked out from his veranda, taking in Alcatraz caught in the late afternoon sun, he thought,

Can't make money without spending some.

LXXVIII

The music wasn't bad. The African rhythms and harmonies filled the auditorium as the sound technicians rung out their system. Scenery was now being loaded into place, the lighting equipment having been hung onto its trusses and flown up into the flies. At seemingly random intervals a light would flash on. The Masked Avenger watched in wonder as the light would then, of its own accord it seemed, move around the stage until it had been focused. It would then blink out.

A lot of activity, he thought. This is a big production.

Suddenly, he heard the ping of metal on metal – only a few yards away from him. He crouched back away from his view port in the ceiling and into the darkness. A couple of stage technicians were up in the catwalks, their wrenches clanging against the steel pipes as they hung their lighting instruments.

"What an asshole," said one of the technicians.

"It makes you wonder how someone like that gets to his level of authority," replied the other between grunts as he tightened the c-clamps down.

"By being an asshole, I'm sure. Hey, did you hear about Lucky Jerry? And the rest of the gang? Word is that Sanders had something to do with it. No one knows how, just that's the word."

"Where'd you hear that?"

"Justin said something. But you have to admit it's sort of strange, isn't it? All the homeless people who used to hang out around here are suddenly gone. Right as we're loading this thing in. More than a coincidence."

The Masked Avenger thought so, too. He slowly moved back to the hole in the ceiling, careful not to make any noise, although the music had resumed, drowning out practically everything else. He could see the first few rows of the auditorium before his view was blocked by the balcony. As he looked down, the heavy-set man entered from a side door and took a seat in the front row.

"There he is," said the first technician.

"We could drop a wrench on his shiny head."

"Wouldn't want *that* lawsuit."

The Masked Avenger watched the man with a great intensity. He was sure he had found his nemesis. Suddenly, the man turned around, seeming to look right at him. The Masked Avenger again pulled back from the hole in the ceiling, but not before freezing the man's visage in his mind. And getting the distinct impression he had been spotted.

*   *   *

John Sanders loved the old auditorium. The arabesque patterns, its majesty, its quiet coolness. The perfect venue for *The Leopard Prince,* he reflected, with its carved, exotic animals and hints of distant lands, magic, and mystery. He sat in the front row, taking in the load-in. He smiled to see the progress of the technicians. On schedule. They would be ready for the invited dress rehearsal by Sunday evening. Then a week of previews as the director and designers made final adjustments and documented their work so that the show could – eventually – transfer to other theatres around the country with little effort. But he loved that he had a cash cow for the next two years, with an option to extend for a third. It was all good.

He suddenly felt a chill, however. As if someone was watching him. He turned around to look over the auditorium. What was that? A flicker of movement up in the ceiling... That house light needs to get fixed, he realized, as he saw the black hole. He pulled out his BlackBerry and tapped in a memo. He was just about to return the BlackBerry to his jacket pocket when it vibrated in his hand. He didn't recognize the number, so he almost hit the disregard button. But during a load-in, anything was possible, so he answered.

"Mr. Sanders," came the voice on the phone.

"Speaking," replied Sanders. Suddenly the sound system in the auditorium came to life again. He waved angrily at the sound technician at the console, who quickly hit the mute button. "Sorry about that, I'm in the middle of a load-in at the theatre. Who's this?"

"Detective James Wang of the San Francisco Police Department."

John Sanders, despite the coolness of the auditorium, suddenly broke into a sweat. His voice quavered a bit as he said, "To what do I owe the honor?"

"I just wanted to set up a time to meet with you. We have a few questions for you – just routine stuff."

"Questions regarding what, exactly?"

"I'd prefer to discuss that with you when we meet," replied Detective Wang. "Do you have time today?"

"I don't. I'm against the clock through the weekend. Can we make it Monday?"

There was a hesitation on the other end of the phone. Finally Detective Wang said, "Yes. We can make it Monday. How about ten in the morning – at your office?"

"That works great. I'll see you then."

"Thanks," replied Detective Wang, who then hung up.

John Sanders suddenly needed to run to the men's room.

*　　　　*　　　　*

As he put his phone down, Jimmy reminded himself:

Let the game come to you. Let the game come to you.

LXXIX

"Where's Little Mary?"

Maddy had run up to Homeless Island. It sucked that there was never any place to park in San Francisco. She had had to park on a side street several blocks away and, now that it was four o'clock, felt the clock ticking against her. Normally, a two-block run wouldn't have winded her, but now she was running completely out of steam – the stimulating effects of the quick shower of the morning and the rush of the press conference having faded, leaving only a fatigue like she had never felt before. Was it only Friday afternoon? It felt like next year.

"I don't know," replied Beth. "Why, what's up? I was just about to head back down the street – afternoon rush, you know."

"I... I have a job for her. And for you. We need to run if we're going to get you interviewed in time."

Beth looked at Maddy for a moment as if she had two heads. Then she burst out laughing. "A job? Who would hire a broken-down wreck like me?"

"The Clarion? Maybe? I don't know, but for a few minutes, I have some pull with them, and I've arranged for interviews with you and Mary. You used to work with accounts, didn't you?"

"That was a long time ago, duck. Another lifetime. What made you think I was looking for a job?"

"You said this was a stupid way to live. A slow death. I have a chance for you to break away from this."

"You are the sweetest little girl on earth," said Beth with a sad smile. "But you still have a lot to learn about the world. You have done me and Mary much kindness, and we are grateful, but there are some things you can't help. I'm out here for a reason. I couldn't hold down a job if my life depended on it. And it would. It does. But I'm cranky and strange and get pissed off at people real easy. I'm a fuck-up. Besides, I couldn't go for an interview now – I smell and look like shit."

"That shouldn't matter. And I know you're a good person, and a kind one, too. I've seen how you look after Mary. Couldn't it be worth the effort?"

Beth looked at Maddy, squinting her eyes into the late afternoon sun. Her weathered face crinkled up with doubt and misgiving. She then looked away, staring at the traffic that was working its way down Van Ness towards the freeway on-ramps.

"I can't do it. I'm sorry. As stupid as it is, this is my life, and this is my home. Not everybody in the world can be saved. I resigned myself to being a statistic long ago. But you can stop by any time, and some French Toast is always welcome."

Maddy burst into tears. Dammit, she thought. I can't be a world class investigative reporter if I'm going to cry all the time. Cut this out.

"Don't cry, duck. It's okay, really."

"What about Mary? She could do the job."

"What's the job?" asked Beth.

"It's in the mail room. Sorting mail."

Beth looked away again, then looked back. "She can't read."

"What?"

"Little Mary. She can't read. I've been trying to teach her, but she's just got some wires crossed somewhere. That's why everyone thought she was stupid. She can't read." As Maddy stood there defeated, Beth wheeled up to her and gave her a hug. "It's okay. You did your best. You're doing your best. Just because we can't do what you hoped we could do doesn't mean you shouldn't have asked. Keep on asking and keep on helping. Acceptance doesn't have to mean defeat. At least for you, it doesn't."

"And for you?" asked Maddy.

"I'll get by. And Mary will, too. And my life is a little better now than it was before."

"How so?"

"I have a new friend." Beth gave Maddy's hand a squeeze. "I've got to go now – it's Showtime." And with that, Beth wheeled herself down the ramp and towards Van Ness. Maddy just watched her go.

*   *   *

Getting home was a nightmare. It was the last Friday of the month, and Maddy was confronted with one of San Francisco's most annoying idiosyncrasies: Critical Mass. Thousands of cyclists – bicycle messengers, mostly - filled the street at a point in the day, in the week, and the month that would cause the most disruption. No one was sure anymore if it was still an act of protest or had just become part of the rhythm of the oddest city in the world, but it was one of those monthly events that San Franciscans had learned to suffer with a certain pride. But the combination of rush hour, thousands of bike riders weaving through the streets on an unplanned and completely random course, and the early movement by a huge portion of the City's population towards TBD Park and the final game of the season caused complete gridlock. Maddy wanted desperately to go home and take another shower and change before heading to the game, but she gave up on the idea. Never could thirty blocks be so far.

"Carlos. Can I borrow your shower?"

"Yes, you can borrow my shower. Where are you?"

"I found a spot on Valencia Street. There's no way I can get home and then to the ballpark by seven."

"No shit. I'm just leaving the office - I'm walking home. It'll be easier than taking the bus. No one's going anywhere right now. It'll take me half an hour, but I can meet you there."

"Can you pick me up a double espresso at Starbucks on your way? I'm dying."

"Whatever it takes, Chica. You going to the game? Word is that Cashman's not going to play. But the game is going to be on national television, just in case. Should be a scene."

"It's a scene out *here*," said Maddy as she watched a never-ending stream of bicycles pour past her. Cars were honking, drivers were cursing the cyclists, sirens were blaring. It was pure chaos.

I love this town, she thought as she started to jog towards the Castro.

LXXX

It was no less chaotic three hours later in front of TBD Park. Maddy had met Carlos at his house, crashed for an hour on his sofa, then reheated the double espresso in his microwave. The shower had then worked its magic, although Carlos had to pound on the bathroom door to remind her to get out.

"Save some for the dolphins!" he had called through the door.

"Sorry!" Maddy had called back.

She had climbed back into her clothes, brushed out her hair and took stock. She didn't have the full make-up kit. Disaster.

"Carlos!"

"All over it, Chica!" He pulled open the top drawer by the sink. A complete complement of powder, eyeliner, mascara, rouge, lip gloss and brushes appeared. "You know…" he said without apology. "For girls' night out."

"Have I ever mentioned how handy it is that you're gay?" said Maddy.

"Watch yourself, or I might just have to give you a make-over," replied Carlos. "I mean. Do you call this hair?"

"What's wrong with my hair?" This was not the way to build confidence, she thought.

"It looks like two rats climbed in there and had a fight. You need a haircut."

"And you're just the man to give it to me, right?"

"Just grab a towel and sit on this stool. You're going to be a professional woman you need to start looking like a professional woman."

"Like you know what you're doing."

Carlos pulled out his license. Expired, but still a cosmetologist's license from New York.

"Dang," said Maddy with not just a little admiration.

*   *   *

Half an hour later and she looked sharp. Gone was the windswept surfer girl look. Instead, the woman looking at her in the mirror had crisp, short hair. A diagonal cut accented her jaw line. Tres chic. With the bags under her eyes, Maddy felt she could easily pass for twenty-nine.

"No time for highlights," said Carlos ruefully.

The back of her neck was cold, though. "I'm going to need a scarf," said Maddy. She swung her head back and forth, watching her hair kick up.

"I pity that poor policeman," said Carlos admiring his work.

He got her a scarf, and to complement her jeans and sweater, he pulled out a blue blazer. "Pretending to be a prep schoolboy," he said, this time apologetically. It was a good combination. Maddy felt like a new woman and felt that she might actually make it through a baseball game and even have some energy to spare for a nightcap.

"And smooches," said Carlos.

Maddy just rolled her eyes, gave Carlos a big hug, and ran out the door. After a few blocks, she jumped on the Number 12 Bus, which dropped her right in front of TBD Park.

*   *   *

Maddy had the extreme pleasure of watching Jimmy search for her in the crowd in vain. When she finally went up to him, his eyes lit up. He couldn't help it. He kissed her immediately. "You look great," he said with

340

a grin. "Really great." Maddy enjoyed being so thoroughly taken in and appreciated. She hooked her arm into his, and they went up to the turnstile.

The crowd around them was buzzing with excitement. The atmosphere in the park was electric. A pennant on the line, the news about Cashman on everyone's lips. Maddy and Jimmy pulled up to the concessions stand and ordered some buffalo wings and Gilroy garlic fries, along with two beers.

"Thank God it's cold tonight," said Maddy. "With a beer in me, I might just fall asleep, otherwise."

Jimmy pretended to look hurt, but then smiled, "I'm right there with you. But should be an interesting game."

They climbed up to the Club Level along the first base line. "Nice seats," said Maddy. "Your dad must have some pull. How come he's not here?"

"He prefers to watch the games on TV. He's not big on crowds."

Maddy almost couldn't blame him. This crowd was restless. Almost angry. Certainly strange. From their vantage point along the first base line, they could see into the Goliaths' dugout. There wasn't much movement in there for ten minutes before the first pitch, just a certain milling about. Funny thing about baseball. The world could be coming to an end and yet baseball players would still move at the same pace, and with almost no change in their facial expressions. A 162-game season would do that. Sure, there could be drama in the clubhouse, but preparation prior to each game in a long season that began with spring training in February was such a routine by early October that no amount of conflagration off the field would change the movements and attitudes on the field.

"You wouldn't know that Benny Cashman was front page news, judging from the players," said Jimmy. The Goliaths were already on the field, tossing the ball around, the starting pitcher warming up on the mound.

All perfectly normal. There was a hole, however, out in left field. The center fielder and the right fielder were playing catch with each other, but out in Cashman's domain, there was no one. One could sense the crowd straining to see into the Goliaths' dugout for any sign of Cashman. He wasn't there.

Suddenly, the voice of the announcer rumbled through the sound system. "And now for the starting line-ups for this evening's game." The crowd, which had been chattering nervously, suddenly grew quiet. With the announcement of each player from Los Angeles, the crowd booed, but their hearts weren't in it. They were waiting for more important things.

"And now the starting line-up for your San Francisco Goliaths!" This was what the crowd had been waiting for, and a shrill cheer went up. The milling about on the concourses stilled. "Batting first..." Cheers for each player named, certainly each player had his fans, but still a sense of restraint. "Batting fourth, playing left field...," a pause. "Jordan Wilson!" The crowd jeered in disapproval. Cashman wasn't starting. Jordan Wilson trotted gamely out to left field, only to be pelted with cups of beer. Security in the left field bleachers looked prepared for such a display and worked quickly to identify and remove any miscreants. Still, it was ugly enough for the announcer to have to make the obligatory warning to the fans, and for the umpire and the third base umpire to jog out to stare them down. The crowd started booing and clapping in rhythm. The booing evolved into chants of "Benny! Benny! Benny!" There was an uncertain moment when it appeared as if things might deteriorate to the point where there could be something of a riot, but the moment passed, and the crowd settled down into a tense watchfulness.

"It's like the lions at the circus," whispered Maddy to Jimmy. "They're cowed for the moment, but they're just waiting for the trainer to turn his back, and they'll take a swipe at him."

"You want live theatre? You got it!" said Jimmy.

The first pitch was thrown, and the game got underway. For the next few hours, things were relatively quiet, with plenty of opportunities to run to the concessions stand for additional fuel. There was the odd burst of excitement – the long fly balls that were caught at the warning track, the double play, a couple of stolen bases. But not much scoring. Jordan Wilson acquitted himself admirably, however, and began to win the crowd over with a couple of base hits and a hustle play on defense, throwing a sacrifice fly caught at the fence to home in time to catch the baserunner for an inning-ending out. He was a trade deadline acquisition by the Goliaths – a solid hitter who had been off-loaded by his former team, a team no longer in the running looking to shed payroll. The Goliaths had picked him up as insurance for the stretch run and the playoffs – a move which, in hindsight, now looked brilliant. He was no Benny Cashman, but he was a solid contributor. Maddy admired his coolness in the face of such initial hostility.

It was actually a good, tight game. There was still much on the line. With a win, the Goliaths took their division, and had home field advantage in the first round of the playoffs, relegating Los Angeles to wild-card status. With a loss, LA took the division, leaving the Goliaths starting the playoffs on the road in St. Louis. And there was the storied rivalry. LA was the team that San Franciscans loved to hate. This had been going on like this for over fifty years, making games between the two teams special events in both cities.

The score, going into the ninth inning, was tied, 2 – 2. Now the crowd got restless again. This was Cashman Time. There was too much at stake, and whereas in games past an appearance by their hero at this juncture was even odds that they would win the game, now much was uncertain.

Los Angeles started the top of the inning strong, and

quickly scored two runs, driving the Goliaths' shaky closer off the mound. The Goliaths managed to stop the bleeding after that, however, and headed into the bottom of the ninth with a chance to still salvage the game. It didn't look good for the home team, though, because the Goliaths were batting the bottom of their order.

But a rally started. LA's fearsome closer, Eric Gaines, uncharacteristically gave up a base hit with the first at-bat. He recovered and proceeded to strike out the next two Goliaths while throwing only eight pitches. The crowd was resigning itself to the loss and was starting to shuffle towards the exits, when a broken-bat single by Armando Rodriguez, the short-stop, suddenly stopped them in their tracks, forcing them to return to their seats. The tying run was suddenly on base, the winning run was at bat. The next batter was scheduled to be the pitcher, but everyone knew that a pinch-hitter would be called.

Suddenly, there was movement deep within the Goliaths' dugout. The crowd froze, electrified. A woman screamed in excitement, then the whole crowd gasped. Out of a shuffling of players within the shadows of the dugout, the familiar figure emerged, slowly, but with stately purpose. The swagger was missing, in fact there was a limp, but there was no doubt who was coming to the plate. His face was heavily bandaged, and he wore a protective mask. Every movement looked like it caused him agony, but he moved relentlessly towards the on-deck circle.

Benny Cashman was going to take one last stab at making history.

As Maddy and Jimmy watched, along with 50,000 others in the ballpark, as well as a national audience on television, Cashman warmed up. It hurt to watch him. Everyone around them was citing the famous Kirk Gibson home run over thirty years earlier, when Gibson was barely able to make his way around the bases, his knees so damaged that he could barely even stand in the batter's box. One of baseball's most heroic moments. Here, with a division title and a home run record on the line, Cashman was looking to secure his place next to Gibson – and Aaron.

As Cashman took his practice swings, the LA infield gathered at the mound, consulting with the pitcher. After a few minutes, the outfielders also joined them. No one could remember a full team meeting at the mound before. There was a strange solemnity to their movements. Eric Gaines looked at each player in turn, and each nodded grimly. Their manager trotted out, causing the crowd to think that Gaines would be pulled. After a few moments of consultation, he trotted back to the dugout alone, as the rest of the players returned to their positions.

Benny Cashman dropped the weights off his bat and approached the batter's box. The crowd was on its feet, not knowing what to think – even whether or not to breathe. Cashman slowly swung his bat back and forth, anticipating the first pitch.

The pitch never came. Gaines stood on the mound, stared at Cashman for what seemed like an eternity, then stepped off the mound. He slowly, deliberately, set the ball on the grass before him, never taking his eyes off Cashman. He then turned his back on the batter and stood in front of the mound with his arms folded. The crowd began to hoot and holler, thinking Gaines was chicken or something. But then each player on the LA team turned their back on Cashman. Cashman, bewildered, turned to the umpire, only to see the catcher also stand up, and face away from him. By this point the crowd began to understand what was happening and fell into a deep silence. George Randolph jogged out of the Goliath's dugout to meet the gathering of the umpires, who were also bewildered. There was a lot of arm waving and gesturing towards the mound. Benny Cashman just stood there.

After a few minutes, the umpire approached the mound. As he did so, however, all the LA players slowly walked towards their dugout. The umpire was jogging beside them, gesticulating wildly. He eventually confronted the manager, who simply shook his head, and headed out of the dugout and into the visitor's locker room with the rest of his team.

They would not play against Benny Cashman.

As the umpires gathered to decide what to do, out of the silence of the hushed crowd was heard the sound of one person clapping. The clapping was soon accompanied by more and more people putting their hands together. No one was clapping for Benny Cashman, no one was clapping for the Goliaths. They were applauding an act of defiance. They were applauding the truth.

The announcer came on to convey the decision of the umpires. Los Angeles had forfeited the game. A lone voice called out "Cheater!" With that, almost as one, the crowd slowly and somberly turned their back on the one Goliaths player still standing on the field.

Cashman did not move. He remained standing in the batter's box. Only when George Randolph slowly walked out to fetch him, did he register what had happened.

Benny Cashman's career was over.

LXXXI

Jimmy and Maddy sat on the step leading to her entry vestibule. They had walked all the way back from the ballpark, deciding that Maddy's car could be picked up in the morning. As they had worked their way down the Embarcadero, and then down Broadway, and then down Columbus Avenue, they had looked in on all the bars and pubs, glimpsing televisions through the windows, and the sad, silent denizens gathered with hunched shoulders in front of them. It was as if an entire city had lost its faith, and was picking its way through the desolation, the denial, and the despair. Never had a division title been won with so little enthusiasm.

It was late, close to midnight, but neither Maddy nor Jimmy felt yet like sleeping. The evening had turned pleasant – after the coldness of the ballpark next to the Bay, the little entry courtyard of Maddy's building was relatively warm. She had run upstairs to fetch a bottle of red wine, two glasses and a candle. They sat together sipping the wine in a tired, but companionable silence. After a while, Maddy spoke.

"I still can't believe what happened," she said in almost a whisper. "I feel it's because of me that Benny Cashman is… I don't know what he is. Do you think he's finished?"

"I can't imagine him playing again. Not until this all gets cleared up."

"I almost feel sorry for him. The way he was standing out there, all alone."

"I don't know. He cheated. But this would never have happened if he wasn't such an asshole. Some people feel that they don't have to play by the rules, or that they're too good for the rest of us. That they can get away with things that the rest of us can't get away with. I have almost always found that the 'truth will out.' Or Karma, if you like. If you, or Little Mary, hadn't been in the right place at the right time, someone else probably would have been. The scales would have eventually balanced."

"It still feels like I'm responsible for the downfall of an icon."

"You just did some solid investigative reporting, using, perhaps, less than standard techniques and unusual resources..."

"Little Mary, The Man Without a Face..." said Maddy with a smile.

"But you did good."

"Why Detective Wang!" said Maddy poking him playfully in the chest. "I believe this would be a complete about face from this past Tuesday evening."

"Why yes... yes it would be. I was wrong in my initial assessment. I'm glad I was wrong. To your continued success." He raised his glass to Maddy, who clinked hers against it.

"To crime," she said with a wink.

Suddenly, out of the open window above them, a woman cried out. Jimmy jumped up quickly, almost spilling his wine.

"It's okay," sighed Maddy. "It's just my roommate." She shrugged her shoulders.

"Wow," whispered Jimmy. The cries grew louder. Embarrassingly loud. "He must be really good." Maddy giggled. She looked at Jimmy. He looked at her. It was something of a turn-on. He settled back down onto the step and leaned in to kiss Maddy. At that moment there was the screech of tires as a limousine pulled quickly into the drive outside the gate. A couple of large men jumped out, one of whom opened the back door of the car. Out of the limo emerged a tall, rangy older man in what looked to be the most expensive suit Maddy had ever seen. One of the large men opened the gate for him, and the trio approached Maddy and Jimmy.

"I'm sorry, didn't mean to break up your party," said the tall man in the expensive suit. He said it with a wry smile, and something of a western twang. He looked profoundly familiar to Maddy, but she couldn't put her finger on where she had seen him before.

"No worries," she replied, as she and Jimmy straightened up. "Just enjoying the fall evening." Maddy pulled out her keys, to open the vestibule door, but the tall man anticipated her and pressed the button for the top floor. After a moment, the door buzzed open. The tall man and his companions went inside, the tall man giving Maddy a wink.

"Who was that?" she asked, after the men had trudged up the stairs.

"You don't know? You haven't seen him on television hundreds of times?" replied Jimmy. "Ever see adds for the new Dream casino?"

"Holy crap! That was Dave Lynn!"

"He looks younger on TV."

"What could he possibly be doing in my building?..." Maddy's eyes got really wide. She pulled out into the courtyard as far from the building as possible and looked up. There was candlelight glowing from the veranda on the top floor. She could hear voices, laughter. As Jimmy joined her, she whispered, "He's gone up to see Peter Kohler. That crate he pulled from the museum last night – perhaps this is another sale!"

"We've got no way of knowing, for sure," whispered Jimmy ruefully.

"Yes, we do," whispered Maddy. She approached the wall of her building. Part of its Italianate flavor came from the trellises that were attached to the walls, covered in creeping vines.

"Maddy, no!" called out Jimmy. "I mean, this is so illegal."

"How is it illegal? I'm not breaking and entering. I may be doing something potentially dangerous and stupid, but I can't see how it's illegal. I live here!"

All Jimmy could do was make a face. He then approached the trellis. "How much do you think this can hold?"

"Why, you want to join me?"

"Yeah. I do."

She smacked his butt. They then tentatively tested the integrity of the trellis. It was actually a metal structure, mounted out from the wall about six inches. Maddy started to climb up. The trellis seemed securely attached to the building. She looked down at Jimmy, gave him the thumb's up and held on tight as he pulled himself up beside her. There was a slight shudder, a sense that perhaps they were testing the structure too much. "I don't think we can both do this," she whispered.

"Then I should go up – it's too dangerous," he whispered back.

"No, I'm a lot lighter. And I've got a camera. You stay on the ground and stand watch." As Jimmy nodded, reluctantly, Maddy stroked his cheek. "Hey. What does it take to get a search warrant?" she asked suddenly.

Jimmy looked thoughtful – as thoughtful as one can look while hanging off the side of a building. "A few phone calls. Could take about an hour. But if this isn't what we think it is, then I would be in a shitload of trouble."

"I'll give you the high sign. If it's a transaction, then you pull the trigger. Start making the calls now."

Jimmy looked at her in a certain wonder, then nodded, and slid back down the trellis to the ground. As Maddy continued her slow ascent up the side of the building, Jimmy started pounding numbers on his cell phone. After a couple more rungs of the trellis, Maddy realized that she was right next to the window to Angelique's room. The noises coming from there were incredible. Maddy was torn as to whether or not to peek in, just to see what could possibly cause that much passionate expression, then thought better of it.

There are just some things that one shouldn't know too much about, she thought.

She was about eight feet from the ledge of Peter Kohler's veranda. She could hear voices overhead, although they seemed to be coming from inside the apartment, not yet outside. Shoot. I might have to hang here longer than I thought, she worried. Let's see what's up there. Maddy looked down at Jimmy, who was talking into his phone. She wasn't sure how the warrant process worked, but she felt that they had sufficient probable cause. She was sure that they had enough circumstantial evidence to make the move.

Maddy climbed the rest of the way up. Nice view, she thought. Really nice view. In that moment, the searchlight from Alcatraz, which she always knew was there but couldn't see from her windows, flashed across her. She flattened herself instinctively, like an escaping prisoner from Stalag 17, then realized that the only people who could possibly see her were their next-door neighbors in the building across the courtyard. She looked nervously over her shoulder, sighing with relief upon seeing that their windows were dark, and the curtains were shut.

She stuck her head slowly over the ledge of the veranda. Her feet were on the second to last rung of the trellis. The only way to hold on was to balance her hands on the top vertical struts of the trellis, or to hang on to the ledge. She thought that the latter option would expose her too much, so she hung on uncomfortably, the top of the trellis making indentations in her palms.

This may not be such a good idea, she thought.

But the sight on the veranda gave her strength. It was a truly remarkable and dramatic image: a dancing, golden figure, lit from below by a cascade of hundreds of votive candles. She had to hand it to Peter Kohler – he knew how to set a scene. She now had to pull out her phone and snap a photo. She was sure, this time, to turn the flash off. Not going to make that mistake twice, she thought, realizing how much her butt still hurt.

Just as she was about to snap the photo, the lights in the apartment went out. What's happening? she wondered. Are they leaving? It took her a moment to realize that the curtains within were being opened. Of course. Lights out in the apartment for the dramatic reveal of the figure outside. Very theatrical. I'm sure Mr. Lynn is loving this, she thought.

And he was. As the French doors opened, Maddy could hear laughing and clapping. "Very nice. Very nice!" went the western twang. "Wow. Wish my interior designers were here. This should be displayed just like this." Dave Lynn walked out onto the veranda and turned to one of his associates. "Take a note. We have to rebuild the whole room to allow for more candles. The ceiling will have to be raised a couple of feet."

"Yes, Mr. Lynn," came the response. Peter Kohler and Madeleine Chang strolled out behind Dave Lynn. Peter Kohler had a glass of wine in one hand, and a glass of whisky in the other. He handed the whisky to Lynn.

"What's this?" asked the casino owner.

"I heard you were partial to single malt. It's an Ardbeg. 30-year-old."

"Nice. At my age, a 30-year-old looks pretty hot to me," joked Lynn. Ew, thought Maddy. They clinked their glasses. They then stood around the statue for a moment in wonder. The perfect shot. Click.

"What was that?" asked Lynn.

"What was what?" asked Kohler. Maddy ducked just in time.

"I thought I heard something." At that moment, Angelique let out a passionate howl, followed by a sequence of little yelps.

"Oh, that. That's just the French girl in the apartment two floors down. She's incredible."

"I'll say," said Dave Lynn with a snort. Maddy realized with panic that footsteps were approaching the

ledge. After giving Jimmy the high sign, she
waved at him to duck into the porch out of sight.
She dropped several rungs down and flattened herself
even flatter than she had when the beacon from Alcatraz
had caught her. She had a moment's grace to drape some
vines over her head. She froze.

"Damn. I'd give anything to watch that action."
Maddy could sense that Dave Lynn was leaning over the
ledge, trying to see into the window below and off to the
side of him.

"You would, I assure you. She's a stunner," said
Kohler between sips of his wine. "Her little room-mate
is pretty hot in her own sort of surfer-girl kind of way."
Double ew, thought Maddy. Either he goes or I go. Can't
live here.

"Well, then, just toss me in the middle," laughed
Dave Lynn. Maddy could hear his footsteps retreating.
"Alright," she heard him continue. "How much am I
paying for this thing?"

Maddy heard Peter Kohler cough theatrically. "It's
the only piece like it outside of Tibet."

"So that means it's worth..."

"One million dollars."

There was a pause. Maddy was dying to see what
Dave Lynn's reaction was to such an astronomical sum.

"Well, shit. What am I doing here?" replied Lynn
eventually. "I don't get out of bed for anything worth
less than five million. Flew all the way to fucking San
Francisco for only a million-dollar whatsit?"

"And some good whisky. And as good a view of the
Golden Gate Bridge as you can find." How smooth was
Peter Kohler?

"Hah!" laughed Dave Lynn. "You're right. And a
sampling of the mating calls of the local fauna. Alright.
Robert, where's the briefcase?"

The briefcase? No shit. Where were the police?

"Some transactions are better done in cash, don't
you think?" said Lynn with a chuckle. "Takes me back

to my early days as a liquor wholesaler." Maddy could hear the click-click of a briefcase being opened. She had to go for it. She scrabbled up the trellis as quietly as she could and stuck her phone up over the ledge. Click.

At that moment, the trellis, which had taken more abuse than it was ever designed for, popped its bolts at the top. As Maddy's stomach went into her mouth, the whole metal structure slowly, but inexorably, peeled its way off the wall of the building. As Maddy's world turned sideways, she was peripherally aware of red lights flashing beyond the gate in the street. The next second she went crashing down thirty feet into the hedge at the far side of the courtyard.

Then everything went black.

LXXXII

"Sheba, come here, girl! Come, Little Sheba!"

Justin laughed at his little joke. He had set out some new food for Robin in a corner of the booth next to a blanket that had been poached from the green room and folded up to make a bed for her. He had also taken a box and filled it with sand from a busted sandbag that had been rotting in the corner of the trap room under the stage. Robin trotted over but sat down next to the little plate without eating. She looked at Justin as if something was missing. "What's the matter, sweetie? You don't like tuna, anymore?"

Robin just made a face, as much as a kitten can make a face. She looked put out, as if she were sitting at the wrong table, or something. "Do you want candles, or an *amuse bouche* before dinner? Have I forgotten the napkins? You're a silly girl." Not knowing what else to do to accommodate the little kitten, he resumed his task of shutting down the lighting console. It had been a hard and long day. He had been working with the assistant lighting designer, revising the programming for the show. It was a big musical with hundreds of lighting cues – all of which had to be adjusted for this new production. He was ready for a good, stiff drink. He had heard that the cast was gathering at a bar down the street, and he was interested in getting to know a few of them. Dancers. He sighed contentedly.

Justin had one last task before calling it a day. To set out the ghost light on the stage. He stroked the kitten behind her ear and left the booth, closing and locking the door behind him. As he clambered down the many flights of stairs, he couldn't help humming the love duet from the show – the big hit that had received massive airplay when covered by two of pop's biggest stars. That was the thing about working on musicals, he thought – the songs got stuck in your head, sometimes even making it hard to go to sleep. Nothing a few drinks wouldn't cure, he laughed to himself.

He finally reached the wings of the stage, now overcrowded with scenery, props and control stations for all of the scenic machinery. In the shadows, the giant scenic elements looked strange and grotesque. The mammoth rock formation where the leopards gathered was especially creepy in the dim light. He thought he was inured to this, but still...

He plugged in the ghost light and took one last look around the auditorium. What was that? He thought he saw some movement out of the corner of his eye. He used his hand to block the glare of the ghost light and scanned the auditorium again, suddenly getting the creeping sensation up the back of his neck that he was being watched. He squinted, then froze. Up in the booth, which he had locked only minutes before, he saw movement. Then he saw something that curdled his blood. A dark shape was standing up in the booth, barely discernible. But he saw its eyes. The eyes glowed in the darkness, staring down at him.

They weren't the eyes of the kitten.

LXXXIII

She was in a little boat, floating through mist-enshrouded water. Candles were rising up all around her and a beautiful voice echoed throughout the cavernous, underground grotto through which she glided, singing softly about dark music. She turned slowly to see a masked figure behind her pushing the boat through the water like a gondolier. Light streamed down upon them from above and behind them, causing the boatman to be no more than a shadow. She turned to face the masked figure fully, and reached out to tear the mask off his face...

"Ow! Hey, now, it's okay. You're going to be okay!" Jimmy appeared before her, rubbing his face where she had just struck out at him. Her phone, which she was still clutching in her hand, was just finishing its Music of the Night ring tone. All around her was mayhem – flashing lights, policemen coming and going, a couple of paramedics leaning over her. As the fog began to lift from her eyes, she could make out Angelique and Jean-Michel standing off to the side, she in the top half of a pair of pajamas, he in the bottoms. Put some clothes on, girl, thought Maddy as she laid her head back.

"What happened?" she croaked.

"You were extremely lucky. The hedge broke your fall."

"That's nice," Maddy sighed. "So, no broken bones, just more massive bruises and scrapes."

"Something like that. You're going to look like some kind of action hero. Bruce Willis, or somebody. Lurching your way to the end of the movie, all banged up and bloodied."

"Yipeekiyay, mother..." Maddy coughed. Jimmy laughed. "So, what's going on?"

"Straight, old-fashioned raid. Was a little dicey with

Mr. Lynn's 'associates,' they wanted to bull-rush us as we came through the door, but Mr. Lynn's a cool customer. He's claiming he was just here for a social gathering. A drink."

"And the briefcase full of cash?"

"Pocket money."

"Nice. He's not the one we're after, anyway... Where's Kohler?"

"He's been asked, along with Madeleine Chang, to accompany us to the station, where their lawyers will be meeting us shortly, I'm sure. The statuette is now in police custody."

Maddy looked over just as two policemen were slowly maneuvering a large crate out the front door. She tried to get up, but the paramedics held her down. "Hang on there, ma'am," one of them said. "You had a nasty knock on the head. Here. Follow my flashlight." Maddy did so and thought to herself that she might have to have accidents more often. She was surrounded by good-looking men. "She checks out okay, but we should still take her to ER for further tests – possible overnight stay for observation."

Maddy just about cried. All she really wanted was to climb into her own bed. And that smooch that she never got. The paramedics brought over a gurney and slid her onto it. She reached out her hand and Jimmy took it. "Will you come with me?"

"I have to do some serious interviewing, going to take a few hours, but I will come and check on you."

"I'll come with," said Angelique. God bless her.

"Can you call Carlos? He needs to cover this story."

Jimmy smiled. "Will do. You just missed a call, by the way. And I'll need to borrow your phone for a bit. You've got some evidence on there, although I'm not sure how admissible it will be."

Maddy looked at her phone. She flipped it open. It was a text message. From Justin.

The Theatre Ghost is real.

Woah, thought Maddy. Wonder what that's all about…

She handed her phone over to Jimmy, who pulled up the two photos. "Nice job, Sherlock. That would be three people toasting around what looks distinctly like contraband. Hey, what speed dial am I?"

"You jerk! What makes you think you're on my speed dial?" Jimmy looked at her with a raised eyebrow. Got that trick from his mother. "All right. It's speed dial 8. Sheesh."

"Thank you." He forwarded the photos onto his phone. "If it's any consolation, you're speed dial 5." He handed the phone back to Maddy. "Now get on with you, I'll catch up with you later."

"Hey," whispered Maddy.

"Hey, what?" answered Jimmy with a smile.

"You gonna send me off like that?"

Jimmy stopped the paramedics for a moment and knelt down like Prince Charming before Sleeping Beauty.

After the best kiss she could remember, Maddy felt profoundly alive. "Hey, do you think we'll make it to our third date?"

Jimmy just smiled and squeezed her hand. The paramedics hefted her up and she floated away towards the ambulance. Just like the movies.

*　　　　　*　　　　　*

"Carlos! I didn't wake you, did I?"

"Hardly, Chica. I'm a…"

"Yes, I know. And you never sleep. Listen, you've got to get down to the station on Vallejo Street, stat."

"Wow, where are you? Sounds like you're right next to an ambulance or something."

"I'm *inside* an ambulance. They're not too happy about me using my phone, but I had to fill you in. We've got another Monster Exclusive." Maddy then told Carlos

---

everything that had transpired.

"Jesus. This is uncanny, the being-in-the-right-place-at-the-right-time thing."

"Yeah, well, it's taking its toll, I assure you."

"You gonna be okay? Do you have someone with you?"

"I've got Angelique riding shotgun, so I'm okay. Just get to the station before all the news is gone."

"Roger that. Looks like another late night."

"Trust me, I'd rather be at my computer right now than going to the emergency room."

"I'll come find you as soon as I can."

"I'm not sure I'll be awake."

"Not if they give you any good drugs, you won't be. Damn, I'm almost jealous."

It would be nice to get a good night's sleep for once, thought Maddy, as the ambulance pulled up to the emergency room entrance. Just wish I could get it some other way.

LXXXIV

She awoke to the sound of a persistent beep. It was warm all around her, she was swaddled in blankets, and she had slept uninterrupted for hours. God, it felt good.

As she became more aware of her surroundings, she saw Angelique, with Jean-Michel next to her. Then at the foot of the bed was Carlos. She slowly turned her head, the room swimming just a little behind, and saw Jimmy.

"Oh, Auntie Em," she croaked. "I had the most incredible dream. You were there," she said to Jean-Michel, and then to Carlos and Jimmy, "and you, and you."

"That is the most gay thing I've ever heard anyone say," said Carlos, who was beaming. He looked very rugged, did Carlos, with the stubble of another all-nighter on his face.

"You should keep that beard," whispered Maddy. "It suits you."

"You doing okay?" asked Jimmy.

"Never better," said Maddy. "What's that beeping?"

"It's your heart," said Carlos. "Seems to be working just fine."

"Can I get out of here?" asked Maddy.

"As soon as you pee, and eat this biscuit," said the nurse coming up. "Must be nice having all these friends."

"It *is* nice," said Maddy. She suddenly started to cry. It really *was* nice. She had been in San Francisco for a month, and she had all these people who cared about her. In spite of everything.

"Now, now," said the nurse. "I'm sending everyone out of here. We'll wheel you up to the curb. You!" she said to everyone. "Go get a car or something, she'll be ready in about twenty minutes."

It took about an hour, actually, but it was good to be heading home. It was really early, still. The sun was rising over the East Bay, once again causing fat shafts of light to cut through the morning mist along the avenues.

"So, what happened with Peter Kohler?" asked Maddy, as Jimmy pulled up in front of her house.

"He's probably upstairs sleeping it off," said Jimmy.

"That's creepy," said Maddy. "What if I meet him on the stairs or something?"

"It is what it is. There's a process, that's all. The Chinese consulate has been contacted, and some experts have been notified to examine the artifact, but no one has been formally charged, pending further investigation. This is the part I hate."

"No clear answers?" asked Maddy.

"Well, the story is still pretty sensational," said Carlos, stirring from his nap in the back seat. "It gets run by legal, and there will be plenty of 'allegeds' and 'preliminarys' and 'suspecteds' and all that bullshit, but the shit stacks up pretty well. The case is very solid."

"He'll have a hard time getting a raise," said Jimmy with a dark chuckle.

"And the woman?"

"Madeleine Chang? Nothing much will happen to her," said Jimmy. "In fact, her stock may rise. She'll be dining out on this experience for years. It all depends on how loyal she is to Kohler. My thinking is that he's a creep and she'll disassociate. There are other charities. There's always the theatre," he chuckled.

Oh. My. Gosh. thought Maddy. The Theatre Ghost. She had almost forgotten. It could wait, though. She would tackle that mystery after a nap, a shower, and a good breakfast.

LXXXV

Breakfast was really dinner. She had slept all day. Crawling out of bed had been the hardest thing she had ever done. The shower had been excruciating, the hot water causing every bruise and scrape and cut to scream out in its own agony. It will feel so much better when I stop, thought Maddy. That turned out not to be true. The stinging had been replaced by an ache in every bone in her body. She had then slowly and gingerly climbed into her softest sweatpants and sweatshirt and wandered out and into the living room.

Somehow her apartment had become a rolling party. As tired as she was, it made perfect sense that Carlos was hanging in the kitchen trading cooking tips with Angelique, while Jimmy and Jean-Michel sat on the sofa sipping beers and watching college football. She accepted this easily as a normal thing, in fact it was comforting. She had a family.

Cal was playing USC. She didn't think that either boy was all that into football, but they both were watching with great intensity. "Hey, look who's up!" smiled Jimmy, as he got up from the sofa. He went over to her to give her a hug.

"Don't touch me!" said Maddy. "I'm sorry – I just hurt all over."

"I won't lie to you, you *don't* look marvelous," said Jimmy. "I think it's the purple and green blotches. They don't do a thing for you."

"Who's winning?" she said, in an effort to change the subject.

"It's tied. Going into the fourth quarter. Great game with championship implications."

"You like football?"

"Not all that much, but I'm a Cal graduate. It's Jean-Michel who's the football fiend."

"Oui," said Jean-Michel raising his Stella Artois in salute to Maddy. "I love this game."

Go figure, thought Maddy.

She shuffled into the kitchen and took a seat at the little table in the corner. The smell was fantastic. "What are you two up to?" asked Maddy.

"Mexican French fusion cuisine," said Carlos, completely seriously. "French onion soup with albondigas."

"Smells incredible," said Maddy.

"Followed by deep fried pork terrine with guacamole."

"You guys are crazy. This is like a Food Network show. You can't bring it on fast enough. I am starving." It had been twenty-four hours since she had eaten anything of substance, not counting the cracker at the hospital.

"Here, have some bread, and a glass of wine," said Angelique.

"What's this?" asked Maddy as Angelique placed a little plate of oil in front of her.

"That's olive oil dusted with chopped cilantro."

"Wow." Maddy plowed into it. "Should I be drinking wine? I'm still on pain killers..."

"Best time to drink a glass or two. Should knock you right back out."

"Just what I want. To be the life of the party."

Jimmy entered the kitchen. "Who says anybody's staying up past 9:00 tonight? I think I've had four hours of sleep this entire week. Jesus, that smells good."

Dinner was laid out, the five of them gathered around the small dining table. Candles were lit, making it profoundly cozy. Maddy could see the fog gathering outside the windows, causing her to feel as if winter had come early, and it was time for sharing good food, wine, and laughter with friends. As sore as she was, she was glad to be alive. She was about to tuck into her onion soup with Mexican meatballs when she stopped, again reminded of how lucky she was. She raised her glass.

"To the Masked Avenger, wherever he is. In his way, he has brought us all together... I hope he's okay."

They all raised their glasses. "To absent friends," said Jimmy.

*   *   *

While Jimmy and Jean-Michel washed the dishes, and Angelique put leftovers into tupperwares, Maddy lounged on the sofa, while Carlos lay on his back on the floor. They were listening to some jazz piano. The music was somewhat melancholy, and Maddy found herself growing a little sad. Or was it sleepy? Probably both.

"So," said Carlos after a song had ended. "The Masked Avenger."

"Yeah? What about him?"

"I think it's time we found out more about him. Started to do the research."

Maddy had gone through the same arguments with herself over and over again. But now she felt that Carlos was right. To do the right thing, they needed to know what they were really dealing with. Whatever the right thing was.

"So where do we start?" she asked.

"We've got the address in West Oakland. I was thinking we should go out there and see what we find. For all we know, that's where he might be hiding."

"If so, he'll be very frustrated to see us. If we can find him, then so could other people." She rolled her eyes in the direction of the kitchen.

"We're just following a wild hair, that's all. No one needs to know unless we find anything. All these secrets are safe with me."

"Secrets? What secrets?" asked Jimmy as came out

of the kitchen, wiping his hands on a dish towel.

"Nothing, Dear," trilled Maddy. It was nice having a boyfriend, albeit one that she kept in the dark about a few things. Just then, her phone rang. It was Justin. She hesitated to pick up, but she remembered his message about the Theatre Ghost. "Excuse me, I should take this," she apologized to her friends.

She took the phone down the hall. "Hey," she said into the phone. "You okay?"

"Yeah," replied Justin. "We're on a break. We've just finished running the first act. We start back up in a few minutes, so I don't have much time."

"So, what's this about the Theatre Ghost?"

"Scared the shit out of me. I actually ran out of the theatre without looking back."

"What did he look like?" Maddy realized she was whispering. Nothing like a good ghost story.

"Just a dark shape with burning eyes. It was up in the booth when I was on the stage turning on the ghost light."

"So, ghost lights don't work, I guess," said Maddy.

"Not with this ghost."

"Have you seen it since?"

"No, and trust me, I'm not hanging in the theatre by myself tonight after rehearsal. Just feed the kitten and get the hell out of here."

"Kitten? What kitten..."

"Listen, I've got to go. The real reason I was calling was I can get you into the invited dress tomorrow night. Want to come?"

"To *The Leopard Prince*? Are you kidding? Of course, I want to come!" She hesitated for a moment. "Can you get me two tickets?"

"Two?... Sure. Who are you bringing?"

"My boyfriend, if that's okay."

After a moment, Justin responded with "Sure. Two tickets. No problem. I'll come find you after the show. We can all go out for a drink."

"Thank you, Justin. This is really..." He had hung up.

*　　　　　*　　　　　*

"I've got to go to bed."

"Sure, Chica, it's getting late, anyway," said Carlos, looking at his watch. It was all of 9:30.

How awkward was this? Jimmy looked at his shoes and then said, "Hey, Carlos. Do you need a ride?"

"No, man, I'm good. I need the walk."

Jimmy looked relieved. But Maddy came up to him. She looked at Carlos, who, by now could take a hint and went out into the hall. "I hurt like nobody's business. Give him a ride."

"But I don't even have to touch you," whispered Jimmy. "Just being next to you would be..."

"But I would want to touch you," whispered Maddy. "I don't think I could keep my hands off you. And then we'd be giving Angelique a run for her money, and I don't mean in a good way."

Jimmy laughed. He nodded. His pride was intact. He called out to Carlos, "Wait up, dude. You're getting a ride!" He looked at Maddy, and the look was pretty classic smoldering. "See you tomorrow?"

"We're going to the show," said Maddy with a sweet smile.

"We are?" asked Jimmy in some surprise. "Tomorrow?"

"Yes, I just scored two tickets to *The Leopard Prince*."

"It's just that my mom... my dad... I'm supposed to have Sunday dinner with them. And my mom wasn't joking when she said I should bring you..."

"It's *The Leopard Prince*!"

"It's my *mom*!"

"So, what do we do?" Another crisis - another test of the relationship - already.

"I put them off until next week – no biggie." With

367

that, he became irresistible, and Maddy was suddenly unwilling to let him out the door. "I'll call you in the morning," he said. He kissed her and was gone.

Damn, thought Maddy.

Best. Boyfriend. Ever.

LXXXVI

Sunday morning was gorgeous. The perfect Bay Area fall day - crystal clear, sunny, but just a little cool in the shadows. Maddy awoke with the sun, feeling profoundly much better. She strolled out to the street in her pajamas, picking her way past the twisted wreckage of the trellis, soaking up the morning sun on her face. God, it felt good. After feeling as if she had become a creature of the night over the last week, she rejoiced in the warmth of the morning sun. She sat on the steps in front of her gate and basked for a few minutes. She was high enough on the hill on Lombard Street that she could see over towards the East Bay, with Mount Diablo clear in the distance. It all made the thought of driving over to West Oakland a little less daunting. There was something about broad daylight that made the task ahead much more comforting.

Another shower - still stinging - but this time the muscles began to unlock, and she found she moved more freely. Nothing much to be done about the scratches on her face, but she put a little extra make-up on the bruises, which just made her look like a victim of domestic abuse. Not quite convincing enough. Oh, well. At least she had stories to tell.

Jean-Michel was making French Toast in the kitchen. Real French Toast. "Oui. Pain Perdu," he said.

"Yum!" said Maddy.

Angelique came in with the Sunday Clarion. A pretty sensational front-page story regarding "questions of propriety" at the Museum of Asian Antiquities opened Maddy's eyes. An investigation under way, with the appropriate disclaimers from everyone's legal counsel. Carlos wove a very convincing tale, and the evidence as presented was pretty damning. Statements already from the Chinese consulate, and from the Secretary/Treasurer of the Museum Board, as Madeleine Chang had been temporarily placed on leave from her position as Chairwoman. All pretty by the numbers, but messy, just the same. Maddy was pleased to see that she received a by-line as well. Not bad for my first month on the job, she thought, sipping her coffee. And thank God for Carlos.

And the Masked Avenger, without whom none of this would have happened.

Her phone rang. "I was just thinking of you," she said to Carlos. "Nice work on the Museum story."

"Still a lot going on – going to have to track this one for some weeks," replied Carlos.

"Nothing like job security."

"No shit. So, are we going to do this? Nice day for a drive, isn't it?

"I'll be over there in an hour. Still got to brush my hair… What's the dress code?"

"I think we want to look like young professionals. We're engendering trust."

"I think I can do that. See you in a bit."

*   *   *

The street in West Oakland was tree lined. That was the only thing good about it. That and maybe the children kicking a dirty volleyball around, laughing and teasing each other. Otherwise, there were too many men standing around on corners doing nothing, and too much trash blowing in the slight breeze. Maddy and Carlos had driven by too many liquor stores and too many storefronts that had been boarded up for Maddy to feel like she was still in Kansas anymore. This was as tough a neighborhood as she had ever seen.

All of this was belied, however, by the beautiful Victorian houses. Or rather, houses that had once been beautiful, still with gorgeous bones, but that had fallen, like the rest of the neighborhood, on hard times. Maddy and Carlos pulled up in front of one such house, its porch sagging, the clapboards starting to fall off, the paint faded and peeling. There was a little chain link fence surrounding the front yard, which had fallen into disrepair. Grass was overgrown everywhere, and the flowerbeds were overflowing with weeds.

As Maddy turned off the engine, she took stock of the men at the corner. Her neon yellow Beetle was an object of interest to them. What had been cute, even adorably spunky in Newport Beach, was suddenly a sore thumb in West Oakland. Maddy felt profoundly self-conscious. "Is it safe, do you think?"

"You're asking me, Miss Batwoman? I don't know. What do you think would be the worst thing that could happen?"

"We get shot."

"Right. Seems like a nice day for it." He sighed. "Alright. Let's cowboy up."

They both put on their best game-faces and got out of the car. Carlos carried a clipboard. He had printed out something with the Verizon logo on it and had some business cards. "Where'd you get that?" asked Maddy.

"I just made it up. Pulled the logo down from their website and just mocked this up in Word. It looks sort of official, doesn't it?"

"I can hardly wait to know you when you're older and more devious," said Maddy.

Carlos just gave her a tight smile. They climbed up onto the porch, set themselves and rang the doorbell. Which worked, much to their surprise. After a minute they heard a voice call out, "Be right there!" There was a shuffling and thumping. The door then opened slowly to reveal an old, small Black woman clutching a walker. Her eyes were bright and clear, though, and her expression of surprise at being visited by two young people was colored by a smile. She was dressed nicely, but from another era. She looked, in fact, as if she had just come from church.

"How can I help you?" the old woman asked brightly.

"We're from Verizon Wireless, ma'am," said Carlos just as brightly. He could have quite the career in sales, thought Maddy. "We're in the neighborhood visiting Verizon Wireless customers to make sure that their needs are being met, and to learn if there is anything more we can do to provide better service." Carlos handed her his card.

"Why, that's funny," said the woman. "They usually just call."

"Well, we're all about community at Verizon, ma'am. We believe in the human connection. We want to be on a face-to-face basis with our customers. In this economy, service is what makes the difference, so we're going the extra mile."

He's really good, thought Maddy. He could run for President.

"Well, that's nice, but I'm not sure how I can help you," said the woman.

Carlos looked at his clipboard. "You are Clarice Bryant, aren't you ma'am?"

"Why, yes I am."

"And this is the address on record for this number?" Carlos showed her the number, which was on the sheet on his clipboard.

"Yes, it is, certainly," said the woman, after putting some glasses on her nose and taking a close look at the number.

"Then you have no dissatisfaction with our service?" asked Maddy, feeling she should jump in and share some of the load.

"I wouldn't know. I pay the bill, but I don't use the service. I don't even have a cell phone."

LXXXVII

Damian Johnson settled into his big recliner. God, I love Sundays, he thought to himself. Six hours of non-stop professional football, preceded by several hours of pre-game analysis, and as much post-game analysis as Georgia would let him have before he had to sit down to dinner. Today felt extra-special, since he was still within his window of being pampered by his wife before she became completely annoyed with him being a big baby. She had set out a large bowl of potato chips, onion dip and a cooler of beer for him, put a pillow behind his head, and handed him the remote. She had then headed off for the afternoon at her sister's. Damian was a new uncle, and his sister-in-law needed an afternoon off. Georgia was happy to oblige her sister and look after her nephew – and to get out of the house.

Doesn't get any better than this, thought Damian.

Big game, too. Early still in the season, but if Oakland could take this one from Kansas City, they would open up a two-game gap between themselves and their hated rivals. Only team Oakland might hate more was San Diego, but then Oakland was hated by everybody. That's what made being a fan of the Knights so special, so much fun. You were automatically a rebel, difficult, ornery and mean. And cool. The Knights fostered this, enjoying being the Bad Boys of the NFL.

The pre-game analysts were talking up the legacy of the Oakland Knights, and the commitment to excellence that had been less than excellent in recent years. They hadn't been to the Super Bowl in over a decade, not since 1998, when they got blown out by Tampa Bay. It had been lean times since then. But this year, they showed promise.

And Damian didn't care *that* much – he wasn't rabid. He enjoyed the ritual of game day as much as anything, and certainly wasn't in a horrible foul mood if the Knights lost. Damian cracked open his first beer – it was now just past noon, so it was okay – and settled back.

*   *   *

The roar of the stadium crowd on the TV was the white noise in the background up in the booth at the Orpheum. Justin listened absent-mindedly - it was more for the spot operators who were hanging out waiting for their next cues while the assistant director yelled at the assistant lighting designer about how the light cues weren't quite the same as they were on Broadway. The original director and original designer had been off working on some production in Berlin, so their assistants were taking the brunt of the remounting effort. Tonight was the night when all the big-wigs would finally be in residence. Justin smiled to himself. The farther down the food chain in the production hierarchy, the more fussy and uptight the people were. He was already over this load-in - everyone involved was a jerk - and he looked forward to several years of a relatively pleasant day-to-day once the show opened and all of them were gone. He lived pretty simply, so he would save a lot of money on this run. Maybe he might even be able to buy a house. Certainly, a new motorcycle.

Sheba was sitting on a stool that they had set up for her next to the booth window. All the commotion onstage was fascinating to her. Was it all the people dressed up like cats? wondered Justin. Huh.

Suddenly the white noise on the TV got louder. It must be kick-off, he thought as he pressed the Go button on the console to initiate another light cue sequence, and sure enough it was. The game was underway.

*   *   *

He could hear the roar of the crowd, the give and take of the play-by-play announcer and the commentators, and something within him stirred. With each passing play, with each tackle, with each crunch of shoulder pad on helmet, he fell deeper and deeper into a reverie. In the darkness, his eyes glowed. He could feel the adrenalin dripping into his bloodstream.

It was time to go back to work.

It was time to pay some debts.

LXXXVIII

She had invited them in to have some lemonade. "It's not fresh, just frozen, but it still tastes pretty good," she said, as she stirred it up in a plastic pitcher. Clarice Bryant got around her kitchen pretty well for using a walker. She didn't really need it, it just helped her from time to time.

"So, whose phone is it?" Maddy had asked after Carlos dropped the clipboard from shock.

"My grandson's. Lincoln's. Don't ask me where he is, I don't know. It's been a long time since I've seen him. A long time since anybody's seen him, from what I can tell."

"Do you ever hear from him?" asked Maddy.

"Every once in a while, he calls. He checks in on me."

"Does he ever tell you what he's doing, or how he is?" asked Carlos, taking the offered lemonade.

"He doesn't talk much. When he does, he keeps it pretty tight. He just says that he's trying to help people out, that's all. Could be in the Peace Corps for all I know." Clarice set herself down in an old, frayed armchair. Maddy helped her, then sat down herself on the sagging sofa next to Carlos.

"But you pay his cell phone bill?" she asked.

"It comes, I pay it."

"It's an impertinent question, ma'am," said Maddy, "but may I ask how you... how you get along?"

"There's still a little bit of money left. There used to be lots of money, but then, well, it kind of went up in smoke. I used to have a nice house for a time, but I had to sell it. Moved back here, and I just dole out the money left over from the sale of my old house to get by."

"You say you moved back here... is this where you're from? I mean originally?" Maddy sipped her lemonade. Clarice was right, it wasn't bad. In fact, it tasted just fine.

"You children ask a lot of questions." Clarice looked at Carlos and then at Maddy. She looked very suspicious. "Who did you say you worked for?"

Before Carlos could say Verizon again, Maddy put her hand on Clarice's. "We're sorry, Mrs. Bryant. We're not really from Verizon. We're friends of Lincoln's and, well, we're worried about him. We haven't seen him ourselves in several days."

Clarice narrowed her eyes and took them both in. "Now why'd you have to come in here and lie to me like that?"

"We're very sorry ma'am," said Carlos. "It was my idea. We weren't sure what we would find. All we had was this phone number, and we were able to trace it here. It was a mean trick, and you've been very kind." Carlos and Maddy stood up to leave.

"You say you're friends of Lincoln's?"

"Yes ma'am," said Maddy. "He pretty much saved my life. Twice."

"Did he now?" Clarice took Maddy's hand. The grip was firm, despite the smallness of the fingers and the tightness of the skin over the bone. She must be almost ninety, thought Maddy. "Have a seat. So, you want to know more about Lincoln? I can only tell you so much. He was a troubled child, surely."

"You are his grandmother? Did you take care of him?"

"I did. He grew up right in this house."

"What happened to his mother?" asked Maddy.

"She was a flighty thing. Bit of a slut, really." Maddy kind of liked Mrs. Bryant. Called it as she saw it, if nothing else. "But it was the late Sixties, and everybody was running around with everybody else. That girl just couldn't get it together. Too many boyfriends. Never could figure out who the father was. Once she had the baby, she just handed it to me and said, 'I got to go now, Momma' and she just took off. Just walked out of our lives. Never saw her again."

"Wow," said Carlos quietly.

"So, he grew up here," Clarice went on. "My husband did his best to take care of us, he was a MUNI driver, but we had our hands full with that boy."

"How so?" asked Maddy.

"He had issues. Not sure if it was caused by all the drugs his momma took when she was pregnant or what, but he had trouble learning. Reading was hard. Making friends was hard. He kept to himself, mostly. He was a big boy, though. Even so, he would get bullied all the time. Come home from school with a broken nose, or with bruises..." Clarice took a long look at Maddy. "You got a man who beats you?" she asked sternly. "Now don't defend a man who beats you. They's the lowest of the low."

Maddy was *so* embarrassed. "No ma'am. I got into an accident just the other day. The bruises are from a fall." Clarice wasn't entirely convinced, and she looked like if there had been someone giving Maddy trouble, she would have taken care of the asshole herself. She was tough.

"So, his grandfather, my husband... a really good man... took the boy under his wing and worked with him. Got him to focus, to take his talents and apply them. He also fed that boy. Wilson would give him as much food as that boy could hold, and Lincoln got big. Between the food and the workouts that Wilson gave him, Lincoln became a big and strong young man."

Maddy and Carlos looked at each other. All made sense so far.

"Was he still bullied after that?" asked Carlos. Carlos knew all about being bullied.

"Funny thing, he still was. He just had too sweet a heart. Was a dreamy boy. Other kids thought he was retarded. He wasn't retarded, just… different. It was football that saved him, if you want to call what happened, saved. That and his books. He loved to read, although he was a terrible slow reader. It was painful to watch him work his way through a sentence, let alone a whole book, but he would just chew and chew on those books 'til he got through them. He could remember some of them word for word, from cover to cover."

"Sounds like some form of autism," said Carlos, writing notes. "What kind of books did he read?"

"I don't know where he got it, and it's not the sort of thing most Black boys pick up, but he was fascinated by this book with this French name." Clarice gestured to a little bookshelf and Maddy went over. On the bottom shelf lay Le Morte D'Arthur by Thomas Malory. Maddy pulled it out. It was a very old cloth covered book, printed in the thirties, with illustrations throughout.

"I love this book," Maddy said, flipping through the pages.

"What is it?" asked Carlos.

"The Death of Arthur. The story of the Knights of the Round Table. Lancelot and Guinevere."

"Oh. My. God," whispered Carlos.

"He read and re-read those stories. He loved that Arthur was a stable boy who became the King. He loved all that chivalry. He was a real gentleman when he was a young man."

"You said football saved him. How so?"

"It gave him discipline. And it made him push himself hard. He grew quite big and strong. And it gave him, finally, something of a family. But his road was a hard one. He had troubles. When he was little, we just thought he was wilful. But there came a day when some kids started to bully him, and, well, he just snapped." Maddy and Carlos exchanged glances. They knew what that meant. "I know those boys were mean, but they didn't deserve what happened to them. All three of them in the hospital. Broken arms and legs. He just threw those kids around like rag dolls."

There was a pause.

"When did you lose track of him?"

"It was after…" At this Clarice started to get misty-eyed. "I can't talk about it. It was about ten years ago. He should have gotten more help. No one would help him. Not even that bitch of a wife, pardon my French. They all walked away from him, leaving him to suffer as he does. I can't do much for him…" she gestured at her frail little body. "But I could give him some love, and a home."

"He's out there, and we're here to help him. Do you have any idea where he could be?"

"I don't. I'm sorry. I wish I did. An old lady could use some family. He's all the family I've got, at this point. I've outlived everybody else."

"Is there anything we can do for you, Mrs. Bryant?"

"Call me Clarice. I'm alright. You two have given me more entertainment this afternoon than I've had in a long time. Just find my boy, I guess."

"We will, ma'am," said Maddy gently. "We'll do our best."

*   *   *

The car was untouched, much to Maddy's relief. Having heard Clarice's story, she wondered if she might be the safest woman in West Oakland. Word was probably on the street that no one should mess with Clarice Bryant, or her friends.

"So, what do we do now?" asked Maddy as she pulled away and headed back towards the Bay Bridge.

"Investigative reporting 101," said Carlos. "When all else fails, Google the guy."

Maddy rolled her eyes. Why hadn't she thought of that? "Your place or mine?" she asked.

"The food's better at your place," said Carlos. He

settled back into the passenger seat and closed his eyes for a quick nap on the way home.

*   *   *

They sat down on her sofa, with her laptop on the coffee table. Maddy typed the name into the little window on the side of her browser and Google took .16 seconds to find over 1.5 million results. There was even a Wikipedia entry, which lay there at the top.

It took her a *minute and sixteen* seconds of staring at the two-line blurb before she could find it in her to click on the entry.

Oh. No.

LXXXIX

It was raining. He had been drinking. When had he last not had a drink? He couldn't remember. That was the point, he had smiled to himself. To not remember.

Another bar. This time it was in Jacksonville. Why was he in Jacksonville? He vaguely remembered something about a friend. Yes. He had come to Jacksonville to visit a friend. He needed a friend right now – he had none. Except this friend.

What was his name?

Where did he live?

Where am I driving now?

It was hard to see through the rain. Harder still with the mist in his eyes. There was something inside him that always challenged him whenever he got behind the wheel of a car after he had been drinking. And he always pushed whatever it was away.

I'm indestructible.

It was a nice car. Very fast and sleek and powerful. It felt good to drive it. Fast. Faster. Fastest. The streets were flooding. The water sprayed in spectacular jets off to his side as he blew through intersection after intersection. He felt free. He felt as if he were about to take flight.

He only saw her eyes.

They were enormous, her eyes. Filled with terror and flooded with the light of his high beams. At the speed with which he was traveling, no amount of pressure on his brakes would stop the car in time.

The thud and the split second of thumping across the roof of his car were sickening. As he slammed on the brakes, the car started to spin round and round along the rain-soaked and oil-slick street. The lights danced in circles around him. A horrible carousel ride.

The car came to a stop, finally. Hundreds of yards later. A lifetime later. He sat for a moment stunned. And then, suddenly, the mist faded, and he could see clearly. More clearly than he had in years.

He leapt out of the car. Years of training had once given him an explosive power off the line, a power that had begun to fade. And yet he never ran faster in his life than he did in that instant. Several hundred yards - several lifetimes - were covered in seconds. His suit – his tailored Armani – was drenched by the rain. The tropical weight wool was plastered to him as he ran.

When he arrived at where she lay, he crumpled to the ground beside her, the asphalt tearing through the soaked fabric at his knees. She was lying on her stomach, face down. When he rolled her over all he could see for the next terrible few seconds were her eyes. Those enormous eyes.

And then he saw the eyes of the dead baby in her arms.

XC

Lincoln Bryant
From Wikipedia, the Free Encyclopedia
Lincoln Bryant (born February 16, 1969, in Oakland, CA) was a former National Football League and Pro Bowl middle linebacker for the Oakland Knights of the American Football Conference, where he played for seven seasons, from 1991 to 1998. Drafted in the middle of the second round out of the University of Southern California, he became one of the most fearsome defensive players in the 90's, leading the league in sacks in 1996 and 1998. He was a member of the American Football Conference Championship team in 1998 that played in the Super Bowl in Phoenix against the Tampa Bay Prowlers.

Bryant gained national notoriety during the week prior to the Super Bowl when he disappeared for three days, causing his dismissal from the team. His absence from the Super Bowl has often been credited for the one-sided loss the Knights sustained.

It had been later determined that Bryant had spent the three days prior to the Super Bowl in Nogales, Mexico, lost and disoriented, suffering from severe bipolar disorder exacerbated by alcohol and painkillers that he had been taking in greater and greater quantities throughout the season.

After his discharge from the Knights, Bryant drifted from team to team, finally closing out his career with the Florida Panthers, an Arena Football League team.

On November 5, 2011, Bryant was involved in a tragic accident in Jacksonville, FL. An unidentified homeless woman and her newborn child were killed by Bryant while he was driving under the influence. He was sentenced to fifteen years in prison, which was commuted to five years in a mental institution. His whereabouts at this time are unknown.

* * *

Maddy and Carlos sat there for what seemed like an hour, without saying anything. Finally, Maddy whispered, mostly to herself, "There are some mistakes…"

Carlos, who was almost always irrepressible, looked profoundly deflated. "There are some stories… We can't tell this story. The pain he must be in. I'm sorry, but I can't imagine what he must be trying to live through."

"We need to find him. And try to get him some help," said Maddy.

"Do we? Maybe Charelle was right. Maybe we should leave him alone. Maybe he's working through his debt the only way he can. The only way he knows how."

"Which will leave him prey to the police, and to his demons. If we could get him the medical attention he needs, he might be okay. Safe, clean, helping Clarice. I don't know." Maddy slumped back onto the sofa.

"How could anyone afford to pay for that?"

Maddy stared off into the middle distance for a bit. She chewed on her lower lip. "We could write the book."

"What?"

"We could write the book, sell the rights to his story. With the money, we could pay for his treatment."

"I just said…"

"I know, and normally I would agree with you. But this could help him and help others."

"And make us famous."

"I don't need that. Do you?"

"No," said Carlos with a shrug. "I like struggling in anonymity."

385

XCI

This was the moment that John Sanders both loved and dreaded. He loved the rush, the energy of an audience filling an auditorium in anticipation of a performance. He dreaded this equally, as for the next few hours almost anything that could go wrong probably would. It was 7:30, and the doors had just opened for the invited dress rehearsal. This was when the cast, crew and staff of the theatre were permitted to invite friends and family to see the show prior to a paying audience. This allowed the cast and production team to get their performance legs without risk.

He covered every inch of the theatre over the next half hour, from the box office to the stage door, to the green room to the crew's lounge, in an effort to make sure, to his satisfaction, that everything that could be done had been. He was also doing everything he could to avoid Cheryl Niederman, who, in such moments, could drive him to complete distraction with her own pre-performance anxieties. Better leave her to entertain the MagicLand upper management, and to hob-nob with the famous director.

His last stop was the booth, from where he preferred to watch the show. This way he could hear the show being called by the stage manager, be tapped into any issues backstage, still see the performance, and curse as much as he wanted without anyone but the stagehands hearing him.

Perfect.

"I don't like that cat up here," he growled at Justin as 'places' was called. Two minutes before the show was about to start.

"Cats are lucky in the theatre, Mr. Sanders. She'll

bring us a three-year run, easily." John Sanders looked at Robin for a moment and decided to give luck a chance. Robin had a funny look on her face, though. Her eyes squinted, and her nose wrinkled.

*   *   *

"I'm so excited I could pop," said Maddy as she nuzzled up against Jimmy's shoulder. They had just taken their seats, which weren't bad. There really wasn't a bad seat in the house. It was fun just to be in the building. Jimmy had never been inside the Orpheum and was completely taken by the ornate decorations and the scale of the auditorium.

"This place is fantastic," he said. "We owe your friend Justin more than just a drink."

"Yeah," said Maddy. "I think he's paid off his karmic debt." Jimmy just arched an eyebrow. "Don't get me started, okay?" pleaded Maddy.

Jimmy smiled. "Okay."

The houselights went to half. Suddenly, a follow spot cut through the hazy air of the auditorium catching a small, intense woman at the side of the stage.

"Hello. I'm Janice Traynor." A roar of approval rose up from the audience. "I'm the director of the show," she continued, although everyone knew that. She was super-famous for her work with puppets, and her artistic credentials were extremely strong. "Tonight is the first night for anyone to see this version of the show. This is still a rehearsal, so we beg your indulgence should we need to stop for any reason. If we feel that anything is unsafe, or if we need to go back to work a transition, the stage manager will stop us, and we will reset. Thank you for joining us on the next phase of the journey of *The Leopard Prince!*" The audience applauded enthusiastically. Nothing like seeing something right at the beginning.

The lights suddenly went to black, causing the

audience to gasp. Then the air was filled with thunderous African drumming, and the auditorium was awash with dappled light. Out of nowhere, animals appeared: monkeys swinging on vines, zebras trotting down the aisles, elephants slowly working their way across the forestage, birds flying through the air. It was pure magic. The curtains parted, revealing a huge, rising sun while the giant rock formation pivoted into view with leopards and their cubs prancing from rock to rock.

"The costumes are amazing," whispered Maddy.

"So is the music," replied Jimmy, who was swaying to the pulsing rhythm.

The story unfolded seamlessly, eliciting oohs and ahs from the audience. More than once, Maddy squeezed Jimmy's arm in excitement. She really is a musical theatre geek, thought Jimmy with a smile. That's not so bad. He was truly enjoying himself, too.

*   *   *

She had seen the show more than a few times and, truth be told, was totally over it. But Cheryl Niederman still had a role to play and would play it as well as she could. She had to be there to massage any first audience jitters, and to direct the various suits from MagicLand to where they needed to be. She also needed to make sure that she was by Mark Eichler's elbow at intermission. Until then, she could pace in the lobby and glance at the show on the closed-circuit monitors that were provided for the latecomers. If there was any buzz for her, it was in hearing the audience reactions – the cheers, the applause, the gasps, even the boos for the evil great white hunter character who is the nemesis of the leopards. Ka-ching.

But was it all about the money? Not really. She had plenty of money. It really was about the power. The power to get things done. The power to play someone like Eichler, who was, himself, one of the most powerful and glamorous CEOs in America. Right up there with Bill Gates, Larry Ellison and Rupert Murdoch. She loved being in such company. Her husband, who was a billionaire in his own right, was not a glamorous man, however. Something of a party-pooper, actually. So, she created her own glamour, her own drama.

Cheryl Niederman glanced up at the monitor. It was getting near the end of the first act. The evil great white hunter was singing his dark aria about how he was going to be wearing a leopard-skin jacket soon. The script was flawless in its manipulation of the audience. People would go into the intermission with concern, excitement, dread, anticipation, hopefulness. Everything that made good theatre.

*   *   *

Up in the booth, John Sanders had only screamed at the stage five times. All in all, a pretty smooth show so far. Robin had jumped every time he uttered a curse. She had finally curled up into a ball at Justin's feet, causing Justin to maintain his posture at the lighting console without adjustment, for fear of scaring her further.

It was a complex show. The dancing, singing, acting, music from the 25-piece orchestra – that was the smallest part of the production. Up in the booth and backstage, dozens of technicians and stage managers were quietly grinding out hundreds of cues. The automation for the scenery alone required a doctorate to run. There were so many moving pieces that one had to monitor every move carefully. Justin had seen the rack of monitors that were next to the main control console for the scenery, and he was impressed with how many different angles of the stage the master scenic technician had. He could see everything. The stage manager also had similar views. Cameras had been placed everywhere.

Justin had only the view from the booth. What he

saw over the next few minutes was only part of what really happened.

*   *   *

The music moved him. Throughout the course of the afternoon, while final preparations had been made, and the Knights of Oakland had slain their foes from Kansas City, he had grown more and more agitated. He had not slept much in the last 48 hours, what with the final preparations for the show, the constant thrum of the TV and the lack of food. Whereas Robin had had her fill, he thought, of cat food, he had gone without. His blood sugar was dangerously low.

*   *   *

"Stop!"

The stage manager had exercised his prerogative. A costume quick change had not happened quickly enough, and the actor, as seen through his monitor, was in danger of being caught in the gigantic scene shift that happened before the final number of the first act. There had also been concern expressed by the head flyman that the giant star drop was not properly weighted. The stars flying in at the end of the first act were what made audiences weep. The flyman was concerned that the drop was out of balance and would require an extra hand to bring into position.

"Goddamnmotherfuckingsonofabitch!" said John Sanders for what was now the sixth time during the first act. "Jesus. I'm going out there to see what the fuck is going on." With that he climbed up the ladder that went to the catwalks, the shortest way to get to the fly rail. He knew the building well and knew that to go down to stage level and then back up to the rail would take much too long.

"Please don't Mr. Sand..." called the stage manager

390

after him, with no success. Justin wasn't sure what to do. He was about to adopt the union stagehand attitude and simply shrug and wait to do what he was told, when the stage manager, looking at his monitor said, "What was that?"

"What was what?" asked Justin.

"Something just flashed by that screen." The stage manager pointed to the monitor that showed the feed from the front of house catwalk that showed the stage in infrared. This was used to tell, during a blackout onstage, if scenery and actors were properly positioned.

"Shit! Did you see that?"

There was the flickering on the monitor that displayed the stage from the vantage point of the loading rail. The distance between the two cameras was one hundred feet of catwalk and stairs, and yet the timing between the two was measured in seconds. The momentary effect on the second monitor was of a black, plastic sheet whipping across the screen.

"What the fuck is going on? If that's the same thing in both places... what could possibly move that fast?"

Justin shivered. He had seen the Ghost.

He then realized that Sheba was no longer at his feet.

*   *   *

Maddy felt chills down her spine. The Great White Hunter was really good. He was more than a little scary. She was startled, as was everyone else, though, when the voice came loudly through the sound system, "Stop!"

The spell had been broken, but, in a funny way, it had been strengthened. There was nothing like being reminded that one was seeing a live event, and that mistakes or accidents could happen. It made the experience of live theatre that much more precious, that much more unique and vital. She suddenly found herself laughing knowingly, having been in more than a few technical rehearsals which came to a crash and burn.

Jimmy looked at her quizzically, not having much experience behind the scenes. Maddy was about to explain, as the audience rustled and buzzed, when she felt something at her feet. She just about jumped out of her skin.

"Robin! What the heck, girl!" The gray kitten was doing a dance at her ankles, trying to get her attention. "Wait. You're the 'Theatre Cat'"? Maddy's stomach dropped through the floor. "Where's... you know... where's your..." At that, Robin poked her with a paw and then bolted down the row towards the aisle. Maddy turned to Jimmy. "He's here. He's got to be. He's the Theatre Ghost."

Jimmy, who had been enjoying the experience immensely, suddenly bristled up. The smile on his face vanished, and he bolted out of his seat. Robin was sitting in the middle of the aisle, waiting for Maddy. As Maddy scrambled over the startled audience members in their row, Robin started running towards the stage. Maddy followed, with Jimmy close behind.

*   *   *

From the time he climbed up onto the catwalks, John Sanders felt a strange sense of vertigo. He reminded himself that there was a ceiling between him and one hundred feet of floor, but that didn't help much. It was still pretty damn high up in the air. But he was on a mission – nothing was going to screw up all of the hard work and sacrifice, nothing was going to disgrace him before his boss or the MagicLand brass. He ran a tight ship, dammit, and if something wasn't working, he wanted to know why. He had evolved, under the tutelage of Cheryl Niederman, to expect heads on plates. He was going to be front row and center in seeing what had gone wrong.

He had just passed through the small steel door that separated the catwalks on the audience side of the proscenium from the loading rail when he saw something out of the corner of his eye. What the fuck was that?

And then he saw it. Or them. The eyes. Glistening in the light emanating from the stage. If he had to guess, John Sanders was now about 80 feet above the stage floor. He wasn't guessing in that moment, however.

A voice hissed. There was something about the acoustics in this part of the theatre that made it sound as if the voice was right next to him, directly next to his ear.

"You. You killed Lucky Jerry. You killed Rodney. You must pay the price."

In that moment, John Sanders let loose his bowels.

* * *

"What the fuck is going on?" snarled Cheryl Niederman to the assistant lighting designer. He was the first person she could get her hands on who was on headset. He was part of the battery of designers and technicians who had tables in the back of the theatre with computer monitors which displayed the status of the sound, scenery, and lighting.

"Nothing much," he stammered. "The stage manager was concerned about actor safety, so he…"

"Actor safety?!" said Cheryl Niederman in disbelief. Actor safety was for pussies. "You tell him from me that he gets this show on the road in ten seconds or I'll personally…" she stopped. "You!" she called out down the aisle. "You! Back in your seat. And no animals in the building!" Everyone in the audience turned to look at her and then started to laugh. No animals in the building… this was *The Leopard Prince*!

* * *

"Robin, no!" Last time she yelled that, all hell had broken loose, and Maddy became immediately

393

apprehensive. That little kitten was more trouble than she could possibly imagine. Robin ran down the aisle and jumped up onto the rail that separated the audience from the orchestra pit. This was covered with a black velour curtain, which gave Robin something she could grip onto. She then balanced effortlessly, turning back to see if Maddy was coming, which she was. Satisfied that Maddy was on her way, Robin then scooted along the rail until she got to where the rail joined the edge of the stage next to the proscenium. She leapt off the rail and onto the stage.

At that point, the audience burst into laughter.

*   *   *

Justin was young, but he had spent some time in the theatre, and seen more than his share of technical snafus. But he had never seen a situation deteriorate so quickly from a couple of simple backstage miscues. He took a philosophical moment, in which he thought that the stakes for such large commercial productions were too high for it to be called theatre anymore. All of the fun was squeezed out of the process at this level by people who were too tightly wound. He preferred the breezy competence of the third national tour teams, or the bus and truck companies. In and out in a week, but practiced and easy.

His momentary reverie was broken when he saw Sheba running onto the stage.

He was *so* fired.

"Justin! Check this out!" The stage manager was pointing to the monitor that was fed by the camera on the loading rail. It was trained across the rail catwalk so that the stage manager and the master carpenters could monitor the movements of the flymen. "Where's Johnny and Rico?" The two flymen were nowhere to be seen. The light levels were low, so the resolution wasn't great, but they could see two shapes up on the rail, neither of them Johnny nor Rico. One was easily recognizable as John Sanders. His lumpy shape in his white shirt and tie was discernible in the half light. The other shape - well, both men had never seen anything like it.

"It's the fucking Theatre Ghost!" said Justin in awe.

"The what?"

"The Theatre Ghost. I've seen him a couple of times before. Jesus, he's big."

It was true. John Sanders was a pretty big man, but he was dwarfed by the creature that was approaching him. This was due, in part, to Sanders cowering like a beaten puppy, but still. The large, black clad, shimmering figure approached Sanders inexorably. Sanders could only fall to his knees in obvious terror.

"Get out there!" called the stage manager.

"What the fuck do you mean, Get out there?" asked Justin incredulously.

"I can't go - I've got to stay on top of this. You and Robert should go."

"And do what?"

"I don't know. Stop that guy!"

Justin looked at Robert, one of the follow spot operators. Both he and Robert were pretty tall guys, but this was not their idea of an easy call. "Got a wrench on you?" Robert patted his back pocket. "Then let's go," sighed Justin. Perhaps, if he saved John Sanders' bacon, he might keep his job.

*   *   *

Maddy had no idea what to do. Robin had landed on stage, and was prancing around, looking at Maddy expectantly. An assistant stage manager, with headset on, came running out to try and catch Robin, but to no avail. The cast, trained not to move during such a technical breakdown unless specifically instructed to do so, stood in place, and watched in amusement. The audience laughing at Robin's antics, and at the screaming woman in the red dress at the back of the auditorium whose face was turning as red as her dress, added to Maddy's sense of discombobulation.

"I'm so sorry!" she called out to the assistant stage manager. "I'll get her – she'll come to me." With that, Maddy ran to the side of the auditorium and climbed up the steps onto stage. "Robin, come here, girl!" At that moment, Robin sat down, looked up into the air, and yowled.

*   *   *

John Sanders began to scream like a little girl. In an instant, the weight of his sins came crashing down upon him. He was going to hell, for sure, and here was the devil's messenger come to take him.

*   *   *

The creature before him on its knees was pleading with him, although he could not make out what it was saying. He had once been on his knees before and was shown no mercy. He had received no mercy from anyone for many years. He would show none now. He knew that the blubbering creature before him was evil and was a source of pain to others.

He would not kill him, however. It was never about killing anyone… there was a moment of pain deep in his soul, then he recovered… just demonstrating strength, prowess, reducing one's opponent to a harmless state. There might not be mercy, but there could be perspective, even magnanimity…

*   *   *

The grip on John Sanders' throat was crushing. He clung to the arm that clutched him in an effort to reduce the pressure, only to find that his feet were no longer on the ground. Oh Jesus, oh Jesus, oh Jesus, he thought over and over. He kicked and tried to scream, but to no avail. And then he suddenly found himself dangling over the rail, more than eight stories over the stage floor. His legs felt hot and wet. As he lost consciousness, he realized with shame that he had just relieved himself all over the cast and scenery of *The Leopard Prince*.

*   *   *

Johnny and Rico were unconscious. They were both handcuffed to the handrail of the first catwalk, directly over the forestage, and on the audience side of the proscenium. How had Sanders missed them? thought Justin. Probably because he hadn't been looking for danger and had gone straight to the loading rail. "Stay with them," Justin said to Robert. "Radio to stage-management. We'll need some medical attention."

"What about you?" said Robert, doubtfully.

"I guess I'm going to go through that door. If I can't handle it, I'll be right back out again. I'm not that stupid."

Robert nodded and went to the two men, who were just starting to come to.

Justin stood outside the steel door that led to the loading rail catwalk and took a deep breath.

*   *   *

Jimmy had no idea what to do. He had run down to the front of the stage, and then stopped. The last thing he wanted to do was to jump up onto the stage waving a badge and shouting 'Police' and telling people to remain calm. For all he knew at that moment it really was a small technical malfunction, and that the little kitten was an added complication. The only one losing her cool completely was some woman in a red dress who was cursing into a headset in the back of the auditorium.

Suddenly, several of the performers started to scream and run off the stage. The actor playing the Great White Hunter was splattered in what looked like mud. He took a moment, then reeled in revulsion. He exited quickly stage left. The performers that remained were all looking up into the flies. Maddy, too, was riveted by what she saw. The audience started to panic.

Jimmy decided it was time to do the 'Police' thing and ran onto the stage, pulling out his badge. He was disoriented by the stage lighting momentarily, and it took him a second to get his bearings. Once his eyes adjusted, though, he had to see what everyone was looking at.

At that moment, there was a loud scream from the collected company as the giant star drop came crashing down out of the fly loft and onto the stage. Dangling in the middle of the drop, like a fly caught in an enormous spider web, was a man.

*   *   *

He had thrown the creature at the glowing stars. Perhaps it might be hurled back into the evil dimension from which it came. As the creature collided with the stars, the whole night sky had fallen. How strange...

Suddenly, he was blinded. Banks of lights over his head came on, revealing the whole theatre. The spell was breaking.

*   *   *

Justin had come through the door onto the rail just as the Theatre Ghost threw John Sanders like a rag doll at the star drop. He knew that the added two hundred plus pounds of Sanders' weight would throw the system out of balance, pop the safety, and send the rig plummeting towards the stage. Woah.

398

He had the presence of mind in that moment to hit the switch that controlled the fly loft work lights. Banks of fluorescent lights flickered on, flooding the loft with a harsh, white light. The Theatre Ghost was suddenly revealed in all his strangeness. A big man, dressed in sweatpants and a garbage bag, stood before him, blinking from the surprise of the lights. As Justin stood there unsure of what to do next, the big man shook off his surprise and lunged at him with a speed that Justin would not have thought possible. In the next instant, Justin found himself struggling in the grip of a gloved fist that had grabbed him by the T-shirt and was pulling him off the catwalk floor.

*   *   *

Maddy, who had been struggling to make out what was happening up on the loading rail high above her, was terrified by what was revealed once the work lights came on. She saw the Masked Avenger lunge at Justin and scoop him up like a puppy. As Maddy, Jimmy and the cast of *The Leopard Prince* watched in terror, the Masked Avenger stood at the rail, holding Justin as if to throw him over the side.

The cry left her before she realized what she was doing.

"Lincoln, no!"

Her voice echoed throughout the building, captured within the sound system, and amplified sufficiently to fill the auditorium. It came through the speakers that the flymen used to hear their calls. It rolled through speakers in the lobbies and even into the restrooms. For a heart-stopping instant that was the only sound anyone heard.

*   *   *

Lincoln.

399

Lincoln. I was... I am... I...

The Masked Avenger released his grip on Justin, who dropped to the grated metal flooring of the catwalk. There was a sickening moment where the Masked Avenger had no idea where he was or how he got there. And then he found himself falling through space, the catwalk receding above him.

There are some mistakes...

Almost a hundred feet – several hundred lifetimes – were covered in seconds.

*   *   *

The impact caused the whole stage to shudder. A chunk of the Leopards' Rock broke away. The entire audience screamed as one, already shocked by the image of the man dangling amongst the stars. Jimmy pulled something from deep inside of him and took command. His voice rang out from the stage, and he was able to make himself heard above the din of the panicked crowd. After a few seconds, he managed, through sheer force of will, to quiet the audience. He directed the ushers to lead the audience out of the auditorium row by row in an orderly sequence. The house was almost clear when the paramedics arrived. Only then did he turn his attention to the center of the stage, where a crowd of performers and stage technicians had gathered around the black and gray clad figure lying within a small crater.

Maddy had pushed her way through the crowd to kneel next to the Masked Avenger. Robin was rubbing up against him, doing all she could to stir him. Blood was leaking from his eyes and ears and from the side of his mouth. But he was breathing.

Maddy took his giant, gloved hand, and took off the glove. She wrapped both hands around his big paw and held it against her cheek. Tears were coursing down her face. The wetness seemed to stir him.

"Oh, please, please, please, please be okay…" Maddy whispered. "We all need you to be okay. It would hurt so much if you weren't okay…"

"You are young," he said, his breathing labored, his voice no more than a whisper. "How many real disappointments have you had?" Maddy could only shake her head. Maybe two or three, she thought to herself. "You have so many dreams," he continued. "Can you imagine being responsible for ending the dreams of others?" He shook violently and was then calm. He whispered, "Can you imagine such a disappointment and what that might do to you?"

Maddy could not imagine such a thing, even though she knew she was living through a profound, sad moment just then. Her heart was breaking – she could barely think. "Please don't die," she said quietly, clutching his giant hand in hers.

"I will," he sighed. "I must."

"Why?!" she wailed, tears streaming down her cheeks.

"Because… because people do. And because there are some mis…"

And with that he slipped away.

XCII

There are few things lonelier or more sad than a baseball field in the off-season. Paul MacDougall took a moment, left his desk and his dark office, and climbed to his favorite seat in the upper deck, with the commanding view of the Bay. He took in the October afternoon. The golden sun was pounding against the hills of the East Bay, and white sails, incandescent in the afternoon light, were strewn about the Bay on cobalt blue water. If he had done nothing else in his entire life, he had built the most beautiful ballpark in the world.

It was a shame about the playoffs. He sighed. Swept in three games. Benny Cashman would have been the difference. But that was all over now. Now there was nothing for the ballpark but a few stadium concerts lined up over the course of the late autumn and early spring. And the odd motocross or X-Games event. A lower-tier bowl game. The Stones were coming, as was U2 – each for several nights. But that was rental income, nothing to savor. Nothing to really feel proud of. Paying the bills – nothing more.

It wasn't all terrible, though. His general manager had explained to him that for all of the lost millions in ticket revenue, he had regained an almost equal sum in incentive bonus money no longer due Cashman. Cashman had been set to make hundreds of thousands of dollars per plate appearance should the Goliaths make The World Series. Plus, a million-dollar bonus for breaking a home run record that would stand now, most likely, forever unbroken. Sure, Cashman had tied the record, but there would always be that asterisk. Hank Aaron's – even Barry Bonds' - legacy would remain secure.

The hills across the Bay were now almost orange in the sunset. Paul MacDougall stood up, shivered a little in the suddenly cool early evening breeze, and took one last look at his field of dreams.

There's always next season, he thought to himself as he slowly climbed up the steps and out of the light.

There's always next season.

XCIII

It was like watching a train wreck in slow motion.

Benny Cashman sat ensconced in his subterranean media room deep in the bowels of his mansion in the exclusive enclave of Blackhawk. He was watching Larry King Live, and having to endure his mistress - check that, former mistress - tell the world her sordid tale of physical and emotional abuse at his hands, and her witnessing multiple incidents of injections of illegal substances.

I *should* have had her killed, he thought as he popped open his billionth beer. Jesus, what a whore.

The whole world had turned against him, not that he cared all that much. He was used to being a loner and an outsider, and he didn't give two shits for what anyone thought of him. The only thing that really bothered him was that he would now never be inducted into the Hall of Fame. Too many hypocrites in the sports media for that to ever happen. It had never been a problem for them to follow his pursuit of the home run record, and sell newspapers, magazines, and advertising with his image. He had given them all that news on a silver platter and taken the heat for it. And now they had turned on him.

They can all fucking go to hell.

He couldn't take it anymore and changed the channel. ESPN2 was showing a special on OJ Simpson. Jesus. He murdered two people, and he still gets to dine out on his fame. And gets all the blonde women he can handle.

Benny Cashman nestled back into his Barcalounger, the leather crinkling as he did so, and closed his eyes. I didn't do anything wrong, he thought to himself.

Greatness is hard.

XCIV

Staring into the fireplace in his cottage in Sonoma, Peter Kohler had the urge to dash his glass of Gewurztraminer onto the hearth. It was all bad, he sighed as he restrained the impulse. Instead, he gulped his wine and set the glass on his belly and gazed at the reflections of the firelight in the cut crystal.

The light reminded him of Greece. The golden light of the late afternoon sun playing across the Aegean Sea. A light he might never see again.

He had been removed from his post and had had to turn over his passport to the police – not to be returned until after the trial, if ever. He had pleaded not guilty and had been released on his own recognizance – he was, after all, one of the more famous people in the Bay Area. It was going to take every dollar he had to provide a legal defense that would keep him out of jail. He might have to sell his building in the City. To add to his humiliation, he had had to endure daily updates regarding his infamy in the Clarion from two kid reporters – one of whom, he learned to his chagrin, was a tenant in his building. Stupid blonde girl. It was all overwhelming. He had repaired to his Russian River Valley retreat to lick his wounds, and to reflect on where he might turn next. His career in the museum world was over...

Wait.

There must be some cachet in being a "defrocked" curator. The positive spin on infamy is notoriety... I've got it, he thought to himself as he poured another glass of wine. I'll be the Anthony Bourdain of the art world. I'll travel the globe – if I ever get my fucking passport back - in search of the most distinctive and unique artifacts and delve into the seamy underbelly of the antiquities trade – about which I know as much as anyone. To Catch a Thief for the arts set. My own Discovery Channel show. It's not as if I don't have the hair.

He was seconds away from calling his agent when he decided to bask in the glow of his own genius. He sipped his Gewurztraminer and sighed.

I'm on top of the world again. I'm on top of the world...

He fell asleep in front of the fire, his glass slipping from his grasp and spilling its contents all over his priceless Turkish carpet.

XCV

Nothing like waking up in the morning with a half-dozen police cars parked in front of your home. There really wasn't enough room for all of them up on the twisty canyon road in the Hollywood Hills. Robert Grant thought they looked like some giant child had been playing with them and dumped them all into a pile in his front yard.

But the police had the warrant, and he had to let them in. And they had found the bodhisattva. He realized, with some frustration, that one doesn't get a receipt or anything for transactions like that. It wasn't like he was going to get his money back.

"If the director of a leading museum says it's okay, you think it should be okay, right? Right?"

The Asian detective looked at him and arched an eyebrow. "Right," he said. "It should be okay. We'll need you to make a statement, sir. Should only take a few minutes. And of course, the statue comes with us."

And with that, he handed Robert Grant a receipt.

XCVI

"Mom, I'm home!"

"I'm in here, sweetie," called out Madeleine Chang. She was dabbling in the kitchen – not that she was much of a cook, but brownies from a mix weren't too hard. Her son – he was too tall by half – came into the kitchen and tossed his backpack onto the floor and gave her a peck on the cheek. He was followed by his father, Bobby Chang, who had uncharacteristically picked him up from swimming practice.

Bobby Chang came up to his wife and slid his arms around her waist. She sighed with contentment.

A funny thing had happened. Instead of disassociating himself from his wife after her involvement in the scandal at the Museum of Asian Antiquities, Bobby Chang woke up. Her dark side had been revealed. She was no longer the boring, bitchy, self-involved lady-who-lunched. She was... interesting and complicated.

Nothing like a scandal to spice up a marriage. She had had to resign from the Museum Board, of course, but there were compensations. Bobby had invited her down to his Malibu beachfront home for a few days to hide from the limelight – the least he could do - and they had rediscovered each other. Madeleine was probably not going to do any jail time – a plea bargain in exchange for testimony had been arranged – but she was going to be under "house arrest" for a few months.

Bobby Chang found the tracking anklet sexy and teased her about being the next Martha Stewart. Madeleine thought that she could finally rest and invest in her family.

The change would do her good.

XCVII

As he lay in his hospital bed in traction, John Sanders had plenty of time to reflect on his choices - and his allegiances.

That bitch, he thought. She knew all along, but she just threw me under the bus. He made as much of a face as his bandaging would allow as he thought, yet again, of the differences between the stars in the firmament and the "little people." That he would forever be one of the "little people" made him weep.

At least he would no longer have to put up with being psychically abused. Now he just got to look forward to spending the next ten years in prison – once he got out of the hospital – and being someone else's bitch.

He stared at the ceiling and began to count the little dots in the acoustic tile. So much for the rush of deadlines and opening nights.

He now had all the time in the world.

XCVIII

"Where to, Ms. Niederman?"

"Just take me home, Ernesto."

"Yes, ma'am." Ernesto eased the limousine away from the curb and into traffic. Another late evening. The gala opening of *The Leopard Prince*. It was two in the morning.

Cheryl Niederman was tired. She gazed out of the window and watched the City pass by as the car made its way across town and up into Pacific Heights. After midnight the City was quiet – felt very much as if it was a small, suburban residential neighborhood and everyone had gone to bed. For her, it had been a brutal week of tap-dancing and spinning after the horrible incident at the invited dress rehearsal. The production had been shut down for several days while the police went through their motions, and no amount of press releases regarding "technical difficulties" could cover over the truth of the events. But, as these things often go, the publicity, as bad as it was, was still publicity, and tickets had been flying out of the box office at a record clip. This was enough to convince MagicLand to open the show as planned, and to sign on for the third-year extension.

Personally, it had been a tough week for her, as well. Her character had been assassinated pretty thoroughly. She was now grateful for all of the hours spent at charity events, and for funding a wing at the Children's Ward of the hospital. These stood her in good stead, and despite the accusations on the part of her former head of production, she had not lost any status or prestige within the highest circles of the community.

If nothing else, she had plausible deniability.

"We're here, Ms. Niederman."

Cheryl Niederman was shaken from her reverie. The gates to her private drive opened before them and Ernesto guided the limousine up to the porte cochere of her palatial home. He leapt out of the front seat and opened the door for her.

"Good night, ma'am."

"Good night, Ernesto." She blew past him and into her house. Ernesto Gonzalez waited for her enormous front door to close with a boom, and then climbed back into the driver's seat.

He sighed from fatigue but shook himself alert.

It was time for him to head home.

XCIX

As he stared at the one remaining chip in his hands, Jason Stillman reflected fuzzily on his lost weekend. How had one hundred thousand dollars vanished so quickly? He staggered up from the blackjack table at the Dream Casino and weaved his way drunkenly towards the elevator lobby. At least his room had been comped.

He did not look forward to telling his girlfriend that their weekend in Vegas was to be cut short a day.

And he did not look forward to going back to work on Monday, and more vials of pee.

C

Clarice Bryant's living room couldn't fit everybody, so the gathering spilled out onto the front porch and into the yard. Clarice worked her way through the group, offering lemonade. Maddy helped her, carrying the pitcher and glasses on a tray.

The service that morning had been remarkable. Maddy and Carlos had put the word out and had organized a van to pick everyone up. It turned out that they needed three vans – Jimmy volunteered to drive the third. People had come out of the woodwork to pay their respects to their fallen hero, the word having spread throughout the homeless community. It moved Maddy deeply to hear voice after voice speak on behalf of the Masked Avenger during the service at the little funeral home in Oakland. He had touched so many lives and had given so much of himself to help others.

Even Damian and Georgia were there. She had insisted on going once she found out more about her husband's former assailant, and he was intrigued by having met – albeit under extremely strange circumstances – one of his football heroes. Both were surprised and deeply affected by the outpouring of goodwill that they saw on behalf of Lincoln Bryant. "Sounds like he was a good man," said Georgia.

"In spite of busting up my nose," said Damian, whose nose was no longer bandaged, but he still had bruises under his eyes. He was helping out on the grill, the wake now in full swing.

Everyone was there: Charelle, Jasmine, Marcus – even old Abe. Benji and Marissa, both of whom had recovered fully, were helping out with the food. Marissa had managed to clean herself up a bit, revealing a weathered, but beautiful face. Beth and Little Mary were there, too. Old Billy, in a new suit, was regaling a small group with his story. Angelique and Jean-Michel wouldn't miss the event but had to leave early – Jean-Michel was flying back to Paris later that afternoon. Justin was there, wanting to meet the grandmother of the Theatre Ghost, and to pay his respects. Even the Man Without a Face was there, and he had spoken eloquently and movingly about his association with the Masked Avenger, and of pain, honor and forgiveness.

And of course, Robin was there. She had been introduced to Clarice and had immediately gone up and rubbed her ankles. Love at first sight for both of them.

Jimmy could only shake his head and smile. He had thought that he knew a lot about people, but he had learned more in the last few days than he had in several years in the SFPD.

It had been a long week. Carlos and Maddy had spent many late nights at the Clarion writing, re-writing, making phone calls, and getting interviews. Carey had done what she did best, offering advice, editing, some punch-ups and the occasional kick in the ass. Jimmy, too, had been busy, and had become something of a celebrity. He had been quoted in the papers daily. There were even rumblings that he might make a jump to Assistant Commissioner. The mayor loved rock stars.

The biggest news, however, was that Carlos had made a few phone calls to the offices of the National Football League and the Player's Union. He had discovered that many hundreds of thousands of dollars had been held on behalf of Lincoln Bryant in pension funds, and now that it was confirmed that he had passed away, these funds were to come to his designate, Clarice Bryant.

"What are you going to do with all that money?" asked Maddy.

"I don't rightly know," said Clarice. "I don't need

much. This house could sure use some fixing up, though. But I'm too old to manage all that."

At this point Marcus spoke up. "Mrs. Bryant, I've been looking for something remotely meaningful to do with myself, and if you would allow me, I'd like to help you fix your house."

"Saint Francis!" laughed Maddy, but she meant it in a nice way.

Benji raised his hand. "I was a carpenter back in the day. 'Fraid I drank too much, and I lost my job, but I think I can get it together. I can still swing a hammer."

"And I can paint," said Abe.

Pretty soon, everyone had identified a task they could take on, and Clarice said that she would sit down with Marcus and work out a plan for the reconstruction of her house. "There's a place down the street that's for sale," Clarice pointed out. It was an enormous, faded yellow Victorian, in worse shape than her own. "Tell you what. I now got the money to buy that place, you live there rent free, and we fix them both up. And I'll still pay you for your labor. Sounds like a good investment to me." Maddy, taking in the neighborhood, wasn't entirely sure that would be true, but then, she thought, some investments weren't as tangible as others. Clarice had created a community for herself after years of loneliness. And it was only money.

Jasmine had been thoughtful for a while. She finally said, "You know... this would be, like, the best reality TV show ever. I should call my dad." Maddy thought it was the most improbable reality TV show ever but didn't even want to risk it.

"Please don't," she said, as kindly as possible. "I mean, call your dad, and all, just don't pitch this. Every single life here has been shattered by some sort of tragedy. I think they need time."

Jasmine nodded. "Could be a good book, though."

That it might be, thought Maddy.

Clarice took especially to Charelle. "That girl is the

nicest little thing," she said. "She could use some more decent clothes, though, but girls these days."

"Yes, ma'am," replied Carlos, suppressing his usual wicked grin. He took extra effort to make sure that Clarice and Charelle had time to talk. Over the course of the afternoon, it became clear that Charelle, whose natural proclivity was to nurse others, had found her calling.

"I can't live here all by myself," said Clarice. "I'm always worried I'm going to fall or something, and there'd be nobody here." She gave Charelle a hug. "Room and board in exchange for some help?"

Charelle's face lit up. "Yes, ma'am!"

"It can be a tough neighborhood, but if we keep track of each other, we'll be okay."

Maddy figured that there might be strength in numbers, and she could already see some signs of gentrification down the street. Perhaps some sweat equity could be the difference in turning the place around. Who knows? Could be a good investment after all.

The afternoon was turning golden. A police car with two of Oakland's Finest pulled up. It turned out that Damian knew the older cop, and they exchanged news. Some lemonade from Clarice, a few bratwursts, and the story of Lincoln Bryant went a long way towards establishing a regular drive-by on the policemen's beat. As Maddy sat on the porch steps, she couldn't help feeling that there was more kindness and hope in the world than she would have believed a few weeks before.

*   *   *

"Some more bruschetta?"

"No, ma'am, I'm saving room for the main course," replied Maddy. Pearl Wang was making one last round with the tray before dinner. Carlos, however, was happy to mop up the antipasti platter. Where does he put it all? thought Maddy, shaking her head. Jimmy was finally making good on his Sunday dinner promise, and both Maddy and Carlos had been expressly invited. James Wang, Sr. in particular wanted to meet them. Pearl teased him that he really just wanted to meet Maddy, to check out Jimmy's new girlfriend. James had pretended to be indignant. But it was true.

Jimmy had been nervous. He wasn't sure what his father would make of a little white, blonde girl, or a little gay Mexican boy for that matter, but his father was a prince. In fact, Jimmy couldn't remember when his father had so obviously enjoyed himself. He regaled Carlos with stories of his own youthful misadventures while Jimmy and Maddy went into the kitchen to offer Pearl some help. The place smelled wonderful, an oven filled with a roast pork loin rubbed with rosemary and garlic, some roast potatoes, and some autumn vegetables – fresh from that morning's farmer's market at the Ferry Building. It was warm, cozy, and inviting. Maddy again felt a sense of community and family. This had turned into a great day.

"You're quite famous," said Pearl to Maddy as she organized a carving platter. Jimmy was pulling down the nice china from the shelves that were too high for either Maddy or Pearl to reach. "What's next on your plate?"

"She's got a voice mail full of messages," said Jimmy. "More than a few offers for her to write the Ballad of the Masked Avenger."

"And will you?"

"I'm thinking about it. Carlos and I have talked about it. It would be a lot of work, though."

"And a lot of money," said Jimmy.

"Maybe – if it sells. We could do some good things with that money. But I've still got my job, and deadlines to meet."

"No shortage of stories in San Francisco," said Pearl.

"Trust me, I know."

"No ma'am," said Maddy. "It's a good town for the improbable."

They finally gathered around the table. Jimmy raised his glass, first to his parents, and then, with a wink to Maddy he said, "To crime!" His father laughed, and his mother tutted.

"To San Francisco!" said Carlos. "I love this town!" Everyone laughed at that. Then there was a pause. An angel had passed.

Maddy raised her glass. "To absent friends," she said.

"To absent friends," they all said as they clinked their glasses once more. Maddy and Carlos exchanged a glance.

To absent friends, indeed.

Acknowledgements

Everything in this tale is just that – a tale. All characters are fictitious – figments of my imagination - with one significant exception. Any resemblance to persons famous, infamous, or dead would be an accident. I promise.

I must confess, though, a great debt to a series of articles that came out in the San Francisco Chronicle in 2003 by Kevin Fagan. They outlined with harsh clarity the hardness of life on the City's streets, and several characters in this book owe their inspiration to the tales of San Francisco's homeless that Fagan recounted.

I am eternally indebted to a group of friends and family who entertained and even supported the notion that I could actually pull this together and were patient with me as I did so. Maryvel Firda, Jennifer LaMoureaux and Lynn Golbetz actually took the time to read the 460-page first draft manuscript and offer their insights – brave souls and good friends. My sister, Claudia Gurevich, who is a great editor (and a lawyer), asked some tough questions – I've ignored some of them at my peril. And my stepchildren, Noah and Fiona, along with my father, were the ones who pushed me to continue to write the story. There were days when the goal was to write enough each day to read to the children at bedtime (with naughty language removed, of course), and when I failed to do so, Fiona, in particular, would make me feel guilty enough to redouble my efforts the next day. My wife, Eileen, is the final piece of the support puzzle. She knew that writing was saving my sanity, and she gave me the time, space and love to allow me to do this. I owe her everything.

The one real character? The Masked Avenger himself. For just one moment, there was a man dressed exactly as I described him, riding a bicycle, exactly as I described him. I saw him on the corner of Hyde and Ellis, many years ago, and he changed my life, for the vision he presented me was so compelling that I had to answer for myself who he might be and how he got there.

Whoever he is, and wherever he might be...

Thank you.

Made in the USA
Las Vegas, NV
09 August 2022

53018775R00236